D0816138

Biographical Essays

ALL RIGHTS RESERVED.

PRINTED IN THE UNITED STATES OF AMERICA.

ISBN 0-15-612616-8 (Harvest/HBJ : pbk.)

B C D E F G H I

Bibliographical Note

Lytton Strachey's shorter essays have previously appeared in three volumes: *Books and Characters, French and English*, published in 1922 and dedicated to John Maynard Keynes; *Portraits in Miniature and Other Essays*, published in 1931 and dedicated 'with gratitude and admiration' to Max Beerbohm; and *Characters and Commentaries*, published posthumously in 1933.

The exigencies of the moment have made it desirable to reduce the three volumes to two. For this purpose their contents have been reshuffled and divided into two collections of approximately equal length made up respectively of 'Biographical' and 'Literary' Essays. In each of these volumes the essays are arranged in the chronological order, not of their composition, but, roughly, of the subjects with which they deal.

Six of the essays in *Characters and Commentaries* have been omitted from the present volumes: 'Versailles', 'Avons-nous changé tout cela?', 'Bonga-Bonga in Whitehall', 'French Poets through Boston Eyes', 'Militarism and Theology' and 'The Claims of Patriotism'. On the other hand an essay on Charles Greville, which was not included in any of the three former books, will be found among the Biographical Essays.

Particulars are given in the table of contents of the date and place at which each essay originally appeared, and acknowledgments are due to the Editors of the various periodicals concerned.

J. S.

Contents

SIR JOHN HARINGTON (*The Nation and The Athenaeum XXXIV*, Nov. 17, 1923. PORTRAITS IN MINIATURE)　　1

MUGGLETON (*The Nation and The Athenaeum XXXV*, July 26, 1924. PORTRAITS IN MINIATURE)　　6

JOHN AUBREY (*The Nation and The Athenaeum XXXIII*, Sept. 15, 1923. PORTRAITS IN MINIATURE)　　11

THE LIFE, ILLNESS, AND DEATH OF DR. NORTH (*The Nation and The Athenaeum XL*, Feb. 19, 1927. PORTRAITS IN MINIATURE)　　17

MADAME DE SÉVIGNÉ'S COUSIN (*The Nation and The Athenaeum XXXVI*, Oct. 4, 1924. PORTRAITS IN MINIATURE)　　23

THE SAD STORY OF DR. COLBATCH (*The Nation and The Athenaeum XXXIV*, Dec. 22, 1923. PORTRAITS IN MINIATURE)　　28

LADY MARY WORTLEY MONTAGU (*The Albany Review I*, Sept., 1907. CHARACTERS AND COMMENTARIES)　　34

HUME (*The Nation and The Athenaeum XLII*, Jan. 7, 1928. PORTRAITS IN MINIATURE)　　43

VOLTAIRE (*The Athenaeum*, Aug. 1, 1919. CHARACTERS AND COMMENTARIES)　　50

VOLTAIRE AND ENGLAND (*Edinburgh Review CCXX*, Oct., 1914. BOOKS AND CHARACTERS)　　56

VOLTAIRE AND FREDERICK THE GREAT (*Edinburgh Review CCXXII*, Oct., 1915. BOOKS AND CHARACTERS)　　80

CONTENTS

A SIDELIGHT ON FREDERICK THE GREAT (*The New Statesman*, Jan. 27, 1917. CHARACTERS AND COMMENTARIES) 106

THE PRÉSIDENT DE BROSSES (*The New Statesman and Nation I*, April 11 & 18, 1931. PORTRAITS IN MINIATURE) 112

THE ROUSSEAU AFFAIR (*The New Quarterly III*, May, 1910. BOOKS AND CHARACTERS) 122

THE ABBÉ MORELLET (*The Nation and The Athenaeum XXXIV*, Jan. 26, 1924. PORTRAITS IN MINIATURE) 133

GIBBON (*The Nation and The Athenaeum XLII*, Jan. 14, 1928. PORTRAITS IN MINIATURE) 139

JAMES BOSWELL (*The Nation and The Athenaeum XXXVI*, Jan. 31, 1925. PORTRAITS IN MINIATURE) 147

MADEMOISELLE DE LESPINASSE (*The Independent Review X*, Sept., 1906. CHARACTERS AND COMMENTARIES) 153

MADAME DU DEFFAND (*Edinburgh Review CCXVII*, Jan., 1913. BOOKS AND CHARACTERS) 165

HORACE WALPOLE (*The Independent Review II*, May, 1904. CHARACTERS AND COMMENTARIES) 187

WALPOLE'S LETTERS (*The Athenaeum*, Aug. 15, 1919. CHARACTERS AND COMMENTARIES) 194

THE EIGHTEENTH CENTURY (*The Nation and The Athenaeum XXXIX*, May 29, 1926. CHARACTERS AND COMMENTARIES) 199

MARY BERRY (*The Nation and The Athenaeum XXXVI*, March 21, 1925. PORTRAITS IN MINIATURE) 204

LADY HESTER STANHOPE (*The Athenaeum*, April 4, 1919. BOOKS AND CHARACTERS) 211

CONTENTS

MADAME DE LIEVEN (*Life and Letters VI*, April, 1931. PORTRAITS IN MINIATURE)   219

AN ADOLESCENT (*The New Statesman*, March 31, 1917. CHARACTERS AND COMMENTARIES)   229

MR. CREEVEY (*The Athenaeum*, June 13, 1919. BOOKS AND CHARACTERS)   236

CHARLES GREVILLE (*The Nation and The Athenaeum XXXIII*, August 11, 1923)   243

CARLYLE (*The Nation and The Athenaeum XLII*, Jan. 28, 1928. PORTRAITS IN MINIATURE)   249

FROUDE (*Life and Letters V*, Dec., 1930. PORTRAITS IN MINIATURE)   257

DIZZY (*The Woman's Leader XII*, July 16, 1920. CHARACTERS AND COMMENTARIES)   264

A DIPLOMATIST: LI HUNG-CHANG (*War and Peace*, March, 1918. CHARACTERS AND COMMENTARIES)   268

CREIGHTON (*Life and Letters II*, June, 1929. PORTRAITS IN MINIATURE)   273

A STATESMAN: LORD MORLEY (*War and Peace*, Feb., 1918. CHARACTERS AND COMMENTARIES)   280

SARAH BERNHARDT (*The Nation and The Athenaeum XXXIII*, May 5, 1923. CHARACTERS AND COMMENTARIES)   284

INDEX   289

SIR JOHN HARINGTON

An old miniature shows a young man's face, whimsically Elizabethan, with tossed-back curly hair, a tip-tilted nose, a tiny point of a beard, and a long single earring, falling in sparkling drops over a ruff of magnificent proportions. Such was John Harington, as he appeared in the happy fifteen-eighties, at Greenwich, or at Nonesuch—a courtier, a wit, a scholar, a poet, and a great favourite with the ladies. Even Gloriana herself usually unbent when he approached her. She liked the foolish fellow. She had known him since he was a child; he was her godson—almost, indeed, a family connection, for his father's first wife had been a natural daughter of her own indefatigable sire. Through this lady the young man had inherited his fine Italian house at Kelston, in Somersetshire, where one day Elizabeth, on her way to Bath, paid him the honour of an extremely expensive visit. He had felt himself obliged to rebuild half the house to lodge his great guest fittingly; but he cared little for that—he wrote a rhyming epigram about it all, which amused the ladies of the bedchamber. He wrote, he found, with extraordinary ease and pleasure; the words came positively running off the end of his pen; and so—to amuse the ladies again, or to tease them—he translated the twenty-eighth book of Ariosto's *Orlando Furioso*, in which the far from decorous history of the fair Fiammetta is told. The Queen soon got wind of this. She read the manuscript and sent for the poet. She was shocked, she said, by this attempt to demoralise her household; and she banished the offender from Court until—could there be a more proper punishment?—he should have completed the translation of the whole poem. Harington hurried off to Kelston, worked away for a month or two, and returned with a fine folio containing the entire everything, and was at last ignominiously ejected by his brother-in-law. King James was equally disappointing. Even the curious lantern, even a learned, elaborate, and fantastic dissertation *On the Succession to the Crown*, failed to win him. After he had been a year in London, the new King granted Sir John an interview, but, though his Majesty was polite, he was not impressed. 'Sir John,' he said, with much gravity, 'do you truly understand why the Devil works more with ancient women than others?' And, unluckily, on that, Sir John 'could not refrain from a scurvy jest.' Nevertheless, though he felt that he had made no headway, he would not despair; a little later, the Lord Chancellorship of Ireland and the Archbishopric of Dublin fell vacant, and the author of *Ajax* bravely requested that he should be appointed to both offices. Oddly enough, his application received no answer. He solaced himself with an endeavour to win the good graces of the young Prince Henry, to whom he addressed a discourse, full of pleasant anecdotes, concerning all the bishops of his acquaintance, followed by a letter describing 'the good deedes and straunge feats' of his 'rare Dogge,' Bungay—how he used to carry messages from London to Kelston, and how, on one occasion, he took a pheasant from a dish at the Spanish Ambassador's table, and then returned it to the very same dish, at a secret sign from his master.

But in truth the days of Bungay were over, and the new times were uncomfortable and strange. 'I ne'er did see such lack of good order, discretion, and sobriety.' There had been jollities and junketings, no doubt, in his youth, but surely, they were different. He remembered the 'heroicall dames,' the 'stately heroyns' whom he had celebrated aforetime—

> These entertayn great Princes; these have learned
> The tongues, toys, tricks of Rome, of Spayn, of Fraunce;
> These can correntos and lavoltas daunce,
> And though they foote it false 'tis ne'er discerned.

More and more his thoughts reverted to his old mistress. 'When she smiled, it was a pure sunshine, that everyone did choose to bask in, if they could; but anon came a storm from a sudden gathering of clouds, and the thunder fell in wondrous manner on all alike.' Yes! Those were great times indeed! And now . . . he was 'olde and infirme'; he was forty-five; he must seek a quiet harbour and lay up his barque. He lingered at Kelston, impoverished, racked by various diseases; he vainly took the Bath waters; he became 'stricken of a dead palsy'; until, in 1612, at the age of fifty-one, he passed into oblivion. And in oblivion he has remained. Nobody reads his *Orlando*; his letters are known to none but a few learned historians; his little books of epigrams lie concealed in the grim recesses of vast libraries; and Englishmen to-day, reflecting on many things, as they enjoy the benefits of a sanitary system unknown to the less fortunate inhabitants of other countries, give never a thought to Sir John Harington.

1923.

MUGGLETON

NEVER did the human mind attain such a magnificent height of self-assertiveness as in England about the year 1650. Then it was that the disintegration of religious authority which had begun with Luther reached its culminating point. The Bible, containing the absolute truth as to the nature and the workings of the Universe, lay open to all; it was only necessary to interpret its assertions; and to do so all that was wanted was the decision of the individual conscience. In those days the individual conscience decided with extraordinary facility. Prophets and prophetesses ranged in crowds through the streets of London, proclaiming, with complete certainty, the explanation of everything. The explanations were extremely varied: so much the better—one could pick and choose. One could become a Behmenist, a Bidellian, a Coppinist, a Salmonist, a Dipper, a Traskite, a Tryonist, a Philadelphian, a Christadelphian, or a Seventh Day Baptist, just as one pleased. Samuel Butler might fleer and flout at

> petulant, capricious sects,
> The maggots of corrupted texts;

but he, too, was deciding according to the light of his individual conscience. By what rule could men determine whether a text was corrupted, or what it meant? The rule of the Catholic Church was gone, and henceforward Eternal Truth might with perfect reason be expected to speak through the mouth of any fish-wife in Billingsgate.

Of these prophets the most famous was George Fox; the most remarkable was Lodowick Muggleton. He was born in 1609, and was brought up to earn his living as a tailor. Becoming religious, he threw over a charming girl, with whom

6

he was in love and whom he was engaged to marry, on the ground that her mother kept a pawnbroker's shop and that usury was sinful. He was persuaded to this by his puritan friends, among whom was his cousin, John Reeve, a man of ardent temperament, fierce conviction, and unflinching holiness. Some years later, in 1650, two peculiar persons, John Tawny and John Robins, appeared in London. Tawny declared that he was the Lord's high priest, that it was his mission to lead the Jews back to Jerusalem, and that, incidentally, he was the King of France. Robins proclaimed that he was something greater; he was Adam, he was Melchizedek, he was the Lord himself. He had raised Jeremiah, Benjamin, and many others from the dead, and did they not stand there beside him, admitting that all he said was true? Serpents and dragons appeared at his command; he rode upon the wings of the wind; he was about to lead 144,000 men and women to the Mount of Olives through the Red Sea, on a diet of dry bread and raw vegetables. These two men, 'greater than prophets,' made a profound impression upon Muggleton and his cousin Reeve. A strange melancholy fell upon them, and then a more strange exaltation. They heard mysterious voices; they were holy; why should not they too be inspired? Greater than prophets. . . . ? Suddenly Reeve rushed into Muggleton's room and declared that they were the chosen witnesses of the Lord, whose appearance had been prophesied in the Book of Revelation, xi. 3. Muggleton agreed that it was so. As for Tawny and Robins, they were devilish impostors, who must be immediately denounced. Sentence of eternal damnation should be passed upon them. The cousins hurried off on their mission, and discovered Robins in gaol, where he had been lodged for blasphemy. The furious embodiment of Adam, Melchizedek, and the Lord glared out at them from a window, clutching the bars with both hands. But Reeve was unabashed. 'That body of thine,' he shouted, pointing at his victim, 'which was thy heaven, must be thy hell; and that proud spirit of thine, which said it was God, must be thy Devil. The one shall be as fire, and the other as brimstone, burning together to all eternity. This is the message of the Lord.' The effect was instantaneous: Robins, letting go the bars, fell back, shattered. 'It is finished.' he groaned; 'the Lord's will be done.' He wrote a letter to Cromwell, recanting; was released from prison, and retired into private life, in the depths of the country. Tawny's fate was equally impressive. Reeve wrote on a piece of paper, 'We pass sentence upon you of eternal damnation,' and left it in his room. The wretched man fled to Holland, in a small boat, *en route* for Jerusalem, and was never heard of again.

After this the success of the new religion was assured. But Reeve did not live long to enjoy his glory. In a few months his fiery spirit had worn itself away, and Muggleton was left alone to carry on the work. He was cast in a very different mould. Tall, thick-set, vigorous, with a great head, whose low brow, high cheekbones, and projecting jowl almost suggested some simian creature, he had never known a day's illness, and lived to be eighty-eight. Tough and solid, he continued, year after year, to earn his living as a tailor, while the words flowed from him which were the final revelation of God. For he preached and he wrote with an inexhaustible volubility. He never ceased, in sermons, in letters, in books, in pamphlets, to declare to the world the divine and absolute truth. His revelations might be incomprehensible, his objurgations frenzied, his argumentations incoherent—no matter; disciples gathered round him in ever-thickening crowds, learning, to their amazement and delight, that there is no Devil but the unclean Reason of men, that Angels are the only beings of Pure Reason, that God is of the stature of a man and made of flesh and bone, that Heaven is situated beyond the stars and six miles above the earth. Schismatics might arise, but they were crushed, cast forth, and sentenced to eternal damnation. Inquiring magistrates were browbeaten with multitudinous texts. George Fox, the miserable wretch, was overwhelmed—or would have been had he not obtained the assistance of the Devil—by thick volumes of intermingled abuse and Pure Reason. The truth was plain—it had been

8

delivered to Muggleton by God; and henceforward, until the Day of Judgment, the Deity would hold no further communication with his creatures. Prayer, therefore, was not only futile, it was blasphemous; and no form of worship was admissible, save the singing of a few hymns of thanksgiving and praise. All that was required of the true believer was that he should ponder upon the Old and the New Testaments, and upon 'The Third and Last Testament of Our Lord Jesus Christ,' by Muggleton.

The English passion for compromise is well illustrated by the attitude of Charles II's Government towards religious heterodoxy. There are two logical alternatives for the treatment of heretics—to let them alone, or to torture them to death; but English public opinion recoiled—it still recoils—from either course. A compromise was the obvious, the comfortable solution; and so it was decided that heretics should be tortured—not to death, oh no!—but . . . to some extent. Accordingly, poor Muggleton became a victim, for years, to the small persecutions of authority. He was badgered by angry justices, he was hunted from place to place, his books were burnt, he was worried by small fines and short imprisonments. At last, at the age of sixty-eight, he was arrested and tried for blasphemy. In the course of the proceedings, it appeared that the prosecution had made a serious blunder: since the publication of the book on which the charge was based an Act of Indemnity had been passed. Thereupon the Judge instructed the jury that, as there was no reason to suppose that the date on the book was not a false imprint, the Act of Indemnity did not apply; and Muggleton was condemned to the pillory. He was badly mauled, for it so happened that the crowd was hostile and pelted the old man with stones. After that, he was set free; his tribulations were at last over. The Prophet spent his closing years writing his autobiography, in the style of the Gospels; and he died in peace.

His doctrines did not die with him. Two hundred and fifty Muggletonians followed him to the grave, and their faith has been handed down, unimpaired through the generations, from

was against him; he was by nature an amiable muddler; in love and in literature, no less than in business, it was always the same—'nothing tooke effect.' Neither Madam Jane Codrington, nor 'that incomparable good conditioned gentlewoman, Mris. M. Wiseman, with whom at first sight I was in love,' would smile upon him; and though 'domina Katherina Ryves,' with a dowry of £2,000, was kinder, just as she was about to marry him she died. He sought distraction abroad, but without success. '1664, in August,' he noted, 'had a terrible fit of the spleen, and piles, at Orleans.' Yet worse was to follow: 'In an ill howre,' he began to make his addresses to Joan Sumner, whose cruelty was more than negative. She had him arrested in Chancery Lane, and for three years pursued him with lawsuits. His ruin followed; all his broad lands vanished; even Easton Piers, the house of his birth, with its terraced gardens, its 'jedeau,' its grotto and 'volant Mercury,' had to be sold; even his books went at last. By 1670 poor Aubrey had lost everything. But then, unexpectedly, happiness descended upon him. Free at last from the struggles of love and law and the tedious responsibilities of property, he found himself in a 'sweet *otium*.' 'I had never quiett, nor anything of happiness till divested of all,' he wrote. 'I was in as much affliction as a mortall could bee, and never quiet till all was gone, and I wholly cast myselfe on God's providence.'

God's providence, in Aubrey's case, took the form of a circle of kindly friends, who were ready enough to give him food and shelter in town and country, in return for the benefit of his 'most ingeniose conversation.' He would spend the winter in London—often with Sir William Petty or Sir Christopher Wren,—and then, with the spring, he would ride off on a round of visits—to Lord Thanet's in Kent, to the Longs in Wiltshire, to Edmund Wylde in Shropshire—until the autumn came, and he would turn his horse's head back to London. Grumpy Anthony Wood might write him down 'a shiftless person, roving and magotieheaded, and sometimes little better than crazed'; but his boon companions thought otherwise. They relished to the full the extraordinary quantity and the delightful variety of his information, and could never tire of his engaging manner of presenting it. 'My head,' he said himself, 'was always working; never idle, and even travelling did glean som observations, of which I have a collection in folio of 2 quiers of paper and a dust basket, some whereof are to be valued.' His inquiries were indeed indefatigable; he was learned in natural history, geology, Gothic architecture, mineralogy, painting, heraldry; he collected statistics, he was a profound astrologer, and a learned geometrician; he wrote a treatise on education; even the mysteries of cookery did not elude him, and he compiled 'a collection of approved receipts.' Before he died he had written sufficient to fill several volumes; but, characteristically enough, he brought only one book to the point of publication: his *Miscellanies*, in which he briefly discussed such fascinating subjects as 'Apparitions, Impulses, Knockings, Blows Invisible, Prophecies, Marvels, Magic, Transportation in the Air, Visions in a Bevil or Glass, Converse with Angels and Spirits, Corps-Candles in Wales, Glances of Love and Envy, and Second-Sighted Persons in Scotland.' It is in this book, in the chapter of Apparitions, that the sentence occurs which so much delighted Mr. Jonathan Oldbuck of Monkbarns: '*Anno* 1670, not far from *Cirencester*, was an Apparition; Being demanded, whether a good Spirit or a bad? Returned no answer, but disappeared with a curious Perfume and most melodious Twang.'

Certainly the learned Ray was right when he said of his friend that he was 'a little inclinable to credit strange relations.' Yet it would be an error to dismiss Aubrey as a mere superstitious trifler; he was something more interesting than that. His insatiable passion for singular odds and ends had a meaning in it; he was groping towards a scientific ordering of phenomena; but the twilight of his age was too confusing, and he could rarely distinguish between a fact and a fantasy. He was clever enough to understand the Newtonian system, but he was not clever enough to understand that a horoscope was an absurdity; and so, in his crowded curiosity-shop of a brain, astronomy and astrology both found a place, and were given equal values. When fortune favoured him, however, he could make real additions to knowledge. He was the first English archæologist, and his most remarkable achievement was the discovery of the hitherto unknown Druidical temple of Avebury. Encouraged by Charles II, he made a careful survey of the great stone circle, writing a dissertation upon it and upon Stonehenge, and refuting the theory of Inigo Jones, who, in order to prove the latter was Roman, had given an entirely factitious account of it. As he rode over the Wiltshire downs, hawking with Colonel Long, he had ample opportunities for these antiquarian investigations. 'Our sport,' he wrote, 'was very good, and in a romantick countrey, for the prospects are noble and vast, the downs stockt with numerous flocks of sheep, the turfe rich and fragrant with thyme and burnet; nor are the nut-brown shepherdesses without their graces. But the flight of the falcons was but a parenthesis to the Colonell's facetious discourse, who was *tam Marti quam Mercurio*, and the Muses did accompany him with his hawkes and spaniells.'

The country was charming; but London too was full of pleasures, and the winter nights passed swiftly with wine and talk. For the company was excellent. There was Robert Hooke 'that invented the Pendulum-Watches, so much more useful than the other watches,' and a calculating machine, and hundreds of other contrivances—'he believes not fewer than a thousand'—and who declared he had forestalled Mr. Newton; and there was Dr. Tonge, who had first taught children to write by means of copper-plates, and left behind him 'two tomes in folio of alchymy'; and Francis Potter, the first to practise the transfusion of blood, who, at 10 o'clock in the morning of December 10, 1625, as he was going upstairs, had discovered 'the mysterie of the Beaste'; and John Pell, the inventor of the division-sign in arithmetic, who 'haz sayd to me that he did believe that he solved some questions *non sine divino auxilio*.' And then the gentle gossip went back to earlier days—to old Mr. Oughtred, Sir Christopher's master, who 'taught all free,' and was an astrologer, though he confessed 'that he was not satisfied how it came about that one might foretell by the starres, but so it was,' and whose 'wife was a penurious woman, and would not allow him to burne candle after supper, by which meanes many a good notion is lost, and many a problem unsolved'; and so back to a still more remote and bizarre past—to Dr. John Dee, of Queen Elizabeth's time, 'who wore a gowne like an artist's gowne, with hanging sleeves and a slit,' made plates of gold 'by projection,' and 'used to distil egge-shells.'

Aubrey lived on into old age—vague, precise, idle, and busy to the last. His state of life, he felt, was not quite satisfactory. He was happy; but he would have been happier still in some other world. He regretted the monasteries. He wished 'the reformers had been more moderate on that point.' It was 'fitt there should be receptacles and provision for contemplative men'; and 'what a pleasure 'twould have been to have travelled from monastery to monastery!' As it was, he did the next best thing—he travelled from country house to country house. In the summer of 1697, when he was over seventy, as he was riding through Oxford on his way to Lady Long's, he was seized with sudden illness, and his journeying was ended for ever.

In the great mass of papers that he left behind him it was hardly to be supposed that there could be anything of permanent value. Most of the antique science was already out of date at his death. But it so happened that Aubrey's appetite for knowledge had carried him into a field of inquiry which, little explored in his own day, attracts the greatest interest in ours. He was an assiduous biographer. Partly to help the ungrateful Anthony Wood in the compilation of his *Athenae Oxonienses*, but chiefly for his own delight, Aubrey was in the habit of jotting down on scraps of paper every piece of information he could acquire concerning both his own contemporaries and and the English worthies of previous generations. He was accurate, he had an unfailing eye for what was interesting, and he possessed—it was almost inevitable in those days—a natural gift of style. The result is that his *Short Lives* (which have been admirably edited for the Clarendon Press by Mr. Andrew Clark) are not only an authority of the highest importance upon seventeenth-century England, but one of the most readable of books. A biography should either be as long as Boswell's or as short as Aubrey's. The method of enormous and elaborate accretion which produced the *Life of Johnson* is excellent, no doubt; but, failing that, let us have no half-measures; let us have the pure essentials—a vivid image, on a page or two, without explanations, transitions, commentaries, or padding. This is what Aubrey gives us; this, and one thing more—a sense of the pleasing, anxious being who, with his odd old alchemy, has transmuted a few handfuls of orts and relics into golden life.

1923.

THE LIFE, ILLNESS, AND
DEATH OF DR. NORTH

JOHN NORTH was a man of eminence in his day—a prebend of Westminster, Professor of Greek at Cambridge, Master of Trinity College, and Clerk of the King's Closet: now totally forgotten. Only the curious inquirer, chancing on the obscure and absurd memoir of him by his admiring younger brother, Roger, catches a glimpse of the intense individual existence of this no longer distinguished man. In the sight of God, we used to be told, a thousand years are as a day; possibly; but notions of the deity are not what they were in the days of King David and Sir Isaac Newton; Evolution, the Life Force, and Einstein have all intervened; so that whether the dictum is still one to which credence should be attached is a problem that must be left to Professor Whitehead (who has studied the subject very carefully) to determine. However that may be, for mortal beings the case is different. In their sight (or perhaps one should say their blindness) a thousand years are too liable to be not as a day but as just nothing. The past is almost entirely a blank. The indescribable complexities, the incalculable extravagances, of a myriad consciousnesses have vanished for ever. Only by sheer accident, when some particular drop from the ocean of empty water is slipped under the microscope—only when some Roger North happens to write a foolish memoir, which happens to survive, and which we happen to open—do we perceive for an amazed moment or two the universe of serried and violent sensations that lie concealed so perfectly in the transparency of oblivion.

Born in 1645, the younger son of an impecunious peer, John North was one of those good little boys who, in the seventeenth century, were invariably destined to Learning, the Universities, and the Church. His goodness, his diligence, his scrupulosity, were perhaps, it is true, the result of a certain ingrained timidity rather than anything else; but that could not be helped. Fear is not easily exorcised. As an undergraduate at Cambridge the youth was still afraid of ghosts in the dark, and slept with the bedclothes over his head. 'For some time,' we are told, 'he lay with his Tutor, who once, coming home, found the Scholar in bed with only his Crown visible. The Tutor, indiscreetly enough, pulled him by the Hair; whereupon the Scholar sunk down, and the Tutor followed, and at last, with a great Outcry, the Scholar sprung up, expecting to see an enorm Spectre.' But in spite of such contretemps the young man pursued his studies with exemplary industry. He was soon a Fellow of his college and a Doctor of Divinity. He continued to work and work; collected a vast library; read the Classics until 'Greek became almost vernacular to him;' wrestled with Hebrew, dived deep into Logic and Metaphysics, and was even 'a Friend to, though no great Scholar in, the Mathematicks.' Unwilling to waste a moment of time, the Doctor found means for turning the most ordinary conversations into matter for improvement, but 'he could not be pleased with such insipid Pastime as Bowls, or less material Discourse, such as Town Tales, Punning, and the Like.' At last his fame as a prodigy of learning spread over the land. He preached before King Charles II, and the great Duke of Lauderdale became his patron. At the early age of twenty-seven, his talents and virtues were rewarded by the Professorship of Greek in the University of Cambridge.

His talents and virtues were indeed great; but still they were informed and dominated by an underlying apprehensiveness. Meticulous, in the true sense of the word, was the nature of the Doctor. An alarmed exactitude kept him continually on the stretch. He was in fear alike for the state of his soul and for his reputation with posterity. He published only one small volume—a commentary on some of Plato's Dialogues; all the rest of the multitudinous fruits of his labours—notes, sermons, treatises, lectures, dissertations—were burnt, by his direction,

18

after his death. A small note-book alone survived by accident, containing the outline of a great work against Socinians, Republics, and Hobbes. But the Doctor had taken care to write on the first page of it—'I beshrew his heart, that gathers my opinion from anything he finds wrote here.' Nor was this strange diffidence merely literary; it extended to his person as well. He would never allow his portrait to be painted, in spite of the entreaties of Sir Peter Lely; 'and, what was very odd, he would not leave the Print in his Bed, where he had lain, remain undefaced.'

Curiously enough, his appearance seemed to belie his character. His complexion was florid, his hair flaxen, and, 'as some used to jest, his Features were scandalous, as showing rather a Madam *entravestie* than a Book-Worm.' At times, indeed, it almost appeared as if his features were a truer index to his soul than the course of his life. His friends were surprised to see that, among his pupils, he 'affected to refresh himself with the society of the young Noblemen,' who gathered round him, in fits of laughter, 'like Younglings about old *Silenus.*' He was arch, too, with the ladies, plying them with raillery. 'Of all the Beasts of the Field,' he said, 'God Almighty thought Woman the fittest Companion for Man'; and the ladies were delighted. But unfortunately no corresponding specimen of his jests with the young noblemen has been preserved.

In 1677, when he was thirty-two, his career reached its climax and he was made Master of Trinity. The magnificent appointment proved to be his ruin. Faced with the governance of the great college over which the omniscient Barrow had lately ruled and which the presence of Newton still made illustrious, the Doctor's sense of responsibility, of duty, and of inadequacy became almost pathological. His days and his nights passed in one ceaseless round of devotion, instruction, and administration, reading, writing, and abstemiousness. He had no longer any time for the young and the fair; no time for a single particle of enjoyment; no time even for breakfast. His rule was strict beyond all measure and precedent. With relentless severity he pursued the undergraduates through their

exercises and punished them for their peccadilloes. His un-
popularity became intense: he was openly jeered at in the
Cloisters, and one evening a stone came whizzing through the
window of the room in the Lodge where he was sitting, and
fell in the fire at his feet. Nor was he consoled by the friendship of his equals. The Senior Fellows were infuriated by his
sour punctilio; a violent feud sprang up; there were shocking
scenes at the council meetings. 'Let me be buried in the ante-
chapel,' exclaimed the Master in his desperation, 'so that they
may trample on me dead as they have living.'

And death was always before his eyes; for now a settled
hypochondria was added to his other miseries. He was a prey
to constant nightmare. He had little doubt that he would
perish of the stone. Taking upon himself the functions of the
Wise Woman, he displayed before his embarrassed friends the
obvious symptoms of fatal disorder. 'Gravel! Red gravel!' he
gasped. In reality his actual weakness lay in quite another
direction. One day he caught cold, it grew worse, his throat
was affected, his uvula swelled. The inflammation continued,
and before long the unhappy Doctor became convinced that
his uvula would have to be cut off. All the physicians of the
University were summoned, and they confessed that the case
was grave. It was the age of Molière, and the practitioners of
Cambridge might well have figured in the *Malade Imagin-
aire.* Their prescriptions were terrific and bizarre: drenches,
'enough to purge a strong man from off his legs,' accompanied
by amber, to be smoked like tobacco in pipes, with astringent
powders blown into the mouth through quills. The Doctor,
who, with all his voluminous reading, had never heard of
Diafoirus, believed every word he was told, and carried out
the fearful orders with elaborate conscientiousness. The
result was plain to all; in a few weeks his health was completely shattered, and his friends, to their amazement, saw him
'come helmeted in Caps upon Caps, and meagre as one newly
crope out of a Fever.' They privately consulted the great Dr.
Lower in London. He threw up his hands. 'I would undertake,' he said, 'by the smoak of Amber alone, to put the

soundest Man in the World into Convulsion Fits.' But it was too late to intervene; the treatment was continued, while the Doctor struggled on with the duties of his office. Two scholars were to be publicly admonished for scandalous conduct; the fellows assembled; the youths stood trembling; the Master appeared. Emaciated, ghastly, in his black gown, and with a mountain of caps upon his head, the extraordinary creature began a tirade of bitter and virulent reproof; when suddenly his left leg swerved beneath him, and he fell in a fit upon the ground. It was apoplexy. He was carried to his bed, where the physicians clustered round him. The one thing, they declared, that was essential was that he should never lose consciousness; if he did he would never regain it; and they therefore ordered that a perpetual noise should be made about his ears. Whereupon 'there was a Consort of Tongs, Firegrate, Wainscote-Drum, and dancing of Curtains and Curtain Rings, such as would have made a sound Man mad.' At that moment, old Lady North, the patient's mother and a formidable dowager, appeared upon the scene. She silenced the incredible tintinnabulation; she even silenced the faculty; and she succeeded in nursing her son back from death.

Yet there were some who averred that it would have been better had she never done so. For now the strangest of the Doctor's transformations came upon him. His recovery was not complete; his body was paralysed on the left side; but it was in his mind that the most remarkable change had occurred. His fears had left him. His scrupulosity, his diffidence, his seriousness, even his morality—all had vanished. He lay on his bed, in reckless levity, pouring forth a stream of flippant observations, and naughty stories, and improper jokes. While his friends hardly knew which way to look, he laughed consumedly, his paralysed features drawn up into a curiously distorted grin. He sent for a gay young scholar of the college, Mr. Warren, to sit by him and regale him with merry tales and readings from light romances. And there was worse still to follow. Attacked by epileptic seizures, he declared that the only mitigation of his sufferings lay in the continued consumption of wine. He, who had been so noted for his austerities, now tossed off, with wild exhilaration, glass after glass of the strongest sherry; the dry ascetic had become a convert to the golden gospel of *la dive bouteille*. In the depth of the night, the studious precincts of the Great Court of Trinity were disturbed by peculiar sounds—the high, triumphant, one-sided cackle of the Master, as he lay, with his flagon in his hand and young Mr. Warren beside him, absorbed in the abandoned, exuberant fantasies of the Curé of Meudon.

After four years of this strange existence, the Doctor died in his sleep. He was buried, as he had directed, in the ante-chapel of the college, where, under a small square stone, engraved with the initials 'J.N.,' so many singular agitations came to their final rest. In his brother Roger's opinion, 'the Consciousness of a well-spent Life was of great service to him,' for otherwise he 'might have fallen into Melancholy, Dejections, Despair, and Misconstructions of Providence.' And probably Roger was right; conscientiousness is apt, in however devious a manner, to have its reward in this world. Whether it also has it in any other is another of those questions that must be referred to Professor Whitehead.

1927.

MADAME DE SEVIGNÉ'S COUSIN

MADAME DE SÉVIGNÉ was one of those chosen beings in whom the forces of life are so abundant and so glorious that they overflow in every direction and invest whatever they meet with the virtue of their own vitality. She was the sun of a whole system, which lived in her light—which lives still for us with a kind of reflected immortality. We can watch—with what a marvellous distinctness!—the planets revolving through that radiance—the greater and the less, and the subordinate moons and dimmest asteroids—from Madame de Grignan herself to the dancing gypsies at Vichy. But then, when the central luminary is withdrawn, what an incredible convulsion! All vanish; we are dimly aware for a little of some obscure shapes moving through strange orbits; and after that there is only darkness.

Emmanuel de Coulanges, for instance. He lived a long life, filled his own place in the world, married, travelled, had his failures and his successes . . . but all those happenings were mere phenomena; the only reality about him lay in one thing —he was Madame de Sévigné's cousin. He was born when she was seven years old, and he never knew a time when he had not loved her. She had petted the little creature when it was a baby, and she had gone on petting it all her life. He had not been quite an ordinary child; he had had strange fancies. There was a fairy, called *Cafut*, so he declared, to whom he was devoted; this was not approved of—it looked like incipient madness; and several whippings had to be administered before *Cafut* was exorcised. In reality, no one could have been saner than the little Emmanuel; but he had ways of amusing himself which seemed unaccountable to the grandly positive generation into which he had been born. There was something about him which made him no fit contemporary of Bossuet. Madame de Sévigné, so completely, so magnificently, a child of her age, while she loved him, could never take him quite seriously. In her eyes, though he might grow old, he could not grow up. At the age of sixty, white-haired and gouty, he remained for her what, in fact, his tiny pink-cheeked rotundity suggested—an infant still. She found him adorable and unimportant. Even his sins—and in those days sins were serious—might, somehow or other, be disregarded; and besides, she observed that he had only one—it was *gaudeamus*; she scolded him with a smile. It was delightful to have anything to do with him—to talk with him, to laugh at him, to write to him. 'Le style qu'on a en lui écrivant,' she said, 'ressemble à la joie et à la santé.' It was true; and some of her most famous, some of her most delicious and life-scattering letters were written to her cousin Coulanges.

He married well—a lady who was related to the great Louvois; but the connection did him little good in the world. For a moment, indeed, an important public office was dangled before his eyes; but it was snapped up by somebody else, and Coulanges, after a few days of disappointment, consoled himself easily enough—with a song. He was very fond of songs, composing them with elegant rapidity to the popular airs of the day; every circumstance of his existence, however grave or however trivial—a journey, a joke, the world's cruelties, his wife's infidelities—he rigged them all out in the bows and ribbons of his little rhymes. His wife was pretty, gay, fashionable, and noted for her epigrams. Her adorers were numerous: there was the Comte de Brancas, famous—immortal, even, as he has his niche in La Bruyère's gallery—for his absent-mindedness; there was the Abbé Têtu, remarkable for two things—for remaining the friend both of Madame de Montespan and of Madame de Maintenon, and for being the first person who was ever afflicted by the vapours; and there was the victorious—the scandalously victorious—Marquis de la Trousse. Decidedly the lady was gay—too gay to be quite to the taste of Madame de Sévigné, who declared that she was a leaf fluttering in the wind. 'Cette feuille,' she said, 'est la plus frivole et la plus légère marchandise que vous ayez jamais vue.' But Coulanges was indifferent to her lightness; what he did feel was her inordinate success at Court. There she gadded, in a blaze of popularity, launching her epigrams and hobnobbing with Madame de Maintenon; he was out of it; and he was growing old, and the gout attacked him in horrid spasms. At times he was almost sad.

Then, gradually and for no apparent reason, there was a change. What was it? Was the world itself changing? Was one age going out and another coming in? From about the year 1690 onwards, one begins to discern the first signs of the petrifaction, the *rigor mortis* of the great epoch of Louis XIV; one begins to detect, more and more clearly in the circum-ambient atmosphere, the scent and savour of the eighteenth century. Already there had been symptoms—there had been the fairy *Cafut*, and the Abbé Têtu's vapours. But now there could be no more doubt about it; the new strange tide was flowing steadily in. And upon it was wafted the cockleshell of Coulanges. At fifty-seven, he found that he had come into his own. No longer was he out of it—far from it: his was now the popularity, the inordinate success. He was asked every-where, and he always fitted in. His songs particularly, his frivolous neat little songs, became the rage; they flew from mouth to mouth; and the young people, at all the fashionable parties, danced as they sang them. At last they were collected by some busybody and printed, to his fury and delight; and his celebrity was redoubled. At the same time a wonderful rejuvenation came upon him; he seemed to grow younger daily; he drank, he guzzled, with astonishing impunity; there must have been a mistake, he said, in his birth certificate—it was ante-dated at least twenty years. As for his gout, it had gone for ever; he had drowned it by bathing, when he was over sixty, all one summer in the Seine. Madame de Sévigné could only be delighted. She had given a great deal of thought to the matter, she told him, and she had come to the conclusion that he was the happiest man in the world. Probably she was right—she almost always was. But, oddly enough, while Coulanges was undergoing this transformation, a precisely contrary one had befallen his wife. She had, in sober truth, grown old—old, and disillusioned, and serious. She could bear the Court no longer—she despised it; she wavered between piety and stoicism; quietly, persistently, she withdrew into herself. Madame de Sévigné, philosophising and quoting La Fontaine, found—it was surprising—that she admired her— the poor brown leaf; and, on her side, Madame de Coulanges grew more and more devoted to Madame de Sévigné. Her husband mildly amused her. As she watched him flying from country-house to country-house, she suggested that it would save time and trouble if he lived in a swing, so that he might whirl backwards and forwards for the rest of his days, without ever having to touch the earth again. 'C'est toujours son plaisir qui le gouverne,' she observed, with an ironical smile; 'et il est heureux: en faut-il davantage?' Apparently not. Coulanges, adored by beautiful young Duchesses, disputed over by enormously wealthy Dowagers, had nothing left to wish for. The gorgeous Cardinal de Bouillon took him up —so did the Duc de Bouillon, and the Chevalier—all the Bouillons, in fact; it was a delightful family. The Cardinal carried him off to his country palace, where there was music all day long, and the servants had the air of noblemen, and the *ragouts* reached a height of ecstatic piquancy—*ragouts* from every country in Europe, it seemed—how they understood each other when they came together on his plate, he had no idea—but no matter; he ate them all.

In the midst of this, the inevitable and the unimaginable happened: Madame de Sévigné died. The source of order, light, and heat was no more; the reign of Chaos and Old Night descended. One catches a hurried vision of Madame de Grignan, pale as ashes, elaborating sentences of grief; and then she herself and all her belongings—her husband, her son, her castle, with its terraces and towers, its Canons, its violins, its Mistral, its hundred guests—are utterly abolished. For a little longer, through a dim penumbra, Coulanges and his wife remain just visible. She was struck down—overwhelmed with grief and horror. Was it possible, was it really possible, that

Madame de Sévigné was dead? She could hardly believe it. It was a reversal of nature. Surely it could not be. She sat alone, considering life and death, silent, harrowed, and sceptical, while her husband—ah! even her husband felt this blow. The little man wrote a piteous letter to Madame de Grignan's daughter, young Madame de Simiane, and tears blotted the page. He was only a shadow now—all too well he knew it; and yet even shadows must obey the law of their being. In a few weeks he wrote to Madame de Simiane again; he was more cheerful; he was staying with Madame de Louvois in her house at Choisy, a truly delicious abode; but Madame de Simiane must not imagine that he did not pass many moments, in spite of all the company, in sad remembrance of his friend. A few weeks more, and he was dancing; the young people danced, and why should not he, who was as young as the youngest? All the Bouillons were in the house. The jigging vision grows fainter; but a few years later one sees him at the height of his felicity, having been provided by one of his kind friends with a room in the Palace at Versailles. More years pass, he is very old, he is very poor, but what does it matter?—

> Je connais de plus en plus
> En faisant très-grande chère,
> Qu'un estomac qui digère
> Vaut plus de cent mille écus.

On his seventy-sixth birthday he sings and dances, and looks forward to being a hundred without any difficulty at all. Then he eats and drinks, and sings and dances again. And so he disappears.

But Madame de Coulanges, ever sadder and more solitary, stayed in her room, thinking, hour after hour, over the fire. The world was nothing to her; success and happiness nothing; heaven itself nothing. She pulled her long fur-trimmed taffeta gown more closely round her, and pushed about the embers, wondering, for the thousandth time, whether it was really possible that Madame de Sévigné was dead.

1924.

THE SAD STORY OF
DR. COLBATCH

THE REV. DR. COLBATCH could not put up with it any more. Animated by the highest motives, he felt that he must intervene. The task was arduous, odious, dangerous; his antagonist most redoubtable; but Dr. Colbatch was a Doctor of Divinity, Professor of Casuistry in the University of Cambridge, a Senior Fellow of Trinity College, and his duty was plain; the conduct of the Master could be tolerated no longer; Dr. Bentley must go.

In the early years of the eighteenth century the life of learning was agitated, violent, and full of extremes. Everything about it was on the grand scale. Erudition was gigantic, controversies were frenzied, careers were punctuated by brutal triumphs, wild temerities, and dreadful mortifications. One sat, bent nearly double, surrounded by four circles of folios, living to edit Hesychius and confound Dr. Hody, and dying at last with a stomach half-full of sand. The very names of the scholars of those days had something about them at once terrifying and preposterous: there was Graevius, there was Wolfius, there was Cruquius; there were Torrentius and Rutgersius; there was the gloomy Baron de Stosch, and there was the deplorable De Pauw. But Richard Bentley was greater than all these. Combining extraordinary knowledge and almost infinite memory with an acumen hardly to be distinguished from inspiration, and a command of logical precision which might have been envied by mathematicians or generals in the field, he revivified with his dæmonic energy the whole domain of classical scholarship. The peer of the mightiest of his predecessors—of Scaliger, of Casaubon—turning, in skilful strength, the magic glass of science, he brought into focus the world's comprehension of ancient literature with a luminous exactitude of which they had never dreamed. His prowess had first declared itself in his *Dissertation upon the Epistles of Phalaris,* in which he had obliterated under cartloads of erudition and ridicule the miserable Mr. Boyle. He had been rewarded, in the year 1700, when he was not yet forty, with the Mastership of Trinity; and then another side of his genius had appeared. It became evident that he was not merely a scholar, that he was a man of action and affairs, and that he intended to dominate over the magnificent foundation of Trinity with a command as absolute as that which he exercised over questions in Greek grammar. He had immediately gathered into his own hands the entire control of the College; he had manipulated the statutes, rearranged the finances, packed the Council; he had compelled the Society to rebuild and redecorate, at great expense, his own Lodge; he had brought every kind of appointment—scholarships, fellowships, livings—to depend simply upon his will. The Fellows murmured and protested in vain; their terrible tyrant treated them with scant ceremony. 'You will die in your shoes!' he had shouted at one tottering Senior who had ventured to oppose him; and another fat and angry old gentleman he had named 'The College Dog.' In fact, he treated his opponents as if they had been corrupt readings in an old manuscript. At last there was open war. The leading Fellows had appealed to the Visitor of the College, the Bishop of Ely, to remove the Master; and the Master had replied by denying the Bishop's competence and declaring that the visitatorial power lay with the Crown. His subtle mind had detected an ambiguity in the Charter; the legal position was, indeed, highly dubious; and for five years, amid indescribable animosities, he was able to hold his enemies at bay. In the meantime, he had not been idle in other directions: he had annihilated Le Clerc, who, ignorant of Greek, was rash enough to publish a Menander; he had produced a monumental edition of Horace; and he had pulverised Freethinking in the person of Anthony Collins. But his foes had pressed upon him; and eventually it had seemed that his hour was come. In 1714 he had been forced to appear before the Bishop's court; his defence had been weak; the Bishop had drawn up a judgment of deprivation. Then there had been a *coup de théâtre*. The Bishop had suddenly died before delivering judgment. All the previous proceedings lapsed, and Bentley ruled once more supreme in Trinity.

It was at this point that the Rev. Dr. Colbatch, animated by the highest motives, felt that he must intervene. Hitherto he had filled the *rôle* of a peacemaker; but now the outrageous proceedings of the triumphant Master—who, in the flush of victory, was beginning to expel hostile Fellows by force from the College, and had even refused to appoint Dr. Colbatch himself to the Vice-Mastership—called aloud for the resistance of every right-thinking man. And Dr. Colbatch flattered himself that he could resist to some purpose. He had devoted his life to the study of the law; he was a man of the world; he was acquainted with Lord Carteret; and he had written a book on Portugal. Accordingly, he hurried to London and interviewed great personages, who were all of them extremely sympathetic and polite; then he returned to Trinity, and, after delivering a fulminating sermon in the chapel, he bearded the Master at a College meeting, and actually had the nerve to answer him back. Just then, moreover, the tide seemed to be turning against the tyrant. Bentley, not content with the battle in his own College, had begun a campaign against the University. There was a hectic struggle, and then the Vice-Chancellor, by an unparalleled exercise of power, deprived Bentley of his degrees: the Master of Trinity College and the Regius Professor of Divinity was reduced to the status of an undergraduate. This delighted the heart of Dr. Colbatch. He flew to London, where Lord Carteret, as usual, was all smiles and agreement. When, a little later, the College living of Orewell fell vacant, Dr. Colbatch gave a signal proof of his power; for Bentley, after refusing to appoint him to the living, at last found himself obliged to give way. Dr. Colbatch entered the rectory in triumph; was it not clear that that villain at the Lodge was a sinking man? But, whether sinking or no, the villain could still use a pen to some purpose. In a pamphlet on a proposed edition of the New Testament, Bentley took occasion to fall upon Dr. Colbatch tooth and nail. The rector of Orewell was 'a casuistic drudge,' a 'plodding pupil of Escobar,' an insect, a snarling dog, a gnawing rat, a maggot, and a cabbage-head. His intellect was as dark as his countenance; his 'eyes, muscles, and shoulders were wrought up into the most solemn posture of gravity'; he grinned horribly; he was probably mad; and his brother's beard was ludicrously long.

On this Dr. Colbatch, chattering with rage, brought an action against the Master for libel in the Court of the Vice-Chancellor. By a cunning legal device Bentley arranged that the action should be stopped by the Court of King's Bench. Was it possible that Dr. Colbatch's knowledge of the law was not impeccable? He could not believe it, and forthwith composed a pamphlet entitled *Jus Academicum*, in which the whole case, in all its bearings, was laid before the public. The language of the pamphlet was temperate, the references to Bentley were not indecently severe; but, unfortunately, in one or two passages some expressions seemed to reflect upon the competence of the Court of King's Bench. The terrible Master saw his opportunity. He moved the Court of King's Bench to take cognisance of the *Jus Academicum* as a contempt of their jurisdiction. A cold shiver ran down Dr. Colbatch's spine. Was it conceivable? . . . But no! He had friends in London, powerful friends, who would never desert him. He rushed to Downing Street; Lord Townshend was reassuring; so was the Lord Chief Justice; and so was the Lord Chancellor. 'Here,' said Lord Carteret, waving a pen, 'is the magician's wand that will always come to the rescue of Dr. Colbatch.' Surely all was well. Nevertheless, he was summoned to appear before the Court of King's Bench in order to explain his pamphlet. The judge was old and testy; he misquoted Horace—'Jura negat sibi nata, nihil non abrogat'; '*Arrogat*, my lord!' said Dr. Colbatch. A little later the judge once more returned to the quotation, making the same error. '*Arrogat*, my lord!' cried Dr. Colbatch for the second time. Yet once again, in the course of his summing-up, the judge pronounced the word 'abrogat'; '*Arrogat*, my lord!' screamed, for the third time, Dr. Colbatch. The interruption was fatal. The unhappy man was fined £50 and imprisoned for a week.

A less pertinacious spirit would have collapsed under such a dire misadventure; but Dr. Colbatch fought on. For ten years more, still animated by the highest motives, he struggled to dispossess the Master. Something was gained when yet another Bishop was appointed to the See of Ely—a Bishop who disapproved of Bentley's proceedings. With indefatigable zeal Dr. Colbatch laid the case before the Bishop of London, implored the Dean and Chapter of Westminster to interfere, and petitioned the Privy Council. In 1729 the Bishop of Ely summoned Bentley to appear before him; whereupon Bentley appealed to the Crown to decide who was the Visitor of Trinity College. For a moment Dr. Colbatch dreamed of obtaining a special Act of Parliament to deal with his enemy; but even he shrank from such a desperate expedient; and at length, in 1732, the whole case came up for decision before the House of Lords. At that very moment Bentley published his edition of *Paradise Lost*, in which all the best passages were emended and rewritten—a book remarkable as a wild aberration of genius, and no less remarkable as containing, for the first time in print, 'tow'ring o'er the alphabet like Saul,' the great Digamma. If Bentley's object had been to impress his judges in his favour, he failed; for the House of Lords decided that the Bishop of Ely was the Visitor. Once more Bentley was summoned to Ely House. Dr. Colbatch was on tenterhooks; the blow was about to fall; nothing could avert it now, unless—he trembled—if the Bishop were to die again? But the Bishop did not die; in 1734 he pronounced judgment; he deposed Bentley.

So, after thirty years, a righteous doom had fallen upon that proud and wicked man. Dr. Colbatch's exultation was inordinate: it was only equalled, in fact, by his subsequent horror, indignation, and fury. For Bentley had discovered in the Statutes of the College a clause which laid it down that, when the Master was to be removed, the necessary steps were to be taken by the Vice-Master. Now the Vice-Master was Bentley's creature; he never took the necessary steps; and Bentley never ceased, so long as he lived, to be Master of Trinity. Dr. Colbatch petitioned the House of Lords, he applied to the Court of King's Bench, he beseeched Lord Carteret—all in vain. His head turned; he was old, haggard, dying. Tossing on his bed at Orewell, he fell into a delirium; at first his mutterings were inarticulate; but suddenly, starting up, a glare in his eye, he exclaimed, with a strange emphasis, to the utter bewilderment of the bystanders, '*Arrogat*, my lord!' and immediately expired.

1923.

LADY MARY WORTLEY MONTAGU

It has often been observed that our virtues and our vices, no less than our clothes, our furniture, and our fine arts, are subject to the laws of fashion. The duties of one age become the temptations of the next; and the historian of manners might draw up an instructive series of moral fashion-plates, which would display, for each preceding generation, the good and evil most in vogue. If, not content with the bare record, he brought to it some touch of inspiration and of art, he would make us, perhaps, begin to feel at home in those strange worlds which lie so far from us, across such seas of time. When we open some old book of memoirs or of letters we are too apt to turn away from it with the same sort of wondering disgust that fills us when we contemplate the faded photographs of thirty years ago. But a Sir Joshua can make even hoops and wigs and powder seem so natural that the wearers of them are no longer futile shadows to us, but beautiful human creatures whom we love. Crinolines and trunk-hose, ruffs and farthingales—these things are not more out of fashion now than the holiness of the Middle Ages which embodied itself in prayer, asceticism, and dirt, or the ancient Roman magnanimity whose highest glory was suicide. To the Italians of the Renaissance virtue meant self-interested force; to us, it means self-sacrifice. Humanity has come into fashion, and it is hard for us to recognise the antiquated cold nobilities. Yet, if we would explore to any purpose the 'famous nations of the dead,' we must leave our insularity behind us. We must descend naked into those abodes, if we would have a wrestling-match with Death.

Lady Mary Wortley Montagu was one of the dominant

figures of an epoch which, in its ideals of conduct and of feeling, affords a curious contrast with our own. The greatest intellect of her age was the author of *Gulliver's Travels*; its greatest poet the author of the *Dunciad*; and Lady Mary herself was for many years the most vital force in the mechanism of its social life. She was, like her age, cold and hard; she was infinitely unromantic; she was often cynical, and sometimes gross. 'I think there are but two pleasures permitted to mortal man,' she wrote at the end of her life—'love and vengeance'; and she used to say that she did not wish her enemies to die: 'Oh no! let them live! let them have the stone, let them have the gout!' She was, in fact, almost devoid of those sympathetic feelings which appear to us to be the essence of all goodness; so that she is read now, when she is read at all, simply for her wit. But, in reality, she was something more than a brilliant letter-writer; she was a moralist. 'This is the strength and blood of virtue,' says the profound and noble Verulam, 'to contemn things that be desired, and to neglect that which is feared.' And, judged by that high criterion, Lady Mary's virtue assuredly deserves a crown.

To write of her adequately were a task demanding no small share of sympathy and wisdom; and, unhappily, these qualities are conspicuously absent from the volume on *Lady Mary Wortley Montagu and her Times*,[1] which Mr. George Paston has lately put together. The book, with its slipshod writing, its uninstructed outlook, its utter lack of taste and purpose, is a fair specimen of the kind of biographical work which seems to give so much satisfaction to large numbers of our reading public. Decidedly, 'they order the matter better in France,' where such a production could never have appeared. Fourfifths of the book—and it is a bulky one—are devoted to a succession of extracts from Lady Mary's printed correspondence, strung together by feeble paraphrases of passages which have not been quoted, and eked out by a number of tedious and irrelevant letters—hitherto very properly unpublished—

[1] *Lady Mary Wortley Montagu and her Times.* By George Paston. Methuen & Co.

concerning the misadventures of Lady Mary's son. Indeed, the volume would be entirely worthless, and undeserving of comment, were it not for the first 150 pages, which contain a series of newly-discovered letters of the deepest interest. Lady Mary's correspondence falls naturally into four sections, determined by four well-marked periods in her life—the letters written to Edward Wortley before her marriage; the letters written during the Embassy to Constantinople; those written while she was reigning in the society of Twickenham and London; and finally those which she wrote during her long retirement in Italy and France. All the new letters of importance belong to the first section of the correspondence. Those in this series which had previously been published indicated clearly enough the main outline of Lady Mary's earliest love-affair—that which ended in her elopement with Edward Wortley; but the new material fills in the details of this remarkable history, and presents us with a picture which is psychologically complete. Unfortunately, however, the compiler has missed his opportunity. He does not print all the letters; he omits portions from those which he does print; and he does not reprint all those which have already been published, so that, in order to follow the whole correspondence, it is necessary to make constant references to the previous editions. He has, moreover, interspersed his quotations with a number of comments which are altogether out of place. If he had been content to collect into one small volume the text— unabridged and unalloyed—of all the existing letters which passed between Lady Mary and her lover, he would have produced something very much more valuable than his present unwieldy and pretentious work.

'L'on n'aime bien,' says La Bruyère, 'qu'une seule fois, c'est la première; les amours qui suivent sont moins involontaires.' That is the key to the part played by Lady Mary in this curious correspondence. When she fell in love with Edward Wortley, she was a girl of twenty, witty, high-spirited, country-bred, and endowed with a taste for serious reading almost unknown among the young ladies of her times.

He was twelve years her senior; and he came upon her as a rising man of the world, the intimate of the wits and politicians of London, and the possessor of an intellect, a character, and an experience, far riper than her own. She was fascinated by his strong intelligence, his high accomplishments, above all, perhaps by his over-mastering force of will. 'I believe,' she wrote to him forty years later, 'there are few men in the world (I never knew any) capable of such a strength of resolution as yourself.' And he, on his side, found in her the one woman who had ever been able, intellectually, to stand up against him. 'There has not yet been,' he burst out to her in one of his rare moments of enthusiasm, 'there never will be, another Lady Mary.' At first sight, it is difficult to understand what impediments there could have been to the marriage of these minds. There was nothing in either to give offence to the other; their tastes were the same; both were sharp-witted, honest, and eminently sensible; and they were in love. Yet for more than two years they hesitated and held back; and, during that time, there was hardly a moment when one or the other was not on the very brink of breaking off for ever. But they were not ordinary lovers; they were intellectual gladiators, and their letters are like the preliminary wary passes of two well-matched wrestlers before they come to grips. If they had been less well-matched, there would have been no such difficulties; but neither could ever be certain that the other was not too strong. She feared that she liked him too much, and he that she liked him too little. 'I own I was very uneasy,' he wrote to her, 'at the beginning of last winter when I saw you and Mr. K. pressing so close upon each other in the Drawing-room, and found that you could not let me speak to you without being overheard by him. What passed between you at the Trial confirmed my suspicions. 'Twould be useless to reckon up all the Passages that gave me pain. The second time I saw you at the Play this year, I was informed of your Passion for him by one that I knew would not conceal it from others. At the Birthnight you remember the many proofs of your affection for him, and

37

cannot have forgot what passed in his favour at the Ball. My observing that you have since been present at the Park, Operas and Assemblies together, and to finish all your contriving, to have him for one of that select number that serenaded you at Acton, and afterwards danced at the Dutchess's—all this had gone a great way in settling my opinion that he and none but he possessed your heart.' Did Lady Mary flirt? Perhaps she did. Among her papers she preserved a note from a humble admirer, whose innocent adoration forms a curious contrast to the severity of Mr. Wortley: 'Dear Charmer, you are very much in the right to imagine I am in perfect health, for nothing contributes so much to it as your good company and a set of fiddles, and am sorry you made so short a stay at the Ball, for I had not half the satisfaction after you was gone.' But the Charmer, though she may have listened for a moment, was soon back again among her arguments and disputations. When Wortley's jealousy had been quieted, there were all her own uneasinesses to be discussed. She speculated on a dozen different subjects—on life in the country, on the ethics of marriage, on poverty and happiness; her anxious spirit surveyed the distant future, and still found matter for doubt. 'In my present opinion, I think if I was yours and you used me well, nothing could be added to my misfortune should I lose you. But when I suffer my reason to speak, it tells me that in any circumstance of life (wretched or happy) there is a certain proportion of money, as the world is made, absolutely necessary for the living in it. . . . Should I find myself forty years hence your widow, without a competency to maintain me in a manner suitable in some degree to my education, I shall not then be so old I may not impossibly live twenty years longer without what is requisite to make life easy—happiness is what I should not think of.' Sentiments like these from a young lady of twenty-two must have delighted good, careful Mr. Wortley. One is reminded of Professor Raleigh's dictum that in the eighteenth century man lived up to his definition, and was a rational animal; and yet nothing could be further from the truth than to suppose that Lady Mary's financial forethought indicated a coldness of heart. Indeed, precisely the reverse was the case. She was in love for the first time; and she was in love not only involuntarily, but against her will. As her feelings deepened in intensity, she became more and more vehement in her determination not to be carried away by them—to be as dispassionately sensible as a mathematician at work on a theorem. Her logic rose like quicksilver as her heat increased, until at last, when it reached the boiling point, the thermometer burst. In a fine letter, written in reply to the suspicious accusations of her lover, it is easy to trace the process. She begins with wit, she goes on to reasoning, she ends in tears: 'The sense of your letter I take to be this. Madam, you are the greatest Coquette I ever knew, and withal very silly; the only happiness you propose to yourself in a Husband is jilting him most abundantly. You must stay till my Lord Hide is a widower or Heaven raises up another Mr. Popham; for my part I know all your tricks. . . . This is the exact miniature of your letter.' After this, Lady Mary proceeds to describe her ideal husband: 'My first and chiefest wish, if I had a Companion, it should be one (now am I going to make you a picture of my own heart) that I very much loved and that loved me; one that thought that the truest wisdom which most conduced to our happiness, and that it was not below a man of sense to take satisfaction in the conversation of a reasonable woman; one who did not think tenderness a disgrace to his understanding . . . one that would be as willing to be happy as I would be to make him so.' And then, suddenly, she breaks out: 'After this description of whom I could like, I need not add that it is not you—you who could suspect where you have the least reason, that thinks so wrong of me, as to believe me everything I abhor. . . . I desire you think no more of me. . . . I am heartily glad I can have no answer to this letter, tho' if I could I should now have the courage to return it unopened. You are unjust and I am unhappy—'tis past—I will never think of you more—never.' Lady Mary's thermometer had burst.

These strange love-letters are full not only of emotion mixed with common sense, but also of a kind of plain-speaking no less remarkable, and, to modern notions, even more out of place. In a subsequent letter—for of course the thermometer had been repaired—Mr. Wortley, still suspecting a rival, and at the same time determined to make his own position clear, wrote to Lady Mary: 'Out of tenderness to you I have forborn to state your case in the plainest light, which is thus. If you have no thoughts of [gallantry] you are mad if you marry him. If you are likely to think of [gallantry] you are mad if you marry me.' To the word in brackets the compiler appends the following note: 'Mr. Wortley uses a word of Elizabethan crudity. In her reply Lady Mary softens it down to "gallantry." Her example is here followed.' This is a piece of unmeaning prudery, but we must be thankful that the passage, even thus mutilated, has been allowed to come to light. For Lady Mary did not flinch before the brutality of her lover; and the reply which she gave to his sharp questioning was actually her final surrender: 'If you please, I will never see another man. . . . I have examined my own heart whether I can leave everything for you; I think I can. If I change my mind, you shall know before Sunday; after that I will not change my mind.'

And, for the first and last time, she did not. In the excitement of the moment, Edward Wortley's usual calm forsook him, and he despatched a letter full of ecstasy and passion and protestations of eternal love. 'The greatest part of my life shall be dedicated to you,' he wrote. 'From everything that can lessen my passion for you I will fly with as much speed as from the Plague. I shall sooner chuse to see my heart torn from my breast than divided from you.' The only difficulties that remained were material ones. Lady Mary's father had set his heart against the match, and, gaining wind of the intentions of the lovers, carried off his daughter at the last moment to his country seat in Wiltshire. Mr. Wortley followed in a post-chaise, came up with the fugitives at an inn on the road, and managed to abstract the lady. 'If we should once get into a coach,' he had written a few days earlier, 'let us not say one word till we come before the parson, lest we should engage in fresh disputes.' The advice was excellent, but who can believe that it was followed? One can imagine the bitter altercations in the flying carriage, as it swept along between the country hedgerows on its way to 'the parson.' Did Lady Mary put out her hand, more than once, towards the cord? Ah! how long ago it is since all that was buried in oblivion!—

> Ay, ages long ago
> These lovers fled away! . . .

But, at any rate, they drew up before the church at a happy moment. For, when they reached the altar, neither the one nor the other refused to say 'I will.'

Lady Mary's subsequent history may be briefly told. Her marriage was a complete failure, and, oddly enough, a failure of the ordinary kind. There were no exciting ruptures; there was only a gradual estrangement, ending at last in almost absolute indifference. Edward Wortley became engrossed in politics and money-making, while his wife, disillusioned, reckless, and brilliant, plunged into the vortex of fashionable London. One day she looked in her looking-glass and found she had grown old; upon which she packed her boxes, retired to an Italian villa, and never looked at a looking-glass again. The last twenty years of her life were spent in that atmosphere of physical and moral laxity which seems in those days to have inevitably surrounded the unattached Englishwoman who lived abroad. Horace Walpole describes her at Florence in language of disgusting minuteness, calls her 'Moll Worthless,' and declares that she was 'so far gone' in her love for a handsome young gentleman that 'she literally took him out to dance country dances last night at a formal ball, where there was no measure kept in laughing at her old, foul, tawdry, painted, plastered personage.' And, though Walpole disliked Lady Mary, there can be little doubt that his account of her represents the superficial truth about her later years. But there was another side of her, which neither Walpole nor the majority of her contemporaries had any conception of—the side revealed in the long series of letters to her daughter, Lady Bute. These letters contain the last act of Lady Mary's tragedy. That tragedy began when, in her early days, she became the battlefield over which her intellect and her emotions furiously fought. It had been her dream that Edward Wortley would satisfy both; and he satisfied neither. The battle continued to the end of her life, and, as she grew older, her emotions became even more arbitrary and sterile, her intellect more penetrating and severe. Her dream of perfect love, which Wortley had shattered, haunted her like a ghost. In her old age she wrote an essay to disprove the maxim of La Rochefoucauld, 'qu'il y a des mariages commodes mais point de délicieux'; she described the exquisite felicity of 'une estime parfaite, fixée par la reconnaissance, soutenue par l'inclination, et éveillée par la tendresse de l'amour'; she lingered over 'la joye de voir qu'on fait le bonheur entier de l'objet aimé—en quel point,' she said, 'je place la jouissance parfaite.' Alas! in her bedraggled Italian adventures, what kind of *jouissance* was it that she found? That she refused to palliate her situation, that she faced her wretched failure without flinching and without pretence—there lay the intellectual eminence which lifts her melancholy history out of the sordid into the sublime. There is something great, something not to be forgotten, about the honesty with which she looked into the worthlessness of things, and the bravery with which she accepted it. In one of her very latest letters she quoted a couplet which might well stand as the motto for the book of her destiny—the summary of what was noblest and most essential in the spirit of her life—

> To dare in fields is valour; but how few
> Dare have the real courage to be true?

1907.

HUME

In what resides the most characteristic virtue of humanity? In good works? Possibly. In the creation of beautiful objects? Perhaps. But some would look in a different direction, and find it in detachment. To all such David Hume must be a great saint in the calendar; for no mortal being was ever more completely divested of the trammels of the personal and the particular, none ever practised with a more consummate success the divine art of impartiality. And certainly to have no axe to grind is something very noble and very rare. It may be said to be the antithesis of the bestial. A series of creatures might be constructed, arranged according to their diminishing interest in the immediate environment, which would begin with the amœba and end with the mathematician. In pure mathematics the maximum of detachment appears to be reached: the mind moves in an infinitely complicated pattern, which is absolutely free from temporal considerations. Yet this very freedom—the essential condition of the mathematician's activity—perhaps gives him an unfair advantage. He can only be wrong—he cannot cheat. But the metaphysician can. The problems with which he deals are of overwhelming importance to himself and the rest of humanity; and it is his business to treat them with an exactitude as unbiased as if they were some puzzle in the theory of numbers. That is his business—and his glory. In the mind of a Hume one can watch at one's ease this superhuman balance of contrasting opposites—the questions of so profound a moment, the answers of so supreme a calm. And the same beautiful quality may be traced in the current of his life, in which the wisdom of philosophy so triumphantly interpenetrated the vicissitudes of the mortal lot.

His history falls into three stages—youth, maturity, repose. The first was the most important. Had Hume died at the age of twenty-six his real work in the world would have been done, and his fame irrevocably established. Born in 1711, the younger son of a small Scottish landowner, he was very early dominated by that passion for literary pursuits which never left him for the rest of his life. When he was twenty-two one of those crises occurred—both physical and mental—which not uncommonly attack young men of genius when their adolescence is over, and determine the lines of their destiny. Hume was suddenly overcome by restlessness, ill-health, anxiety and hesitation. He left home, went to London, and then to Bristol, where, with the idea of making an independent fortune, he became a clerk in a merchant's office. 'But,' as he wrote long afterwards in his autobiography, 'in a few months I found that scene totally unsuitable to me.' No wonder; and then it was that, by a bold stroke of instinctive wisdom, he took the strange step which was the starting-point of his career. He went to France, where he remained for three years—first at Rheims, then at La Flèche, in Anjou —entirely alone, with only just money enough to support an extremely frugal existence, and with only the vaguest prospects before him. During those years he composed his *Treatise of Human Nature*, the masterpiece which contains all that is most important in his thought. The book opened a new era in philosophy. The last vestiges of theological prepossessions— which were still faintly visible in Descartes and Locke—were discarded; and reason, in all her strength and all her purity, came into her own. It is in the sense that Hume gives one of being committed absolutely to reason—of following wherever reason leads, with a complete, and even reckless, confidence— that the great charm of his writing consists. But it is not only that: one is not alone; one is in the company of a supremely competent guide. With astonishing vigour, with heavenly lucidity, Hume leads one through the confusion and the darkness of speculation. One has got into an aeroplane, which has glided imperceptibly from the ground; with thrilling ease one mounts and mounts; and, supported by the mighty power of intellect, one looks out, to see the world below one, as one has never seen it before. In the Treatise there is something that does not appear again in Hume's work—a feeling of excitement—the excitement of discovery. At moments he even hesitates, and stands back, amazed at his own temerity. 'The *intense* view of these manifold contradictions and imperfections in human reason has so wrought upon me, and heated my brain, that I am ready to reject all belief and reasoning, and can look upon no opinion even as more probable or likely than another. Where am I, or what? From what causes do I derive my existence, and to what condition shall I return? Whose favour shall I court, and whose anger must I dread? What beings surround me? and on whom have I any influence, or who have influence on me? I am confounded with all these questions, and begin to fancy myself in the most deplorable condition imaginable, environed with the deepest darkness, and utterly deprived of the use of every member and faculty.' And then his courage returns once more, and he speeds along on his exploration.

The Treatise, published in 1738, was a complete failure. For many years more Hume remained in poverty and insignificance. He eked out a living by precarious secretaryships, writing meanwhile a series of essays on philosophical, political and æsthetic subjects, which appeared from time to time in small volumes, and gradually brought him a certain reputation. It was not till he was over forty, when he was made librarian to the Faculty of Advocates in Edinburgh, that his position became secure. The appointment gave him not only a small competence, but the command of a large library; and he determined to write the history of England—a task which occupied him for the next ten years.

The History was a great success; many editions were printed; and in his own day it was chiefly as a historian that Hume was known to the general public. After his death his work continued for many years the standard history of England, until, with a new age, new fields of knowledge were opened up and a new style of historical writing became fashionable. The book is highly typical of the eighteenth century. It was an attempt—one of the very earliest—to apply intelligence to the events of the past. Hitherto, with very few exceptions (Bacon's *Henry the Seventh* was one of them) history had been in the hands of memoir writers like Commines and Clarendon, or moralists like Bossuet. Montesquieu, in his *Considérations sur les Romains*, had been the first to break the new ground; but his book, brilliant and weighty as it was, must be classed rather as a philosophical survey than a historical narration. Voltaire, almost exactly contemporary with Hume, was indeed a master of narrative, but was usually too much occupied with discrediting Christianity to be a satisfactory historian. Hume had no such *arrière pensée*; he only wished to tell the truth as he saw it, with clarity and elegance. And he succeeded. In his volumes—especially those on the Tudors and Stuarts—one may still find entertainment and even instruction. Hume was an extremely intelligent man, and anything that he had to say on English history could not fail to be worth attending to. But, unfortunately, mere intelligence is not itself quite enough to make a great historian. It was not simply that Hume's knowledge of his subjects was insufficient—that an enormous number of facts, which have come into view since he wrote, have made so many of his statements untrue and so many of his comments unmeaning; all that is serious, but it is not more serious than the circumstance that his cast of mind was in reality ill-fitted for the task he had undertaken. The virtues of a metaphysician are the vices of a historian. A generalised, colourless, unimaginative view of things is admirable when one is considering the law of causality, but one needs something else if one has to describe Queen Elizabeth.

This fundamental weakness is materialised in the style of the History. Nothing could be more enchanting than Hume's style when he is discussing philosophical subjects. The grace and clarity of exquisite writing are enhanced by a touch of colloquialism—the tone of a polished conversation. A personality—a most engaging personality—just appears. The cat-like touches of ironic malice—hints of something very sharp behind the velvet—add to the effect. 'Nothing,' Hume concludes, after demolishing every argument in favour of the immortality of the soul, 'could set in a fuller light the infinite obligations which mankind have to divine revelation, since we find that no other medium could ascertain this great and important truth.' The sentence is characteristic of Hume's writing at its best, where the pungency of the sense varies in direct proportion with the mildness of the expression. But such effects are banished from the History. A certain formality, which Hume doubtless supposed was required by the dignity of the subject, is interposed between the reader and the author; an almost completely latinised vocabulary makes vividness impossible; and a habit of *oratio obliqua* has a deadening effect. We shall never know exactly what Henry the Second said—in some uncouth dialect of French or English—in his final exasperation against Thomas of Canterbury; but it was certainly something about 'a set of fools and cowards,' and 'vengeance,' and 'an upstart clerk.' Hume, however, preferred to describe the scene as follows: 'The King himself being vehemently agitated, burst forth with an exclamation against his servants, whose want of zeal, he said, had so long left him exposed to the enterprises of that ungrateful and imperious prelate.' Such phrasing, in conjunction with the Middle Ages, is comic. The more modern centuries seem to provide a more appropriate field for urbanity, aloofness and common sense. The measured cynicism of Hume's comments on Cromwell, for instance, still makes good reading—particularly as a corrective to the *O, altitudo!* sentimentalities of Carlyle.

Soon after his completion of the History Hume went to Paris as the secretary to the English Ambassador. He was now a celebrity, and French society fell upon him with delirious delight. He was flattered by princes, worshipped by fine ladies, and treated as an oracle by the *philosophes*. To such an extent did he become the fashion that it was at last positively *de rigueur* to have met him, and a lady who, it was discovered, had not even seen the great philosopher, was banished from Court. His appearance, so strangely out of keeping with mental agility, added to the fascination. 'His face,' wrote one of his friends, 'was broad and flat, his mouth wide, and without any other expression than that of imbecility. His eyes vacant and spiritless, and the corpulence of his whole person was far better fitted to communicate the idea of a turtle-eating alderman than of a refined philosopher.' All this was indeed delightful to the French. They loved to watch the awkward affability of the uncouth figure, to listen in rapt attention to the extraordinary French accent, and when, one evening, at a party, the adorable man appeared in a charade as a sultan between two lovely ladies and could only say, as he struck his chest, over and over again 'Eh bien, mesdemoiselles, eh bien, vous voilà donc!' their ecstasy reached its height. It seemed indeed almost impossible to believe in this combination of the outer and inner man. Even his own mother never got below the surface. 'Our Davie,' she is reported to have said, 'is a fine good-natured cratur, but uncommon wake-minded.' In no sense whatever was this true. Hume was not only brilliant as an abstract thinker and a writer; he was no less competent in the practical affairs of life. In the absence of the Ambassador he was left in Paris for some months as *chargé d'affaires*, and his despatches still exist to show that he understood diplomacy as well as ratiocination.

Entirely unmoved by the raptures of Paris, Hume returned to Edinburgh, at last a prosperous and wealthy man. For seven years he lived in his native capital, growing comfortably old amid leisure, books, and devoted friends. It is to this final period of his life that those pleasant legends belong which reveal the genial charm, the happy temperament, of the philosopher. There is the story of the tallow-chandler's wife, who arrived to deliver a monitory message from on High, but was diverted from her purpose by a tactful order for an enormous number of candles. There is the well-known tale of the weighty philosopher getting stuck in the boggy ground at the base of the Castle rock, and calling on a passing old woman to help him out. She doubted whether any help should be given to the author of the Essay on Miracles. 'But, my good woman, does not your religion as a Christian teach you to do good, even to your enemies?' 'That may be,' was the reply, 'but ye

shallna get out of that till ye become a Christian yersell: and
repeat the Lord's Prayer and the Belief'—a feat that was
accomplished with astonishing alacrity. And there is the vision
of the mountainous metaphysician seated, amid a laughing
party of young ladies, on a chair that was too weak for him,
and suddenly subsiding to the ground.

In 1776, when Hume was sixty-five, an internal complaint, to which he had long been subject, completely undermined his health, and recovery became impossible. For many
months he knew he was dying, but his mode of life remained
unaltered, and, while he gradually grew weaker, his cheerful-
ness continued unabated. With ease, with gaiety, with the
simplicity of perfect taste, he gently welcomed the inevitable.
This wonderful equanimity lasted till the very end. There
was no ostentation of stoicism, much less any Addisonian
dotting of death-bed i's. Not long before he died he amused
himself by writing his autobiography—a model of pointed
brevity. In one of his last conversations—it was with Adam
Smith—he composed an imaginary conversation between
himself and Charon, after the manner of Lucian: ' "Have a
little patience, good Charon, I have been endeavouring to
open the eyes of the Public. If I live a few years longer, I may
have the satisfaction of seeing the downfall of some of the
prevailing systems of superstition." But Charon would then
lose all temper and decency. "You loitering rogue, that will
not happen these many hundred years. Do you fancy I will
grant you a lease for so long a term? Get into the boat this
instant, you lazy, loitering rogue." ' Within a few days of his
death he wrote a brief letter to his old friend, the Comtesse de
Boufflers; it was the final expression of a supreme detachment.
'My disorder,' he said, 'is a diarrhœa, or disorder in my
bowels, which has been gradually undermining me these two
years; but, within these six months, has been visibly hasten-
ing me to my end. I see death approach gradually, without
anxiety or regret. I salute you, with great affection and
regard, for the last time.'

1928.

VOLTAIRE

BETWEEN the collapse of the Roman Empire and the Industrial Revolution three men were the intellectual masters of Europe—Bernard of Clairvaux, Erasmus, and Voltaire. In Bernard the piety and the superstition of the Middle Ages attained their supreme embodiment; in Erasmus the learning and the humanity of the Renaissance. But Erasmus was a tragic figure. The great revolution in the human mind, of which he had been the presiding genius, ended in failure; he lived to see the tide of barbarism rising once more over the world; and it was left to Voltaire to carry off the final victory. By a curious irony, the Renaissance contained within itself the seeds of its ruin. That very enlightenment which seemed to be leading the way to the unlimited progress of the race involved Europe in the internecine struggles of nationalism and religion. England alone, by a series of accidents, of which the complexion of Anne Boleyn, a storm in the Channel, and the character of Charles I were the most important, escaped disaster. There the spirit of Reason found for itself a not too precarious home; and by the beginning of the eighteenth century a civilisation had been evolved which, in essentials, was not very far distant from the great ideals of the Renaissance. In the meantime the rest of Europe had relapsed into mediævalism. If Bernard of Clairvaux had returned to life at the end of the seventeenth century, he would have been perfectly at home at Madrid, and not at all uncomfortable at Versailles. At last, in France, the beginnings of a change became discernible. The incompetence of Louis XIV's government threw discredit upon the principles of bigotry and obscurantism; with the death of the old King there was a reaction among thinking men towards scepticism and toleration;

and the movement was set on foot which ended, seventy-five years later, in the French Revolution. Of this movement Voltaire was the master spirit. For a generation he was the commander-in-chief in the great war against mediævalism. Eventually, by virtue of his extraordinary literary skill, his incredible energy, and his tremendous force of character, he dominated Europe, and the Victory was won. The upheaval which followed, though it was perhaps inevitable, would certainly not have pleased him; but the violence of the French Revolution and its disastrous consequences were evils of small magnitude compared with the new and terrible complication in which, at the very moment, mankind became involved. The ironical Fates were at work again. By a strange chance, no sooner was mediævalism dead than industrialism was born. The mechanical ingenuity of a young man in Glasgow plunged the world into a whole series of enormous and utterly unexpected difficulties, which are still clamouring to be solved. Thus the progress which the Renaissance had envisioned, and which had seemed assured at the end of the eighteenth century, was once more side-tracked. Yet the work of Voltaire was not undone. Short of some overwhelming catastrophe, the doctrine which he preached—that life should be ruled, not by the dictates of tyranny and superstition, but by those of reason and humanity—can never be obliterated from the minds of men.

Voltaire's personal history was quite as remarkable as his public achievement. Sense and sensibility were the two qualities which formed the woof and the warp of his life. Good sense was the basis of his being—that supreme good sense which shows itself not only in taste and judgment, but in every field of activity—in an agile adaptation of means to ends, in an unerring acumen in the practical affairs of the world; and Voltaire would probably have become a great lawyer, or possibly a great statesman, had not this fundamental characteristic of his been shot through and through by a vehement sensitiveness—a nervous susceptibility of amazing intensity, which impregnated his solidity with a fierce electric fluid, and made him an artist, an egotist, a delirious enthusiast, dancing, screaming, and gesticulating to the last moment of an extreme old age. This latter quality was no doubt largely the product of physical causes—of an overstrung nervous system and a highly capricious digestion. He was in fact an excellent example of his own theory, propounded when he was over eighty in the delicious *Les Oreilles du Comte de Chesterfield,* that the prime factor in the world's history has always been *la chaise percée.* So constituted, it was almost inevitable that he should take to the profession of letters—the obvious career for a lively and intelligent young man—and, in particular, that he should write tragedies, the tragedy holding in those days the place of the novel in our own. Naturally he was precocious; and by the time he was thirty he was a successful dramatist and a fashionable poet, enjoying a royal pension and the flattering attentions of high society. Then there was a catastrophe which changed his whole life. He quarrelled with the Chevalier de Rohan, was beaten by hired roughs, found himself ridiculed and cut by his fine friends, and finally shut up in the Bastille. This was the first of a long chain of circumstances which ultimately made him the champion of liberty in Europe. But for the Chevalier de Rohan he might have been engulfed in the successes and pleasures of the capital. The *coups de bâton* suddenly made him serious: never again was he satisfied with the state of the world.

The importance of his English exile, which followed, has usually been exaggerated. Voltaire did not need to learn infidelity from the English deists, and he never did learn very much about English political institutions. England was not a cause, but a symbol of his discontent. His book upon the subject was his first definite declaration of war upon the old *régime,* and it was burnt accordingly by the common hangman. It might have been supposed that his course was now clear, that he was embarked, once and for all, on a career of struggle and propaganda. But this was not the case. Circumstance intervened once more, in the shape of the eccentric and terrific Madame du Châtelet, who carried him off to her remote country house, and kept him there for fifteen years engaged on scientific experiments. This long period, which filled the middle years of his life (from forty to fifty-five), though it seems at first sight to have been almost wasted, was in reality a blessing in disguise, for it gave him what was absolutely essential for his future work—a European reputation. When Madame du Châtelet died (at exactly the right moment), Voltaire was recognised not merely as the greatest living dramatist and poet, and as a brilliant exponent of new ideas, but as a man of encyclopædic knowledge, whose claim to rank as a solid and serious thinker it was impossible to dismiss. All that was needed to put the crown upon his celebrity was some piece of resoundingly personal *réclame*; and this was provided by the Berlin episode, with its splendid opening, its preposterous developments, its hectic climax, and its violent close.

At the age of sixty Voltaire was the most famous man in the world. Yet it is strange to think that his fame was founded on achievements that were almost entirely ephemeral, and that if he had died then he would be remembered now merely as an overrated poet and a very clever man. His first sixty years were in reality nothing but an apprenticeship for those that were to follow. Settled down at last at Ferney, on the borders of France and Switzerland, perfectly independent, with the large fortune which his business shrewdness had amassed for him, with his colossal reputation, and his pen, Voltaire began the work of his life. Apart from his personal prowess, most of the elements in the situation were favourable to him. The time was ripe: the new movement was like an engine which had slowly risen up a long and steep ascent, and was standing at the top, waiting for a master hand to propel it forward and downward with irresistible force. But there were two contingencies, either of which might at any moment have proved fatal. Everything depended upon Voltaire's continuing at Ferney for a considerable time: it was clearly impossible to *écraser l'infâme* in a year or so. Yet how many years could he count upon? With his abominable health, he had very little reason to hope for a long old age. Nevertheless, a very long old age was granted him. Incredible as it seemed, he lived to be eighty-four, maintaining the whole vigour of his extra-ordinary vitality to the last second of his existence: for a quarter of a century he worked with his full power. The other danger lay in the curious fact that he himself never quite realised the strength of his position. In his restless egotism he was perpetually trying to get leave to return to Paris; and if he had succeeded the greater part of his influence would almost certainly have disappeared. At Ferney he was his own master; he was safe from the intrigues of the capital; and his remoteness invested him and everything about him with the mysterious grandeur of a myth. If the authorities had had the slightest foresight, they would have welcomed him with open arms to Paris, where his time would have been wasted in society, where his quarrelsomeness would have landed him sooner or later in some dreadful mess, where, inevitably, the 'patriarch' would at last have vanished altogether in the very fallible old gentleman. It was the final stroke of luck in an amazingly lucky life that Voltaire should have been saved from his own folly by the folly of his enemies.

The history of the years at Ferney is written at large in that gigantic correspondence which forms one of the most impressive monuments of human energy known to the world. Besides the vast body of facts which it contains, besides the day-to-day record of a moving and memorable struggle, besides the exquisite beauty, the æsthetic perfection, of its form, there emerges from it, with peculiar distinctness, the vision of a human spirit. It cannot be said that that vision is altogether a pleasing one. There is a natural tendency—visible in England, perhaps, especially—towards the elegant embellishment of great men; and Voltaire has not escaped the process. In Miss Tallentyre's translation, for instance, of a small selection from his letters, with an introduction and notes,[1] Voltaire is presented to us as a kindly, gentle, respectable personage, a tolerant, broad-minded author, who ended his life as a country gentleman much interested in the drama and social reform.

[1] *Voltaire in his Letters. Being a Selection from his Correspondence.* Translated with a Preface and Forewords by S. G. Tallentyre. Murray.

Such a picture would be merely ridiculous, if it were not calculated to mislead. The fact that Voltaire devoted his life to one of the noblest of causes must not blind us to another fact—that he was personally a very ugly customer. He was a frantic, desperate fighter, to whom all means were excusable; he was a trickster, a rogue; he lied, he blasphemed, and he was extremely indecent. He was, too, quite devoid of dignity, adopting, whenever he saw fit, the wildest expedients and the most extravagant postures; there was, in fact, a strong element of farce in his character, which he had the wit to exploit for his own ends. At the same time he was inordinately vain, and mercilessly revengeful; he was as mischievous as a monkey, and as cruel as a cat. At times one fancies him as a puppet on wires, a creature raving in a mechanical frenzy—and then one remembers that lucid, piercing intellect, that overwhelming passion for reason and liberty. The contradiction is strange; but the world is full of strange contradictions; and, on the whole, it is more interesting, and also wiser, to face them than to hush them up.

1919.

VOLTAIRE AND ENGLAND[1]

THE visit of Voltaire to England marks a turning-point in the history of civilisation. It was the first step in a long process of interaction—big with momentous consequences—between the French and English cultures. For centuries the combined forces of mutual ignorance and political hostility had kept the two nations apart: Voltaire planted a small seed of friendship which, in spite of a thousand hostile influences, grew and flourished mightily. The seed, no doubt, fell on good ground, and no doubt, if Voltaire had never left his native country, some chance wind would have carried it over the narrow seas, so that history in the main would have been unaltered. But actually his was the hand which did the work.

It is unfortunate that our knowledge of so important a period of Voltaire's life should be extremely incomplete. Carlyle, who gave a hasty glance at it in his life of Frederick, declared that he could find nothing but 'mere inanity and darkness visible'; and since Carlyle's day the progress has been small. A short chapter in Desnoiresterres' long Biography and an essay by Churton Collins did something to co-ordinate the few known facts. Another step was taken a few years ago with the publication of M. Lanson's elaborate and exhaustive edition of the *Lettres Philosophiques*, the work in which Voltaire gave to the world the distilled essence of his English experiences. And now M. Lucien Foulet has brought together all the extant letters concerning the period, which he has collated with scrupulous exactitude and to which he has added a series of valuable appendices upon various obscure and disputed points. M. Lanson's great attainments are well

[1] *Correspondance de Voltaire* (1726–1729). By Lucien Foulet. Paris; Hachette, 1913.

known, and to say that M. Foulet's work may fitly rank as a supplementary volume to the edition of the *Lettres Philosophiques* is simply to say that he is a worthy follower of that noble tradition of profound research and perfect lucidity which has made French scholarship one of the glories of European culture.

Upon the events in particular which led up to Voltaire's departure for England, M. Foulet has been able to throw considerable light. The story, as revealed by the letters of contemporary observers and the official documents of the police, is an instructive and curious one. In the early days of January 1726 Voltaire, who was thirty-one years of age, occupied a position which, so far as could be seen upon the surface, could hardly have been more fortunate. He was recognised everywhere as the rising poet of the day; he was a successful dramatist; he was a friend of Madame de Prie, who was all-powerful at Court, and his talents had been rewarded by a pension from the royal purse. His brilliance, his gaiety, his extraordinary capacity for being agreeable had made him the pet of the narrow and aristocratic circle which dominated France. Dropping his middle-class antecedents as completely as he had dropped his middle-class name, young Arouet, the notary's offspring, floated at his ease through the palaces of dukes and princes, with whose sons he drank and jested, and for whose wives—it was *de rigueur* in those days—he expressed all the ardours of a passionate and polite devotion. Such was his roseate situation when, all at once, the catastrophe came. One night at the Opéra the Chevalier de Rohan-Chabot, of the famous and powerful family of the Rohans, a man of forty-three, quarrelsome, blustering, whose reputation for courage left something to be desired, began to taunt the poet upon his birth—'Monsieur Arouet, Monsieur Voltaire—what *is* your name?' To which the retort came quickly—'Whatever my name may be, I know how to preserve the honour of it.' The Chevalier muttered something and went off, but the incident was not ended. Voltaire had let his high spirits and his sharp tongue carry him too far, and he was to pay the penalty. It was not an age in which it was safe to be too witty with lords. 'Now mind, Dancourt,' said one of those *grands seigneurs* to the leading actor of the day, 'if you're more amusing than I am at dinner to night, *je te donnerai cent coups de bâtons.*' It was dangerous enough to show one's wits at all in the company of such privileged persons, but to do so at their expense—! A few days later Voltaire and the Chevalier met again, at the Comédie, in Adrienne Lecouvreur's dressing-room. Rohan repeated his sneering question and 'the Chevalier has had his answer' was Voltaire's reply. Furious, Rohan lifted his stick, but at that moment Adrienne very properly fainted, and the company dispersed. A few days more and Rohan had perfected the arrangements for his revenge. Voltaire, dining at the Duc de Sully's, where, we are told, he was on the footing of a son of the house, received a message that he was wanted outside in the street. He went out, was seized by a gang of lackeys, and beaten before the eyes of Rohan, who directed operations from a cab. 'Epargnez la tête,' he shouted, 'elle est encore bonne pour faire rire le public'; upon which, according to one account, there were exclamations from the crowd which had gathered round of 'Ah! le bon seigneur!' The sequel is known to everyone: how Voltaire rushed back, dishevelled and agonised, into Sully's dining-room, how he poured out his story in an agitated flood of words, and how that high-born company, with whom he had been living up to that moment on terms of the closest intimacy, now only displayed the signs of a frigid indifference. The caste-feeling had suddenly asserted itself. Poets, no doubt, were all very well in their way, but really, if they began squabbling with noblemen, what could they expect? And then the callous and stupid convention of that still half-barbarous age—the convention which made misfortune the proper object of ridicule—came into play no less powerfully. One might take a poet seriously, perhaps—until he was whipped; then, of course, one could only laugh at him. For the next few days, wherever Voltaire went he was received with icy looks, covert smiles, or exaggerated politeness.

The Prince de Conti, who, a month or two before, had written an ode in which he placed the author of *Œdipe* side by side with the authors of *Le Cid* and *Phèdre*, now remarked, with a shrug of the shoulders, that 'ces coups de bâtons étaient bien reçus et mal donnés.' 'Nous serions bien malheureux,' said another well-bred personage, as he took a pinch of snuff, 'si les poètes n'avaient pas des épaules.' Such friends as remained faithful were helpless. Even Madame de Prie could do nothing. 'Le pauvre Voltaire me fait grande pitié,' she said; 'dans le fond il a raison.' But the influence of the Rohan family was too much for her, and she could only advise him to disappear for a little into the country, lest worse should befall. Disappear he did, remaining for the next two months concealed in the outskirts of Paris, where he practised swordsmanship against his next meeting with his enemy. The situation was cynically topsy-turvy. As M. Foulet points out, Rohan had legally rendered himself liable, under the edict against duelling, to a long term of imprisonment, if not to the penalty of death. Yet the law did not move, and Voltaire was left to take the only course open in those days to a man of honour in such circumstances—to avenge the insult by a challenge and a fight. But now the law, which had winked at Rohan, began to act against Voltaire. The police were instructed to arrest him so soon as he should show any sign of an intention to break the peace. One day he suddenly appeared at Versailles, evidently on the lookout for Rohan, and then as suddenly vanished. A few weeks later, the police reported that he was in Paris, lodging with a fencing-master, and making no concealment of his desire to 'insulter incessamment et avec éclat M. le chevalier de Rohan.' This decided the authorities, and accordingly on the night of the 17th of April, as we learn from the *Police Gazette*, 'le sieur Arrouët de Voltaire, fameux poète,' was arrested, and conducted 'par ordre du Roi' to the Bastille.

A letter, written by Voltaire to his friend Madame de Bernières while he was still in hiding, reveals the effect which these events had produced upon his mind. It is the first letter in the series of his collected correspondence which is not all Epicurean elegance and caressing wit. The wit, the elegance, the finely turned phrase, the shifting smile—these things are still visible there no doubt, but they are informed and over-mastered by a new, an almost ominous spirit: Voltaire, for the first time in his life, is serious.

J'ai été à l'extrémité; je n'attends que ma convalescence pour abandonner à jamais ce pays-ci. Souvenez-vous de l'amitié tendre que vous avez eue pour moi; au nom de cette amitié informez-moi par un mot de votre main de ce qui se passe, ou parlez à l'homme que je vous envoi, en qui vous pouvez prendre une entière confiance. Présentez mes respects à Madame du Deffand; dites à Thieriot que je veux absolument qu'il m'aime, ou quand je serai mort, ou quand je serai heureux; jusque-là, je lui pardonne son indifférence. Dites à M. le chevalier des Alleurs que je n'oublierai jamais la générosité de ses procédés pour moi. Comptez que tout détrompé que je suis de la vanité des amitiés humaines, la vôtre me sera à jamais précieuse. Je ne souhaite de revenir à Paris que pour vous voir, vous embrasser encore une fois, et vous faire voir ma constance dans mon amitié et dans mes malheurs.

'Présentez mes respects à Madame du Deffand!' Strange indeed are the whirligigs of Time! Madame de Bernières was then living in none other than that famous house at the corner of the Rue de Beaune and the Quai des Théatins (now Quai Voltaire) where, more than half a century later, the writer of those lines was to come, bowed down under the weight of an enormous celebrity, to look for the last time upon Paris and the world; where, too, Madame du Deffand herself, decrepit, blind, and bitter with the disillusionments of a strange lifetime, was to listen once more to the mellifluous enchantments of that extraordinary intelligence, which—so it seemed to her as she sat entranced—could never, never grow old.[1]

Voltaire was not kept long in the Bastille. For some time

---

[1] 'Il est aussi animé qu'il ait jamais été. Il a quatre-vingt-quatre ans, et en vérité je le crois immortel; il jouit de tous ses sens, aucun même n'est affaibli; c'est un être bien singulier, et en vérité fort supérieur.' Madame du Deffand to Horace Walpole, 12 Avril 1778.

he had entertained a vague intention of visiting England, and he now begged for permission to leave the country. The authorities, whose one object was to prevent an unpleasant *fracas*, were ready enough to substitute exile for imprisonment; and thus, after a fortnight's detention, the 'fameux poète' was released on condition that he should depart forthwith, and remain, until further permission, at a distance of at least fifty leagues from Versailles.

It is from this point onwards that our information grows scanty and confused. We know that Voltaire was in Calais early in May, and it is generally agreed that he crossed over to England shortly afterwards. His subsequent movements are uncertain. We find him established at Wandsworth in the middle of October, but it is probable that in the interval he had made a secret journey to Paris with the object—in which he did not succeed—of challenging the Chevalier de Rohan to a duel. Where he lived during these months is unknown, but apparently it was not in London. The date of his final departure from England is equally in doubt; M. Foulet adduces some reasons for supposing that he returned secretly to France in November 1728, and in that case the total length of the English visit was just two and a half years. Churton Collins, however, prolongs it until March 1729. A similar obscurity hangs over all the details of Voltaire's stay. Not only are his own extant letters during this period unusually few, but allusions to him in contemporary English correspondences are almost entirely absent. We have to depend upon scattered hints, uncertain inferences, and conflicting rumours. We know that he stayed for some time at Wandsworth with a certain Everard Falkener in circumstances which he described to Thieriot in a letter in English—an English quaintly flavoured with the gay impetuosity of another race. 'At my coming to London,' he wrote, 'I found my damned Jew was broken.' (He had depended upon some bills of exchange drawn upon a Jewish broker.)

I was without a penny, sick to dye of a violent ague, stranger, alone, helpless, in the midst of a city wherein I was known to nobody;

my Lord and Lady Bolingbroke were into the country; I could not make bold to see our ambassadour in so wretched a condition. I had never undergone such distress; but I am born to run through all the misfortunes of life. In these circumstances my star, that among all its direful influences pours allways on me some kind refreshment, sent to me an English gentleman unknown to me, who forced me to receive some money that I wanted. Another London citisen that I had seen but once at Paris, carried me to his own country house, wherein I lead an obscure and charming life since that time, without going to London, and quite given over to the pleasures of indolence and friendshipp. The true and generous affection of this man who soothes the bitterness of my life brings me to love you more and more. All the instances of friendshipp indear my friend Tiriot to me. I have seen often mylord and mylady Bolinbroke; I have found their affection still the same, even increased in proportion to my un-happiness; they offered me all, their money, their house; but I have refused all, because they are lords, and I have accepted all from Mr. Faulknear because he is a single gentleman.

We know that the friendship thus begun continued for many years, but as to who or what Everard Falkener was— besides the fact that he was a 'single gentleman'—we have only just information enough to make us wish for more.

'I am here,' he wrote after Voltaire had gone, 'just as you left me, neither merrier nor sadder, nor richer nor poorer, enjoying perfect health, having everything that makes life agreeable, without love, without avarice, without ambition, and without envy; and as long as all this lasts I shall take the liberty to call myself a very happy man.' This stoical English-man was a merchant who eventually so far overcame his distaste both for ambition and for love, as to become first Ambassador at Constantinople and then Postmaster-General —has anyone, before or since, ever held such a singular suc-cession of offices?—and to wind up by marrying, as we are intriguingly told, at the age of sixty-three, 'the illegitimate daughter of General Churchill.'

We have another glimpse of Voltaire at Wandsworth in a curious document brought to light by M. Lanson. Edward Higginson, an assistant master at a Quaker's school there, remembered how the excitable Frenchman used to argue with him for hours in Latin on the subject of 'water-baptism,' until at last Higginson produced a text from St. Paul which seemed conclusive.

Some time after, Voltaire being at the Earl Temple's seat in Fulham, with Pope and others such, in their conversation fell on the subject of water-baptism. Voltaire assumed the part of a quaker, and at length came to mention that assertion of Paul. They questioned there being such an assertion in all his writings; on which was a large wager laid, as near as I remember of £500: and Voltaire, not retaining where it was, had one of the Earl's horses, and came over the ferry from Fulham to Putney. . . . When I came he desired me to give him in writing the place where Paul said, *he was not sent to baptize*; which I presently did. Then courteously taking his leave, he mounted and rode back—

and, we must suppose, won his wager.

He seemed so taken with me (adds Higginson) as to offer to buy out the remainder of my time. I told him I expected my master would be very exorbitant in his demand. He said, let his demand be what it might, he would give it on condition I would yield to be his companion, keeping the same company, and I should always, in every respect, fare as he fared, wearing my clothes like his and of equal value: telling me then plainly, he was a Deist; adding, so were most of the noblemen in France and in England; deriding the account given by the four Evangelists concerning the birth of Christ, and his miracles, etc., so far that I desired him to desist: for I could not bear to hear my Saviour so reviled and spoken against. Whereupon he seemed under a disappointment and left me with some reluctance.

In London itself we catch fleeting visions of the eager gesticulating figure, hurrying out from his lodgings in Billiter Square—'Belitery Square' he calls it—or at the sign of the 'White Whigg' in Maiden Lane, Covent Garden, to go off to the funeral of Sir Isaac Newton in Westminster Abbey, or to pay a call on Congreve, or to attend a Quaker's Meeting. One would like to know in which street it was that he found himself surrounded by an insulting crowd, whose jeers at the 'French dog' he turned to enthusiasm by jumping upon a milestone, and delivering a harangue beginning—'Brave Englishmen! Am I not sufficiently unhappy in not having been born among you?' Then there are one or two stories of him in the great country houses—at Bubb Dodington's where he met Dr. Young and disputed with him upon the episode of Sin and Death in *Paradise Lost* with such vigour that at last Young burst out with the couplet:

> You are so witty, profligate, and thin,
> At once we think you Milton, Death, and Sin;

and at Blenheim, where the old Duchess of Marlborough hoped to lure him into helping her with her decocted memoirs, until she found that he had scruples, when in a fury she snatched the papers out of his hands. 'I thought,' she cried, 'the man had sense; but I find him at bottom either a fool or a philosopher.'

It is peculiarly tantalising that our knowledge should be almost at its scantiest in the very direction in which we should like to know most, and in which there was most reason to hope that our curiosity might have been gratified. Of Voltaire's relations with the circle of Pope, Swift, and Bolingbroke only the most meagre details have reached us. His correspondence with Bolingbroke, whom he had known in France and whose presence in London was one of his principal inducements in coming to England—a correspondence which must have been considerable—has completely disappeared. Nor, in the numerous published letters which passed about between the members of that distinguished group, is there any reference to Voltaire's name. Now and then some chance remark raises our expectations, only to make our disappointment more acute. Many years later, for instance, in 1765, a certain Major Broome paid a visit to Ferney, and made the following entry in his diary:

Dined with Mons. Voltaire, who behaved very politely. He is very old, was dressed in a robe-de-chambre of blue sattan and gold spots on it, with a sort of blue sattan cap and tassle of gold. He spoke all the time in English.... His house is not very fine, but genteel, and

64

stands upon a mount close to the mountains. He is tall and very thin, has a piercing eye, and a look singularly vivacious. He told me of his acquaintance with Pope, Swift (with whom he lived for three months at Lord Peterborough's) and Gay, who first showed him the *Beggar's Opera* before it was acted. He says he admires Swift, and loved Gay vastly. He said that Swift had a great deal of the ridiculum acre.

And then Major Broome goes on to describe the 'handsome new church' at Ferney, and the 'very neat waterworks' at Geneva. But what a vision has he opened out for us, and, in that very moment, shut away for ever from our gaze in that brief parenthesis—'with whom he lived for three months at Lord Peterborough's'! What would we not give now for no more than one or two of the bright intoxicating drops from that noble river of talk which flowed then with such a careless abundance!—that prodigal stream, swirling away, so swiftly and so happily, into the empty spaces of forgetfulness and the long night of Time!

So complete, indeed, is the lack of precise and well-authenticated information upon this, by far the most obviously interesting side of Voltaire's life in England, that some writers have been led to adopt a very different theory from that which is usually accepted, and to suppose that his relations with Pope's circle were in reality of a purely superficial, or even of an actually disreputable, kind. Voltaire himself, no doubt, was anxious to appear as the intimate friend of the great writers of England; but what reason is there to believe that he was not embroidering upon the facts, and that his true position was not that of a mere literary hanger-on, eager simply for money and *réclame*, with, perhaps, no particular scruples as to his means of getting hold of those desirable ends? The objection to this theory is that there is even less evidence to support it than there is to support Voltaire's own story. There are a few rumours and anecdotes; but that is all. Voltaire was probably the best-hated man in the eighteenth century, and it is only natural that, out of the enormous mass of mud that was thrown at him, some handfuls should have been particularly aimed at his life in England. Accordingly, we learn that somebody was told by somebody else—'avec des détails que je ne rapporterai point'—that 'M. de Voltaire se conduisit très-irrégulièrement en Angleterre: qu'il s'y est fait beaucoup d'ennemis, par des procédés qui n'accordaient pas avec les principes d'une morale exacte.' And we are told that he left England 'under a cloud'; that before he went he was 'cudgelled' by an infuriated publisher; that he swindled Lord Peterborough out of large sums of money, and that the outraged nobleman drew his sword upon the miscreant, who only escaped with his life by a midnight flight. A more circumstantial story has been given currency by Dr. Johnson. Voltaire, it appears, was a spy in the pay of Walpole, and was in the habit of betraying Bolingbroke's political secrets to the Government. The tale first appears in a third-rate life of Pope by Owen Ruffhead, who had it from Warburton, who had it from Pope himself. Oddly enough Churton Collins apparently believed it, partly from the evidence afforded by the 'fulsome flattery' and 'exaggerated compliments' to be found in Voltaire's correspondence, which, he says, reveal a man in whom 'falsehood and hypocrisy are of the very essence of his composition. There is nothing, however base, to which he will not stoop: there is no law in the code of social honour which he is not capable of violating.' Such an extreme and sweeping conclusion, following from such shadowy premises, seems to show that some of the mud thrown in the eighteenth century was still sticking in the twentieth. M. Foulet, however, has examined Ruffhead's charge in a very different spirit, with conscientious minuteness, and has concluded that it is utterly without foundation.

It is, indeed, certain that Voltaire's acquaintanceship was not limited to the extremely bitter Opposition circle which centred about the disappointed and restless figure of Bolingbroke. He had come to London with letters of introduction from Horace Walpole, the English Ambassador at Paris, to various eminent persons in the Government. 'Mr. Voltaire, a poet and a very ingenious one,' was recommended by Walpole to the favour and protection of the Duke of Newcastle, while Dodington was asked to support the subscription to 'an excellent poem, called "Henry IV," which, on account of some bold strokes in it against persecution and the priests, cannot be printed here.' These letters had their effect, and Voltaire rapidly made friends at Court. When he brought out his London edition of the *Henriade*, there was hardly a great name in England which was not on the subscription list. He was allowed to dedicate the poem to Queen Caroline, and he received a royal gift of £240. Now it is also certain that just before this time Bolingbroke and Swift were suspicious of a 'certain pragmatical spy of quality, well known to act in that capacity by those into whose company he insinuates himself,' who, they believed, was betraying their plans to the Government. But to conclude that this detected spy, whose favour at Court was known to be the reward of treachery to his friends, was Voltaire is, apart from the inherent improbability of the supposition, rendered almost impossible, owing to the fact that Bolingbroke and Swift were themselves subscribers to the *Henriade*—Bolingbroke took no fewer than twenty copies—and that Swift was not only instrumental in obtaining a large number of Irish subscriptions, but actually wrote a preface to the Dublin edition of another of Voltaire's works. What inducement could Bolingbroke have had for such liberality towards a man who had betrayed him? Who can conceive of the redoubtable Dean of St. Patrick's, then at the very summit of his fame, dispensing such splendid favours to a wretch he knew to be engaged in the shabbiest of all traffics at the expense of himself and his friends?

Voltaire's literary activities were as insatiable while he was in England as during every other period of his career. Besides the edition of the *Henriade*, which was considerably altered and enlarged—one of the changes was the silent removal of the name of Sully from its pages—he brought out a volume of two essays, written in English, upon the French Civil Wars and upon Epic Poetry, he began an adaptation of *Julius Caesar* for the French stage, he wrote the opening acts of his tragedy of *Brutus*, and he collected a quantity of material for his History of Charles XII. In addition to all this, he was busily engaged with the preparations for his *Lettres Philosophiques*. The *Henriade* met with a great success. Every copy of the magnificent quarto edition was sold before publication; three octavo editions were exhausted in as many weeks; and Voltaire made a profit of at least ten thousand francs. M. Foulet thinks that he left England shortly after this highly successful transaction, and that he established himself secretly in some town in Normandy, probably Rouen, where he devoted himself to the completion of the various works which he had in hand. Be this as it may, he was certainly in France early in April 1729; a few days later he applied for permission to return to Paris; this was granted on the 9th of April, and the remarkable incident which had begun at the Opéra more than three years before came to a close.

It was not until five years later that the *Lettres Philosophiques* appeared. This epoch-making book was the lens by means of which Voltaire gathered together the scattered rays of his English impressions into a focus of brilliant and burning intensity. It so happened that the nation into whose midst he had plunged, and whose characteristics he had scrutinised with so avid a curiosity, had just reached one of the culminating moments in its history. The great achievement of the Revolution and the splendid triumphs of Marlborough had brought to England freedom, power, wealth, and that sense of high exhilaration which springs from victory and self-confidence. Her destiny was in the hands of an aristocracy which was not only capable and enlightened, like most successful aristocracies, but which possessed the peculiar attribute of being deep-rooted in popular traditions and popular sympathies and of drawing its life-blood from the popular will. The agitations of the reign of Anne were over; the stagnation of the reign of Walpole had not yet begun. There was a great outburst of intellectual activity and æsthetic energy. The amazing discoveries of Newton seemed to open out boundless possibilities of speculation; and in the meantime the great nobles were building palaces and reviving the magnificence of the Augustan Age, while men of letters filled the offices of State. Never, perhaps, before or since, has England been so thoroughly English; never have the national qualities of solidity and sense, independence of judgment and idiosyncrasy of temperament, received a more forcible and complete expression. It was the England of Walpole and Carteret, of Butler and Berkeley, of Swift and Pope. The two works which, out of the whole range of English literature, contain in a supreme degree those elements of power, breadth, and common sense, which lie at the root of the national genius—'Gulliver's Travels' and the 'Dunciad'—both appeared during Voltaire's visit. Nor was it only in the high places of the nation's consciousness that these signs were manifest; they were visible everywhere, to every stroller through the London streets—in the Royal Exchange, where all the world came crowding to pour its gold into English purses, in the Meeting Houses of the Quakers, where the Holy Spirit rushed forth untrammelled to clothe itself in the sober garb of English idiom, and in the taverns of Cheapside, where the brawny fellow-countrymen of Newton and Shakespeare sat, in an impenetrable silence, over their English beef and English beer.

It was only natural that such a society should act as a powerful stimulus upon the vivid temperament of Voltaire, who had come to it with the bitter knowledge fresh in his mind of the mediæval futility, the narrow-minded cynicism of his own country. Yet the book which was the result is in many ways a surprising one. It is almost as remarkable for what it does not say as for what it does. In the first place, Voltaire makes no attempt to give his readers an account of the outward surface, the social and spectacular aspects of English life. It is impossible not to regret this, especially since we know, from a delightful fragment which was not published until after his death, describing his first impressions on arriving in London, in how brilliant and inimitable a fashion he would have accomplished the task. A full-length portrait of Hanoverian England from the personal point of view, by Voltaire, would have been a priceless possession for posterity; but it was never to be painted. The first sketch revealing in its perfection the hand of the master, was lightly drawn, and then thrown aside for ever. And in reality it is better so. Voltaire decided to aim at something higher and more important, something more original and more profound. He determined to write a book which should be, not the sparkling record of an ingenious traveller, but a work of propaganda and a declaration of faith. That new mood, which had come upon him first in Sully's dining-room and is revealed to us in the quivering phrases of the note to Madame de Bernières, was to grow, in the congenial air of England, into the dominating passion of his life. Henceforth, whatever quips and follies, whatever flouts and mockeries might play upon the surface, he was to be in deadly earnest at heart. He was to live and die a fighter in the ranks of progress, a champion in the mighty struggle which was now beginning against the powers of darkness in France. The first great blow in that struggle had been struck ten years earlier by Montesquieu in his *Lettres Persanes*; the second was struck by Voltaire in the *Lettres Philosophiques*. The intellectual freedom, the vigorous precision, the elegant urbanity which characterise the earlier work appear in a yet more perfect form in the later one. Voltaire's book, as its title indicates, is in effect a series of generalised reflections upon a multitude of important topics, connected together by a common point of view. A description of the institutions and manners of England is only an incidental part of the scheme: it is the fulcrum by means of which the lever of Voltaire's philosophy is brought into operation. The book is an extremely short one—it fills less than two hundred small octavo pages; and its tone and style have just that light and airy gaiety which befits the ostensible form of it—a set of private letters to a friend. With an extraordinary width of comprehension, an extraordinary pliability of intelligence, Voltaire touches upon a hundred subjects of the most varied interest and importance—from the theory of gravitation to the satires of Lord Rochester, from the effects of inoculation to the immortality of the soul—and every touch tells. It is the spirit of Humanism carried to its furthest, its quintessential point; indeed, at first sight, one is tempted to think that this quality of rarefied universality has been exaggerated into a defect. The matters treated of are so many and so vast, they are disposed of and dismissed so swiftly, so easily, so unemphatically, that one begins to wonder whether, after all, anything of real significance can have been expressed. But, in reality, what, in those few small pages, has been expressed is simply the whole philosophy of Voltaire. He offers one an exquisite dish of whipped cream; one swallows down the unsubstantial trifle, and asks impatiently if that is all? At any rate, it is enough. Into that frothy sweetness his subtle hand has insinuated a single drop of some strange liquor—is it a poison or is it an elixir of life?—whose penetrating influence will spread and spread until the remotest fibres of the system have felt its power. Contemporary French readers, when they had shut the book, found somehow that they were looking out upon a new world; that a process of disintegration had begun among their most intimate beliefs and feelings; that the whole rigid framework of society—of life itself—the hard, dark, narrow, antiquated structure of their existence—had suddenly, in the twinkling of an eye, become a faded, shadowy thing.

It might have been expected that, among the reforms which such a work would advocate, a prominent place would certainly have been given to those of a political nature. In England a political revolution had been crowned with triumph, and all that was best in English life was founded upon the political institutions which had been then established. The moral was obvious: one had only to compare the state of England under a free government with the state of France, disgraced, bankrupt, and incompetent, under autocratic rule. But the moral is never drawn by Voltaire. His references to political questions are slight and vague; he gives a sketch of English history, which reaches Magna Charta, suddenly mentions Henry VII, and then stops; he has not a word to say upon the responsibility of Ministers, the independence of the judicature, or even the freedom of the press. He approves of the English financial system, whose control by the Commons he mentions, but he fails to indicate the importance of the fact. As to the underlying principles of the constitution, the account which he gives of them conveys hardly more to the reader than the famous lines in the *Henriade*:

> Aux murs de Westminster on voit paraître ensemble
> Trois pouvoirs étonnés du nœud qui les rassemble.

Apparently Voltaire was aware of these deficiencies, for in the English edition of the book he caused the following curious excuses to be inserted in the preface:

> Some of his *English* Readers may perhaps be dissatisfied at his not expatiating farther on their Constitution and their Laws, which most of them revere almost to Idolatry; but, this Reservedness is an effect of *M. de Voltaire's* Judgment. He contented himself with giving his opinion of them in general Reflexions, the Cast of which is entirely new, and which prove that he had made this Part of the *British* Polity his particular Study. Besides, how was it possible for a Foreigner to pierce thro' their Politicks, that gloomy Labyrinth, in which such of the *English* themselves as are best acquainted with it, confess daily that they are bewilder'd and lost?

Nothing could be more characteristic of the attitude, not only of Voltaire himself, but of the whole host of his followers in the later eighteenth century, towards the actual problems of politics. They turned away in disgust from the 'gloomy labyrinth' of practical fact to take refuge in those charming 'general Reflexions' so dear to their hearts, 'the Cast of which was entirely new'—and the conclusion of which was also entirely new, for it was the French Revolution.

It was, indeed, typical of Voltaire and of his age that the *Lettres Philosophiques* should have been condemned by the authorities, not for any political heterodoxy, but for a few remarks which seemed to call in question the immortality of the soul. His attack upon the *ancien régime* was, in the main, a theoretical attack; doubtless its immediate effectiveness was thereby diminished, but its ultimate force was increased. And the *ancien régime* itself was not slow to realise the danger: to touch the ark of metaphysical orthodoxy was in its eyes the unforgivable sin. Voltaire knew well enough that he must be careful.

Il n'y a qu'une lettre touchant M. Loke [he wrote to a friend]. La seule matière philosophique que j'y traite est la petite bagatelle de l'immortalité de l'âme; mais la chose a trop de conséquence pour la traiter sérieusement. Il a fallu l'égorger pour ne pas heurter de front nos seigneurs les théologiens, gens qui voient si clairement la spiritualité de l'âme qu'ils feraient brûler, s'ils pouvaient, les corps de ceux qui en doutent.

Nor was it only 'M. Loke' whom he felt himself obliged to touch so gingerly; the remarkable movement towards Deism, which was then beginning in England, Voltaire only dared to allude to in a hardly perceivable hint. He just mentions, almost in a parenthesis, the names of Shaftesbury, Collins, and Toland, and then quickly passes on. In this connection, it may be noticed that the influence upon Voltaire of the writers of this group has often been exaggerated. To say, as Lord Morley says, that 'it was the English onslaught which sowed in him the seed of the idea . . . of a systematic and reasoned attack' upon Christian theology, is to misjudge the situation. In the first place it is certain both that Voltaire's opinions upon those matters were fixed, and that his proselytising habits had begun, long before he came to England. There is curious evidence of this in an anonymous letter, preserved among the archives of the Bastille, and addressed to the head of the police at the time of Voltaire's imprisonment.

Vous venez de mettre à la Bastille [says the writer, who, it is supposed, was an ecclesiastic] un homme que je souhaitais y voir il y a plus de 15 années.

The writer goes on to speak of the

métier que faisait l'homme en question, prêchant le déisme tout à découvert aux toilettes de nos jeunes seigneurs . . . L'Ancien Testament, selon lui, n'est qu'un tissu de contes et de fables, les apôtres étaient de bonnes gens idiots, simples, et crédules, et les pères de l'Eglise, Saint Bernard surtout, auquel ien veut le lplus, n'étaient que des charlatans et des suborneurs.

'Je voudrais être homme d'authorité,' he adds, 'pour un jour seulement, afin d'enfermer ce poète entre quatre murailles pour toute sa vie.' That Voltaire at this early date should have already given rise to such pious ecclesiastical wishes shows clearly enough that he had little to learn from the deists of England. And, in the second place, the deists of England had very little to teach a disciple of Bayle, Fontenelle, and Montesquieu. They were, almost without exception, a group of second-rate and insignificant writers whose 'onslaught' upon current beliefs was only to a faint extent 'systematic and reasoned.' The feeble and fluctuating rationalism of Toland and Wollaston, the crude and confused rationalism of Collins, the half-crazy rationalism of Woolston, may each and all, no doubt, have furnished Voltaire with arguments and suggestions, but they cannot have seriously influenced his thought. Bolingbroke was a more important figure, and he was in close personal relation with Voltaire; but his contro-versial writings were clumsy and superficial to an extra-ordinary degree. As Voltaire himself said, 'in his works there are many leaves and little fruit; distorted expressions and periods intolerably long.' Tindal and Middleton were more vigorous; but their work did not appear until a later period. The masterly and far-reaching speculations of Hume belong, of course, to a totally different class.

Apart from politics and metaphysics, there were two direc-tions in which the *Lettres Philosophiques* did pioneer work of a highly important kind: they introduced both Newton and Shakespeare to the French public. The four letters on Newton show Voltaire at his best—succinct, lucid, persuasive, and bold. The few paragraphs on Shakespeare, on the other hand, show him at his worst. Their principal merit is that they mention his existence—a fact hitherto unknown in France; otherwise they merely afford a striking example of the singular contradiction in Voltaire's nature which made him a revolutionary in intellect and kept him a high Tory in taste. Never was such speculative audacity combined with such æsthetic timidity; it is as if he had reserved all his superstition for matters of art. From his account of Shakespeare, it is clear that he had never dared to open his eyes and frankly look at what he should see before him. All was 'barbare, dépourvu de bienséances, d'ordre, de vraisemblance'; in the hurly-burly he was dimly aware of a figured and elevated style, and of some few 'lueurs étonnantes'; but to the true significance of Shakespeare's genius he remained utterly blind.

Characteristically enough, Voltaire, at the last moment, did his best to reinforce his tentative metaphysical observations on 'M. Loke' by slipping into his book, as it were accidentally, an additional letter, quite disconnected from the rest of the work, containing reflections upon some of the *Pensées* of Pascal. He no doubt hoped that these reflections, into which he had distilled some of his most insidious venom, might, under cover of the rest, pass unobserved. But all his subterfuges were useless. It was in vain that he pulled wires and intrigued with high personages; in vain that he made his way to the aged Minister, Cardinal Fleury, and attempted, by reading him some choice extracts on the Quakers, to obtain permission for the publication of his book. The old Cardinal could not help smiling, though Voltaire had felt that it would be safer to skip the best parts—'the poor man!' he said afterwards, 'he didn't realise what he had missed'—but the permission never came. Voltaire was obliged to have recourse to an illicit publication; and then the authorities acted with full force. The *Lettres Philosophiques* were officially condemned; the book was declared to be scandalous and 'contraire à la religion, aux bonnes mœurs, et au respect dû aux puissances,' and it was ordered to be publicly burned by the executioner. The result was precisely what might have been expected: the prohibitions and fulminations, so far from putting a stop to the sale of such exciting matter, sent it up by leaps and bounds. England suddenly became the fashion; the theories of M. Loke and Sir Newton began to be discussed; even the plays of 'ce fou de

Shakespeare' began to be read. And, at the same time, the whispered message of tolerance, of free inquiry, of enlightened curiosity, was carried over the land. The success of Voltaire's work was complete.

He himself, however, had been obliged to seek refuge from the wrath of the government in the remote seclusion of Madame du Châtelet's country house at Cirey. In this retirement he pursued his studies of Newton, and a few years later produced an exact and brilliant summary of the work of the great English philosopher. Once more the authorities intervened, and condemned Voltaire's book. The Newtonian system destroyed that of Descartes, and Descartes still spoke in France with the voice of orthodoxy; therefore, of course, the voice of Newton must not be heard. But, somehow or other, the voice of Newton *was* heard. The men of science were converted to the new doctrine; and thus it is not too much to say that the wonderful advances in the study of mathematics which took place in France during the later years of the eighteenth century were the result of the illuminating zeal of Voltaire.

With his work on Newton, Voltaire's direct connection with English influences came to an end. For the rest of his life, indeed, he never lost his interest in England; he was never tired of reading English books, of being polite to English travellers, and of doing his best, in the intervals of more serious labours, to destroy the reputation of that deplorable English buffoon, whom, unfortunately, he himself had been so foolish as first to introduce to the attention of his countrymen. But it is curious to notice how, as time went on, the force of Voltaire's nature inevitably carried him further and further away from the central standpoints of the English mind. The stimulus which he had received in England only served to urge him into a path which no Englishman has ever trod. The movement of English thought in the eighteenth century found its perfect expression in the profound, sceptical, and yet essentially conservative, genius of Hume. How different was the attitude of Voltaire! With what a reckless audacity, what a fierce uncompromising passion he charged and fought and charged again! He had no time for the nice discriminations of an elaborate philosophy, and no desire for the careful balance of the judicial mind; his creed was simple and explicit, and it also possessed the supreme merit of brevity: 'Écrasez l'infâme!' was enough for him.

1914.

A DIALOGUE

BETWEEN

MOSES, DIOGENES, AND MR. LOKE

DIOGENES

Confess, oh *Moses!* Your Miracles were but conjuring-tricks, your Prophecies lucky Hazards, and your Laws a *Gallimaufry* of Commonplaces and Absurdities.

MR. LOKE

Confess that you were more skill'd in flattering the Vulgar than in ascertaining the Truth, and that your Reputation in the World would never have been so high, had your Lot fallen among a Nation of Philosophers.

DIOGENES

Confess that when you taught the *Jews* to spoil the *Egyptians* you were a sad rogue.

MR. LOKE

Confess that it was a Fable to give Horses to Pharaoh and an uncloven hoof to the Hare.

DIOGENES

Confess that you did never see the *Back Parts* of the Lord.

MR. LOKE

Confess that your style had too much Singularity and too little Taste to be that of the Holy Ghost.

Moses

All this may be true, my good Friends; but what are the Conclusions you would draw from your Raillery? Do you suppose that I am ignorant of all that a Wise Man might urge against my Conduct, my Tales, and my Language? But alas! my path was chalk'd out for me not by Choice but by Necessity. I had not the Happiness of living in *England* or a *Tub*. I was the Leader of an ignorant and superstitious People, who would never have heeded the sober Counsels of Good Sense and Toleration, and who would have laughed at the Refinements of a nice Philosophy. It was necessary to flatter their Vanity by telling them that they were the favour'd Children of God, to satisfy their Passions by allowing them to be treacherous and cruel to their Enemies, and to tickle their Ears by Stories and Farces by turns ridiculous and horrible, fit either for a Nursery or *Bedlam*. By such Contrivances I was able to attain my Ends and to establish the Welfare of my Countrymen. Do you blame me? It is not the business of a Ruler to be truthful, but to be politick; he must fly even from Virtue herself, if she sit in a different Quarter from Expediency. It is his Duty to *sacrifice* the Best, which is impossible, to a *little Good*, which is close at hand. I was willing to lay down a Multitude of foolish Laws, so that, under their Cloak, I might slip in a few Wise ones; and, had I not shown myself to be both Cruel and Superstitious, the *Jews* would never have escaped from the Bondage of the *Egyptians*.

Diogenes

Perhaps that would not have been an overwhelming Disaster. But, in truth, you are right. There is no viler Profession than the Government of Nations. He who dreams that he can lead a great Crowd of Fools without a great Store of Knavery is a Fool himself.

Mr. Loke

Are not you too hasty? Does not History show that there have been great Rulers who were good Men? Solon, Henry of *Navarre*, and Milord Somers were certainly not Fools, and yet I am unwilling to believe that they were Knaves either.

Moses

No, not Knaves; but Dissemblers. In their different degrees, they all juggled; but 'twas not because Jugglery pleas'd 'em; 'twas because Men cannot be governed without it.

Mr. Loke

I would be happy to try the Experiment. If Men were told the Truth, might they not believe it? If the Opportunity of Virtue and Wisdom is never to be offer'd 'em, how can we be sure that they would not be willing to take it? Let Rulers be *bold* and *honest*, and it is possible that the Folly of their Peoples will disappear.

Diogenes

A pretty phantastick Vision! But History is against you.

Moses

And Prophecy.

Diogenes

And Common Observation. Look at the World at this moment, and what do we see? It is as it has always been, and always will be. So long as it endures, the World will continue to be rul'd by Cajolery, by Injustice, and by Imposture.

Mr. Loke

If that be so, I must take leave to lament the *Destiny* of the Human Race.

*** *A note in* Books and Characters *explains that this Dialogue 'is now* [*1922*] *printed for the first time, from a manuscript, apparently in the handwriting of Voltaire and belonging to his English period.'*

VOLTAIRE AND FREDERICK
THE GREAT

At the present time,[1] when it is so difficult to think of anything but of what is and what will be, it may yet be worth while to cast occasionally a glance backward at what was. Such glances may at least prove to have the humble merit of being entertaining: they may even be instructive as well. Certainly it would be a mistake to forget that Frederick the Great once lived in Germany. Nor is it altogether useless to remember that a curious old gentleman, extremely thin, extremely active, and heavily bewigged, once decided that, on the whole, it would be as well for him *not* to live in France. For, just as modern Germany dates from the accession of Frederick to the throne of Prussia, so modern France dates from the establishment of Voltaire on the banks of the Lake of Geneva. The intersection of those two momentous lives forms one of the most curious and one of the most celebrated incidents in history. To English readers it is probably best known through the few brilliant paragraphs devoted to it by Macaulay; though Carlyle's masterly and far more elaborate narrative is familiar to every lover of *The History of Friedrich II*. Since Carlyle wrote, however, fifty years have passed. New points of view have arisen, and a certain amount of new material—including the valuable edition of the correspondence between Voltaire and Frederick published from the original documents in the Archives at Berlin—has become available. It seems, therefore, in spite of the familiarity of the main outlines of the story, that another rapid review of it will not be out of place.

Voltaire was forty-two years of age, and already one of the most famous men of the day, when, in August 1736, he received a letter from the Crown Prince of Prussia. This letter

[1] October 1915.

80

was the first in a correspondence which was to last, with a few remarkable intervals, for a space of over forty years. It was written by a young man of twenty-four, of whose personal qualities very little was known, and whose importance seemed to lie simply in the fact that he was heir-apparent to one of the secondary European monarchies. Voltaire, however, was not the man to turn up his nose at royalty, in whatever form it might present itself; and it was moreover clear that the young prince had picked up at least a smattering of French culture, that he was genuinely anxious to become acquainted with the tendencies of modern thought, and, above all, that his admiration for the author of the *Henriade* and *Zaïre* was unbounded.

La douceur et le support [wrote Frederick] que vous marquez pour tous ceux qui se vouent aux arts et aux sciences, me font espérer que vous ne m'exclurez pas du nombre de ceux que vous trouvez dignes de vos instructions. Je nomme ainsi votre commerce de lettres, qui ne peut être que profitable à tout être pensant. J'ose même avancer, sans déroger au mérite d'autrui, que dans l'univers entier il n'y aurait pas d'exception à faire de ceux dont vous ne pourriez être le maître.

The great man was accordingly delighted; he replied with all that graceful affability of which he was a master, declared that his correspondent was 'un prince philosophe qui rendra les hommes heureux,' and showed that he meant business by plunging at once into a discussion of the metaphysical doctrines of 'le sieur Wolf,' whom Frederick had commended as 'le plus célèbre philosophe de nos jours.' For the next four years the correspondence continued on the lines thus laid down. It was a correspondence between a master and a pupil: Frederick, his passions divided between German philosophy and French poetry, poured out with equal copiousness disquisitions upon Free Will and *la raison suffisante*, odes *sur la Flatterie*, and epistles *sur l'Humanité*, while Voltaire kept the ball rolling with no less enormous philosophical replies, together with minute criticisms of His Royal Highness's mistakes in French metre and French orthography. Thus, though the interest of these early letters must have been intense to the young Prince, they have far too little personal flavour to be anything but extremely tedious to the reader of to-day. Only very occasionally is it possible to detect, amid the long and careful periods, some faint signs of feeling or of character. Voltaire's *empressement* seems to take on, once or twice, the colours of something like a real enthusiasm; and one notices that, after two years, Frederick's letters begin no longer with 'Monsieur' but with 'Mon cher ami,' which glides at last insensibly into 'Mon cher Voltaire'; though the careful poet continues with his 'Monseigneur' throughout. Then, on one occasion, Frederick makes a little avowal, which reads oddly in the light of future events.

> Souffrez [he says] que je vous fasse mon caractère, afin que vous ne vous y mépreniez plus . . . J'ai peu de mérite et peu de savoir; mais j'ai beaucoup de bonne volonté, et un fonds inépuisable d'estime et d'amitié pour les personnes d'une vertu distinguée, et avec cela je suis capable de toute la constance que la vraie amitié exige. J'ai assez de jugement pour vous rendre toute la justice que vous méritez; mais je n'en ai pas assez pour m'empêcher de faire de mauvais vers.

But this is exceptional; as a rule, elaborate compliments take the place of personal confessions; and, while Voltaire is never tired of comparing Frederick to Apollo, Alcibiades, and the youthful Marcus Aurelius, of proclaiming the rebirth of 'les talents de Virgile et les vertus d'Auguste,' or of declaring that 'Socrate ne m'est rien, c'est Frédéric que j'aime,' the Crown Prince is on his side ready with an equal flow of protestations, which sometimes rise to singular heights. 'Ne croyez pas,' he says, 'que je pousse mon scepticisime à outrance . . . Je crois, par exemple, qu'il n'y a qu'un Dieu et qu'un Voltaire dans le monde; je crois encore que ce Dieu avait besoin dans ce siècle d'un Voltaire pour le rendre aimable.' Decidedly the Prince's compliments were too emphatic, and the poet's too ingenious; as Voltaire himself said afterwards, 'les épithètes ne nous coûtaient rien'; yet neither was without a little residue of sincerity. Frederick's admiration bordered upon the sentimental; and Voltaire had begun to allow himself to hope that some day, in a provincial German court, there might be found a crowned head devoting his life to philosophy, good sense, and the love of letters. Both were to receive a curious awakening.

In 1740 Frederick became King of Prussia, and a new epoch in the relations between the two men began. The next ten years were, on both sides, years of growing disillusionment. Voltaire very soon discovered that his phrase about 'un prince philosophe qui rendra les hommes heureux' was indeed a phrase and nothing more. His *prince philosophe* started out on a career of conquest, plunged all Europe into war, and turned Prussia into a great military power. Frederick, it appeared, was at once a far more important and a far more dangerous phenomenon than Voltaire had suspected. And, on the other hand, the matured mind of the King was not slow to perceive that the enthusiasm of the Prince needed a good deal of qualification. This change of view, was, indeed, remarkably rapid. Nothing is more striking than the alteration of the tone in Frederick's correspondence during the few months which followed his accession: the voice of the raw and inexperienced youth is heard no more, and its place is taken— at once and for ever—by the self-contained caustic utterance of an embittered man of the world. In this transformation it was only natural that the wondrous figure of Voltaire should lose some of its glitter—especially since Frederick now began to have the opportunity of inspecting that figure in the flesh with his own sharp eyes. The friends met three or four times, and it is noticeable that after each meeting there is a distinct coolness on the part of Frederick. He writes with a sudden brusqueness to accuse Voltaire of showing about his manuscripts, which, he says, had only been sent him on the condition of *un secret inviolable*. He writes to Jordan complaining of Voltaire's avarice in very stringent terms. 'Ton avare boira la lie de son insatiable désir de s'enrichir . . . Son apparition de six jours me coûtera par journée cinq cent cinquante écus. C'est bien payer un fou; jamais bouffon de grand seigneur n'eut de pareils gages.' He declares that 'la cervelle du poète est aussi légère que le style de ses ouvrages,' and remarks sarcastically that he is indeed a man *extraordinaire en tout.*

Yet, while his opinion of Voltaire's character was rapidly growing more and more severe, his admiration of his talents remained undiminished. For, though he had dropped metaphysics when he came to the throne, Frederick could never drop his passion for French poetry; he recognised in Voltaire the unapproachable master of that absorbing art; and for years he had made up his mind that, some day or other, he would *posséder*—for so he put it—the author of the *Henriade,* would keep him at Berlin as the brightest ornament of his court, and, above all, would have him always ready at hand to put the final polish on his own verses. In the autumn of 1743 it seemed for a moment that his wish would be gratified. Voltaire spent a visit of several weeks in Berlin; he was dazzled by the graciousness of his reception and the splendour of his surroundings; and he began to listen to the honeyed overtures of the Prussian Majesty. The great obstacle to Frederick's desire was Voltaire's relationship with Madame du Châtelet. He had lived with her for more than ten years; he was attached to her by all the ties of friendship and gratitude; he had constantly declared that he would never leave her—no, not for all the seductions of princes. She would, it is true, have been willing to accompany Voltaire to Berlin; but such a solution would by no means have suited Frederick. He was not fond of ladies—even of ladies like Madame du Châtelet—learned enough to translate Newton and to discuss by the hour the niceties of the Leibnitzian philosophy; and he had determined to *posséder* Voltaire either completely or not at all. Voltaire, in spite of repeated temptations, had remained faithful; but now, for the first time, poor Madame du Châtelet began to be seriously alarmed. His letters from Berlin grew fewer and fewer, and more and more ambiguous; she knew nothing of his plans; 'il est ivre absolument' she burst out in her distress to d'Argental, one of his oldest friends. By every post she dreaded to learn at last that he had deserted her for ever. But suddenly Voltaire returned. The spell of

Berlin had been broken, and he was at her feet once more.

What had happened was highly characteristic both of the Poet and of the King. Each had tried to play a trick on the other, and each had found the other out. The French Government had been anxious to obtain an insight into the diplomatic intentions of Frederick, in an unofficial way; Voltaire had offered his services, and it had been agreed that he should write to Frederick declaring that he was obliged to leave France for a time owing to the hostility of a member of the Government, the Bishop of Mirepoix, and asking for Frederick's hospitality. Frederick had not been taken in: though he had not disentangled the whole plot, he had perceived clearly enough that Voltaire's visit was in reality that of an agent of the French Government; he also thought he saw an opportunity of securing the desire of his heart. Voltaire, to give verisimilitude to his story, had, in his letter to Frederick, loaded the Bishop of Mirepoix with ridicule and abuse; and Frederick now secretly sent this letter to Mirepoix himself. His calculation was that Mirepoix would be so outraged that he would make it impossible for Voltaire ever to return to France; and in that case—well, Voltaire would have no other course open to him but to stay where he was, in Berlin, and Madame du Châtelet would have to make the best of it. Of course, Frederick's plan failed, and Voltaire was duly informed by Mirepoix of what had happened. He was naturally very angry. He had been almost induced to stay in Berlin of his own accord, and now he found that his host had been attempting, by means of treachery and intrigue, to force him to stay there whether he liked it or not. It was a long time before he forgave Frederick. But the King was most anxious to patch up the quarrel; he still could not abandon the hope of ultimately securing Voltaire; and besides, he was now possessed by another and a more immediate desire—to be allowed a glimpse of that famous and scandalous work which Voltaire kept locked in the innermost drawer of his cabinet and revealed to none but the most favoured of his intimates —*La Pucelle.*

Accordingly the royal letters became more frequent and more flattering than ever; the royal hand cajoled and implored. 'Ne me faites point injustice sur mon caractère; d'ailleurs il vous est permis de badiner sur mon sujet comme il vous plaira.' '*La Pucelle! La Pucelle! La Pucelle!* et encore *La Pucelle!*' he exclaims. 'Pour l'amour de Dieu, ou plus encore pour l'amour de vous-même, envoyez-la-moi.' And at last Voltaire was softened. He sent off a few fragments of his *Pucelle*—just enough to whet Frederick's appetite—and he declared himself reconciled. 'Je vous ai aimé tendrement,' he wrote in March 1749; 'j'ai été fâché contre vous, je vous ai pardonné, et actuellement je vous aime à la folie.' Within a year of this date his situation had undergone a complete change. Madame du Châtelet was dead; and his position at Versailles, in spite of the friendship of Madame de Pompadour, had become almost as impossible as he had pretended it to have been in 1743. Frederick eagerly repeated his invitation; and this time Voltaire did not refuse. He was careful to make a very good bargain; obliged Frederick to pay for his journey; and arrived at Berlin in July 1750. He was given rooms in the royal palaces both at Berlin and Potsdam; he was made a Court Chamberlain, and received the Order of Merit, together with a pension of £800 a year. These arrangements caused considerable amusement in Paris; and for some days hawkers, carrying prints of Voltaire dressed in furs, and crying 'Voltaire le prussien! Six sols le fameux prussien!' were to be seen walking up and down the Quays.

The curious drama that followed, with its farcical περιπέτεια and its tragi-comic *dénouement*, can hardly be understood without a brief consideration of the feelings and intentions of the two chief actors in it. The position of Frederick is comparatively plain. He had now completely thrown aside the last lingering remnants of any esteem which he may once have entertained for the character of Voltaire. He frankly thought him a scoundrel. In September 1749, less than a year before Voltaire's arrival, and at the very period of Frederick's most urgent invitations, we find him using the following language in a letter to Algarotti: 'Voltaire vient de faire un tour qui est indigne.' (He had been showing to all his friends a garbled copy of one of Frederick's letters.)

Il mériterait d'être fleurdelisé au Parnasse. C'est bien dommage qu'une âme aussi lâche soit unie à un aussi beau génie. Il a les gentillesses et les malices d'un singe. Je vous conterai ce que c'est, lorsque je vous reverrai; cependant je ne ferai semblant de rien, car j'en ai besoin pour l'étude de l'élocution française. On peut apprendre de bonnes choses d'un scélérat. Je veux savoir son français; que m'importe sa morale? Cet homme a trouvé le moyen de réunir tous les contraires. On admire son esprit, en même temps qu'on méprise son caractère.

There is no ambiguity about this. Voltaire was a scoundrel; but he was a scoundrel of genius. He would make the best possible teacher of *l'élocution française*; therefore it was necessary that he should come and live in Berlin. But as for anything more—as for any real interchange of sympathies, any genuine feeling of friendliness, of respect, or even of regard— all that was utterly out of the question. The avowal is cynical, no doubt; but it is at any rate straightforward, and above all it is peculiarly devoid of any trace of self-deception. In the face of these trenchant sentences, the view of Frederick's attitude which is suggested so assiduously by Carlyle—that he was the victim of an elevated misapprehension, that he was always hoping for the best, and that, when the explosion came he was very much surprised and profoundly disappointed— becomes obviously untenable. If any man ever acted with his eyes wide open, it was Frederick when he invited Voltaire to Berlin.

Yet, though that much is clear, the letter to Algarotti betrays, in more than one direction, a very singular state of mind. A warm devotion to *l'élocution française* is easy enough to understand; but Frederick's devotion was much more than warm; it was so absorbing and so intense that it left him no rest until by hook or by crook, by supplication, or by trickery, or by paying down hard cash, he had obtained the close and constant proximity of—what?—of a man whom he himself described as a 'singe' and a 'scélérat,' a man of base soul and despicable character. And Frederick appears to see nothing surprising in this. He takes it quite as a matter of course that he should be, not merely willing, but delighted to run all the risks involved by Voltaire's undoubted roguery, so long as he can be sure of benefiting from Voltaire's no less undoubted mastery of French versification. This is certainly strange; but the explanation of it lies in the extraordinary vogue—a vogue, indeed, so extraordinary that it is very difficult for the modern reader to realise it—enjoyed throughout Europe by French culture and literature during the middle years of the eighteenth century. Frederick was merely an extreme instance of a universal fact. Like all Germans of any education, he habitually wrote and spoke in French; like every lady and gentleman from Naples to Edinburgh, his life was regulated by the social conventions of France; like every amateur of letters from Madrid to St. Petersburg, his whole conception of literary taste, his whole standard of literary values, was French. To him, as to the vast majority of his contemporaries, the very essence of civilisation was concentrated in French literature, and especially in French poetry; and French poetry meant to him, as to his contemporaries, that particular kind of French poetry which had come into fashion at the court of Louis XIV. For this curious creed was as narrow as it was all-pervading. The *Grand Siècle* was the Church Infallible; and it was heresy to doubt the Gospel of Boileau.

Frederick's library, still preserved at Potsdam, shows us what literature meant in those days to a cultivated man: it is composed entirely of the French Classics, of the works of Voltaire, and of the masterpieces of antiquity translated into eighteenth-century French. But Frederick was not content with mere appreciation; he too would create; he would write alexandrines on the model of Racine, and madrigals after the manner of Chaulieu; he would press in person into the sacred sanctuary, and burn incense with his own hands upon

88

the inmost shrine. It was true that he was a foreigner; it was true that his knowledge of the French language was incomplete and incorrect; but his sense of his own ability urged him forward, and his indefatigable pertinacity kept him at his strange task throughout the whole of his life. He filled volumes, and the contents of those volumes afford probably the most complete illustration in literature of the very trite proverb—*Poeta nascitur, non fit.* The spectacle of that heavy German Muse, with her feet crammed into pointed slippers, executing, with incredible conscientiousness, now the stately measure of a Versailles minuet, and now the spritely steps of a Parisian jig, would be either ludicrous or pathetic—one hardly knows which—were it not so certainly neither the one nor the other, but simply dreary with an unutterable dreariness, from which the eyes of men avert themselves in shuddering dismay. Frederick himself felt that there was something wrong—something, but not really very much. All that was wanted was a little expert advice; and obviously Voltaire was the man to supply it—Voltaire, the one true heir of the Great Age, the dramatist who had revived the glories of Racine (did not Frederick's tears flow almost as copiously over *Mahomet* as over *Britannicus?*), the epic poet who had eclipsed Homer and Virgil (had not Frederick every right to judge, since he had read the 'Iliad' in French prose and the 'Æneid' in French verse?), the lyric master whose odes and whose epistles occasionally even surpassed (Frederick confessed it with amazement) those of the Marquis de la Fare. Voltaire, there could be no doubt, would do just what was needed; he would know how to squeeze in a little further the waist of the German Calliope, to apply with his deft fingers precisely the right dab of rouge to her cheeks, to instil into her movements the last *nuances* of correct deportment. And, if he did that, of what consequence were the blemishes of his personal character? 'On peut apprendre de bonnes choses d'un scélérat.'

And, besides, though Voltaire might be a rogue, Frederick felt quite convinced that he could keep him in order. A crack

or two of the master's whip—a coldness in the royal de-
meanour, a hint at a stoppage of the pension—and the monkey
would put an end to his tricks soon enough. It never seems to
have occurred to Frederick that the possession of genius
might imply a quality of spirit which was not that of an
ordinary man. This was his great, his fundamental error. It
was the ingenuous error of a cynic. He knew that he was
under no delusion as to Voltaire's faults, and so he supposed
that he could be under no delusion as to his merits. He inno-
cently imagined that the capacity for great writing was something that could be as easily separated from the owner of it as
a hat or a glove. 'C'est bien dommage qu'une âme aussi lâche
soit unie à un aussi beau génie.' *C'est bien dommage!*—as if
there was nothing more extraordinary in such a combination
than that of a pretty woman and an ugly dress. And so
Frederick held his whip a little tighter, and reminded himself
once more that, in spite of that *beau génie*, it was a monkey
that he had to deal with. But he was wrong: it was not a
monkey; it was a devil, which is a very different thing.

A devil—or perhaps an angel? One cannot be quite sure.
For, amid the complexities of that extraordinary spirit, where
good and evil were so mysteriously interwoven, where the
elements of darkness and the elements of light lay crowded
together in such ever-deepening ambiguity, fold within fold,
the clearer the vision the greater the bewilderment, the more
impartial the judgment the profounder the doubt. But one
thing at least is certain: that spirit, whether it was admirable
or whether it was odious, was moved by a terrific force.
Frederick had failed to realise this; and indeed, though Voltaire was fifty-six when he went to Berlin, and though his
whole life had been spent in a blaze of publicity, there was
still not one of his contemporaries who understood the true
nature of his genius; it was perhaps hidden even from himself. He had reached the threshold of old age, and his life's
work was still before him; it was not as a writer of tragedies
and epics that he was to take his place in the world. Was he,
in the depths of his consciousness, aware that this was so? Did

some obscure instinct urge him forward, at this late hour, to break with the ties of a lifetime, and rush forth into the unknown?

What his precise motives were in embarking upon the Berlin adventure it is very difficult to say. It is true that he was disgusted with Paris—he was ill-received at Court, and he was pestered by endless literary quarrels and jealousies; it would be very pleasant to show his countrymen that he had other strings to his bow, that, if they did not appreciate him, Frederick the Great did. It is true, too, that he admired Frederick's intellect, and that he was flattered by his favour. 'Il avait de l'esprit,' he said afterwards, 'des grâces, et, de plus, il était roi; ce qui fait toujours une grande séduction, attendu la faiblesse humaine.' His vanity could not resist the prestige of a royal intimacy; and no doubt he relished to the full even the increased consequence which came to him with his Chamberlain's key and his order—to say nothing of the addition of £800 to his income. Yet, on the other hand, he was very well aware that he was exchanging freedom for servitude, and that he was entering into a bargain with a man who would make quite sure that he was getting his money's worth; and he knew in his heart that he had something better to do than to play, however successfully, the part of a courtier. Nor was he personally attached to Frederick; he was personally attached to no one on earth. Certainly he had never been a man of feeling, and now that he was old and hardened by the uses of the world he had grown to be completely what in essence he always was—a fighter, without tenderness, without scruples, and without remorse. No, he went to Berlin for his own purposes—however dubious those purposes may have been.

And it is curious to observe that in his correspondence with his niece, Madame Denis, whom he had left behind him at the head of his Paris establishment and in whom he confided —in so far as he can be said to have confided in anyone—he repeatedly states that there is nothing permanent about his visit to Berlin. At first he declares that he is only making a

stay of a few weeks with Frederick, that he is going on to
Italy to visit 'sa Sainteté' and to inspect 'la ville souterraine,'
that he will be back in Paris in the autumn. The autumn
comes, and the roads are too muddy to travel by; he must
wait till the winter, when they will be frozen hard. Winter
comes, and it is too cold to move; but he will certainly return
in the spring. Spring comes, and he is on the point of finishing
his *Siècle de Louis XIV*; he really must wait just a few weeks
more. The book is published; but then how can he appear in
Paris until he is quite sure of its success? And so he lingers on,
delaying and prevaricating, until a whole year has passed, and
still he lingers on, still he is on the point of going, and still he
does not go. Meanwhile, to all appearances, he was definitely
fixed, a salaried official, at Frederick's court; and he was
writing to all his other friends, to assure them that he had
never been so happy, that he could see no reason why he
should ever come away. What were his true intentions?
Could he himself have said? Had he perhaps, in some secret
corner of his brain, into which even he hardly dared to look, a
premonition of the future? At times, in this Berlin adventure,
he seems to resemble some great buzzing fly, shooting suddenly into a room through an open window and dashing
frantically from side to side; when all at once, as suddenly, he
swoops away and out through another window which opens in
quite a different direction, towards wide and flowery fields;
so that perhaps the reckless creature knew where he was
going after all.

In any case, it is evident to the impartial observer that
Voltaire's visit could only have ended as it did—in an explosion. The elements of the situation were too combustible
for any other conclusion. When two confirmed egotists decide, for purely selfish reasons, to set up house together, everyone knows what will happen. For some time their sense of
mutual advantage may induce them to tolerate each other, but
sooner or later human nature will assert itself, and the *ménage*
will break up. And, with Voltaire and Frederick, the difficulties inherent in all such cases were intensified by the fact

that the relationship between them was, in effect, that of servant and master; that Voltaire, under a very thin disguise, was
a paid menial, while Frederick, condescend as he might, was
an autocrat whose will was law. Thus the two famous and
perhaps mythical sentences, invariably repeated by historians
of the incident, about orange-skins and dirty linen, do in fact
sum up the gist of the matter. 'When one has sucked the
orange, one throws away the skin,' somebody told Voltaire
that the King had said, on being asked how much longer he
would put up with the poet's vagaries. And Frederick, on his
side, was informed that Voltaire, when a batch of the royal
verses were brought to him for correction, had burst out with
'Does the man expect me to go on washing his dirty linen for
ever?' Each knew well enough the weak spot in his position,
and each was acutely and uncomfortably conscious that the
other knew it too. Thus, but a very few weeks after Voltaire's
arrival, little clouds of discord become visible on the horizon;
electrical discharges of irritability begin to take place, growing more and more frequent and violent as time goes on; and
one can overhear the pot and the kettle, in strictest privacy,
calling each other black. 'The monster,' whispers Voltaire
to Madame Denis, 'he opens all our letters in the post'—
Voltaire, whose light-handedness with other people's correspondence was only too notorious. 'The monkey,' mutters
Frederick, 'he shows my private letters to his friends'—
Frederick, who had thought nothing of betraying Voltaire's
letters to the Bishop of Mirepoix. 'How happy I should be
here,' exclaims the callous old poet, 'but for one thing—his
Majesty is utterly heartless!' And meanwhile Frederick, who
had never let a farthing escape from his close fist without some
very good reason, was busy concocting an epigram upon the
avarice of Voltaire.

It was, indeed, Voltaire's passion for money which brought
on the first really serious storm. Three months after his
arrival in Berlin, the temptation to increase his already considerable fortune by a stroke of illegal stock-jobbing proved
too strong for him; he became involved in a series of shady

financial transactions with a Jew; he quarrelled with the Jew; there was an acrimonious lawsuit, with charges and counter-charges of the most discreditable kind; and, though the Jew lost his case on a technical point, the poet certainly did not leave the court without a stain upon his character. Among other misdemeanours, it is almost certain—the evidence is not quite conclusive—that he committed forgery in order to support a false oath. Frederick was furious, and for a moment was on the brink of dismissing Voltaire from Berlin. He would have been wise if he had done so. But he could not part with his *beau génie* so soon. He cracked his whip, and, setting the monkey to stand in the corner, contented himself with a shrug of the shoulders and the exclamation 'C'est l'affaire d'un fripon qui a voulu tromper un filou.' A few weeks later the royal favour shone forth once more, and Voltaire, who had been hiding himself in a suburban villa, came out and basked again in those refulgent beams.

And the beams were decidedly refulgent—so much so, in fact, that they almost satisfied even the vanity of Voltaire. Almost, but not quite. For, though his glory was great, though he was the centre of all men's admiration, courted by nobles, flattered by princesses—there is a letter from one of them, a sister of Frederick's, still extant, wherein the trembling votaress ventures to praise the great man's works, which, she says, 'vous rendent si célèbre et immortel'—though he had ample leisure for his private activities, though he enjoyed every day the brilliant conversation of the King, though he could often forget for weeks together that he was the paid servant of a jealous despot—yet, in spite of all, there was a crumpled rose-leaf amid the silken sheets, and he lay awake o' nights. He was not the only Frenchman at Frederick's court. That monarch had surrounded himself with a small group of persons—foreigners for the most part—whose business it was to instruct him when he wished to improve his mind, to flatter him when he was out of temper, and to entertain him when he was bored. There was hardly one of them that was not thoroughly second-rate. Algarotti was an elegant dabbler in scientific matters—he had written a book to explain Newton to the ladies; d'Argens was an amiable and erudite writer of a dull free-thinking turn; Chasot was a retired military man with too many debts, and Darget was a good-natured secretary with too many love affairs; La Mettrie was a doctor who had been exiled from France for atheism and bad manners; and Pöllnitz was a decaying baron who, under stress of circumstances, had unfortunately been obliged to change his religion six times.

These were the boon companions among whom Frederick chose to spend his leisure hours. Whenever he had nothing better to do, he would exchange rhymed epigrams with Algarotti, or discuss the Jewish religion with d'Argens, or write long improper poems about Darget, in the style of *La Pucelle*. Or else he would summon La Mettrie, who would forthwith prove the irrefutability of materialism in a series of wild paradoxes, shout with laughter, suddenly shudder and cross himself on upsetting the salt, and eventually pursue his majesty with his buffooneries into a place where even royal persons are wont to be left alone. At other times Frederick would amuse himself by first cutting down the pension of Pöllnitz, who was at the moment a Lutheran, and then writing long and serious letters to him suggesting that if he would only become a Catholic again he might be made a Silesian Abbot. Strangely enough, Frederick was not popular, and one or other of the inmates of his little menagerie was constantly escaping and running away. Darget and Chasot both succeeded in getting through the wires; they obtained leave to visit Paris, and stayed there. Poor d'Argens often tried to follow their example; more than once he set off for France, secretly vowing never to return; but he had no money, Frederick was blandishing, and the wretch was always lured back to captivity. As for La Mettrie, he made his escape in a different manner—by dying after supper one evening of a surfeit of pheasant pie. 'Jésus! Marie!' he gasped, as he felt the pains of death upon him. 'Ah!' said a priest who had been sent for, 'vous voilà enfin retourné à ces noms consolateurs.'

La Mettrie, with an oath, expired; and Frederick, on hearing of this unorthodox conclusion, remarked, 'J'en suis bien aise, pour le repos de son âme.'

Among this circle of down-at-heel eccentrics there was a single figure whose distinction and respectability stood out in striking contrast from the rest—that of Maupertuis, who had been, since 1745, the President of the Academy of Sciences at Berlin. Maupertuis has had an unfortunate fate: he was first annihilated by the ridicule of Voltaire, and then recreated by the humour of Carlyle; but he was an ambitious man, very anxious to be famous, and his desire has been gratified in overflowing measure. During his life he was chiefly known for his voyage to Lapland, and his observations there, by which he was able to substantiate the Newtonian doctrine of the flatness of the earth at the poles. He possessed considerable scientific attainments, he was honest, he was energetic; he appeared to be just the man to revive the waning glories of Prussian science; and when Frederick succeeded in inducing him to come to Berlin as President of his Academy the choice seemed amply justified. Maupertuis had, moreover, some pretensions to wit; and in his earlier days his biting and elegant sarcasms had more than once overwhelmed his scientific adversaries. Such accomplishments suited Frederick admirably. Maupertuis, he declared, was an *homme d'esprit*, and the happy President became a constant guest at the royal supper-parties. It was the happy—the too happy—President who was the rose-leaf in the bed of Voltaire. The two men had known each other slightly for many years, and had always expressed the highest admiration for each other; but their mutual amiability was now to be put to a severe test. The sagacious Buffon observed the danger from afar: 'ces deux hommes,' he wrote to a friend, 'ne sont pas faits pour demeurer ensemble dans la même chambre.' And indeed to the vain and sensitive poet, uncertain of Frederick's cordiality, suspicious of hidden enemies, intensely jealous of possible rivals, the spectacle of Maupertuis at supper, radiant, at his ease, obviously protected, obviously superior to the shady mediocrities who sat around—that sight was gall and wormwood; and he looked closer, with a new malignity; and then those piercing eyes began to make discoveries, and that relentless brain began to do its work.

Maupertuis had very little judgment; so far from attempting to conciliate Voltaire, he was rash enough to provoke hostilities. It was very natural that he should have lost his temper. He had been for five years the dominating figure in the royal circle, and now suddenly he was deprived of his pre-eminence and thrown completely into the shade. Who could attend to Maupertuis while Voltaire was talking?—Voltaire, who as obviously outshone Maupertuis as Maupertuis outshone La Mettrie and Darget and the rest. In his exasperation the President went to the length of openly giving his protection to a disreputable literary man, La Beaumelle, who was a declared enemy of Voltaire. This meant war, and war was not long in coming.

Some years previously Maupertuis had, as he believed, discovered an important mathematical law—the 'principle of least action.' The law was, in fact, important, and has had a fruitful history in the development of mechanical theory; but, as Mr. Jourdain has shown in a recent monograph, Maupertuis enunciated it incorrectly without realising its true import, and a far more accurate and scientific statement of it was given, within a few months, by Euler. Maupertuis, however, was very proud of his discovery, which, he considered, embodied one of the principal reasons for believing in the existence of God; and he was therefore exceedingly angry when, shortly after Voltaire's arrival in Berlin, a Swiss mathematician, Koenig, published a polite memoir attacking both its accuracy and its originality, and quoted in support of his contention an unpublished letter by Leibnitz, in which the law was more exactly expressed. Instead of arguing upon the merits of the case, Maupertuis declared that the letter of Leibnitz was a forgery, and that therefore Koenig's remarks deserved no further consideration. When Koenig expostulated, Maupertuis decided upon a more drastic step. He summoned a meeting of the Berlin Academy of Sciences, of which Koenig was a member, laid the case before it, and moved that it should solemnly pronounce Koenig a forger, and the letter of Leibnitz supposititious and false. The members of the Academy were frightened; their pensions depended upon the President's good will; and even the illustrious Euler was not ashamed to take part in this absurd and disgraceful condemnation.

Voltaire saw at once that his opportunity had come. Maupertuis had put himself utterly and irretrievably in the wrong. He was wrong in attributing to his discovery a value which it did not possess; he was wrong in denying the authenticity of the Leibnitz letter; above all he was wrong in treating a purely scientific question as the proper subject for the disciplinary jurisdiction of an Academy. If Voltaire struck now, he would have his enemy on the hip. There was only one consideration to give him pause, and that was a grave one: to attack Maupertuis upon this matter was, in effect, to attack the King. Not only was Frederick certainly privy to Maupertuis' action, but he was extremely sensitive of the reputation of his Academy and of its President, and he would certainly consider any interference on the part of Voltaire, who himself drew his wages from the royal purse, as a flagrant act of disloyalty. But Voltaire decided to take the risk. He had now been more than two years in Berlin, and the atmosphere of a Court was beginning to weigh upon his spirit; he was restless, he was reckless, he was spoiling for a fight; he would take on Maupertuis singly or Maupertuis and Frederick combined—he did not much care which, and in any case he flattered himself that he would settle the hash of the President.

As a preparatory measure, he withdrew all his spare cash from Berlin, and invested it with the Duke of Würtemberg. 'Je mets tout doucement ordre à mes affaires,' he told Madame Denis. Then, on September 18, 1752, there appeared in the papers a short article entitled 'Réponse d'un Académicien de Berlin à un Académicien de Paris.' It was a statement, deadly in its bald simplicity, its studied coldness, its concentrated force, of Koenig's case against Maupertuis. The President must have turned pale as he read it; but the King turned crimson. The terrible indictment could, of course, only have been written by one man, and that man was receiving a royal pension of £800 a year and carrying about a Chamberlain's gold key in his pocket. Frederick flew to his writing-table, and composed an indignant pamphlet which he caused to be published with the Prussian arms on the title-page. It was a feeble work, full of exaggerated praises of Maupertuis, and of clumsy invectives against Voltaire: the President's reputation was gravely compared to that of Homer; the author of the 'Réponse d'un Académicien de Berlin' was declared to be a 'faiseur de libelles sans génie,' an 'imposteur effronté,' a 'malheureux écrivain'; while the 'Réponse' itself was a 'grossièreté plate,' whose publication was an 'action malicieuse, lâche, infâme,' a 'brigandage affreux.' The presence of the royal insignia only intensified the futility of the outburst. 'L'aigle, le sceptre, et la couronne,' wrote Voltaire to Madame Denis, 'sont bien étonnés de se trouver là.' But one thing was now certain: the King had joined the fray. Voltaire's blood was up, and he was not sorry. A kind of exaltation seized him; from this moment his course was clear—he would do as much damage as he could, and then leave Prussia for ever. And it so happened that just then an unexpected opportunity occurred for one of those furious onslaughts so dear to his heart, with that weapon which he knew so well how to wield. 'Je n'ai point de sceptre,' he ominously shot out to Madame Denis, 'mais j'ai une plume.'

Meanwhile the life of the Court—which passed for the most part at Potsdam, in the little palace of Sans Souci which Frederick had built for himself—proceeded on its accustomed course. It was a singular life, half military, half monastic, rigid, retired, from which all the ordinary pleasures of society were strictly excluded. 'What do you do here?' one of the royal princes was once asked. 'We conjugate the verb *s'ennuyer*,' was the reply. But, wherever he might be, that was a verb unknown to Voltaire. Shut up all day in the strange little room, still preserved for the eyes of the curious, with its windows opening on the formal garden, and its yellow walls thickly embossed with the brightly coloured shapes of fruits, flowers, birds, and apes, the indefatigable old man worked away at his histories, his tragedies, his *Pucelle*, and his enormous correspondence. He was, of course, ill—very ill; he was probably, in fact, upon the brink of death; but he had grown accustomed to that situation; and the worse he grew the more furiously he worked. He was a victim, he declared, of erysipelas, dysentery, and scurvy; he was constantly attacked by fever, and all his teeth had fallen out. But he continued to work. On one occasion a friend visited him, and found him in bed. 'J'ai quatre maladies mortelles,' he wailed. 'Pourtant,' remarked the friend, 'vous avez l'œil fort bon.' Voltaire leapt up from the pillows: 'Ne savez-vous pas,' he shouted, 'que les scorbutiques meurent l'œil enflammé?' When the evening came it was time to dress, and, in all the pomp of flowing wig and diamond order, to proceed to the little music-room, where his Majesty, after the business of the day, was preparing to relax himself upon the flute. The orchestra was gathered together; the audience was seated; the concerto began. And then the sounds of beauty flowed and trembled, and seemed, for a little space, to triumph over the pains of living and the hard hearts of men; and the royal master poured out his skill in some long and elaborate cadenza, and the adagio came, the marvellous adagio, and the conqueror of Rossbach drew tears from the author of *Candide*. But a moment later it was suppertime; and the night ended in the oval dining-room, amid laughter and champagne, the ejaculations of La Mettrie, the epigrams of Maupertuis, the sarcasms of Frederick, and the devastating coruscations of Voltaire.

Yet, in spite of all the jests and roses, everyone could hear the rumbling of the volcano under the ground. Everyone could hear, but nobody would listen; the little flames leapt up through the surface, but still the gay life went on; and then the irruption came. Voltaire's enemy had written a book. In the intervals of his more serious labours, the President had put together a series of 'Letters,' in which a number of miscellaneous scientific subjects were treated in a mildly speculative and popular style. The volume was rather dull, and very unimportant; but it happened to appear at this particular moment, and Voltaire pounced upon it with the swift swoop of a hawk on a mouse. The famous *Diatribe du Docteur Akakia* is still fresh with a fiendish gaiety after a hundred and fifty years; but to realise to the full the skill and malice which went to the making of it, one must at least have glanced at the flat insipid production which called it forth, and noted with what a diabolical art the latent absurdities in poor Maupertuis' *rêveries* have been detected, dragged forth into the light of day, and nailed to the pillory of an immortal ridicule. The *Diatribe*, however, is not all mere laughter; there is a real criticism in it, too. For instance, it was not simply a farcical exaggeration to say that Maupertuis had set out to prove the existence of God by 'A plus B divided by Z'; in substance, the charge was both important and well founded. 'Lorsque la métaphysique entre dans la géometrie,' Voltaire wrote in a private letter some months afterwards, 'c'est Arimane qui entre dans le royaume d'Oromasde, et qui y apporte des ténèbres'; and Maupertuis had in fact vitiated his treatment of the 'principle of least action' by his metaphysical pre-occupations. Indeed, all through Voltaire's pamphlet, there is an implied appeal to true scientific principles, an underlying assertion of the paramount importance of the experimental method, a consistent attack upon *a priori* reasoning, loose statement, and vague conjecture. But of course, mixed with all this, and covering it all, there is a bubbling, sparkling fountain of effervescent raillery—cruel, personal, insatiable—the raillery of a demon with a grudge. The manuscript was shown to Frederick, who laughed till the tears ran down his cheeks. But, between his gasps, he forbade Voltaire to publish it on pain of his most terrible displeasure. Naturally Voltaire was profuse with promises, and a few days later, under a royal licence obtained for another work, the little book appeared in print. Frederick still managed to keep his wrath within bounds: he collected all the copies of the edition and had them privately destroyed; he gave a furious wigging to Voltaire; and he flattered himself that he had heard the last of the business.

Ne vous embarrassez de rien, mon cher Maupertuis [he wrote to the President in his singular orthography]; l'affaire des libelles est finie. J'ai parlé si vrai à l'hôme, je lui ai lavé si bien la tête que je ne crois pas qu'il y retourne, et je connais son âme lache, incapable de sentiments d'honneur. Je l'ai intimidé du côté de la boursse, ce qui a fait tout l'effet que j'attendais. Je lui ai déclaré enfin nettement que ma maison devait être un sanctuaire et non une retraite de brigands ou de célérats qui distillent des poissons.

Apparently it did not occur to Frederick that this declaration had come a little late in the day. Meanwhile Maupertuis, overcome by illness and by rage, had taken to his bed. 'Un peu trop d'amour-propre,' Frederick wrote to Darget, 'l'a rendu trop sensible aux manœuvres d'un singe qu'il devait mépriser après qu'on l'avait fouetté.' But now the monkey *had* been whipped, and doubtless all would be well. It seems strange that Frederick should still, after more than two years observation, have had no notion of the material he was dealing with. He might as well have supposed that he could stop a mountain torrent in spate with a wave of his hand, as have imagined that he could impose obedience upon Voltaire in such a crisis by means of a lecture and a threat 'du côté de la boursse.' Before the month was out all Germany was swarming with *Akakias*; thousands of copies were being printed in Holland; and editions were going off in Paris like hot cakes. It is difficult to withhold one's admiration from the audacious old spirit who thus, on the mere strength of his mother-wits, dared to defy the enraged master of a powerful state. 'Votre effronterie m'étonne,' fulminated Frederick in a furious note, when he suddenly discovered that all Europe was ringing with the absurdity of the man whom he had chosen to be the President of his favourite Academy, whose cause he had publicly espoused, and whom he had privately assured of his royal protection. 'Ah! Mon Dieu, Sire,' scribbled Voltaire on the same sheet of paper, 'dans l'état où je suis!' (He was, of course, once more dying.) 'Quoi! vous me jugeriez sans entendre! Je demande justice et la mort.' Frederick replied by having copies of *Akakia* burnt by the common hangman in the streets of Berlin. Voltaire thereupon returned his Order, his gold key, and his pension. It might have been supposed that the final rupture had now really come at last. But three months elapsed before Frederick could bring himself to realise that all was over, and to agree to the departure of his extraordinary guest. Carlyle's suggestion that this last delay arose from the unwillingness of Voltaire to go, rather than from Frederick's desire to keep him, is plainly controverted by the facts. The King not only insisted on Voltaire's accepting once again the honours which he had surrendered, but actually went so far as to write him a letter of forgiveness and reconciliation. But the poet would not relent; there was a last week of suppers at Potsdam—'soupers de Damoclès' Voltaire called them; and then, on March 26, 1753, the two men parted for ever.

The storm seemed to be over; but the tail of it was still hanging in the wind. Voltaire, on his way to the waters of Plombières, stopped at Leipzig, where he could not resist, in spite of his repeated promises to the contrary, the temptation to bring out a new and enlarged edition of *Akakia*. Upon this Maupertuis utterly lost his head: he wrote to Voltaire, threatening him with personal chastisement. Voltaire issued yet another edition of *Akakia*, appended a somewhat unauthorised version of the President's letter, and added that if the dangerous and cruel man really persisted in his threat he would be received with a vigorous discharge from those instruments of intimate utility which figure so freely in the comedies of Molière. This stroke was the *coup de grâce* of Maupertuis. Shattered in body and mind, he dragged himself from Berlin to die at last in Basle under the ministration of a couple of Capuchins and a Protestant valet reading aloud the Genevan Bible. In the meantime Frederick had decided on a violent measure. He had suddenly remembered that Voltaire

had carried off with him one of the very few privately printed
copies of those poetical works upon which he had spent so
much devoted labour; it occurred to him that they contained
several passages of a highly damaging kind; and he could feel
no certainty that those passages would not be given to the
world by the malicious Frenchman. Such, at any rate, were
his own excuses for the step which he now took; but it seems
possible that he was at least partly swayed by feelings of resent-
ment and revenge which had been rendered uncontrollable by
the last onslaught upon Maupertuis. Whatever may have been
his motives, it is certain that he ordered the Prussian Resident
in Frankfort, which was Voltaire's next stopping-place, to
hold the poet in arrest until he delivered over the royal
volume. A multitude of strange blunders and ludicrous incidents followed, upon which much controversial and patriotic
ink has been spilt by a succession of French and German
biographers. To an English reader it is clear that in this
little comedy of errors none of the parties concerned can
escape from blame—that Voltaire was hysterical, undignified,
and untruthful, that the Prussian Resident was stupid and
domineering, that Frederick was careless in his orders and
cynical as to their results. Nor, it is to be hoped, need any
Englishman be reminded that the consequences of a system
of government in which the arbitrary will of an individual
takes the place of the rule of law are apt to be disgraceful and
absurd.

After five weeks' detention at Frankfort, Voltaire was free
—free in every sense of the word—free from the service of
Kings and the clutches of Residents, free in his own mind,
free to shape his own destiny. He hesitated for several months,
and then settled down by the Lake of Geneva. There the
fires, which had lain smouldering so long in the profundities
of his spirit, flared up, and flamed over Europe, towering and
inextinguishable. In a few years letters began to flow once
more to and from Berlin. At first the old grievances still
rankled; but in time even the wrongs of Maupertuis and the
misadventures of Frankfort were almost forgotten. Twenty

years passed, and the King of Prussia was submitting his verses as anxiously as ever to Voltaire, whose compliments and cajoleries were pouring out in their accustomed stream. But their relationship was no longer that of master and pupil, courtier and King; it was that of two independent and equal powers. Even Frederick the Great was forced to see at last in the Patriarch of Ferney something more than a monkey with a genius for French versification. He actually came to respect the author of *Akakia*, and to cherish his memory. 'Je lui fais tous les matins ma prière,' he told d'Alembert, when Voltaire had been two years in the grave; 'je lui dis, Divin Voltaire, *ora pro nobis.*'

1915.

A SIDELIGHT ON
FREDERICK THE GREAT

THE Memoirs of Henri de Catt have long been familiar to scholars; they were used by Carlyle in his *Life of Friedrich*, and an elaborate edition of the original manuscript forms one of the valuable series of publications issued from the Prussian State Archives. The book is an extremely interesting one, and the present translation,[1] which makes it for the first time accessible to the ordinary English reader, deserves to be widely read. The translation itself is of a decidedly unpretentious kind. Occasionally, it is somewhat misleading. The rendering, for instance, throughout the book, of Frederick's familiar and affectionate *mon cher* by the stiff formality of 'my dear sir' gives a seriously false impression of the King's attitude towards his secretary. Stylistically, however, the excellent Catt has nothing to lose from any translation, however pedestrian. It is not as a piece of literature that his work is to be judged. Nor, except incidentally and indirectly, is it of any real importance from the historical and political point of view. The Frederick of history reaches us through other channels, and our estimate of that extraordinary career does not depend upon the kind of information which Catt provides. The interest of his book is entirely personal and psychological. It is like one of those photographs—old-fashioned and faded, perhaps, but still taken *sur le vif*—which one turns to with an eager curiosity, of some remarkable and celebrated man. The historian neglects Oliver Cromwell's warts; but it is just such queer details of a physiognomy that the amateur of human

---

[1] *Frederick the Great: the Memoirs of his Reader, Henri de Catt* (1758–1760). Translated by F. S. Flint. With an Introduction by Lord Rosebery. Constable. 2 vols.

nature most delights in. Catt shows us the queer details of Frederick's mental physiognomy, and some of them are very queer indeed.

His portrait has both the merits and the drawbacks of a photograph: it is true, and it is stupid; and its very stupidity is the measure of its truth. There is not a trace of Boswellian artistry about it—of that power of selection and evocation which clothes its object with something of the palpable reality of life. There is hardly even a trace of criticism. 'Let me have men about me that are . . . not too clever,' must have been Frederick's inward resolution after his disastrous experience with Voltaire; and obviously it was with some such feeling in his mind that, after a chance meeting on a boat in Holland, he engaged as his 'reader' the pious, ingenuous, good-natured Swiss young man. The King's choice was amply justified: the young man was certainly not too clever; one gathers that Frederick actually almost liked him; and, though the inevitable rupture came at last, it was delayed for more than twenty years. Catt was indeed the precise antithesis of Voltaire. And his Memoirs are the precise antithesis of Voltaire's famous lampoon. The Frenchman's devastating sketch is painted with such brilliance that nobody can believe in it, and nobody can help believing in the bland acceptance of Catt's photographic plate.

The Memoirs only cover a period of two years, but it so happens that those years contained the crisis of Frederick's life. Between 1758 and 1761 the hideous convulsion of the Seven Years' War reached its culmination. Frederick, attacked simultaneously by France, Austria and Russia, faced his enemies like a bear tied to the stake: disaster after disaster fell upon him; bloody defeats punctuated his ruinous marches and desperate manœuvrings; Berlin itself was taken; for many months it seemed certain that the doom of Prussia was sealed; more than once the hopeless King was on the brink of escaping the final humiliation by suicide. Catt, with a few brief intervals, was in daily intercourse with Frederick all through this period, and it is against this lurid background of frenzied struggle and accumulating horror that he shows us his portrait of his master. Every day, whether in camp under canvas, or in the cramped quarters of some wretched village, or amid the uncongenial splendours of some momentarily conquered palace, he was summoned at about five in the evening to the royal presence, where he remained, usually for at least two, and sometimes for four or five hours. His duties as 'reader' were of a purely passive kind: it was his business, not to read, but to listen. And listen he did, while the King, putting aside at last the labours and agitations of the day, the coils of strategy and high politics, relaxed himself in literary chat, French declamations, and philosophical arguments. Clearly enough, these evening *tête-à-têtes* with Catt were the one vestige left to him, in his terrible surroundings, of the pleasures of private life—of the life of intellectual cultivation and unofficial intercourse; and the spectacle of this grim old conqueror seeking out the company of a mediocre young man from Switzerland, with whom to solace himself in rhymes and rhapsodies, would be pathetic, if such a word were not so totally inapplicable to such a character. No, the spectacle is not pathetic; it is simply exceedingly curious. For what Catt shows us is a man for whom literature was not merely a pastime but a passion, a man of exaggerated sensibilities, a man who would devote ungrudging hours to the laborious imitation of French poetry, a man who would pass the evenings of days spent in scheming and slaughter reading aloud the plays of his favourite dramatist, until at last he would be overcome by emotion, and break down, in floods of tears. Frederick, in fact, appears in Catt's pages as a literary sentimentalist; he weeps at every opportunity, and is never tired of declaiming high sentiments in alexandrine verse. When he is cheerful, he quotes Chaulieu; when he is satirical, he misquotes *Athalie*; when he is defeated in battle and within an ace of utter destruction, he greets his astonished Reader with a long tirade from *Mithridate*. After Frederick himself, Racine is the real hero of these Memoirs. His exquisite, sensuous, and high-resounding oratory flows through them in a perpetual stream. It is a strange triumph for that most refined of poets: the sobs of Burrhus are heard in the ruined hamlets of Saxony, and the agonies of Zorndorf mingle with those of Phèdre.

And after Racine, Voltaire. Again and again, Frederick recurs, in accents of mingled anger and regret, to the Master whose art he worshipped, whose person he had once held in his clutches, and who had now escaped him for ever. Voltaire was a rogue, no doubt, a heartless scoundrel, capable of any villainy—but his genius!—'Si son cœur égalait ses talents, quel homme, mon ami, quel homme! Et comme il nous humilierait tous!' And so Majesty bent once more over the screed of halting verses, struggling to polish them according to the precepts of the Patriarch; and so, when a letter came from Ferney, the royal countenance beamed with pleasure, and soldiers who had pilfered hen-roosts might hope for fewer lashes that day. Sometimes, when Frederick was particularly pleased with his compositions, he ventured to submit them to the critical eye of the great man. 'Mon cher, croyez-vous que ma pièce soit assez bonne pour être envoyée au patriarche?' On one occasion he allowed his author's vanity to interfere even with his policy. He had concocted some highly scurrilous verses on Louis XV and Madame de Pompadour, and was so delighted with them that he proposed at once to send them to Ferney. He had never, he told Catt, done anything better; even the Patriarch would be unable to detect a single fault. Catt allowed the excellence of the verses, but sagaciously pointed out the danger of putting them into the hands of Voltaire—that heartless scoundrel, as his Majesty had so constantly remarked, capable of any villainy—at the very moment when the disasters of the campaign made it important to capture, if possible, the good graces of the French Court. Frederick reflected; agreed that Catt was right; and then, in a day or two, unable to resist the temptation, secretly sent off the verses to Voltaire. The inevitable followed. On the receipt of the verses, Voltaire immediately despatched them to the French authorities, while he wrote to Frederick informing him that the royal letter had been apparently opened in the post, and that therefore, if copies had been taken of it and forwarded to certain quarters, he at any rate was not to blame. Frederick at once realised his folly. Voltaire, he declared to Catt, was a monster, a traitor, and an old monkey. A few months later, a copy of *Candide* arrived from the author. Frederick read it; he read it again, and yet again. It was the best novel, he told Catt, that had ever been written, and Voltaire was the greatest man alive.

Never, surely, was the eighteenth-century theory of the 'ruling passion' more signally falsified than in the case of Frederick the Great. He was ambitious, no doubt; but ambitious for what? For political power? For military prestige? Or for the glory of satisfying an old monkey at Ferney that he could write a good alexandrine if he tried? The European bandit who sits up all night declaiming the noble sentiments of Racine's heroes, the hardened cynic who weeps for hours over his own elegies, is certainly a puzzling creature, hard to fit into any cut-and-dried system of psychology. So glaring, indeed, are these contradictions that Lord Rosebery, in his Introduction to the present translation, suggests that Frederick posed to his Reader, that the tears and the literary emotions which Catt chronicles were 'the result of dramatic art.' When, in particular, Frederick expatiates on his desire for a life of retirement, devoted to the delights of friendship and æsthetic cultivation, Lord Rosebery is disposed to agree with the comment of the Swiss young man that 'the whole was a little comedy.' It may be so; but it is difficult to believe it. It is hard to see what object Frederick could have had in deluding Catt; and it is easier to suppose that a man should contradict himself, both in his thoughts and his feelings, than that he should spend years in keeping up an elaborate mystification with an insignificant secretary, for no apparent purpose. As a whole, the impression, produced by the Memoirs, of Frederick's sincerity is overwhelming. And perhaps the contradictions in his character, extreme as they were, are more apparent than real. Cynicism and sentimentality, so opposite in their effects, share at their root in a certain crudity; and Frederick, intellectually and spiritually, was crude. His ambitions, his scepticisms, his admirations, his tastes—all were crude; on the one side, this underlying quality came out in public Macchiavellisms and private cruelties, and on the other in highfalutin pathos and a schoolgirl's prostration before the literary man. On a smaller scale, such characters are not uncommon; what makes Frederick's case so extraordinary and at first sight so baffling is the extremity of difference to which the opposite tendencies were pushed. The explanation of this no doubt lies in the portentous, the terrific, energy of the man. His vehemence could be content with no ordinary moderation either in the callous or the lachrymose; and the same amazing force which made Prussia a Great Power created, in spite of incredible difficulties, in a foreign idiom, under the bondage of the harshest literary conventions ever known, that vast mass of fifth-rate poetising from which shuddering History averts her face.

1917.

THE PRÉSIDENT DE BROSSES

A CHARMING and sometimes forgotten feature of the world as it used to be before the age of trains and telephones was the provincial capital. When Edinburgh was as far from London as Vienna is to-day, it was natural—it was inevitable—that it should be the centre of a local civilisation, which, while it remained politically and linguistically British, developed a colour and a character of its own. In France there was the same pleasant phenomenon. Bordeaux, Toulouse, Aix-en-Provence—up to the end of the eighteenth century each of these was in truth a capital, where a peculiar culture had grown up that was at once French and idiosyncratic. An impossibility to-day! It is hard to believe, as one whisks through Dijon in a tram, that here, a hundred and fifty years ago, was the centre of a distinct and vigorous civilisation—until, perhaps, one leaves the tram, and turns aside into the rue de la Préfecture. Ah! One has come upon a vanished age. The houses, so solid and yet so vivacious, with their cobbled courts and coloured tiles, seem to be withdrawn into an aristocratic resignation. Memory and forgetfulness are everywhere. It is the moment to reflect upon the Président de Brosses.

Dijon, the capital of Burgundy, had become in the eighteenth century pre-eminently a city of magistrates. There the provincial *parlement* assembled and the laws were administered by the hereditary judges, the nobility of the long robe, whose rule was more immediate, more impressive, and almost more powerful, than the King's. Charles de Brosses was born into this aristocracy, and grew up to be a perfect representative of its highest traditions. He was extremely intelligent, admirably conscientious, and crammed full of life.

He was at once a wit, a scholar, a lawyer, and a man of the world. He resembled the generous wine of the country in his combination of gay vitality with richness and strength. His tiny figure and his satirical face lost in the forest of a judicial wig might prompt to laughter—'the corners of one's mouth,' said Diderot, 'couldn't help going up when one looked at him'; but he was impressive on the bench; and, late in life, was to prove his patriotism by his intrepid resistance when the privileges of his province were attacked by the royal authority. In his leisure, he devoted himself to every kind of literary and scientific work. A tour in Italy produced a series of amusing letters, which, published posthumously, are still read and remembered; his book on the newly discovered Herculaneum (1750) was the first on the subject; his *Histoire des navigations des Terres Australes* (1756) was of use to both Cook and Bougainville; his *Culte des Dieux Fétiches* (1760) contained a curious speculation on the origin of the religion of Egypt; his *Traité de la formation mécanique des langues* (1765) was the earliest attempt at a science of etymology; and his labours were concluded with an elaborate edition of *Sallust* (1777) upon which he had worked for thirty years. The growth of knowledge has converted his researches and his speculations into mere curiosities; but it was natural that the citizens of Dijon should have honoured him as one of their most splendid luminaries, and that the Président de Brosses should have been compared in his day to that other great provincial figure of a previous generation—the Président de Montesquieu. Of course, though Dijon was select and Dijon was magnificent, it had to be admitted that there did exist a higher tribunal, at whose bar taste, learning, and behaviour received their final doom or their crowning approbation: the drawing-rooms of Paris reigned supreme. In those drawing-rooms the Président was well thought of; he had powerful friends at Court; was it not to be expected that at last, in the fullness of time, his worth would be completely recognised and receive its due reward in the highest honour that could fall to a man of his pretensions—a seat in the Academy?

A prize, indeed, that it was impossible not to hope for! The promises of other worlds had grown dim and dubious; but here, among the glorious forty, was a definite, an indisputable immortality—and one, moreover, that possessed the singular advantage of being enjoyable here and now, while the eighteenth-century sun still shone on the rue de la Préfecture.

The Président was at the height of his exuberant manhood —he was not yet fifty—when something occurred which had a strange and unexpected effect upon his history. Voltaire, having quarrelled with Frederick the Great and shaken the dust of Potsdam from his feet, had been wandering for some years in uncertainty among the minor states that lay between France and Germany. He had settled for a time at Colmar; he had moved to Lausanne; then he had gone to Geneva and taken a country house in its neighbourhood. But the Calvinism of the townspeople, who frowned at his passion for private theatricals, annoyed him; and his eye fell on the house and territory of Ferney, which was just inside the borders of France, but, lying on the eastern slopes of the Jura mountains, was so remote as to be almost independent of French control and within a drive of the free city of Geneva. This was exactly what he wanted—a secluded abode, where he would have elbow-room for his activities, and from which he could bolt at any moment, if things became too hot for him. Accordingly, in 1758, he bought Ferney, where he lived for the rest of his life; and at the same time he entered into negotiations for the purchase of a neighbouring property—that of Tournay —which belonged to the Président de Brosses. The Président, who already had a slight acquaintance with the great man— his wife, a Crévecœur, was the daughter of one of Voltaire's oldest friends—declared that he would be delighted to oblige him. There was some stiff haggling, for each party prided himself on his business capacity, but eventually Voltaire, for 35,000 francs, became possessed of the domain of Tournay —which included the right to the title of Count—on a life-tenancy. The bargain, obviously, was something of a gamble; the new Comte de Tournay was sixty-four, and, so he declared, on the point of death; but then he had been on the point of death ever since any one could remember. When it was all over, the Président had an uneasy feeling that he had been done. The feeling increased as time went on, and his agent informed him that the estate was being allowed to go to rack and ruin. He complained; but the poet replied with a flat denial, declared—what was quite true—that he had built a theatre at Tournay, and begged the Président to come and see his latest tragedy performed in it. A little later, a new manœuvre began: Voltaire proposed that he should buy the property outright. The Président was not altogether averse; but this time he was far more cautious; as the negotiations proceeded, he became privately convinced that an attempt was being made to cheat him; but he said nothing, and the proposal lapsed. Voltaire, on his side, was none too pleased with his bargain. The land of Tournay was poor, and the Countship had brought with it various responsibilities and expenses not at all to his taste. He was vexed; and his vexation took the form of bothering the Président, in letter after letter, with a multitude of legal questions upon points connected with the property. The Président was also vexed; but he answered every letter and every question with extreme civility.

In this way two years passed—two years during which the Président published his *Culte des Dieux Fétiches* and Voltaire his *Candide*. The old creature at Ferney was at last beginning to settle down to the final and by far the most important period of his immense and extraordinary career. Free, rich, happy, with his colossal reputation and his terrific energy, he was starting on the great adventure of his life—his onslaught upon Christianity. Meanwhile his vitality and his pugnacity were satisfying themselves in a multitude of minor ways. He was belabouring Rousseau, torturing Fréron, annihilating le Franc de Pompignan; he was corresponding with all the world, he was composing half a dozen tragedies, he was writing the life of Peter the Great, he was preparing a

monumental edition of Corneille. When, in the midst of these
and a hundred other activities, he received a bill for 281 francs
from a peasant called Charlot Baudy for fourteen loads of
wood from Tournay, he brushed the matter on one side.
More bother from Tournay! But it was ridiculous—why
should he pay for wood from his own estate? And besides, he
remembered quite well that the Président, before the sale was
completed, had told him that he could have as much wood as
he wanted. He did nothing, and when Charlot Baudy pressed
for the money, refused to pay. Then, early in 1761, a letter
arrived from the Président. 'Agreez, Monsieur,' he began,
'que je vous demande l'explication d'une chose tout-à-fait
singulière.' Charlot Baudy, he continued, had, *before the sale
of Tournay*, bought from the Président the cut wood on the
estate; Baudy had now sent in his account of what he owed
the Président, and had subtracted from it the sum of 281
francs for wood supplied to M. de Voltaire; his reason for this
was that M. de Voltaire had told him that the wood was a
gift from the Président. 'Je vous demande excuse,' the letter
went on, 'si je vous répète un tel propos: car vous sentez bien
que je suis fort éloigné de croire que vous l'ayez tenu, et je
n'y ajoute pas la moindre foi. Je ne prends ceci que pour le
discours d'un homme rustique fait pour ignorer les usages du
monde et les convenances; qui ne sait pas qu'on envoie bien
à son ami et son voisin un panier de pêches, mais que si on
s'avisait de lui faire la galanterie de quatorze moules de bois,
il le prendrait pour une absurdité contraire aux bienséances.'
The sarcasm was clear and cutting, and the Président proceeded to give his own account of what had occurred. He
distinctly remembered, he said, that Voltaire, at the time
of the negotiations about Tournay, had in the course of conversation, complained of a lack of firewood, and that he had
thereupon recommended Baudy as the man who would supply
Voltaire with as much as he wanted. That was all; the offen-
sive notion of a present had never entered his head. 'J'espère,'
he concluded, 'que vous voudrez bien faire incontinent payer
cette bagatelle à Charlot, parce que, comme je me ferai

certainement payer de lui, il aurait infailliblement aussi son recours contre vous; ce qui ferait une affaire du genre de celles qu'un homme tel que vous ne veut point avoir.'

It was obvious to anyone in his senses that the Président was right: that his account of the matter was the true one, and that, as he had said, the only reasonable thing for Voltaire to do was to pay Baudy the money—the miserable sum of money!—and finish the business. But Voltaire was not in his senses—he never was when even the most miserable sum of money was concerned. He could not bear to think of parting with 281 francs. It was monstrous; the land and everything on it was his; the wood had been given him; he would not be set down; and this wretched man had dared to be ironical! At any rate, he had had the wood and burnt it, and the Président de Brosses might do what he liked. Accordingly, in his next letter, he airily dismissed the subject. 'It is no longer a question,' he said, 'of Charles Baudy and four loads of wood'—and proceeded to discuss an entirely different matter. The Président replied in detail, and then reverted for a moment to Baudy—'Four loads—read *fourteen*; you dropped a figure; we call this a *lapsus linguae*';—and he begged Voltaire once more to avoid the painful publicity of a lawsuit. Voltaire made no reply; he hoped the whole thing was over; but he was wrong. In June, the Président sued Baudy for 281 francs, and in July Baudy sued Voltaire for the same sum. The cases came on at the local court, and were adjourned.

And now the fury of the frantic old desperado flamed up sky-high. Seizing his pen, he poured out, in letter after letter to all the lawyers in Dijon, his account of what had happened —the swindling to which he had been subjected—the insults to which he had been exposed. To a particular friend, the Président de Ruffey, he sent a long formal statement of his case, followed by a private sheet of enraged argumentation. As for his enemy, he was no longer a président—the little bewigged monster—he was a fetish. He would see to it that the nickname stuck. 'Le Fétiche,' he shrieked, 'demande de l'argent de ses moules et de ses fagots. . . . Le misérable m'accable d'exploits.' He had put up Baudy, who was a man of straw, to do his dirty work. 'Songez qu'il faisait cette in-fâmie dans le temps qu'il recevait de moi 47 mille livres! . . . Qu'il tremble! Il ne s'agit pas de le rendre ridicule: il s'agit de le déshonorer. Cela m'afflige. Mais il payera cher la bassesse d'un procédé si coupable et si lâche.' Finally he addressed the Fetish himself in a letter composed in his most magnificent style. 'Vous n'êtes donc venu chez moi, Monsieur, vous ne m'avez offert votre amitié, que pour empoisonner par des procès la fin de ma vie.' In great detail he went over the whole dispute. With singular violence, and no less singular obtuse-ness, he asserted the hopelessly contradictory propositions, both that the wood was his own and that the Président had given it him; he hinted that his enemy would make use of his position to pervert the course of justice; and he ended with threats. 'S'il faut que M. le Chancelier, et les Ministres, et tout Paris, soient instruits de votre procédé, ils le seront; et, s'il se trouve dans votre Compagnie respectable une personne qui vous approuve, je me condamne.'

The Président's moment had come—the testing moment of his life. What was he to do? It was still not too late to with-draw, to pay the money with a shrug of the shoulders and put an end to this fearful hubbub and this terrifying enmity. For a short space, he wavered. It was true that Voltaire was the greatest writer of the age, and perhaps he deserved some allow-ances on that score. In any case, he was an extremely danger-ous antagonist—a man who had made mincemeat of all his literary opponents and fought on equal terms with Frederick the Great. But no! It was intolerable! His Burgundian blood boiled, and the proud traditions of aristocracy and the judicial habits of a lifetime asserted themselves. 'Là-dessus on dit':— so he explained later to a friend—'c'est un homme dangereux. Et à cause de cela, faut-il donc le laisser être méchant im-punément? Ce sont au contraire ces sortes de gens-là qu'il faut châtier. Je ne le crains pas. . . . On l'admire, parce qu'il fait d'excellents vers. Sans doute il les fait excellents. Mais ce sont ses vers qu'il faut admirer.' And so, taking Voltaire's letter, he wrote upon the margin of it a reply, in which he not only rebutted his arguments but told him exactly what he thought of him. Point by point he exposed the futility of Voltaire's contentions. He showed that there was actually a clause in the lease, by which the cut wood on the estate was specifically excepted from the sale. He offered to drop the matter if Voltaire would send him a receipt in the following terms: 'Je soussigné, François-Marie Arouet de Voltaire, chevalier, seigneur de Ferney, gentilhomme ordinaire de la chambre du Roi, reconnois que M. de Brosses, président du Parlement, m'a fait présent de . . . voies de bois de moule, pour mon chauffage, en valeur de 281 f., dont je le remercie.' He pointed out that otherwise he had nothing to do with the business, that Voltaire owed the money to Charlot Baudy, and that it was indeed extraordinary to see 'un homme si riche et si illustre se tourmenter à tel excès pour ne pas payer à un paysan 280 livres pour du bois de chauffage qu'il a fourni.' His incidental remarks were nothing if not outspoken. 'En vérité,' he wrote, 'je gémis pour l'humanité de voir un si grand génie avec un cœur si petit sans cesse tiraillé par des misères de jalousie et de lésine. C'est vous-même qui empoisonnez une vie si bien faite d'ailleurs pour être heureuse.' As for the suggestion that he would bring undue influence to bear upon the case,—'il ne convient pas de parler ainsi: soyez assez sage à l'avenir pour ne rien dire de pareil à un magistrat.' 'Tenez vous pour dit,' the letter concluded, 'de ne m'écrire plus ni sur cette matière ni surtout de ce ton. Je vous fais, Monsieur, le souhait de Perse: *Mens sana in corpore sano.*'

It is difficult indeed to imagine the scene at Ferney while Voltaire was deciphering, on the edges of his own letter, this devastating reply. But there was worse to follow. A note came from the Président de Ruffey, in which, with infinite politeness, he made it clear that in his opinion Voltaire had no case, and that he had better pay. At the same time Ruffey wrote to Madame Denis, Voltaire's niece, advising her to give the money privately to Baudy. Madame Denis had not the courage to do so; she showed the letter to her uncle, who, in a dictated reply, still tried to keep up an appearance of self-confidence. 'Je ne crains point les Fétiches,' he added in his own hand. 'Et les Fétiches doivent me craindre.' And again, at the bottom of the paper, he scribbled, 'N.B. Il n'y a qu'une voix sur le Fétiche.' But such screams were useless; the game was up. The Président's letter remained unanswered; Voltaire swallowed in silence the incredible affront; and when, a little later, the Président, feeling that he could afford to be magnanimous, informed a common friend that he would cancel his account with Baudy if Voltaire gave 281 francs to the poor of Tournay, the great man was glad enough to fall in with the suggestion.

The Président had triumphed; but could he really have supposed that he would escape from such an antagonist unscathed? The sequel came ten years later, when the Président Hénault died and left a seat vacant at the Academy. There was a strong movement in favour of electing the Président de Brosses. There appeared to be no other very suitable candidate; his friends rallied round him; and d'Alembert, writing to Voltaire from Paris, assured him that there was every likelihood that 'ce plat Président' would be chosen for the vacant place. The serious feature of the case was that the old Maréchal de Richelieu, who, after a lifetime of fighting and gallantry, amused his decrepitude by making his influence felt in affairs of this kind, supported him. What was to be done? Voltaire was equal to the occasion: his letters flew. At all costs the Fetish must be kept out. He wrote repeatedly to Richelieu, in that tone of delicate cajolery of which he was a master, touching upon their ancient friendship, and spinning a strange tale of the perfidies committed by 'ce petit persécuteur nasilloneur,' until the Maréchal melted, and promised to withdraw his support. Finally Voltaire despatched to d'Alembert a signed declaration to the effect that he would himself resign from the Academy if Brosses was elected. This settled the matter, and no more was heard of the candidature of the Président. It seems likely that he never knew what it was that had baulked him of the ambition of his life. For 281 francs he had lost the immortality of the Academy. A bad bargain, no doubt; and yet, after all, the transaction had gained him another, and in fact a unique, distinction: he would go down to history as the man who had got the better of Voltaire.

1931

THE ROUSSEAU AFFAIR

No one who has made the slightest expedition into that curious and fascinating country, Eighteenth-Century France, can have come away from it without at least *one* impression strong upon him—that in no other place and at no other time have people ever squabbled so much. France in the eighteenth century, whatever else it may have been—however splendid in genius, in vitality, in noble accomplishment and high endeavour—was certainly not a quiet place to live in. One could never have been certain, when one woke up in the morning, whether, before the day was out, one would not be in the Bastille for something one had said at dinner, or have quarrelled with half one's friends for something one had never said at all.

Of all the disputes and agitations of that agitated age none is more remarkable than the famous quarrel between Rousseau and his friends, which disturbed French society for so many years, and profoundly affected the life and the character of the most strange and perhaps the most potent of the precursors of the Revolution. The affair is constantly cropping up in the literature of the time; it occupies a prominent place in the later books of the *Confessions;* and there is an account of its earlier phases—an account written from the anti-Rousseau point of view—in the *Mémoires* of Madame d'Epinay. The whole story is an exceedingly complex one, and all the details of it have never been satisfactorily explained; but the general verdict of subsequent writers has been decidedly hostile to Rousseau, though it has not subscribed to all the virulent abuse poured upon him by his enemies at the time of the quarrel. This, indeed, is precisely the conclusion which an unprejudiced reader of the *Confessions* would naturally come to. Rousseau's story, even as he himself tells it, does not carry conviction. He would have us believe that he was the victim of a vast and diabolical conspiracy, of which Grimm and Diderot were the moving spirits, which succeeded in alienating from him his dearest friends, and which eventually included all the ablest and most distinguished persons of the age. Not only does such a conspiracy appear, upon the face of it, highly improbable, but the evidence which Rousseau adduces to prove its existence seems totally insufficient; and the reader is left under the impression that the unfortunate Jean-Jacques was the victim, not of a plot contrived by rancorous enemies, but of his own perplexed, suspicious, and deluded mind. This conclusion is supported by the account of the affair given by contemporaries, and it is still further strengthened by Rousseau's own writings subsequent to the *Confessions*, where his endless recriminations, his elaborate hypotheses, and his wild inferences bear all the appearance of mania. Here the matter has rested for many years; and it seemed improbable that any fresh reasons would arise for reopening the question. Mrs. F. Macdonald, however, in a recently-published work,[1] has produced some new and important evidence, which throws entirely fresh light upon certain obscure parts of this doubtful history; and is possibly of even greater interest. For it is Mrs. Macdonald's contention that her new discovery completely overturns the orthodox theory, establishes the guilt of Grimm, Diderot, and the rest of the anti-Rousseau party, and proves that the story told in the *Confessions* is simply the truth.

If these conclusions really do follow from Mrs. Macdonald's newly-discovered data, it would be difficult to overestimate the value of her work, for the result of it would be nothing less than a revolution in our judgments upon some of the principal characters of the eighteenth century. To make it certain that Diderot was a cad and a cheat, that d'Alembert was a dupe, and Hume a liar—that, surely, were no small achievement. And, even if these conclusions do not follow

---

[1] *Jean Jacques Rousseau: a New Criticism*, by Frederika Macdonald. In two volumes. Chapman and Hall. 1906.

from Mrs. Macdonald's data, her work will still be valuable, owing to the data themselves. Her discoveries are important, whatever inferences may be drawn from them; and for this reason her book, 'which represents,' as she tells us, 'twenty years of research,' will be welcome to all students of that remarkable age.

Mrs. Macdonald's principal revelations relate to the *Mémoires* of Madame d'Epinay. This work was first printed in 1818, and the concluding quarter of it contains an account of the Rousseau quarrel, the most detailed of all those written from the anti-Rousseau point of view. It has, however, always been doubtful how far the *Mémoires* were to be trusted as accurate records of historical fact. The manuscript disappeared; but it was known that the characters who, in the printed book, appear under the names of real persons, were given pseudonyms in the original document; and many of the minor statements contradicted known events. Had Madame d'Epinay merely intended to write a *roman à clef*? What seemed, so far as concerned the Rousseau narrative, to put this hypothesis out of court was the fact that the story of the quarrel as it appears in the *Mémoires* is, in its main outlines, substantiated both by Grimm's references to Rousseau in his *Correspondance Littéraire*, and by a brief memorandum of Rousseau's misconduct, drawn up by Diderot for his private use, and not published until many years after Madame d'Epinay's death. Accordingly most writers on the subject have taken the accuracy of the *Mémoires* for granted; Sainte-Beuve, for instance, prefers the word of Madame d'Epinay to that of Rousseau, when there is a direct conflict of testimony; and Lord Morley, in his well-known biography, uses the *Mémoires* as an authority for many of the incidents which he relates. Mrs. Macdonald's researches, however, have put an entirely different complexion on the case. She has discovered the manuscript from which the *Mémoires* were printed, and she has examined the original draft of this manuscript, which had been unearthed some years ago, but whose full import had been unaccountably neglected by previous scholars. From these researches, two facts have come to light. In the first place, the manuscript differs in many respects from the printed book, and, in particular, contains a conclusion of two hundred sheets, which has never been printed at all; the alterations were clearly made in order to conceal the inaccuracies of the manuscript; and the omitted conclusion is frankly and palpably a fiction. And in the second place, the original draft of the manuscript turns out to be the work of several hands; it contains, especially in those portions which concern Rousseau, many erasures, corrections, and notes, while several pages had been altogether cut out; most of the corrections were made by Madame d'Epinay herself; but in nearly every case these corrections carry out the instruction in the notes; and the notes themselves are in the handwriting of Diderot and Grimm. Mrs. Macdonald gives several facsimiles of pages in the original draft, which amply support her description of it; but it is to be hoped that before long she will be able to produce a new and complete edition of the *Mémoires*, with all the manuscript alterations clearly indicated; for until then it will be difficult to realise the exact condition of the text. However, it is now beyond dispute both that Madame d'Epinay's narrative cannot be regarded as historically accurate, and that its agreement with the statements of Grimm and Diderot is by no means an independent confirmation of its truth, for Grimm and Diderot themselves had a hand in its compilation.

Thus far we are on firm ground. But what are the conclusions which Mrs. Macdonald builds up from these foundations? The account, she says, of Rousseau's conduct and character, as it appears in the printed version, is hostile to him, but it was not the account which Madame d'Epinay herself originally wrote. The hostile narrative was, in effect, composed by Grimm and Diderot, who induced Madame d'Epinay to substitute it for her own story; and thus her own story could not have agreed with theirs. Madame d'Epinay knew the truth; she knew that Rousseau's conduct had been honourable and wise; and so she had described it in her book;

until, falling completely under the influence of Grimm and Diderot, she had allowed herself to become the instrument for blackening the reputation of her old friend. Mrs. Macdonald paints a lurid picture of the conspirators at work—of Diderot penning his false and malignant instructions, of Madame d'Epinay's half-unwilling hand putting the last touches to the fraud, of Grimm, rushing back to Paris at the time of the Revolution, and risking his life in order to make quite certain that the result of all these efforts should reach posterity. Well! it would be difficult—perhaps it would be impossible—to prove conclusively that none of these things ever took place. The facts upon which Mrs. Macdonald lays so much stress—the mutilations, the additions, the instructing notes, the proved inaccuracy of the story the manuscripts tell—these facts, no doubt, may be explained by Mrs. Macdonald's theories; but there are other facts—no less important, and no less certain—which are in direct contradiction to Mrs. Macdonald's view, and over which she passes as lightly as she can. Putting aside the question of the *Mémoires*, we know nothing of Diderot which would lead us to entertain for a moment the supposition that he was a dishonourable and badhearted man; we do know that his writings bear the imprint of a singularly candid, noble, and fearless mind; we do know that he devoted his life, unflinchingly and unsparingly, to a great cause. We know less of Grimm; but it is at least certain that he was the intimate friend of Diderot, and of many more of the distinguished men of the time. Is all this evidence to be put on one side as of no account? Are we to dismiss it as Mrs. Macdonald dismisses it, as merely 'psychological'? Surely Diderot's reputation as an honest man is as much a fact as his notes in the draft of the *Mémoires*. It is quite true that his reputation *may* have been ill-founded, that d'Alembert, and Turgot, and Hume *may* have been deluded, or *may* have been bribed, into admitting him to their friendship; but is it not clear that we ought not to believe any such hypotheses as these until we have before us such convincing proof of Diderot's guilt that we *must* believe them? Mrs.

Macdonald declares that she has produced such proof; and she points triumphantly to her garbled and concocted manuscripts. If there is indeed no explanation of these garblings and concoctions other than that which Mrs. Macdonald puts forward—that they were the outcome of a false and malicious conspiracy to blast the reputation of Rousseau—then we must admit that she is right, and that all our general 'psychological' considerations as to Diderot's reputation in the world must be disregarded. But, before we come to this conclusion, how careful must we be to examine every other possible explanation of Mrs. Macdonald's facts, how rigorously must we sift her own explanation of them, how eagerly must we seize upon every loophole of escape!

It is, I believe, possible to explain the condition of the d'Epinay manuscript without having recourse to the iconoclastic theory of Mrs. Macdonald. To explain everything, indeed, would be out of the question, owing to our insufficient data, and the extreme complexity of the events; all that we can hope to do is to suggest an explanation which will account for the most important of the known facts. Not the least interesting of Mrs. Macdonald's discoveries went to show that the *Mémoires*, so far from being historically accurate, were in reality full of unfounded statements, that they concluded with an entirely imaginary narrative, and that, in short, they might be described, almost without exaggeration, in the very words with which Grimm himself actually did describe them in his *Correspondance Littéraire*, as 'l'ébauche d'un long roman.' Mrs. Macdonald eagerly lays emphasis upon this discovery, because she is, of course, anxious to prove that the most damning of all accounts of Rousseau's conduct is an untrue one. But she has proved too much. The *Mémoires*, she says, are a fiction; therefore the writers of them were liars. The answer is obvious: why should we not suppose that the writers were not liars at all, but simply novelists? Will not this hypothesis fit into the facts just as well as Mrs. Macdonald's? Madame d'Epinay, let us suppose, wrote a narrative, partly imaginary and partly true, based upon her own experiences, but without any strict adherence to the actual course of events, and filled with personages whose actions were, in many cases, fictitious, but whose characters were, on the whole, moulded upon the actual characters of her friends. Let us suppose that when she had finished her work—a work full of subtle observation and delightful writing—she showed it to Grimm and Diderot. They had only one criticism to make: it related to her treatment of the character which had been moulded upon that of Rousseau. 'Your Rousseau, chère Madame, is a very poor affair indeed! The most salient points in his character seem to have escaped you. We know what that man really was. We know how he behaved at that time. *C'était un homme à faire peur.* You have missed a great opportunity of drawing a fine picture of a hypocritical rascal.' Whereupon they gave her their own impressions of Rousseau's conduct, they showed her the letters that had passed between them, and they jotted down some notes for her guidance. She rewrote the story in accordance with their notes and their anecdotes; but she rearranged the incidents, she condensed or amplified the letters, as she thought fit—for she was not writing a history, but 'l'ébauche d'un long roman.' If we suppose that this, or something like this, was what occurred, shall we not have avoided the necessity for a theory so repugnant to common sense as that which would impute to a man of recognised integrity the meanest of frauds?

To follow Mrs. Macdonald into the inner recesses and elaborations of her argument would be a difficult and tedious task. The circumstances with which she is principally concerned—the suspicions, the accusations, the anonymous letters, the intrigues, the endless problems as to whether Madame d'Epinay was jealous of Madame d'Houdetot, whether Thérèse told fibs, whether, on the 14th of the month, Grimm was grossly impertinent, and whether, on the 15th, Rousseau was outrageously rude, whether Rousseau revealed a secret to Diderot, which Diderot revealed to Saint-Lambert, and whether, if Diderot revealed it, he believed that Rousseau had revealed it before—these circumstances form, as Lord

Morley says, 'a tale of labyrinthine nightmares,' and Mrs. Macdonald has done very little to mitigate either the contortions of the labyrinths or the horror of the dreams. Her book is exceedingly ill-arranged; it is enormously long, filling two large volumes, with an immense apparatus of appendices and notes; it is full of repetitions and of irrelevant matter; and the argument is so indistinctly set forth that even an instructed reader finds great difficulty in following its drift. Without, however, plunging into the abyss of complications which yawns for us in Mrs. Macdonald's pages, it may be worth while to touch upon one point with which she has dealt (perhaps wisely for her own case!) only very slightly—the question of the motives which could have induced Grimm and Diderot to perpetuate a series of malignant lies.

It is, doubtless, conceivable that Grimm, who was Madame d'Epinay's lover, was jealous of Rousseau, who was Madame d'Epinay's friend. We know very little of Grimm's character, but what we do know seems to show that he was a jealous man and an ambitious man; it is possible that a close alliance with Madame d'Epinay may have seemed to him a necessary step in his career; and it is conceivable that he may have determined not to rest until his most serious rival in Madame d'Epinay's affections was utterly cast out. He was probably prejudiced against Rousseau from the beginning, and he may have allowed his prejudices to colour his view of Rousseau's character and acts. The violence of the abuse which Grimm and the rest of the Encyclopædists hurled against the miserable Jean-Jacques was certainly quite out of proportion to the real facts of the case. Whenever he is mentioned one is sure of hearing something about *traître* and *mensonge* and *scélératesse*. He is referred to as often as not as if he were some dangerous kind of wild beast. This was Grimm's habitual language with regard to him; and this was the view of his character which Madame d'Epinay finally expressed in her book. The important question is—did Grimm know that Rousseau was in reality an honourable man, and, knowing this, did he deliberately defame him in order to drive him out of Madame d'Epinay's affections? The answer, I think, must be in the negative, for the following reason. If Grimm had known that there was something to be ashamed of in the notes with which he had supplied Madame d'Epinay, and which led to the alteration of her *Mémoires*, he certainly would have destroyed the draft of the manuscript, which was the only record of those notes having ever been made. As it happens, we know that he had the opportunity of destroying the draft, and he did not do so. He came to Paris at the risk of his life in 1791, and stayed there for four months, with the object, according to his own account, of collecting papers belonging to the Empress Catherine, or, according to Mrs. Macdonald's account, of having the rough draft of the *Mémoires* copied out by his secretary. Whatever his object, it is certain that the copy—that from which ultimately the *Mémoires* were printed—was made either at that time, or earlier; and that there was nothing on earth to prevent him, during the four months of his stay in Paris, from destroying the draft. Mrs. Macdonald's explanation of this difficulty is lamentably weak. Grimm, she says, must have wished to get away from Paris 'without arousing suspicion by destroying papers.' This is indeed an 'exquisite reason,' which would have delighted that good knight Sir Andrew Aguecheek. Grimm had four months at his disposal; he was undisturbed in his own house; why should he not have burnt the draft page by page as it was copied out? There can be only one reply: Why *should* he?

If it is possible to suggest some fairly plausible motives which might conceivably have induced Grimm to blacken Rousseau's character, the case of Diderot presents difficulties which are quite insurmountable. Mrs. Macdonald asserts that Diderot was jealous of Rousseau. Why? Because he was tired of hearing Rousseau described as 'the virtuous'; that is all. Surely Mrs. Macdonald should have been the first to recognise that such an argument is a little too 'psychological.' The truth is that Diderot had nothing to gain by attacking Rousseau. He was not, like Grimm, in love with Madame d'Epinay; he was not a newcomer who had still to win for himself a position in the Parisian world. His acquaintance with Madame d'Epinay was slight; and, if there were any advances, they were from her side, for he was one of the most distinguished men of the day. In fact, the only reason that he could have had for abusing Rousseau was that he believed Rousseau deserved abuse. Whether he was right in believing so is a very different question. Most readers, at the present day, now that the whole noisy controversy has long taken its quiet place in the perspective of Time, would, I think, agree that Diderot and the rest of the Encyclopædists were mistaken. As we see him now, in that long vista, Rousseau was not a wicked man; he was an unfortunate, a distracted, a deeply sensitive, a strangely complex, creature; and, above all else, he possessed one quality which cut him off from his contemporaries, which set an immense gulf betwixt him and them: he was modern. Among those quick, strong, fiery people of the eighteenth century, he belonged to another world—to the new world of self-consciousness, and doubt, and hesitation, of mysterious melancholy and quiet intimate delights, of long reflections amid the solitudes of Nature, of infinite introspections amid the solitudes of the heart. Who can wonder that he was misunderstood, and buffeted, and driven mad? Who can wonder that, in his agitations, his perplexities, his writhings, he seemed, to the pupils of Voltaire, little less than a frenzied fiend? 'Cet homme est un forcené!' Diderot exclaims. 'Je tâche en vain de faire de la poésie, mais cet homme me revient tout à travers mon travail; il me trouble, et je suis somme si j'avais à côté de moi un damné: il est damné, cela est sûr. . . . J'avoue que je n'ai jamais éprouvé un trouble d'âme si terrible que celui que j'ai . . . Que je ne revoie plus cet homme-là, il me ferait croire au diable et à l'enfer. Si je suis jamais forcé de retourner chez lui, je suis sûr que je frémirai tout le long du chemin: j'avais la fièvre en revenant . . . On entendait ses cris jusqu'au bout du jardin; et je le voyais! . . . Les poètes ont bien fait de mettre un intervalle immense entre le ciel et les enfers. En vérité, la main me tremble.' Every word of that is stamped with sincerity; Diderot was writing from his heart. But he was wrong; the 'intervalle immense,' across which, so strangely and so horribly, he had caught glimpses of what he had never seen before, was not the abyss between heaven and hell, but between the old world and the new.

1910.

THE ABBÉ MORELLET

TALLEYRAND once remarked that only those who had lived in France before the Revolution had really experienced *la douceur de vivre*. The Abbé Morellet would have agreed with him. Born in 1727 at Lyons, the son of a small paper merchant, how was it possible, in that age of caste and privilege, that André Morellet should have known anything of life but what was hard, dull, and insignificant? So one might have supposed; but the contrary was the case. Before he was thirty this young man, without either fortune or connections, and without taking very much trouble about it, found himself a member of the most brilliant society in Paris, the close friend of the famous and the great, with a rosy future before him. The secret of it was simple: he had shown that he was intelligent; and in those days a little intelligence went a long way. So, indeed, did a little—a very little—money. A thousand francs from a generous cousin had opened Paris to him, by enabling him to go to the Sorbonne, whence, after five years, he had emerged an Abbé and an infidel. A chance meeting with Diderot did the rest. The great *philosophe*, forty years of age and at the height of his intellectual power, completely captivated a youth whose eager mind was only waiting for new ideas and new activities. Every Sunday morning the Abbé scaled the stairs to Diderot's lodging, to sit entranced for hours, while the Master poured forth the irresistible floods of his amazing conversation. 'J'ai éprouvé peu de plaisirs de l'esprit au-dessus de celui-là,' wrote Morellet long afterwards; 'et je m'en souviendrai toujours.' One can well believe it. The young man listened so intelligently that Diderot soon saw he would do; enrolled him among his disciples; introduced him to all his friends; and set him to write articles for his great Encyclopædia. *La douceur de vivre* had begun.

Thirty delightful years followed—years of exciting work, delicious friendship, and ever-growing optimism. The great battle for liberty, tolerance, reason, and humanity was in full swing; the forces of darkness were yielding more and more rapidly; and Morellet was in the forefront of the fight. He wrote with untiring zeal. Besides his Encyclopædia articles, he produced pamphlets in favour of the Protestants, he brought out a *Manuel des Inquisiteurs* exposing the methods of the Inquisition, he translated Beccaria's great work. But his principal interest was political economy. A close friend of Turgot, he was one of the earliest believers in Free Trade. He translated *The Wealth of Nations*; though the cast of his mind contrasted curiously with Adam Smith's. The Abbé like most of the *philosophes*, preferred the *a priori* mode of argument. The reasons which led him to favour Free Trade are characteristic. The rights of property, he argued, are fundamental to the very existence of civilised society; now to interfere with the freedom of exchange is to attack one of the rights of property; therefore Protection and civilisation are incompatible. This extremely complete argument seems to have escaped the notice of Tory Free Traders.

But the Abbé was not merely enlightened and argumentative; he had another quality which was essential in those days if one was to make any figure at all: he was malicious—though only, of course, at the expense of 'the enemies of reason.' Some particularly biting little flysheets of his actually brought a word of praise from the mighty Patriarch of Ferney. 'Embrassez pour moi l'Abbé Mords-les,' wrote Voltaire to a common friend; 'je ne connais personne qui soit plus capable de rendre service à la raison.' This was a testimonial indeed! Morellet's reputation went up with a bound, and he himself declared that the sentence was all he wanted by way of an epitaph.

Only one thing more was needed to make his success complete; and that a kindly fate provided. Palissot, a *protégé* of a certain great lady, the Princesse de Robecq, attacked the *philosophes* in a satirical farce. Morellet, among the rest, replied with a stinging pamphlet; but he was unwise enough to direct some of his sharp remarks, not at Palissot, but at the Princess. This could not be allowed. Madame de Robecq had been the mistress of the Duc de Choiseul, who was all-powerful with Madame de Pompadour and, through her, with the King. A *lettre de cachet* sent Morellet to the Bastille. One can imagine no more striking example of the corruption and tyranny of the *ancien régime*—if only the poor Abbé had been treated properly—thrown into an underground dungeon, let us say, loaded with chains, and fed on bread and water. Unfortunately, nothing of the sort occurred. The victim was given a comfortable room, plenty of excellent food, a bottle of wine a day, provided with writing materials, and allowed all the books he asked for, besides being given the run of the Bastille library, which was especially strong in novels. He spent three months in peaceful study; and returned to liberty with the added glory of martyrdom.

Liberty and martyrdom—one hardly knew which was the pleasanter. In Paris one's mornings passed in reading and writing—the quill dashing over the paper with a heavenly speed; and one's afternoons and evenings were spent in company. There were dinners at d'Holbach's; there were the nightly gatherings in the little rooms of Mademoiselle de Lespinasse; there were lunches with Madame Geoffrin; and everywhere and always the conversation was copious and audacious to an intoxicating degree. Madame Geoffrin, indeed, insisted upon limits. 'Voilà qui est bien!' she used to exclaim, when the talk grew too wild and high. Then the more reckless spirits, headed by d'Alembert, would go out into the Tuileries Gardens, and, sitting under the trees, continue the discourse until the exploded ruins of religions, philosophies, and conventions fell in showers about their ears. If Paris grew too hot or too noisy, there was always, close at hand, Auteuil. There lived Madame Helvétius, the widow of one of the leading *philosophes*, in a charming little villa, with a garden and all the simple pleasures of a country life. A curious *ménage*, highly typical of the nation and the age, was gathered together between those friendly walls. Morellet spent every summer and all his week-ends there; another clever Abbé also had rooms in the house; and so had a younger man, Cabanis, to whom Madame Helvétius was particularly attached. The elements of sentiment and friendship were so perfectly balanced between the four that their harmony and happiness were complete. Year after year the summers waxed and waned in the Auteuil garden, while Morellet lingered there, with peace, wit, kindness, and beauty around him. What was there left to wish for? Well! it would be nice, he sometimes thought, to have a little—a very little—more money. His income—made up of a few small pensions and legacies—was about £100 a year.

A most pleasant interlude was a visit to England, where Morellet spent several months as the guest of Lord Shelburne. Shelburne was a failure at politics (he was a Prime Minister and a man of intellect—a hazardous combination); but he made an admirable host. Garrick and Franklin were asked down to Bowood to meet the Abbé, and then he was carried off on a driving tour all over England. One day, near Plymouth, there was a picnic on the banks of the Tamar. After the meal, as the company lay on the grass, and the evening fell, three country girls made their appearance; on which the Abbé, offering them a basket of cherries, asked them, in his broken English, for a song. They smiled, and blushed; but sing they did, in unison, with the sweetest voices. The description of the scene in Morellet's *Mémoires* reads like a page from the *Vicar of Wakefield*.

Even affluence came at last. The incumbent of a priory, the reversion of which had been given to Morellet by Turgot twenty years before, died, and the Abbé found himself in the possession of a spacious country house, with land, and an income of £600 a year. This was in 1788. In less than a year all was over. The Abbé never lived in his priory. The tempest of the Revolution engulfed both him and it. The rights of property were violated, and the priest was deprived of a sinecure that he was enjoying as a member of a Church in which he disbelieved. Morellet's surprised indignation at this catastrophe—his absolute unconsciousness that the whole effort of his life had been in reality directed towards this very goal—makes comic reading—comic, and pathetic too. For still worse was to follow. The happy *ménage* at Auteuil was broken up. Cabanis and the other Abbé believed in the Revolution; Madame Helvétius agreed with them; and Morellet, finding himself in a minority of one, after a violent scene left the villa for ever. His plight was serious; but he weathered the storm. A revolutionary tribunal, before which he was haled, treated him gently, partly because it transpired in the course of the proceedings that he had been a friend of Turgot, '*ce bon citoyen*'; he was dismissed with a caution. Then, besides saving his own neck, he was able to do a good turn to the *Académie Française*, of which he was the Director. When that body was broken up, the care of its valuable possessions—its papers and its portraits—fell to him. He concealed everything in various hiding-places, from which he drew forth the precious relics in triumph, when the days of order returned.

For they did return; and the Abbé, very old and very tired, found his way, with one or two others, to young Madame de Rémusat's drawing-room. There he sat dozing by the fire, while the talk sped on around him; dozing, and nodding; then suddenly waking up to denounce Monsieur de Chateaubriand and lament the ruin of French prose. He was treated with great respect by everybody; even the First Consul was flattering; even the Emperor was polite, and made him a Senator. Then the Emperor vanished, and a Bourbon ruled once more on the throne of his fathers. With that tenacity of life which seems to have been the portion of the creatures of the eighteenth century, Morellet continued in this world until his ninety-second year. But this world was no longer what it used to be: something had gone wrong. Those agitations, those arrangements and rearrangements, they seemed hardly worth attending to. One might as well doze. All his young friends were very kind certainly, but did they understand?

How could they? What had been their experience of life?
As for him, ah! *he* had listened to Diderot—used to sit
for hours talking in the Tuileries Gardens with d'Alembert
and Mademoiselle de Lespinasse—mentioned by Voltaire—
spent half a lifetime at Auteuil with dear Madame Helvétius
—imprisoned in the Bastille . . . he nodded. Yes! *He* had
known *la douceur de vivre*.

1924.

GIBBON

Happiness is the word that immediately rises to the mind at the thought of Edward Gibbon: and happiness in its widest connotation—including good fortune as well as enjoyment. Good fortune, indeed, followed him from the cradle to the grave in the most tactful way possible; occasionally it appeared to fail him; but its absence always turned out to be a blessing in disguise. Out of a family of seven he alone had the luck to survive—but only with difficulty; and the maladies of his childhood opened his mind to the pleasures of study and literature. His mother died; but her place was taken by a devoted aunt, whose care brought him through the dangerous years of adolescence to a vigorous manhood. His misadventures at Oxford saved him from becoming a don. His exile to Lausanne, by giving him a command of the French language, initiated him into European culture, and at the same time enabled him to lay the foundations of his scholarship. His father married again; but his stepmother remained childless and became one of his dearest friends. He fell in love; the match was forbidden; and he escaped the dubious joys of domestic life with the future Madame Necker. While he was allowed to travel on the Continent, it seemed doubtful for some time whether his father would have the resources or the generosity to send him over the Alps into Italy. His fate hung in the balance; but at last his father produced the necessary five hundred pounds and, in the autumn of 1764, Rome saw her historian. His father died at exactly the right moment, and left him exactly the right amount of money. At the age of thirty-three Gibbon found himself his own master, with a fortune just sufficient to support him as an English gentleman of leisure and fashion. For ten years he lived in London, a member of Parliament, a placeman, and a diner-out, and during those ten years he produced the first three volumes of his History. After that he lost his place, failed to obtain another, and, finding his income unequal to his expenses, returned to Lausanne, where he took up his residence in the house of a friend, overlooking the Lake of Geneva. It was the final step in his career, and no less fortunate than all the others. In Lausanne he was rich once more, he was famous, he enjoyed a delightful combination of retirement and society. Before another ten years were out he had completed his History; and in ease, dignity, and absolute satisfaction his work in this world was accomplished.

One sees in such a life an epitome of the blessings of the eighteenth century—the wonderful μηδὲν ἄγαν of that most balmy time—the rich fruit ripening slowly on the sun-warmed wall, and coming inevitably to its delicious perfection. It is difficult to imagine, at any other period in history, such a combination of varied qualities, so beautifully balanced —the profound scholar who was also a brilliant man of the world—the votary of cosmopolitan culture, who never for a moment ceased to be a supremely English 'character.' The ten years of Gibbon's life in London afford an astonishing spectacle of interacting energies. By what strange power did he succeed in producing a masterpiece of enormous erudition and perfect form, while he was leading the gay life of a man about town, spending his evenings at White's or Boodle's or the Club, attending Parliament, oscillating between his house in Bentinck Street, his country cottage at Hampton Court, and his little establishment at Brighton, spending his summers in Bath or Paris, and even, at odd moments, doing a little work at the Board of Trade, to show that his place was not entirely a sinecure? Such a triumph could only have been achieved by the sweet reasonableness of the eighteenth century. 'Monsieur Gibbon n'est point mon homme,' said Rousseau. Decidedly! The prophet of the coming age of sentiment and romance could have nothing in common with such a nature. It was not that the historian was a mere frigid

observer of the golden mean—far from it. He was full of fire
and feeling. His youth had been at moments riotous—night
after night he had reeled hallooing down St. James's Street.
Old age did not diminish the natural warmth of his affections;
the beautiful letter—a model of its kind—written on the death
of his aunt, in his fiftieth year, is a proof of it. But the fire and
the feeling were controlled and co-ordinated. Boswell was a
Rousseau-ite, one of the first of the Romantics, an inveterate
sentimentalist, and nothing could be more complete than the
contrast between his career and Gibbon's. He, too, achieved
a glorious triumph; but it was by dint of the sheer force of
native genius asserting itself over the extravagance and disorder of an agitated life—a life which, after a desperate
struggle, seemed to end at last in darkness and shipwreck.
With Gibbon there was never any struggle: everything came
naturally to him—learning and dissipation, industry and indolence, affection and scepticism—in the correct proportions;
and he enjoyed himself up to the very end.

To complete the picture one must notice another antithesis: the wit, the genius, the massive intellect, were housed
in a physical mould that was ridiculous. A little figure, extraordinarily rotund, met the eye, surmounted by a top-heavy
head, with a button nose, planted amid a vast expanse of cheek
and ear, and chin upon chin rolling downward. Nor was this
appearance only; the odd shape reflected something in the
inner man. Mr. Gibbon, it was noticed, was always slightly
over-dressed; his favourite wear was flowered velvet. He was
a little vain, a little pompous; at the first moment one almost
laughed; then one forgot everything under the fascination of
that even flow of admirably intelligent, exquisitely turned,
and most amusing sentences. Among all his other merits this
obviously ludicrous egotism took its place. The astonishing
creature was able to make a virtue even of absurdity. Without
that touch of nature he would have run the risk of being too
much of a good thing; as it was there was no such danger; he
was preposterous and a human being.

It is not difficult to envisage the character and figure; what seems strange, and remote, and hard to grasp is the connection between this individual and the decline and fall of the Roman Empire. The paradox, indeed, is so complete as to be almost romantic. At a given moment—October 15, 1764—at a given place—the Capitoline Hill, outside the church of Aracoeli—the impact occurred between the serried centuries of Rome and Edward Gibbon. His life, his work, his fame, his place in the history of civilisation, followed from that circumstance. The point of his achievement lay precisely in the extreme improbability of it. The utter incongruity of those combining elements produced the masterpiece—the gigantic ruin of Europe through a thousand years, mirrored in the mind of an eighteenth-century English gentleman.

How was the miracle accomplished? Needless to say, Gibbon was a great artist—one of those rare spirits, with whom a vital and penetrating imagination and a supreme capacity for general conceptions express themselves instinctively in an appropriate form. That the question has ever been not only asked but seriously debated, whether History was an art, is certainly one of the curiosities of human ineptitude. What else can it possibly be? It is obvious that History is not a science: it is obvious that History is not the accumulation of facts, but the relation of them. Only the pedantry of incomplete academic persons could have given birth to such a monstrous supposition. Facts relating to the past, when they are collected without art, are compilations; and compilations, no doubt, may be useful; but they are no more History than butter, eggs, salt and herbs are an omelette. That Gibbon was a great artist, therefore, is implied in the statement that he was a great historian; but what is interesting is the particular nature of his artistry. His whole genius was pre-eminently classical; order, lucidity, balance, precision—the great classical qualities—dominate his work; and his History is chiefly remarkable as one of the supreme monuments of Classic Art in European literature.

'L'ordre est ce qu'il y a de plus rare dans les opérations de l'esprit.' Gibbon's work is a magnificent illustration of the splendid dictum of Fénelon. He brought order out of the enormous chaos of his subject—a truly stupendous achievement! With characteristic good fortune, indeed, the material with which he had to cope was still just not too voluminous to be digested by a single extremely competent mind. In the following century even a Gibbon would have collapsed under the accumulated mass of knowledge at his disposal. As it was, by dint of a superb constructive vision, a serene self-confidence, a very acute judgment, and an astonishing facility in the manipulation of material, he was able to dominate the known facts. To dominate, nothing more; anything else would have been foreign to his purpose. He was a classicist; and his object was not comprehension but illumination. He drove a straight, firm road through the vast unexplored forest of Roman history; his readers could follow with easy pleasure along the wonderful way; they might glance, as far as their eyes could reach, into the entangled recesses on either side of them; but they were not invited to stop, or wander, or camp out, or make friends with the natives; they must be content to look and to pass on.

It is clear that Gibbon's central problem was the one of exclusion: how much, and what, was he to leave out? This was largely a question of scale—always one of the major difficulties in literary composition—and it appears from several passages in the Autobiographies that Gibbon paid particular attention to it. Incidentally, it may be observed that the six Autobiographies were not so much excursions in egotism—though no doubt it is true that Gibbon was not without a certain fondness for what he himself called 'the most disgusting of the pronouns'—as exercises on the theme of scale. Every variety of compression and expansion is visible among those remarkable pages; but apparently, since the manuscripts were left in an unfinished state, Gibbon still felt, after the sixth attempt, that he had not discovered the right solution. Even with the scale of the History he was not altogether satisfied; the chapters on Christianity, he thought, might, with further labour, have been considerably reduced. But, even more fundamental than the element of scale, there was something else that, in reality, conditioned the whole treatment of his material, the whole scope and nature of his History; and that was the style in which it was written. The style once fixed, everything else followed. Gibbon was well aware of this. He wrote his first chapter three times over, his second and third twice; then at last he was satisfied, and after that he wrote on without a hitch. In particular the problem of exclusion was solved. Gibbon's. style is probably the most exclusive in literature. By its very nature it bars out a great multitude of human energies. It makes sympathy impossible, it takes no cognisance of passion, it turns its back upon religion with a withering smile. But that was just what was wanted. Classic beauty came instead. By the penetrating influence of style— automatically, inevitably—lucidity, balance and precision were everywhere introduced; and the miracle of order was established over the chaos of a thousand years.

Of course, the Romantics raised a protest. 'Gibbon's style,' said Coleridge, 'is detestable; but,' he added, 'it is not the worst thing about him.' Critics of the later nineteenth century were less consistent. They admired Gibbon for everything except his style, imagining that his History would have been much improved if it had been written in some other way; they did not see that, if it had been written in any other way, it would have ceased to exist; just as St. Paul's would cease to exist if it were rebuilt in Gothic. Obsessed by the colour and movement of romantic prose, they were blind to the subtlety, the clarity, the continuous strength of Gibbon's writing. Gibbon could turn a bold phrase with the best of them—'the fat slumbers of the Church,' for instance—if he wanted to; but he very rarely wanted to; such effects would have disturbed the easy, close-knit, homogeneous surface of his work. His use of words is, in fact, extremely delicate. When, describing St. Simeon Stylites on his pillar, he speaks of 'this last and lofty station,' he succeeds, with the least possible emphasis, merely by the combination of those two alliterative epithets with that particular substantive, in making the whole affair ridiculous. One can almost see his shoulders shrug. The nineteenth century found him pompous; they did not relish the irony beneath the pomp. He produces some of his most delightful effects by rhythm alone. In the *Vindication*—a work which deserves to be better known, for it shows us Gibbon, as one sees him nowhere else, really letting himself go—there is an admirable example of this. 'I still think,' he says, in reply to a criticism by Dr. Randolph, 'I still think that an hundred Bishops, with Athanasius at their head, were as competent judges of the discipline of the fourth century, as even the Lady Margaret's Professor of Divinity in the University of Oxford.' Gibbon's irony, no doubt, is the salt of his work; but, like all irony, it is the product of style. It was not for nothing that he read through every year the *Lettres Provinciales* of Pascal. From this point of view it is interesting to compare him with Voltaire. The irony of the great Frenchman was a flashing sword—extreme, virulent, deadly—a terrific instrument of propaganda. Gibbon uses the weapon with far more delicacy; he carves his enemy 'as a dish fit for the Gods'; his mocking is aloof, almost indifferent, and perhaps, in the long run, for that very reason, even more effective.

At every period of his life Gibbon is a pleasant thing to contemplate, but perhaps most pleasant of all in the closing weeks of it, during his last visit to England. He had hurried home from Lausanne to join his friend Lord Sheffield, whose wife had died suddenly, and who, he felt, was in need of his company. The journey was no small proof of his affectionate nature; old age was approaching; he was corpulent, gouty, and accustomed to every comfort; and the war of the French Revolution was raging in the districts through which he had to pass. But he did not hesitate, and after skirting the belligerent armies in his chaise, arrived safely in England. After visiting Lord Sheffield he proceeded to Bath, to stay with his stepmother. The amazing little figure, now almost spherical, bowled along the Bath Road in the highest state of exhilaration. 'I am always,' he told his friend, 'so much delighted and improved with this union of ease and motion, that, were not the expense enormous, I would travel every year some hundred miles, more especially in England.' Mrs. Gibbon, a very old lady, but still full of vitality, worshipped her stepson, and the two spent ten days together, talking, almost always *tête-à-tête*, for ten hours a day. Then the historian went off to Althorpe, where he spent a happy morning with Lord Spencer, looking at early editions of Cicero. And so back to London. In London a little trouble arose. A protuberance in the lower part of his person, which, owing to years of characteristic *insouciance*, had grown to extraordinary proportions, required attention; an operation was necessary; but it went off well, and there seemed to be no danger. Once more Mr. Gibbon dined out. Once more he was seen, in his accustomed attitude, with advanced forefinger, addressing the company, and rapping his snuff box at the close of each particularly pointed phrase. But illness came on again—nothing very serious. The great man lay in bed discussing how much longer he would live—he was fifty-six—ten years, twelve years, or perhaps twenty. He ate some chicken and drank three glasses of madeira. Life seemed almost as charming as usual. Next morning, getting out of bed for a necessary moment, 'Je suis plus adroit,' he said with his odd smile to his French valet. Back in bed again, he muttered something more, a little incoherently, lay back among the pillows, dozed, half-woke, dozed again, and became unconscious—for ever.

1928.

JAMES BOSWELL

IT would be difficult to find a more shattering refutation of
the lessons of cheap morality than the life of James Boswell.
One of the most extraordinary successes in the history of
civilization was achieved by an idler, a lecher, a drunkard, and
a snob. Nor was this success of that sudden explosive kind
which is frequent enough with youthful genius—the inspired
efflorescence of a Rimbaud or a Swinburne; it was essentially
the product of long years of accumulated energy; it was the
supreme expression of an entire life. Boswell triumphed by
dint of abandoning himself, through fifty years, to his instincts.
The example, no doubt, is not one to be followed rashly.
Self-indulgence is common, and Boswells are rare. The precise character of the rarity we are now able, for the first time,
to estimate with something like completeness. Boswell's
nature and inner history cannot be fully understood from the
works published by himself. It is only in his letters that the
whole man is revealed. Professor Tinker, by collecting together Boswell's correspondence and editing it with scholarly
exactitude, has done a great service to English literature.[1]
There is, in fact, only one fault to be found with this admirable book. Professor Tinker shows us more of Boswell than
any previous editor, but he does not show us all that he might.
Like the editors of Walpole's Letters and Pepys's Diary, while
giving himself credit for rehabilitating the text of his author,
he admits in the same breath that he has mutilated it. When
will this silly and barbarous prudery come to an end?

Boswell's career was completely dominated by his innate
characteristics. Where they came from it is impossible to

[1] *Letters of James Boswell.* Collected and edited by Chauncey
Brewster Tinker. 2 vols. (Oxford: Clarendon Press.)

guess. He was the strangest sport: the descendant of Scotch barons and country gentlemen, the son of a sharp lowland lawyer, was an artist, a spendthrift, a buffoon, with a passion for literature, and without any dignity whatever. So he was born, and so he remained; life taught him nothing—he had nothing to learn; his course was marked out, immutably, from the beginning. At the age of twenty-three he discovered Dr. Johnson. A year later he was writing to him, at Wittenberg, 'from the tomb of Melancthon': 'My paper rests upon the gravestone of that great and good man. . . . At this tomb, then, my ever dear and respected friend! I vow to thee an eternal attachment.' The rest of Boswell's existence was the history of that vow's accomplishment. But his connection with Dr. Johnson was itself only the crowning instance of an overwhelming predisposition, which showed itself in a multitude of varied forms. There were other great men, for instance—there was Mr. Wilkes, and General Paoli, and Sir David Dalrymple. One of Professor Tinker's most delightful discoveries is a series of letters from the youthful Boswell to Jean-Jacques Rousseau, in which all the writer's most persistent qualities—his literary skill, his psychological perspicacity, his passion for personalities, and his amazing aptitude for self-revelation—are exquisitely displayed. 'Dites-moi,' he asked the misanthropic sentimentalist, 'ne ferai-je bien de m'appliquer véritablement à la musique, jusques à un certain point? Dites-moi quel doit être mon instrument. C'est tard je l'avoue. Mais n'aurai-je pas le plaisir de faire un progrès continuel, et ne serai-je pas capable d'adoucir ma vieillesse par les sons de ma lyre?' Rousseau was completely melted. The elder Pitt, however, was made of sterner stuff. When Boswell appeared before him in the costume of a Corsican chieftain, 'Lord Chatham,' we are told, 'smiled, but received him very graciously in his Pompous manner'—and there the acquaintance ended; in spite of Boswell's modest suggestion that the Prime Minister should 'honour me now and then with a letter. . . . To correspond with a Paoli and with a Chatham is enough to keep a young man ever ardent in the pursuit of virtuous fame.'

Fame—though perhaps it was hardly virtuous—Boswell certainly attained; but his ardent pursuit of it followed the track of an extraordinary zigzag which could never have had anything in common with letters from Lord Chatham. His own letters to his friend Temple lay bare the whole unique peregrination, from start to finish. To confess is the desire of many; but it is within the power of few. A rare clarity of vision, a still rarer candour of expression—without these qualities it is vain for a man to seek to unburden his heart. Boswell possessed them in the highest degree; and, at the same time, he was untroubled by certain other qualities, which, admirable though they be in other connections, are fatal for this particular purpose. He had no pride, no shame, and no dignity. The result was that a multitude of inhibitions passed him by. Nevertheless he was by no means detached. His was not the method of the scientific observer, noting his introspections with a cold exactness—far from it; he was intimately fascinated by everything to do with himself—his thoughts, his feelings, his reactions; and yet he was able to give expression to them all with absolute ingenuousness, without a shade of self-consciousness, without a particle of reserve. Naturally enough the picture presented in such circumstances is full of absurdities, for no character which had suppressed its absurdities could possibly depict itself so. Boswell was *ex hypothesi* absurd: it was his absurdity that was the essential condition of his consummate art.

It was in the description of his love affairs that this truly marvellous capacity found its fullest scope. The succession of his passions, with all their details, their variations, their agitations, and their preposterousnesses, fill the letters to Temple (a quiet clergyman in the depths of Devonshire) with a constant effervescence of delight. One progresses with wonderful exhilaration from Miss W——t ('just such a young lady as I could wish for the partner of my soul') to Zelide ('upon my soul, Temple, I must have her'), and so to the Signora, and the Moffat woman ('can I do better than keep a dear infidel for my hours of Paphian bliss?'), and the Princess ('here every flower is united'), and the gardener's daughter, and Mrs. D., and Miss Bosville, and La Belle Irlandaise ('just sixteen, formed like a Grecian nymph, with the sweetest countenance, full of sensibility, accomplished, with a Dublin education'), and Mrs. Boswell ('I am fully sensible of my happiness in being married to so excellent a woman'), and Miss Silverton ('in the fly with me, an amiable creature who has been in France. I can unite little fondnesses with perfect conjugal love'), and Miss Bagnal ('*a Ranelagh girl*, but of excellent principles, in so much that she reads prayers to the servants in her father's family, every Sunday evening. "Let me see such a woman," cried I'), and Miss Milles ('*d'une certaine âge*, and with a fortune of £10,000'), and—but the catalogue is endless. These are the pages which record the sunny hours of Boswell's chequered day. Light and warmth sparkle from them; but, even in the noon of his happiness, there were sudden clouds. Hypochondria seized him; he would wake in the night 'dreading annihilation, or being thrown into some horrible state of being.' His conscience would not leave him alone; he was attacked by disgraceful illnesses; he felt 'like a man ordered for ignominious execution'; he feared that his infidelities to Mrs. Boswell would not be excused hereafter. And then his vital spirits rushed to his rescue, and the shadow fled. Was he not the friend of Paoli? Indeed he was; and he was sitting in a library forty feet long, dressed in green and gold. The future was radiant. 'My warm imagination looks forward with great complacency on the sobriety, the healthfulness, and the worth of my future life.' As for his infidelities, were they so reprehensible after all? 'Concubinage is almost universal. If it was *morally* wrong, why was it permitted to the pious men under the Old Testament? Why did our Saviour never say a word against it?'

As his life went on, however, the clouds grew thicker and more menacing, and the end was storm and darkness. The climax came with the death of his wife. Boswell found himself at the age of fifty alone in the world with embarrassed fortunes, a family of young children to bring up, and no sign that any of the 'towering hopes' of his youth had been realised. Worse still, he had become by this time a confirmed drunkard. His self-reproaches were pitiable; his efforts at amendment never ceased; he took a vow of sobriety under 'a venerable yew'; he swore a solemn oath that he would give up drinking altogether—that he would limit himself to four glasses of wine at dinner and a pint afterwards; but it was all in vain. His way of life grew more and more disorderly, humiliating, and miserable. If he had retired to Scotland, and lived economically on his estate, he might have retrieved his position; but that was what he could not do; he could not be out of London. His ambitions seemed to multiply with his misfortunes. He exchanged the Scotch bar for the English, and lost all his professional income at a blow. He had wild hopes of becoming a Member of Parliament, if only he toadied Lord Lonsdale sufficiently; and Lord Lonsdale promised much, asked him to his castle, made a butt of him, hid his wig, was gravely concerned, and finally threw him off after 'expressing himself in the most degrading manner in presence of a low man from Carlisle and one of his menial servants.' Consolations now were few indeed. It was something, no doubt, to be able to go to Court. 'I was the *great man* at the late drawing-room in a suit of imperial blue lined with rose-coloured silk, and ornamented with rich gold-wrought buttons. What a motley scene is life!' And at Eton, where he was 'carried to dine at the Fellows' table,' it was pleasant enough to find that in spite of a Scotch education one could still make a creditable figure. 'I had my classical quotations very ready.' But these were fleeting gleams. 'Your kindness to me,' he burst out to Temple, in April, 1791, 'fairly makes me shed tears. Alas, I fear that my constitutional melancholy, which returns in such dismal fits and is now aggravated by the loss of my valuable wife, must prevent me from any permanent felicity in this life. I snatch *gratifications*; but have no *comfort*, at least very little. . . . I get bad rest in the night, and then I brood over all my complaints—the *sickly mind* which I have had from my early years—the disappointment of my hopes of success in life—the irrevocable separation between me and that excellent woman who was my cousin, my friend, and my wife—the embarrassment of my affairs—the disadvantage to my children in having so wretched a father—nay, the want of *absolute certainty* of being happy after death, the *sure prospect* of which is *frightful*. No more of this.'

The tragedy was closing; but it was only superficially a sordid one. Six weeks later the writer of these lines published, in two volumes quarto, the *Life of Dr. Johnson*. In reality, Boswell's spirit had never failed. With incredible persistence he had carried through the enormous task which he had set himself thirty years earlier. Everything else was gone. He was burnt down to the wick, but his work was there. It was the work of one whose appetite for life was insatiable—so insatiable that it proved in the end self-destructive. The same force which produced the *Life of Johnson* plunged its author into ruin and desperation. If Boswell had been capable of retiring to the country and economising we should never have heard of him. It was Lord Lonsdale's butt who reached immortality.

1925.

MADEMOISELLE DE LESPINASSE

'Oh! je m'en vais vous paraître folle: je vais vous parler avec
la franchise et l'abandon qu'on aurait, si l'on croyait mourir le
lendemain; écoutez-moi donc avec cette indulgence et cet
intérêt qu'on a pour les mourants.' So wrote Mademoiselle de
Lespinasse; and the words might well be taken as a motto for
the volume of letters which has made her name imperishable.
The book, for all its tenderness and pathos, is in many ways a
terrible one; it is gloomy, morbid, and remorseless; after one
has read it, it is horrible to think that it is true. Yet it is its
truth—its uncompromising truth—which gives it an immense
and unique value: it is the most complete analysis the world
possesses of a passion which actually existed in a human mind.
Thus, when one thinks of Mademoiselle de Lespinasse, it is
towards passion, and all the fearful accompaniments of passion,
that one's imagination naturally turns. One is apt to forget
that she was not merely 'une amante insensée,' that she was
also a brilliant and fascinating woman of the world. The Marquis de Ségur, in the biography of her which he has recently
published,[1] has been careful to avoid this error. He has drawn a
full-length portrait of Julie de Lespinasse; and he has drawn
it with a subtlety and a sympathy which compels a delighted
attention. His book is enriched with a great mass of information never before made public; his researches have been rewarded with the discovery of authentic documents of the
deepest interest; and every reader of the present volume will
await with anxious expectation the publication, which he
promises us, of a new and enlarged edition of the Letters
themselves. One of the most important results of M. de
Ségur's labours is the additional knowledge which they have

---

[1] Marquis de Ségur. *Julie de Lespinasse*. Paris: Calmann-Lévy.

153

given us upon the subject of the Comte de Guibert, to whom the letters were addressed. This alone would have made the book indispensable to any one who is interested in Mademoiselle de Lespinasse. But it would be idle to attempt to recapitulate all the fresh points of importance which M. de Ségur has brought out; it were best to go to the book itself. In the meantime, it may be worth while to trace, however rapidly and imperfectly, the outline of that tragical history which M. de Ségur has done so much to put in its proper light.

Julie de Lespinasse was born at Lyons on November 9, 1732. She was the illegitimate daughter of the Comtesse d'Albon, a lady of distinguished family, who, some years earlier, had separated from her husband, and established herself in the neighbourhood of Lyons in the château of Avauges. So much is certain; but the obscurity which hung over Julie's birth has never been completely withdrawn. Who was her father? According to the orthodox tradition, she was the child of Cardinal de Tencin, whose sister, the famous Madame de Tencin, was the mother of d'Alembert. This story has the advantage of discovering a strange and concealed connection between two lives which were afterwards to be intimately bound together; but it has the disadvantage of not being true. M. de Ségur shows conclusively that, whoever else may have been the father of Mademoiselle de Lespinasse, Cardinal de Tencin was not; and he produces some weighty reasons for believing that Julie was the niece, not of Madame de Tencin, but of a woman equally remarkable and equally celebrated— Madame du Deffand. If M. de Ségur's hypothesis be correct —and the evidence which he adduces is, I think, conclusive —the true history of Julie's parentage is even more extraordinary than the orthodox one. Besides Julie herself, Madame d'Albon had two legitimate children, one of whom was a daughter; this daughter married, in 1739, the Comte Gaspard de Vichy, the eldest brother of Madame du Deffand. The Comte de Vichy was the father of Mademoiselle de Lespinasse. Once or twice, in her correspondence, she touches upon the strange circumstances of her early life. Her history, she said, outdid the novels of Prévost and of Richardson; it proved that 'le vrai n'est souvent pas vraisemblable'; it was 'un composé de circonstances funestes,' which would produce, in the mind of her correspondent, 'une grande horreur pour l'espèce humaine.' These phrases lose their appearance of exaggeration in the light of the Marquis de Ségur's theory. 'Ce sont des horreurs!' exclaimed Gaspard's son, when his mother had told him all. Even for the eighteenth century, there was something horrible in Julie's situation. When, at the age of sixteen, she lost Madame d'Albon, she was obliged to take up her abode with her sister and the Comte de Vichy. They treated her as a dependant, as a governess for their children, as some one to be made use of and kept in place. There, in her father's strange old castle, with its towers and its terraces and its moat, amid the quiet Macon country, neglected, wretched, alone, Julie de Lespinasse grew up into womanhood; she was waiting for her fate.

Her fate came in the shape of Madame du Deffand. That great lady was entering upon the final stage of her long career. She was beginning to grow old, she was beginning to grow blind, and, in spite of her glory and her dominion, she was beginning to grow tired of Paris. Disgusted and ill, she fled into the depths of the country; she spent a summer with the Vichys, and became acquainted with Mademoiselle de Lespinasse. The two women seem to have felt almost at once that they were made for one another. Julie was now twenty-one; she was determined to escape at all hazards from an intolerable position; and she confided in the brilliant and affectionate marquise. With all her cynicism and all her icy knowledge of the world, Madame du Deffand was nothing if not impulsive. Julie had every virtue and every accomplishment; she was 'ma reine'; with her, it would be once more possible to exist; she must come to Paris; it was the only thing to do. For a year Julie hesitated, and then she took the final plunge. In April, 1754, she went to Paris, to live with Madame du Deffand in her apartments in the Convent of St. Joseph.

The famous salon was now reaching the highest point of its glory. Nowhere else in Paris were the forces of intellect and the forces of the world so completely combined. That was Madame du Deffand's great achievement: she was able to mingle every variety of distinction into an harmonious whole. Her drawing-room was filled with eminent diplomatists, with beautiful women of fashion, with famous men of letters; it was the common meeting-place for great ladies like the Duchesse de Choiseul, for politicians like Turgot, for arbiters of taste like the Maréchale de Luxembourg, for philosophers like d'Alembert. Amid these brilliant assemblies, Mademoiselle de Lespinasse very soon obtained an established place. She possessed all the qualities necessary for success in such a society; she had tact, refinement, wit and penetration; she was animated and she was sympathetic; she could interest and she could charm. Madame du Deffand's experiment seemed to be amply justified by the event. Yet, after ten years, Julie's connection with the Convent of St. Joseph came to a sudden and violent termination. The story of the quarrel is sufficiently well known: the informal and surreptitious gatherings in Julie's private room, the discovery of the secret, the fury of the blind old woman, the cold hostility of the younger one, the eternal separation—these things need no further description here. M. de Ségur dwells on them with his usual insight; and his account is peculiarly valuable because it makes quite clear what had always been ambiguous before—the essential points of the situation. The discovery of the secret salon only brought to a head a profound disagreement which had been gathering strength for years; Julie's flight was not the result of a vulgar squabble, it was the outcome of an inherent antagonism pregnant with inevitable disaster. The two women were too much alike for a tolerable partnership; they were both too clever, too strong, and too fond of their own will. In the drawing-room of St. Joseph it was a necessary condition that Julie should play second fiddle; and how could she do that? She was born—it was clear enough—to be nothing less than the leader of an orchestra. Thus the question at issue was a question of spiritual domination; and the dilemma was a tragic one, because it was insoluble except by force. The struggle—the long, the desperate struggle—centred round d'Alembert, who, supreme alike in genius and in conversation, was the keystone of Madame du Deffand's elaborate triumphal arch. When the time came, it was for him to make the momentous decision. He did not hesitate. He knew well how much he owed to Madame du Deffand —fifteen years of unwavering friendship and his position in the world; but his indebtedness to Julie—her sympathy, her attachment, her affection—these things surpassed his computations; and, in exchange, he had given her his heart. He followed where she led, carrying with him in his defection the whole body of the encyclopædists. The salon of St. Joseph was shattered; it became a wilderness, and, in the eyes of its ruler, life itself grew waste. To the miserable lady, infinitely disillusioned and eternally alone, it must have seemed that she at any rate had experienced the last humiliation. She was wrong. She was yet to know, in what remained to her of life, a suffering far deeper than any that had gone before. She—but this is not the history of Madame du Deffand.

Julie was victorious and free. Her friends closed round her, gallantly subscribed towards her maintenance, established her in a little set of rooms on the upper storey of a house in the rue Saint-Dominique. The years which followed were the happiest of her life. They passed in a perpetual round of visits and conversations, of theatres and operas, of gaiety and success. Her drawing-room became the intellectual centre of Paris, perhaps of the world. Every evening, from six to ten, there assembled within it a circle of illustrious persons. D'Alembert was always there; Condorcet and Turgot constantly, sometimes Malesherbes and Diderot, often Chastellux and Suard and Marmontel. One might find there the charming Duchesse de Châtillon, and the amazing Comtesse de Boufflers, and even sometimes the great Madame Geoffrin herself. In addition, there were the distinguished strangers —Caraccioli, the Neapolitan ambassador, the witty and inexhaustible Galiani, the penetrating Lord Shelburne, and the potentate of potentates, David Hume. Oh! It was a place worth visiting—the little salon in the *rue* Saint-Dominique. And, if one were privileged to go there often, one found there what one found nowhere else—a sense of freedom and intimacy which was the outcome of a real equality, a real understanding, a real friendship such as have existed, before or since, in few societies indeed. Mademoiselle de Lespinasse, inspiring and absorbing all, was the crowning wonder, the final delight. To watch the moving expressions of her face was to watch the conversation itself, transmuted to a living thing by the glow of an intense intelligence. 'There is a flame within her!' was the common exclamation of her friends. Nor were they mistaken; she burnt with an inward fire. It was a steady flame, giving out a genial warmth, a happy brilliance. What wind could shake it? What sudden gust transform it to an instrument of devastation? whirl it, with horror and with blindness, into the path of death?

About two years after Julie's establishment in the rue Saint-Dominique, the Marquis de Mora, a young Spaniard of rank and fortune, paid a visit to Paris. He was handsome, clever, and *sensible*; he delighted the French *philosophes*, he fascinated the French ladies; among his conquests was Mademoiselle de Lespinasse. He departed, returned two years later, renewed acquaintance with Julie, and, this time, fell deeply in love. All that is known of him goes to show that he was a man of high worth, endowed with genuine talents, and capable of strong and profound emotions. To Julie, then and ever afterwards, he appeared to be a perfect being, a creature of almost superhuman excellence. She returned his passion with all the force of her nature; her energies had suddenly carried her into a new and splendid universe; she loved him with the intensity of a woman who has lost her youth, and loves for the first time. In spite of the disparity of age, of wealth, and of position, Mora had determined upon marriage. There was only one bar to the completion of their happiness —his ill-health, which perpetually harassed him and was beginning to display the symptoms of consumption. At last, after four years of waiting, everything was prepared; they were about to take the final step; and at that very moment Mora was stricken down by a violent attack of illness. He was obliged to depart from Paris, and return to his native air. The separation was terrible. Julie, worn out with anxiety and watching, her nerves shattered, her hopes crushed, was ready to presage the worst. Yet, however dreadful her fears may have been, they fell far short of the event. After a few weeks of collapse, she managed to pull herself together. She dragged herself to a garden party, in the hope of meeting some of her friends. She met the Comte de Guibert, and her fate was sealed.

The Comte de Guibert was at that moment at the height of his celebrity. A wonderful book on military tactics—now, alas! known no more—had made him the fashion; every one was at his feet; even ladies, in their enthusiasm, read (or pretended to read) his great work. 'Oh, M. de Guibert,' said one of them, 'que votre tic-tac est admirable!' But it was not only his book, it was the compelling charm of his manner and his conversation which secured him his distinguished place in the Parisian world. His talk was copious, brilliant, and extraordinarily impressive; one came away from him wondering what splendid future was in store for so remarkable a man. In addition, he was young, and gallant in every sense of the word. Mademoiselle de Lespinasse, wandering and dejected, came upon him suddenly, and, with a flash of intuition, recognised his qualities as precisely those of which she stood most in need. He seemed to her a tower of strength and sympathy; she felt him to be something she might cling to for support. She showed it, and he was flattered, attracted, at last charmed. They very soon became friends. Before long she had poured out to him the whole history of her agitations and her sorrows; and when, after a few months of constant intercourse, he left Paris to make a tour in Germany, she immediately continued the stream of her confidence in a series of letters. Thus began the famous and terrible correspondence which has made her immortal. The opening letters are charged with dramatic import and premonitions of approaching disaster. They are full of Mora; but, as they succeed one another, it is easy to observe in them a latent uneasiness rising gradually to the surface—a growing, dreadful doubt. As one peers into their depths, one can see, forming itself ever more and more distinctly, the image of the absent Guibert, the intruding symbol of a new, inexplicable desire. The mind of Julie, lonely, morbid, and hysterical, was losing itself among its memories and imaginations and obsessions; it was falling under a spell. 'Dites-moi,' she breaks out at last, 'est-ce là le ton de l'amitié? Est-ce celui de la confiance? Qui est-ce qui m'entraine? Faites-moi connaître à moi-même; aidez-moi à me remettre en mesure. Mon âme est bouleversée; sont-ce mes remords? Est-ce ma faute? Est-ce vous? Serait-ce votre départ? Qu'est-ce donc qui me persécute?' Such was her language when Guibert was still absent; but when he returned, when, triumphant with fresh laurels, he besieged her, adored her, when she felt the pressure of his presence and heard the music of his voice, then indeed there was an end of all doubt and hesitation; blinded, intoxicated, overwhelmed, she forgot what should never be forgotten, she forgot Mora, she forgot the whole world.

C'est Vénus tout entière à sa proie attachée!

By a cruel irony, the one event which, in other circumstances, might have come as a release, proved, in Julie's case, nothing less than the final misfortune. Mora died, and his death took away from her for ever all hope of escape from an intolerable situation. For, in the months which followed, it became clear enough that Guibert, whatever else he may have been, was no Mora. Sainte-Beuve, led astray by insufficient knowledge, has painted Guibert as a callous and dunder-headed donkey, a half-grotesque figure, dropping love-letters out of his pockets, and going to the grave without a notion of the tumult he had created. Such a person could never have obtained dominion over Julie de Lespinasse. The truth is that Guibert's character was infinitely better calculated to bring a woman of high intelligence and violent emotions to disaster and destruction. He was really a clever man; he was really well-meaning and warm-hearted; but that was all. He was attractive, affectionate, admirable, everything, in fact, that a man should be; he had, like most men, his moments of passion; like most men, he was ambitious: and he looked forward, like most men, to a comfortable and domestic old age. It is easy to understand how such a character as that worked havoc with Mademoiselle de Lespinasse. It seemed to offer so much, and, when it came to the point, it provided so little—and to her, who asked either for nothing or for all! She had swallowed the bait of his charm and his excellence, and she was hooked with the deadly compromise which they concealed. 'Je n'aime rien de ce qui est à demi,' she wrote of herself, 'de ce qui est indécis, de ce qui n'est qu'un peu. Je n'entends pas la langue des gens du monde: ils s'amusent et ils bâillent; ils ont des amis, et ils n'aiment rien. Tout cela me paraît déplorable. Oui, j'aime mieux le tourment qui consume ma vie, que le plaisir qui engourdit la leur; mais avec cette manière d'être, on n'est point aimable; eh bien! on s'en passe; non, on n'est point aimable, mais on est aimé, et cela vaut mille fois mieux que de plaire.' This was written when Mora was still alive; but, when she had lost him, she discovered soon enough that even passion might go without its recompense from one who was, precisely, a man of the world. 'Ah! mon ami,' she exclaimed to Guibert, summing up her tragedy in a single sentence, 'mon malheur, c'est que vous n'avez pas besoin d'être aimé comme je sais aimer.' No, assuredly, he was never tempted to ask for such dangerous delights. 'Mon ami,' she told him, 'je vous aime, *comme il faut aimer*, avec excès, avec folie, transport, et désespoir.'

Her complete consciousness of the situation made her position more pitiable, but it did not help her to escape. She was bound to him by too many ties; and he, youthful and complaisant, found it beyond his force to break her bondage. Even when she despised him most, her senses fought against her reason, and she lost herself in shame. The phantom of Mora was perpetually before her eyes, torturing her with vanished happiness and visionary upbraidings. 'Oh! Combien j'ai été aimée! une âme de feu, pleine d'énergie, qui avait tout jugé, tout apprécié, et qui, revenue et dégoûtée de tout, s'était abandonnée au besoin et au plaisir d'aimer: mon ami, voilà comme j'étais aimée. Plusieurs années s'étaient écoulées, remplies du charme et de la douleur inséparables d'une passion aussi forte que profonde, lorsque vous êtes venu verser du poison dans mon cœur, ravager mon âme par le trouble et le remords. Mon Dieu! que ne m'avez-vous point fait souffrir! Vous m'arrachiez à mon sentiment, et je voyais que vous n'étiez pas à moi: comprenez-vous toute l'horreur de cette situation? comment trouve-t-on encore de la douceur à dire: mon ami, je vous aime, mais avec tant de vérité et de tendresse qu'il n'est pas possible que votre âme soit froide en m'écoutant?'

His unfaithfulness, and his marriage, were, after all, little more than incidents in her anguish; they were the symptoms of an incurable disease. They stimulated her to fresh efforts towards detachment, but it was in vain. She was a wild animal struggling in a net, involving herself, with every twist and every convulsion, more and more inextricably in the toils. Sometimes she sank into a torpor; existence became a weariness; she drugged herself with opium to escape a pain which was too great to bear. Evening after evening she spent at the opera, drinking in the music of Orpheus, the divine melodies of Gluck. 'Il n'y a qu'une chose dans le monde,' she wrote, 'qui me fasse du bien, c'est la musique, mais c'est un bien qu'on appelerait douleur. Je voudrais entendre dix fois par jour cet air qui me déchire, et qui me fait jouir de tout ce que je regrette: *J'ai perdu mon Euridice.*' But she could never shake off her nightmare. Among her friends, in her charming salon, she would suddenly be overcome with tears, and forced to hurry from the room. Every knock upon the door brought desire and terror to her heart. The postman was a minister of death. 'Non, les effets de la passion ou de la raison (car je ne sais laquelle m'anime dans ce moment) sont incroyables. Après avoir entendu le facteur avec ce besoin, cette agitation, qui font de l'attente le plus grand tourment, j'en étais malade physiquement: ma toux et ma rage de tête m'en avaient avancée de cinq ou six heures. Et bien! après cet état violent, qui n'est susceptible ni de distraction ni d'adoucissement, le facteur est arrivé, j'ai eu des lettres. Il n'y en avoit point de vous; j'en ai reçu une violente commotion intérieure et extérieure, et puis je ne sais ce qui est arrivé, mais je me suis sentie calmée: il me semble que j'éprouve une sorte de douceur à vous trouver encore plus froid et plus indifférent que vous ne pouvez me trouver bizarre.' Who does not discover, beneath these dreadful confidences, a superhuman power moving mysteriously to an appointed doom? a veiled and awful voice of self-immolation?

> Je suis la plaie et le couteau!
> Je suis le soufflet et la joue!
> Je suis les membres et la roue,
> Et la victime et le bourreau!

Her last letters are one long wail of agony.—'Je ne sais si c'est vous ou la mort que j'implore: j'ai besoin d'être secourue, d'être délivrée du malheur qui me tue.'—'Mon ami, *je vous aime.* Quand vous verrai-je? Voilà le résultat du passé, du présent, et de l'avenir, s'il y a un avenir! Ah! mon ami, que j'ai souffert, que je souffre! Mes maux sont affreux; mais je sens que je vous aime.'—'Ah! s'il vous reste quelque bonté, plaignez-moi: je ne sais plus, je ne puis plus vous répondre; mon corps et mon âme sont anéantis. . . . Ah! Mon Dieu, je ne me connais plus.' Yet, in spite of all the pains of her existence she was glad that she had lived. 'J'en mourrai peut-être,' she had written, when she could still hope, 'mais cela vaut mieux que de n'avoir jamais vécu'; and, in the depth of her despair, it was still the same.—'Ah! ces souvenirs me tuent! Cependant je voudrais bien pouvoir recommencer, et à des conditions plus cruelles encore.' She regretted nothing; she was insatiable. Shattered in body and in mind, she fell at last into complete and irremediable collapse. Guibert, helpless and overwhelmed, hurried to her, declared he could never survive her; she forbade him her presence; the faithful d'Alembert alone watched beside her bed. 'Adieu, mon ami,' she wrote to Guibert, when the end was approaching. 'Si jamais je revenais à la vie, j'aimerais encore à l'employer à vous aimer; mais il n'y a plus de temps.' The wretched man, imprisoned in her ante-chamber, awaited the inevitable hour. With a supreme effort, she wrote him her valediction. She implored him to let her die at last.—'Ah! mon ami, faites que je vous doive le repos! Par vertu, soyez cruel une fois.' She sank into the arms of d'Alembert, thanking him tenderly for that long kindness, that unalterable devotion; then, begging from him some strange forgiveness, she seemed, for a moment, to be struggling to an avowal of unutterable things. The ghastly secret trembled; but it was too late.

She died on the 22nd of May, 1776, in the forty-fourth year of her life. She was buried quietly in the cemetery of Saint-Sulpice, d'Alembert and Condorcet performing the final rites. For d'Alembert, however, there was one more duty. She had named him her executor; it was his task to examine her papers; and, when he did so, he made a discovery which cut him to the heart. Not a single letter of his own had been preserved among all the multitude; instead, it was Mora, Mora, Mora, and nothing else. He had fondly imagined that, among her friends, his own place had been the first. In his distress, he rushed to Guibert, pouring out his disappointment, his cruel disillusionment: 'Oh! we were all of us mistaken; it was Mora that she loved!' Guibert was silent. The tragic irony was complete. A thousand memories besieged him, a thousand thoughts of past delights, of vanished conversations, of delicious annihilated hours; he was stifled by regrets, by remorse, by vain possibilities; he was blinded by endless visions of a pearl richer than all his tribe; a dreadful mist of tears, of desecration, of horror, rose up and clouded him for ever from his agonised and deluded friend.

> O lasso,
> Quanti dolci pensier, quanto disio
> Menò costoro al doloroso passo!

1906.

MADAME DU DEFFAND[1]

WHEN Napoleon was starting for his campaign in Russia, he ordered the proof-sheets of a forthcoming book, about which there had been some disagreement among the censors of the press, to be put into his carriage, so that he might decide for himself what suppressions it might be necessary to make. 'Je m'ennuie en route; je lirai ces volumes, et j'écrirai de Mayence ce qu'il y aura à faire.' The volumes thus chosen to beguile the imperial leisure between Paris and Mayence contained the famous correspondence of Madame du Deffand with Horace Walpole. By the Emperor's command a few excisions were made, and the book—reprinted from Miss Berry's original edition which had appeared two years earlier in England—was published almost at once. The sensation in Paris was immense; the excitement of the Russian campaign itself was half forgotten; and for some time the blind old inhabitant of the Convent of Saint Joseph held her own as a subject of conversation with the burning of Moscow and the passage of the Berezina. We cannot wonder that this was so. In the Parisian drawing-room of those days the letters of Madame du Deffand must have exercised a double fascination —on the one hand as a mine of gossip about numberless persons and events still familiar to many a living memory, and, on the other, as a detailed and brilliant record of a state of society which had already ceased to be actual and become historical. The letters were hardly more than thirty years old; but the world which they depicted in all its intensity and all

[1] *Lettres de la Marquise du Deffand à Horace Walpole* (1766–80). Première Édition complète, augmentée d'environ 500 Lettres inédites, publiées, d'après les originaux, avec une introduction, des notes, et une table des noms, par Mrs. Paget Toynbee. 3 vols. Methuen, 1912.

its singularity—the world of the old régime—had vanished
for ever into limbo. Between it and the eager readers of the
First Empire a gulf was fixed—a narrow gulf, but a deep one,
still hot and sulphurous with the volcanic fires of the Revolution. Since then a century has passed; the gulf has widened;
and the vision which these curious letters show us to-day
seems hardly less remote—from some points of view, indeed,
even more—than that which is revealed to us in the Memoirs
of Cellini or the correspondence of Cicero. Yet the vision is
not simply one of a strange and dead antiquity: there is a personal and human element in the letters which gives them a
more poignant interest, and brings them close to ourselves.
The soul of man is not subject to the rumour of periods; and
these pages, impregnated though they be with the abolished
life of the eighteenth century, can never be out of date.

A fortunate chance enables us now, for the first time, to
appreciate them in their completeness. The late Mrs. Paget
Toynbee, while preparing her edition of Horace Walpole's
letters, came upon the trace of the original manuscripts, which
had long lain hidden in obscurity in a country house in
Staffordshire. The publication of these manuscripts in full,
accompanied by notes and indexes in which Mrs. Toynbee's
well-known accuracy, industry, and tact are everywhere conspicuous, is an event of no small importance to lovers of
French literature. A great mass of new and deeply interesting
material makes its appearance. The original edition produced
by Miss Berry in 1810, from which all the subsequent editions
were reprinted with varying degrees of inaccuracy, turns out
to have contained nothing more than a comparatively small
fraction of the whole correspondence; of the 838 letters
published by Mrs. Toynbee, 485 are entirely new, and of the
rest only 52 were printed by Miss Berry in their entirety.
Miss Berry's edition was, in fact, simply a selection, and as a
selection it deserves nothing but praise. It skims the cream of
the correspondence; and it faithfully preserves the main outline of the story which the letters reveal. No doubt that was
enough for the readers of that generation; indeed, even for the

more exacting reader of to-day, there is something a little overwhelming in the closely packed 2000 pages of Mrs. Toynbee's volumes. Enthusiasm alone will undertake to grapple with them, but enthusiasm will be rewarded. In place of the truthful summary of the earlier editions, we have now the truth itself—the truth in all its subtle gradations, all its long-drawn-out suspensions, all its intangible and irremediable obscurities: it is the difference between a clear-cut drawing in black-and-white and a finished painting in oils. Probably Miss Berry's edition will still be preferred by the ordinary reader who wishes to become acquainted with a celebrated figure in French literature; but Mrs. Toynbee's will always be indispensable for the historical student, and invaluable for anyone with the leisure, the patience, and the taste for a detailed and elaborate examination of a singular adventure of the heart.

The Marquise du Deffand was perhaps the most typical representative of that phase of civilisation which came into existence in Western Europe during the early years of the eighteenth century, and reached its most concentrated and characteristic form about the year 1750 in the drawing-rooms of Paris. She was supremely a woman of her age; but it is important to notice that her age was the first, and not the second, half of the eighteenth century: it was the age of the Regent Orleans, Fontenelle, and the young Voltaire; not that of Rousseau, the 'Encyclopædia,' and the Patriarch of Ferney. It is true that her letters to Walpole, to which her fame is mainly due, were written between 1766 and 1780; but they are the letters of an old woman, and they bear upon every page of them the traces of a mind to which the whole movement of contemporary life was profoundly distasteful. The new forces to which the eighteenth century gave birth in thought, in art, in sentiment, in action—which for us form its peculiar interest and its peculiar glory—were anathema to Madame du Deffand. In her letters to Walpole, whenever she compares the present with the past her bitterness becomes extreme. 'J'ai eu autrefois,' she writes in 1778, 'des plaisirs indicibles aux opéras de Quinault et de Lulli, et au jeu de

Thévenart et de la Lemaur. Pour aujourd'hui, tout me paraît détestable: acteurs, auteurs, musiciens, beaux esprits, philosophes, tout est de mauvais goût, tout est affreux, affreux.' That great movement towards intellectual and political emancipation which centred in the 'Encyclopædia' and the *Philosophes* was the object of her particular detestation. She saw Diderot once—and that was enough for both of them. She could never understand why it was that M. de Voltaire would persist in wasting his talent for writing over such a dreary subject as religion. Turgot, she confessed, was an honest man, but he was also a 'sot animal.' His dismissal from office—that fatal act, which made the French Revolution inevitable—delighted her: she concealed her feelings from Walpole, who admired him, but she was outspoken enough to the Duchesse de Choiseul. 'Le renvoi du Turgot me plaît extrêmement,' she wrote; 'tout me paraît en bon train.' And then she added, more prophetically than she knew, 'Mais, assurément, nous n'en resterons pas là.' No doubt her dislike of the Encyclopædists and all their works was in part a matter of personal pique—the result of her famous quarrel with Mademoiselle de Lespinasse, under whose opposing banner d'Alembert and all the intellectual leaders of Parisian society had unhesitatingly ranged themselves. But that quarrel was itself far more a symptom of a deeply rooted spiritual antipathy than a mere vulgar struggle for influence between two rival *salonnières*. There are indications that, even before it took place, the elder woman's friendship for d'Alembert was giving way under the strain of her scorn for his advanced views and her hatred of his proselytising cast of mind. 'Il y a de certains articles,' she complained to Voltaire in 1763—a year before the final estrangement—'qui sont devenus pour lui affaires de parti, et sur lesquels je ne lui trouve pas le sens commun.' The truth is that d'Alembert and his friends were moving, and Madame du Deffand was standing still. Mademoiselle de Lespinasse simply precipitated and intensified an inevitable rupture. She was the younger generation knocking at the door.

Madame du Deffand's generation had, indeed, very little in common with that ardent, hopeful, speculative, sentimental group of friends who met together every evening in the drawing-room of Mademoiselle de Lespinasse. Born at the close of the seventeenth century, she had come into the world in the brilliant days of the Regent, whose witty and licentious reign had suddenly dissipated the atmosphere of gloom and bigotry imposed upon society by the moribund Court of Louis XIV. For a fortnight (so she confessed to Walpole) she was actually the Regent's mistress; and a fortnight, in those days, was a considerable time. Then she became the intimate friend of Madame de Prie—the singular woman who, for a moment, on the Regent's death, during the government of M. le Duc, controlled the destinies of France, and who committed suicide when that amusement was denied her. During her early middle age Madame du Deffand was one of the principal figures in the palace of Sceaux, where the Duchesse du Maine, the grand-daughter of the great Condé and the daughter-in-law of Louis XIV, kept up for many years an almost royal state among the most distinguished men and women of the time. It was at Sceaux, with its endless succession of entertainments and conversations—supper-parties and water-parties, concerts and masked balls, plays in the little theatre and picnics under the great trees of the park—that Madame du Deffand came to her maturity and established her position as one of the leaders of the society in which she moved. The nature of that society is plainly enough revealed in the letters and the memoirs that have come down to us. The days of formal pomp and vast representation had ended for ever when the 'Grand Monarque' was no longer to be seen strutting, in periwig and red-heeled shoes, down the glittering gallery of Versailles; the intimacy and seclusion of modern life had not yet begun. It was an intermediate period, and the comparatively small group formed by the élite of the rich, refined, and intelligent classes led an existence in which the elements of publicity and privacy were curiously combined. Never, certainly, before or since, have any set of persons lived

so absolutely and unreservedly with and for their friends as
these high ladies and gentlemen of the middle years of the
eighteenth century. The circle of one's friends was, in those
days, the framework of one's whole being; within which was
to be found all that life had to offer, and outside of which no
interest, however fruitful, no passion, however profound, no
art, however soaring, was of the slightest account. Thus
while in one sense the ideal of such a society was an eminently
selfish one, it is none the less true that there have been very
few societies indeed in which the ordinary forms of personal
selfishness have played so small a part. The selfishness of the
eighteenth century was a communal selfishness. Each individual was expected to practise, and did in fact practise to a
consummate degree, those difficult arts which make the
wheels of human intercourse run smoothly—the arts of tact
and temper, of frankness and sympathy, of delicate compliment and exquisite self-abnegation—with the result that a
condition of living was produced which, in all its superficial
and obvious qualities, was one of unparalleled amenity. Indeed,
those persons who were privileged to enjoy it showed their
appreciation of it in an unequivocal way—by the tenacity
with which they clung to the scene of such delights and graces.
They refused to grow old; they almost refused to die. Time
himself seems to have joined their circle, to have been infected with their politeness, and to have absolved them, to the
furthest possible point, from the operation of his laws. Voltaire, d'Argental, Moncrif, Hénault, Madame d'Egmont,
Madame du Deffand herself—all were born within a few
years of each other, and all lived to be well over eighty, with
the full zest of their activities unimpaired. Pont-de-Veyle, it
is true, died young—at the age of seventy-seven. Another contemporary, Richelieu, who was famous for his adventures while
Louis XIV was still on the throne, lived till within a year of the
opening of the States-General. More typical still of this singular and fortunate generation was Fontenelle, who, one morning
in his hundredth year, quietly observed that he felt a difficulty
in existing, and forthwith, even more quietly, ceased to do so.

Yet, though the wheels of life rolled round with such an alluring smoothness, they did not roll of themselves; the skill and care of trained mechanicians were needed to keep them going; and the task was no light one. Even Fontenelle himself, fitted as he was for it by being blessed (as one of his friend's observed) with two brains and no heart, realised to the full the hard conditions of social happiness. 'Il y a peu de choses,' he wrote, 'aussi difficiles et aussi dangereuses que le commerce des hommes.' The sentence, true for all ages, was particularly true for his own. The graceful, easy motions of that gay company were those of dancers balanced on skates, gliding, twirling, interlacing, over the thinnest ice. Those drawing-rooms, those little circles, so charming with the familiarity of their privacy, were themselves the rigorous abodes of the deadliest kind of public opinion—the kind that lives and glitters in a score of penetrating eyes. They required in their votaries the absolute submission that reigns in religious orders—the willing sacrifice of the entire life. The intimacy of personal passion, the intensity of high endeavour—these things must be left behind and utterly cast away by all who would enter that narrow sanctuary. Friendship might be allowed there, and flirtation disguised as love; but the overweening and devouring influence of love itself should never be admitted to destroy the calm of daily intercourse and absorb into a single channel attentions due to all. Politics were to be tolerated, so long as they remained a game; so soon as they grew serious and envisaged the public good, they became insufferable. As for literature and art, though they might be excellent as subjects for recreation and good talk, what could be more preposterous than to treat such trifles as if they had a value of their own? Only one thing; and that was to indulge, in the day-dreams of religion or philosophy, the inward ardours of the soul. Indeed, the scepticism of that generation was the most uncompromising that the world has known; for it did not even trouble to deny: it simply ignored. It presented a blank wall of perfect indifference alike to the mysteries of the universe and to the solutions of them. Madame du Deffand gave early proof that she shared to the full this propensity of her age. While still a young girl in a convent school, she had shrugged her shoulders when the nuns began to instruct her in the articles of their faith. The matter was considered serious, and the great Massillon, then at the height of his fame as a preacher and a healer of souls, was sent for to deal with the youthful heretic. She was not impressed by his arguments. In his person the generous fervour and the massive piety of an age that could still believe felt the icy and disintegrating touch of a new and strange indifference. 'Mais qu'elle est jolie!' he murmured as he came away. The Abbess ran forward to ask what holy books he recommended. 'Give her a threepenny Catechism,' was Massillon's reply. He had seen that the case was hopeless.

An innate scepticism, a profound levity, an antipathy to enthusiasm that wavered between laughter and disgust, combined with an unswerving devotion to the exacting and arduous ideals of social intercourse—such were the characteristics of the brilliant group of men and women who had spent their youth at the Court of the Regent, and dallied out their middle age down the long avenues of Sceaux. About the middle of the century the Duchesse du Maine died, and Madame du Deffand established herself in Paris at the Convent of Saint Joseph in a set of rooms which still showed traces—in the emblazoned arms over the great mantelpiece—of the occupation of Madame de Montespan. A few years later a physical affliction overtook her: at the age of fifty-seven she became totally blind; and this misfortune placed her, almost without a transition, among the ranks of the old. For the rest of her life she hardly moved from her drawing-room, which speedily became the most celebrated in Europe. The thirty years of her reign there fall into two distinct and almost equal parts. The first, during which d'Alembert was pre-eminent, came to an end with the violent expulsion of Mademoiselle de Lespinasse. During the second, which lasted for the rest of her life, her salon, purged of the Encyclopædists, took on a more decidedly worldly tone; and the influence of Horace Walpole was supreme.

It is this final period of Madame du Deffand's life that is reflected so minutely in the famous correspondence which the labours of Mrs. Toynbee have now presented to us for the first time in its entirety. Her letters to Walpole form in effect a continuous journal covering the space of fifteen years (1766–1780). They allow us, on the one hand, to trace through all its developments the progress of an extraordinary passion, and on the other to examine, as it were under the microscope of perhaps the bitterest perspicacity on record, the last phase of a doomed society. For the circle which came together in her drawing-room during those years had the hand of death upon it. The future lay elsewhere; it was simply the past that survived there—in the rich trappings of fashion and wit and elaborate gaiety—but still irrevocably the past. The radiant creatures of Sceaux had fallen into the yellow leaf. We see them in these letters, a collection of elderly persons trying hard to amuse themselves, and not succeeding very well. Pont-de-Veyle, the youthful septuagenarian, did perhaps succeed; for he never noticed what a bore he was becoming with his perpetual cough, and continued to go the rounds with indefatigable animation, until one day his cough was heard no more. Hénault—once notorious for his dinner-parties, and for having written an historical treatise—which, it is true, was worthless, but he had written it—Hénault was beginning to dodder, and Voltaire, grinning in Ferney, had already dubbed him 'notre délabré Président.' Various dowagers were engaged upon various vanities. The Marquise de Boufflers was gambling herself to ruin; the Comtesse de Boufflers was wringing out the last drops of her reputation as the mistress of a Royal Prince; the Maréchale de Mirepoix was involved in shady politics; the Maréchale de Luxembourg was obliterating a highly dubious past by a scrupulous attention to 'bon ton,' of which, at last, she became the arbitress: 'Quel ton! Quel effroyable ton!' she is said to have exclaimed after a shuddering glance at the Bible; 'ah, Madame, quel dommage que le Saint Esprit eût aussi peu de goût!' Then there was the floating company of foreign diplomats, some of whom were invariably to be found at Madame du Deffand's: Caraccioli, for instance, the Neapolitan Ambassador—'je perds les trois quarts de ce qu'il dit,' she wrote, 'mais comme il en dit beaucoup, on peut supporter cette perte'; and Bernstorff, the Danish envoy, who became the fashion, was lauded to the skies for his wit and fine manners, until, says the malicious lady, 'à travers tous ces éloges, je m'avisai de l'appeler Puffendorf,' and Puffendorf the poor man remained for evermore. Besides the diplomats, nearly every foreign traveller of distinction found his way to the renowned *salon*; Englishmen were particularly frequent visitors; and among the familiar figures of whom we catch more than one glimpse in the letters to Walpole are Burke, Fox, and Gibbon. Sometimes influential parents in England obtained leave for their young sons to be admitted into the centre of Parisian refinement. The English cub, fresh from Eton, was introduced by his tutor into the red and yellow drawing-room, where the great circle of a dozen or more elderly important persons, glittering in jewels and orders, pompous in powder and rouge, ranged in rigid order round the fireplace, followed with the precision of a perfect orchestra the leading word or smile or nod of an ancient Sibyl, who seemed to survey the company with her eyes shut, from a vast chair by the wall. It is easy to imagine the scene, in all its terrifying politeness. Madame du Deffand could not tolerate young people; she declared that she did not know what to say to them; and they, no doubt, were in precisely the same difficulty. To an English youth, unfamiliar with the language and shy as only English youths can be, a conversation with that redoubtable old lady must have been a grim ordeal indeed. One can almost hear the stumbling, pointless observations, almost see the imploring looks cast, from among the infinitely attentive company, towards the tutor, and the pink ears growing still more pink.

But such awkward moments were rare. As a rule the days flowed on in easy monotony—or rather, not the days, but the nights. For Madame du Deffand rarely rose till five o'clock in the evening; at six she began her reception; and at nine or half-past the central moment of the twenty-four hours arrived—the moment of supper. Upon this event the whole of her existence hinged. Supper, she used to say, was one of the four ends of man, and what the other three were she could never remember. She lived up to her dictum. She had an income of £1400 a year, and of this she spent more than half—£720—on food. These figures should be largely increased to give them their modern values; but, economise as she might, she found that she could only just manage to rub along. Her parties varied considerably in size; sometimes only four or five persons sat down to supper—sometimes twenty or thirty. No doubt they were elaborate meals. In a moment of economy we find the hospitable lady making pious resolutions: she would no longer give 'des repas'—only ordinary suppers for six people at the most, at which there should be served nothing more than two entrées, one roast, two sweets, and—mysterious addition—'la pièce du milieu.' This was certainly moderate for those days (Monsieur de Jonsac rarely provided fewer than fourteen entrées), but such resolutions did not last long. A week later she would suddenly begin to issue invitations wildly, and, day after day, her tables would be loaded with provisions for thirty guests. But she did not always have supper at home. From time to time she sallied forth in her vast coach and rattled through the streets of Paris to one of her still extant dowagers—a Maréchale, or a Duchesse—or the more and more 'délabré Président.' There the same company awaited her as that which met in her own house; it was simply a change of decorations; often enough for weeks together she had supper every night with the same half-dozen persons. The entertainment, apart from the supper itself, hardly varied. Occasionally there was a little music, more often there were cards and gambling. Madame du Deffand disliked gambling, but she loathed going to bed, and, if it came to a choice between the two, she did not hesitate: once, at the age of seventy-three, she sat up till seven o'clock in the morning playing vingt-et-un with Charles Fox. But distractions of that kind were merely incidental to the grand business of the night—the conversation. In the circle that, after an eight hours' sitting, broke up reluctantly at two or three every morning to meet again that same evening at six, talk continually flowed. For those strange creatures it seemed to form the very substance of life itself. It was the underlying essence, the circumambient ether, in which alone the pulsations of existence had their being; it was the one eternal reality; men might come and men might go, but talk went on for ever. It is difficult, especially for those born under the Saturnine influence of an English sky, quite to realise the nature of such conversation. Brilliant, charming, easy-flowing, gay and rapid it must have been; never profound, never intimate, never thrilling; but also never emphatic, never affected, never languishing, and never dull. Madame du Deffand herself had a most vigorous flow of language. 'Écoutez! Écoutez!' Walpole used constantly to exclaim, trying to get in his points; but in vain; the sparkling cataract swept on unheeding. And indeed to listen was the wiser part—to drink in deliciously the animation of those quick, illimitable, exquisitely articulated syllables, to surrender one's whole soul to the pure and penetrating precision of those phrases, to follow without a breath the happy swiftness of that fine-spun thread of thought. Then at moments her wit crystallised; the cataract threw off a shower of radiant jewels, which one caught as one might. Some of these have come down to us. Her remark on Montesquieu's great book—'C'est de l'esprit sur les lois'—is an almost final criticism. Her famous 'mot de Saint Denis,' so dear to the heart of Voltaire, deserves to be once more recorded. A garrulous and credulous Cardinal was describing the martyrdom of Saint Denis the Areopagite: when his head was cut off, he took it up and carried it in his hands. That, said the Cardinal, was well known; what was not well known was the extraordinary fact that he walked with his head under his arm all the way from Montmartre to the Church of Saint Denis— a distance of six miles. 'Ah, Monseigneur!' said Madame du Deffand, 'dans une telle situation, il n'y a que le premier pas qui coûte.' At two o'clock the brilliance began to flag; the

guests began to go; the dreadful moment was approaching. If
Madame de Gramont happened to be there, there was still
some hope, for Madame de Gramont abhorred going to bed
almost as much as Madame du Deffand. Or there was just a
chance that the Duc de Choiseul might come in at the last
moment, and stay on for a couple of hours. But at length it
was impossible to hesitate any longer; the chariot was at the
door. She swept off, but it was still early; it was only half-past
three; and the coachman was ordered to drive about the
Boulevards for an hour before going home.

It was, after all, only natural that she should put off going
to bed, for she rarely slept for more than two or three hours.
The greater part of that empty time, during which conversation was impossible, she devoted to her books. But she hardly
ever found anything to read that she really enjoyed. Of the
two thousand volumes she possessed—all bound alike, and
stamped on the back with her device of a cat—she had only
read four or five hundred; the rest were impossible. She perpetually complained to Walpole of the extreme dearth of
reading matter. In nothing, indeed, is the contrast more
marked between that age and ours than in the quantity of
books available for the ordinary reader. How the eighteenth
century would envy us our innumerable novels, our biographies, our books of travel, all our easy approaches to knowledge and entertainment, our translations, our cheap reprints!
In those days even for a reader of catholic tastes, there was
really very little to read. And, of course, Madame du Deffand's tastes were far from catholic—they were fastidious to
the last degree. She considered that Racine alone of writers
had reached perfection, and that only once—in *Athalie*.
Corneille carried her away for moments, but on the whole
he was barbarous. She highly admired 'quelques centaines de
vers de M. de Voltaire.' She thought Richardson and Fielding
excellent, and she was enraptured by the style—but only by
the style—of *Gil Blas*. And that was all. Everything else
appeared to her either affected or pedantic or insipid. Walpole
recommended to her a History of Malta; she tried it, but she

soon gave it up—it mentioned the Crusades. She began Gibbon, but she found him superficial. She tried Buffon, but he was 'd'une monotonie insupportable; il sait bien ce qu'il sait, mais il ne s'occupe que des bêtes; il faut l'être un peu soi-même pour se dévouer à une telle occupation.' She got hold of the memoirs of Saint-Simon in manuscript, and these amused her enormously; but she was so disgusted by the style that she was very nearly sick. At last, in despair, she embarked on a prose translation of Shakespeare. The result was unexpected; she was positively pleased. *Coriolanus*, it is true, 'me semble, sauf votre respect, épouvantable, et n'a pas le sens commun'; and 'pour *La Tempête*, je ne suis pas touchée de ce genre.' But she was impressed by *Othello*; she was interested by *Macbeth*; and she admired *Julius Caesar*, in spite of its bad taste. At *King Lear*, indeed, she had to draw the line. 'Ah, mon Dieu! Quelle pièce! Réellement la trouvez-vous belle? Elle me noircit l'âme à un point que je ne puis exprimer; c'est un amas de toutes les horreurs infernales.' Her reader was an old soldier from the Invalides, who came round every morning early, and took up his position by her bedside. She lay back among the cushions, listening, for long hours. Was there ever a more incongruous company, a queerer trysting-place, for Goneril and Desdemona, Ariel and Lady Macbeth?

Often, even before the arrival of the old pensioner, she was at work dictating a letter, usually to Horace Walpole, occasionally to Madame de Choiseul or Voltaire. Her letters to Voltaire are enchanting; his replies are no less so; and it is much to be regretted that the whole correspondence has never been collected together in chronological order, and published as a separate book. The slim volume would be, of its kind, quite perfect. There was no love lost between the two old friends; they could not understand each other; Voltaire, alone of his generation, had thrown himself into the very vanguard of thought; to Madame du Deffand progress had no meaning, and thought itself was hardly more than an unpleasant necessity. She distrusted him profoundly, and he returned the compliment. Yet neither could do without the other: through her, he kept in touch with one of the most influential circles in Paris; and even she could not be insensible to the glory of corresponding with such a man. Besides, in spite of all their differences, they admired each other genuinely, and they were held together by the habit of a long familiarity. The result was a marvellous display of epistolary art. If they had liked each other any better, they never would have troubled to write so well. They were on their best behaviour—exquisitely courteous and yet punctiliously at ease, like dancers in a minuet. His cajoleries are infinite; his deft sentences, mingling flattery with reflection, have almost the quality of a caress. She replies in the tone of a worshipper, glancing lightly at a hundred subjects, purring out her 'Monsieur de Voltaire,' and seeking his advice on literature and life. He rejoins in that wonderful strain of epicurean stoicism of which he alone possessed the secret: and so the letters go on. Sometimes one just catches the glimpse of a claw beneath the soft pad, a grimace under the smile of elegance; and one remembers with a shock that, after all, one is reading the correspondence of a monkey and a cat.

Madame du Deffand's style reflects, perhaps even more completely than that of Voltaire himself, the common sense of the eighteenth century. Its precision is absolute. It is like a line drawn in one stroke by a master, with the prompt exactitude of an unerring subtlety. There is no breadth in it —no sense of colour and the concrete mass of things. One cannot wonder, as one reads her, that she hardly regretted her blindness. What did she lose by it? Certainly not

> The sweet approach of even or morn,
> Or sight of vernal bloom, or Summer's rose;

for what did she care for such particulars when her eyes were at their clearest? Her perception was intellectual; and to the penetrating glances of her mental vision the objects of the sensual world were mere irrelevance. The kind of writing produced by such a quality of mind may seem thin and barren to those accustomed to the wealth and variety of the Romantic school. Yet it will repay attention. The vocabulary is very small; but every word is the right one; this old lady of high society, who had never given a thought to her style, who wrote—and spelt—by the light of nature, was a past mistress of that most difficult of literary accomplishments—'l'art de dire en un mot tout ce qu'un mot peut dire.' The object of all art is to make suggestions. The romantic artist attains that end by using a multitude of different stimuli, by calling up image after image, recollection after recollection, until the reader's mind is filled and held by a vivid and palpable evocation; the classic works by the contrary method of a fine economy, and, ignoring everything but what is essential, trusts, by means of the exact propriety of his presentation, to produce the required effect. Madame du Deffand carries the classical ideal to its furthest point. She never strikes more than once, and she always hits the nail on the head. Such is her skill that she sometimes seems to beat the Romantics even on their own ground: her reticences make a deeper impression than all the dottings of their i's. The following passage from a letter to Walpole is characteristic:

Nous eûmes une musique charmante, une dame qui joue de la harpe à merveille; elle me fit tant de plaisir que j'eus du regret que vous ne l'entendissiez pas; c'est un instrument admirable. Nous eûmes aussi un clavecin, mais quoiqu'il fût touché avec une grande perfection, ce n'est rien en comparaison de la harpe. Je fus fort triste toute la soirée; j'avais appris en partant que Mme. de Luxembourg, qui était allée samedi à Montmorency pour y passer quinze jours, s'était trouvée si mal qu'on avait fait venir Tronchin, et qu'on l'avait ramenée le dimanche à huit heures du soir, qu'on lui croyait de l'eau dans la poitrine. L'ancienneté de la connaissance; une habitude qui a l'air de l'amitié; voir disparaître ceux avec qui l'on vit; un retour sur soi-même; sentir que l'on ne tient à rien, que tout fuit, que tout échappe, qu'on reste seule dans l'univers, et que malgré cela on craint de le quitter; voilà ce qui m'occupa pendant la musique.

Here are no coloured words, no fine phrases—only the most flat and ordinary expressions—'un instrument admirable'—'une grande perfection'—'fort triste.' Nothing is described;

and yet how much is suggested! The whole scene is conjured up—one does not know how; one's imagination is switched on to the right rails, as it were, by a look, by a gesture, and then left to run of itself. In the simple, faultless rhythm of that closing sentence, the trembling melancholy of the old harp seems to be lingering still.

While the letters to Voltaire show us nothing but the brilliant exterior of Madame du Deffand's mind, those to Walpole reveal the whole state of her soul. The revelation is not a pretty one. Bitterness, discontent, pessimism, cynicism, boredom, regret, despair—these are the feelings that dominate every page. To a superficial observer Madame du Deffand's lot must have seemed peculiarly enviable; she was well off, she enjoyed the highest consideration, she possessed intellectual talents of the rarest kind which she had every opportunity of displaying, and she was surrounded by a multitude of friends. What more could anyone desire? The harsh old woman would have smiled grimly at such a question. 'A little appetite,' she might have answered. She was like a dyspeptic at a feast; the finer the dishes that were set before her, the greater her distaste; that spiritual gusto which lends a savour to the meanest act of living, and without which all life seems profitless, had gone from her for ever. Yet—and this intensified her wretchedness—though the banquet was loathsome to her, she had not the strength to tear herself away from the table. Once, in a moment of desperation, she had thoughts of retiring to a convent, but she soon realised that such an action was out of the question. Fate had put her into the midst of the world, and there she must remain. 'Je ne suis point assez heureuse,' she said, 'de me passer des choses dont je ne me soucie pas.' She was extremely lonely. As fastidious in friendship as in literature, she passed her life among a crowd of persons whom she disliked and despised. 'Je ne vois que des sots et des fripons,' she said; and she did not know which were the most disgusting. She took a kind of deadly pleasure in analysing 'les nuances des sottises' among the people with whom she lived. The varieties were many, from the foolishness of her

companion, Mademoiselle Sanadon, who would do nothing
but imitate her—'elle fait des définitions,' she wails—to that of
the lady who hoped to prove her friendship by unending
presents of grapes and pears—'comme je n'y tâte pas, cela
diminue mes scrupules du peu de goût que j'ai pour elle.'
Then there were those who were not quite fools but something very near it. 'Tous les Matignon sont des sots,' said
somebody one day to the Regent, 'excepté le Marquis de
Matignon.' 'Cela est vrai,' the Regent replied, 'il n'est pas
sot, mais on voit bien qu'il est le fils d'un sot.' Madame du
Deffand was an expert at tracing such affinities. For instance,
there was Necker. It was clear that Necker was not a fool, and
yet—what was it? Something was the matter—yes, she had it:
he made you feel a fool yourself—'l'on est plus bête avec lui
que l'on ne l'est tout seul.' As she said of herself: 'elle est
toujours tentée d'arracher les masques qu'elle rencontre.'
Those blind, piercing eyes of hers spied out unerringly the
weakness or the ill-nature or the absurdity that lurked behind
the gravest or the most fascinating exterior; then her fingers
began to itch, and she could resist no longer—she gave way
to her besetting temptation. It is impossible not to sympathise
with Rousseau's remark about her—'J'aimai mieux encore
m'exposer au fléau de sa haine qu'à celui de son amitié.' There,
sitting in her great Diogenes-tub of an armchair—her
'tonneau' as she called it—talking, smiling, scattering her
bons mots, she went on through the night, in the remorseless
secrecy of her heart, tearing off the masks from the faces that
surrounded her. Sometimes the world in which she lived displayed itself before her horrified inward vision like some
intolerable and meaningless piece of clock-work mechanism:

J'admirais hier au soir la nombreuse compagnie qui était chez
moi; hommes et femmes me paraissaient des machines à ressorts,
qui allaient, venaient, parlaient, riaient, sans penser, sans réfléchir,
sans sentir; chacun jouait son rôle par habitude: Madame la
Duchesse d'Aiguillon crevait de rire, Mme. de Forcalquier dédaig-
nait tout, Mme. de la Vallière jabotait sur tout. Les hommes ne
jouaient pas de meilleurs rôles, et moi j'étais abîmée dans les

réflexions les plus noires; je pensai que j'avais passé ma vie dans les illusions; que je m'étais creusée tous les abîmes dans lesquels j'étais tombée.

At other times she could see around her nothing but a mass of mutual hatreds, into which she was plunged herself no less than her neighbours:

Je ramenai la Maréchale de Mirepoix chez elle; j'y descendis, je causai une heure avec elle; je n'en fus pas mécontente. Elle hait la petite Idole, elle hait la Maréchale de Luxembourg; enfin, sa haine pour tous les gens qui me déplaisent me fit lui pardonner l'indifférénce et peut-être la haine qu'elle a pour moi. Convenez que voilà une jolie société, un charmant commerce.

Once or twice for several months together she thought that she had found in the Duchesse de Choiseul a true friend and a perfect companion. But there was one fatal flaw even in Madame de Choiseul: she *was* perfect!—'Elle est parfaite; et c'est un plus grand défaut qu'on ne pense et qu'on ne saurait imaginer.' At last one day the inevitable happened—she went to see Madame de Choiseul, and she was bored. 'Je rentrai chez moi à une heure, pénétrée, persuadée qu'on ne peut être content de personne.'

One person, however, there was who pleased her; and it was the final irony of her fate that this very fact should have been the last drop that caused the cup of her unhappiness to overflow. Horace Walpole had come upon her at a psychological moment. Her quarrel with Mademoiselle de Lespinasse and the Encyclopædists had just occurred; she was within a few years of seventy; and it must have seemed to her that, after such a break, at such an age, there was little left for her to do but to die quietly. Then the gay, talented, fascinating Englishman appeared, and she suddenly found that, so far from her life being over, she was embarked for good and all upon her greatest adventure. What she experienced at that moment was something like a religious conversion. Her past fell away from her a dead thing; she was overwhelmed by an ineffable vision; she, who had wandered for so many years in the ways of worldly indifference, was uplifted all at once on to a strange summit, and pierced with the intensest pangs of an unknown devotion. Henceforward her life was dedicated; but, unlike the happier saints of a holier persuasion, she was to find no peace on earth. It was, indeed, hardly to be expected that Walpole, a blasé bachelor of fifty, should have reciprocated so singular a passion; yet he might at least have treated it with gentleness and respect. The total impression of him which these letters produce is very damaging. It is true that he was in a difficult position; and it is also true that, since only the merest fragments of his side of the correspondence have been preserved, our knowledge of the precise details of his conduct is incomplete; nevertheless, it is clear that, on the whole, throughout the long and painful episode, the principal motive which actuated him was an inexcusable egoism. He was obsessed by a fear of ridicule. He knew that letters were regularly opened at the French Post Office, and he lived in terror lest some spiteful story of his absurd relationship with a blind old woman of seventy should be concocted and set afloat among his friends, or his enemies, in England, which would make him the laughing-stock of society for the rest of his days. He was no less terrified by the intensity of the sentiment of which he had become the object. Thoroughly superficial and thoroughly selfish, immersed in his London life of dilettantism and gossip, the weekly letters from France with their burden of a desperate affection appalled him and bored him by turns. He did not know what to do; and his perplexity was increased by the fact that he really liked Madame du Deffand—so far as he could like anyone—and also by the fact that his vanity was highly flattered by her letters. Many courses were open to him, but the one he took was probably the most cruel that he could have taken : he insisted with an absolute rigidity on their correspondence being conducted in the tone of the most ordinary friendship—on those terms alone, he said, would he consent to continue it. And of course such terms were impossible to Madame du Deffand. She accepted them—what else could she do?—but every line she wrote was a denial of them. Then, periodically, there was an explosion. Walpole stormed, threatened, declared he would write no more; and on her side there were abject apologies, and solemn promises of amendment. Naturally, it was all in vain. A few months later he would be attacked by a fit of the gout, her solicitude would be too exaggerated, and the same fury was repeated, and the same submission. One wonders what the charm could have been that held that proud old spirit in such a miserable captivity. Was it his very coldness that subdued her? If he had cared for her a little more, perhaps she would have cared for him a good deal less. But it is clear that what really bound her to him was the fact that they so rarely met. If he had lived in Paris, if he had been a member of her little clique, subject to the unceasing searchlight of her nightly scrutiny, who can doubt that, sooner or later, Walpole too would have felt 'le fléau de son amitié'? His mask, too, would have been torn to tatters like the rest. But, as it was, his absence saved him; her imagination clothed him with an almost mythic excellence; his brilliant letters added to the impression; and then, at intervals of about two years, he appeared in Paris for six weeks—just long enough to rivet her chains, and not long enough to loosen them. And so it was that she fell before him with that absolute and unquestioning devotion of which only the most dominating and fastidious natures are capable. Once or twice, indeed, she did attempt a revolt, but only succeeded in plunging herself into a deeper subjection. After one of his most violent and cruel outbursts, she refused to communicate with him further, and for three or four weeks she kept her word; then she crept back and pleaded for forgiveness. Walpole graciously granted it. It is with some satisfaction that one finds him, a few weeks later, laid up with a peculiarly painful attack of the gout.

About half-way through the correspondence there is an acute crisis, after which the tone of the letters undergoes a marked change. After seven years of struggle, Madame du Deffand's indomitable spirit was broken; henceforward she would hope for nothing; she would gratefully accept the few crumbs that might be thrown her; and for the rest she resigned herself to her fate. Gradually sinking into extreme old age, her self-repression and her bitterness grew ever more and more complete. She was always bored; and her later letters are a series of variations on the perpetual theme of 'ennui.' 'C'est une maladie de l'âme,' she says, 'dont nous afflige la nature en nous donnant l'existence; c'est le ver solitaire qui absorbe tout.' And again, 'l'ennui est l'avant-goût du néant, mais le néant lui est préférable.' Her existence had become a hateful waste—a garden, she said, from which all the flowers had been uprooted and which had been sown with salt. 'Ah! Je le répète sans cesse, il n'y a qu'un malheur, celui d'être né.' The grasshopper had become a burden; and yet death seemed as little desirable as life. 'Comment est-il possible,' she asks, 'qu'on craigne la fin d'une vie aussi triste?' When Death did come at last, he came very gently. She felt his approaches, and dictated a letter to Walpole, bidding him, in her strange fashion, an infinitely restrained farewell: 'Divertissez-vous, mon ami, le plus que vous pourrez; ne vous affligez point de mon état, nous étions presque perdus l'un pour l'autre; nous ne nous devions jamais revoir; vous me regretterez, parce qu'on est bien aise de se savoir aimé.' That was her last word to him. Walpole might have reached her before she finally lost consciousness, but, though he realised her condition and knew well enough what his presence would have been to her, he did not trouble to move. She died as she had lived—her room crowded with acquaintances and the sound of a conversation in her ears. When one reflects upon her extraordinary tragedy, when one attempts to gauge the significance of her character and of her life, it is difficult to know whether to pity most, to admire, or to fear. Certainly there is something at once pitiable and magnificent in such an unflinching perception of the futilities of living, such an uncompromising refusal to be content with anything save the one thing that it is impossible to have. But there is something alarming too; was she perhaps right after all?

1913.

HORACE WALPOLE

Lovers of Walpole will not fail to welcome the first instalment of Mrs. Toynbee's new edition of the incomparable *Letters*.[1] The Clarendon Press is to be congratulated on the production of these charming and comfortable volumes, which, on the score of form alone, are worthy of precedence over the cumbrous tomes of Peter Cunningham. It is pleasant to think that henceforward it will be possible to read with ease the most readable of books, and that the lightest of writers is no longer too heavy to carry. But the present edition has other claims to superiority: it is far more nearly complete than any of its predecessors; it may be supposed, indeed, to be the penultimate Walpole. Peter Cunningham's nine volumes contain 2654 letters; there will be as many as 3061 in Mrs. Toynbee's sixteen, and, out of this new material, no less than 111 letters have never before been printed. In the volumes at present published, the most interesting additions are some early letters to Charles Lyttelton, afterwards Bishop of Carlisle, among them being the first extant letter of Walpole, written while he was still at Eton. But the most important part of the unprinted matter has yet to appear—seven letters, written in French, to Madame du Deffand. At the death of his 'dear old friend,' Walpole came into the possession of all her papers; his terror of ridicule made him anxious to destroy such evidence as they contained of the lady's strange attachment and his own bad French. The forthcoming letters, however, seem to have survived by accident, and are all that remains, on Walpole's part, of a correspondence of sixteen years.

The excellence of Mrs. Toynbee's work makes it all the

[1] *The Letters of Horace Walpole, Fourth Earl of Orford.* Chronologically arranged and edited, with notes and indices, by Mrs. Paget Toynbee, in sixteen volumes, with portraits and facsimiles. Vols. I.–IV. The Oxford University Press. 1903.

more to be regretted that she has been unable to make use of some unpublished manuscripts still lying at Holland House; for, with their addition, none of the known letters of Walpole would have been absent from her collection. In one other respect alone the present edition seems to fall short of the ideal. A great many passages 'quite unfit for publication' have been omitted from the letters to Sir Horace Mann. It is true that these passages have never been printed before; but it is difficult to believe that there is any adequate reason for their not being printed now. The *jeune fille* is certainly not an adequate reason, and, even if she were, the *jeune fille* does not read Walpole. Whoever does read him must feel that these constant omissions are so many blots upon perfection, and distressing relics of an age of barbarous prudery.

The panorama of the correspondence is so vast, that it is almost a relief to be able to look at it in sections. Never, indeed, was such exquisite delicacy combined with such enormous bulk; and there can be no doubt that it is owing to their mass, as well as to their matter, that the letters hold the place they do in English literature. No other English letter writer except Byron—and in fact no other in the world except Voltaire, who stands supreme—ever approached the productiveness of Walpole. But Byron's exuberance of vitality forms a curious contrast to Walpole's prolific ease. The former is all vigour and hurry, all chops and changes, all multitudinous romance; he is salt and breezy and racy as the sea. Walpole flows like a delightful river through his endless pages, between shady lawns and luxurious villas, dimpling all the way. One common characteristic, and one alone, unites the two men; they both possess a vivid and peculiar imagination. It is this quality in Walpole, this 'ease,' to use the words of Macaulay, 'with which he yokes together ideas between which there would seem, at first sight, to be no connection,' that makes him so distinctively English a writer. His fancy roams, indeed, as constantly as that of Keats, though it roams in a different direction. From the letters of his early Cambridge days to the letters of his extreme old age, there is a perpetual procession of sparkling imagery.

'Youthful passages of life,' he writes to Montagu, from King's, 'are the chippings of Pitt's diamond, set into little heart-rings with mottoes; the stone itself more worth, the filings more gentle and agreeable.'

In the letter he wrote to Lady Ossory six weeks before his death, though the style has reached perfection, it is the same style. She had been praising his letters, and he writes to her:

'Pray send me no more such laurels, which I desire no more than their leaves when decked with a scrap of tinsel, and stuck on Twelfth-cakes that lie on the shop-boards of pastrycooks at Christmas. I shall be quite content with a sprig of rosemary thrown after me, when the parson of the parish commits my dust to dust.'

This mastery of decoration never deserts him. Whatever his theme—the Opposition, or Madame de Sévigné, or the weather, or nothing at all—he contrives to beautify it in a hundred wonderful ways. His writing, as he might have said himself, is like lace; the material is of very little consequence, the embroidery is all that counts; and it shares with lace the happy faculty of coming out sometimes in yards and yards.

The period covered by the present volumes extends over the twenty years which preceded the death of George II. At the beginning of it, Sir Robert was still in power; at the end of it the triumphant Ministry of Pitt was drawing to its close. The political changes during that interval had been immense: in Asia and in America, as well as in Europe, a vast transformation had taken place; the imperial power of Britain, which had hardly been dreamt of in 1740, had become, in 1760, an established fact. Yet the social change during the same period had been almost equally profound. The accession of George III is the dividing point between two distinct ages: the age of Fielding and Hogarth and Warburton on the one hand, and the age of Sterne and Reynolds and Hume on the other. The difference is curiously illustrated by the contrast between Sir Robert Walpole and his son Horace, who each possessed, to a somewhat exaggerated degree, the peculiar characteristics of his generation. All over England, during these years of transition, coarse and vigorous fathers were being succeeded by refined and sentimental sons; sceptics were everywhere stepping into the shoes of deists; in France the same movement at the same time brought about the triumph of the Encyclopædia. Whatever may have been the causes of this remarkable revolution, there can be no doubt that the latter half of the eighteenth century attained to a height of civilisation unknown in Europe since the days of Hadrian. Horace Walpole was, in England at any rate, the true prophet of the movement. Already, in his earliest letters, he is over-civilised; he is a dilettante, a connoisseur who purchases alabaster gladiators and Domenichinos; he languishes among the boors of Houghton like a creature from another world.

'I literally seem to have murdered a man whose name was Ennui, for his ghost is ever before me,' he writes at the age of twenty-six; 'I fear 'tis growing old. They say there is no English word for *ennui*,' he goes on; 'I think you may translate it most literally by what is called "entertaining people," and "doing the honours." '

Twenty years later he was still 'entertaining'; but the 'people' were different, and he was no longer bored. 'My resolutions of growing old and staid,' he writes to Lady Hervey, 'are admirable; I wake with a sober plan, and intend to pass the day with my friends—then comes the Duke of Richmond, and hurries me down to Whitehall to dinner—then the Duchess of Grafton sends for me to loo in Upper Grosvenor Street—before I can get thither, I am begged to step to Kensington, to give Mrs. Anne Pitt my opinion about a bow-window—after the loo, I am to march back to Whitehall to supper—and after that, am to walk with Miss Pelham on the terrace till two in the morning, because it is moonlight and her chair is not come. All this does not help my morning laziness; and, by the time I have breakfasted, fed my birds and my squirrels, and dressed, there is an auction ready. In short, Madam, this was my life last week, and is I think every week, with the addition of forty episodes.'

Thirty years later still, he was 'doing the honours' as happily as ever—to the French *émigrés* at Berkeley Square, to Queen Charlotte at Strawberry Hill: he had come into his kingdom with the new age.

If the contrast is great between the first half of the eighteenth century and the last, it is even greater between the latter and the first half of the nineteenth; and nothing shows this more clearly than the treatment which Walpole received in the *Edinburgh*, hardly forty years after his death, at the hands of Macaulay. The criticism is written in the great reviewer's most trenchant style; it contains passages which stand, for cleverness and brilliancy, on the level of his cleverest and most brilliant work; every other sentence is an epigram, and all the paragraphs go off like Catherine-wheels; everything is present, in fact, that could be desired, except the remotest understanding of the subject. Macaulay, stepping out for a moment from his world of machinery and progress, found himself face to face with a phenomenon which scarcely presented anything to his mind. Here was a writer who was not literary, a member of Parliament who was not a politician, an aristocrat who declared himself a Republican, and a Whig who took more interest in a new snuff-box than in the French Revolution. What could the meaning of this portent possibly be? The solution was only too obvious—the creature must be a mere *poseur*, with an empty head, and an empty heart, and a few tricks to amuse the public. In this case, at any rate, Macaulay employed the very method of portraiture with which he charges Walpole himself:

'He copied from the life only those glaring and obvious peculiarities which could not escape the most superficial observation. The rest of the canvas he filled up, in a careless dashing way, with knave and fool, mixed in such proportions as pleased Heaven.'

The accusation most commonly raised against Walpole— that he was devoid of true feeling in his intercourse with others—is of course reiterated by Macaulay, though even he feels obliged to admit parenthetically that to Conway at least Walpole 'appears to have been sincerely attached.' But the truth seems to be, in spite of 'those glaring and obvious peculiarities which could not escape the most superficial observation'—his angry, cutting sentences, his constant mockery of his enemies, his constant quarrels with his friends, and his perpetual reserve—that Walpole's nature was in reality peculiarly affectionate. There can be no doubt that he was sensitive to an extraordinary degree; and it is much more probable that the defects—for defects they certainly were—which he showed in social intercourse, were caused by an excess of this quality of sensitiveness, rather than by a lack of sincere feeling. It is impossible to quarrel with one's friends unless one likes them; and it is impossible to like some people very much without disliking other people a good deal. These elementary considerations are quite enough to account for the vagaries and the malice of Walpole. But there was another element in his character which gave his malice all the appearance of a deep malignity, and made his vagaries seem to be the outcome of a callous nature: it was his pride. At heart he was a complete aristocrat; it was impossible for him to be unreserved. The masks he wore were imposed upon him by his caste, by his breeding, by his own intimate sense of the decencies and proprieties of life; so that his hatreds and loves, so easily aroused and so intensely cherished, were forced to express themselves in spiteful little taunts and in artificial compliments. His letter to Mason is an exquisite proof alike of how much he could feel, and how much he could keep back. The account he gives of his own misconduct is utterly dispassionate and polite; he makes no protestations of affection, he expresses not a word of regret; it is only at last, when he touches upon the feelings of Gray, that the veil seems for a moment to be withdrawn. 'I treated him insolently. *He loved me, and I did not think he did.*' One must be very blind indeed to see in such words as those nothing more than a frigid indifference; and one must suffer from a strange obliquity of vision to be able to trace in them a likeness to the ape of

Macaulay's caricature, mopping and mowing, spitting and gibbering, dressed out in its master's finery, and keeping an eye upon the looking-glass.

There is a portrait of him, taken in later life, which gives a clearer idea of the real Walpole. He is sitting cross-legged on his chair, with a book open in his hand, and Madame du Deffand's dog beside him; in the background, through the window, one catches a glimpse of the Thames, and a barge sailing past amid the spring foliage. It is a pretty picture; and the thin face, with its high forehead and its tiny nervous mouth, is a curiously kind one. Looking at it, it is easy to return in spirit to that little world of Walpole, that happy society of five hundred personages which seems to move and dance perpetually before our gaze, and yet remains fixed for us for ever in a strange fixity, like a fly in amber. To Macaulay, indeed, fresh and victorious from the great fight of the Reform Bill, that society must have seemed a narrow and a petty one, remote from the realities of life. Yet, after all, what could be more real, for instance, than to sit down to cards with 'the Archbishopess of Canterbury and Mr. Gibbon'? Or to entertain the Duchess of Hamilton at Strawberry? Or to write verses in honour of the Princess Amelia? Or to exchange confidences with Madame du Deffand? Or to watch long hours from the bow-window in the great room at Isleworth the ferries passing to and fro across the river? Or to print a new edition of the poems of Mr. Gray? Or to scribble notes to Lady Ossory? Or to spend the evening with Mary Berry over the old Duchess of Queensberry and the old Duchess of Marlborough, till the candles expire in their sockets, and one begins to feel that one is getting old one's self? Are these things really less real, Walpole might have asked, than shouting at elections, and writing articles for the magazines?

'One passes away so soon, and worlds succeed to worlds, in which the occupiers build the same castles in the air. What is ours but the present moment? And how many of mine are gone!'

1904.

WALPOLE'S LETTERS

THESE two long-expected volumes,[1] which complete and perfect Mrs. Paget Toynbee's great edition of Horace Walpole's Letters, will be welcomed by every lover of English scholarship. They contain a hundred and eleven hitherto unpublished letters, of which the most interesting are a series written in Italy to Sir Horace Mann and two childish letters to Lady Walpole, reproduced in facsimile. Among the letters published elsewhere, but not contained in Mrs. Toynbee's edition, are an important group addressed to Henry Fox and all that is still extant of Walpole's part in his correspondence with Madame du Deffand. But the volumes are chiefly valuable for their mass of *corrigenda* and for the new light which they throw upon a multitude of minor matters. This additional information is almost entirely derived from the remarkable and only lately discovered collection of Walpole MSS. in the possession of Sir Wathen Waller—a collection containing, as Mr. Toynbee tells us, 'private journals, note-books, and commonplace books of Horace Walpole, together with numerous letters addressed to him, marked "for illustration," which had been carefully preserved by Walpole in a series of letter-books, evidently with a view to their eventual utilisation in the annotation of his own letters'; and we are glad to hear that we may look forward to the appearance of 'the most interesting portions of this material in two further supplementary volumes.' It would be impossible to overrate Mr. Toynbee's erudition, industry, and exactness; owing to his labours and those of the late Mrs. Toynbee, we now possess an edition of

[1] *Supplement to the Letters of Horace Walpole, Fourth Earl of Orford.* Chronologically arranged and edited, with notes and indices, by Paget Toynbee, D.Litt. 2 vols. Oxford: Clarendon Press.

this great classic truly worthy of its immense and varied interests—historical, biographical, political, psychological—and its potent literary charm. The reader who merely reads for entertainment will find a volume of this edition a perfect companion for a holiday; while its elaborate apparatus of notes, indices, and tables will supply the learned inquirer with everything that his heart can desire. One blemish, and one only, can we discover in it: the omission of numerous passages on the score of impropriety. Surely, in a work of such serious intention and such monumental proportions the publication of the *whole* of the original material was not only justifiable, but demanded by the nature of the case.

Good letters are like pearls: they are admirable in themselves, but their value is infinitely enhanced when there is a string of them. Therefore, to be a really great letter writer it is not enough to write an occasional excellent letter; it is necessary to write constantly, indefatigably, with ever-recurring zest; it is almost necessary to live to a good old age. What makes a correspondence fascinating is the cumulative effect of slow, gradual, day-to-day development—the long, leisurely unfolding of a character and a life. The Walpole correspondence has this merit in a peculiar degree; its enormous progression carries the reader on and on through sixty years of living. Even if the individual letters had been dull, and about tedious things, a collection on such a scale could hardly have failed to be full of interest. But Walpole's letters are far from dull, and, placed as he was in the very centre of a powerful and brilliant society, during one of the most attractive epochs of English history, the topics upon which he writes are very far from tedious. The result is something that is certainly unique in our literature. Though from the point of view of style, or personal charm, or originality of observation, other letter writers may deserve a place at least on an equality with that of Walpole, it is indisputable that the collected series of his letters forms by far the most important single correspondence in the language.

The achievement was certainly greater than the man.

Walpole, in fact, was not great at all; though it would be a mistake to suppose that he was the fluttering popinjay of Macaulay's picture. He had great ability and great industry. Though it amused him to pose as a mere fine gentleman, he was in reality a learned antiquary and a shrewd politician; in the history of taste he is remarkable as one of the originators of the Gothic revival; as a writer, apart from his letters, he is important as the author of a series of memoirs which are both intrinsically interesting and of high value as historical material. Personally, he was, of course, affected and foppish in a variety of ways; he had the narrowness and the self-complacency of an aristocrat; but he also had an aristocrat's distinction and reserve; he could be affectionate in spite of his politeness, and towards the end of his life, in his relations with Miss Berry, he showed himself capable of deep feeling. Nevertheless, compare him with the master-spirits of his generation, and it becomes clear at once that he was second-rate. He was as far removed from the humanity of Johnson as from the passion of Burke and the intellectual grasp of Gibbon. His dealings with Chatterton were not particularly discreditable (though he lied heavily in his subsequent account of them); but, in that odd momentary concatenation, beside the mysterious and tragic figure of the 'marvellous boy,' the worldly old creature of Strawberry Hill seems to wither away into limbo.

The mediocrity of the man has sometimes—by Macaulay among others—been actually suggested as the cause of the excellence of his letters. But this will not do. There is no necessary connection between second-rateness and good letter-writing. The correspondences of Voltaire and of Keats—to take two extremely dissimilar examples—show that it is possible to write magnificent letters, and also to be a man of genius. Perhaps the really essential element in the letter writer's make-up is a certain strain of femininity. The unmixed male—the great man of action, the solid statesman—does not express himself happily on those little bits of paper that go by the post. The medium is unsuitable. Nobody ever could have expected to get a good letter from Sir Robert Peel. It is true that the

Duke of Wellington wrote very good letters; but the Duke, who was an exception to all rules, holds a peculiar place in the craft: he reminds one in his letters of a music-hall comedian who has evolved a single inimitable trick, which has become his very own, which is invariably produced, and as invariably goes down. The female element is obvious in Cicero, the father—or should we say the mother?—of the familiar letter. Among English writers, Swift and Carlyle, both of whom were anxious to be masculine, are disappointing correspondents; Swift's letters are too dry (a bad fault), and Carlyle's are too long (an even worse one). Gray and Cowper, on the other hand, in both of whom many of the qualities of the gentler sex are visible, wrote letters which reached perfection; and in the curious composition of Gibbon (whose admirable correspondence is perhaps less read than it deserves) there was decidedly a touch of the she-cat, the naughty old maid. In Walpole himself it is easy to perceive at once the sinuosity and grace of a fine lady, the pettishness of a dowager, the love of trifles of a maiden aunt, and even, at moments, the sensitiveness of a girl.

Another quality is perhaps equally important: the great letter writer must be an egotist. Only those who are extremely interested in themselves possess the overwhelming pertinacity of the born correspondent. No good letter was ever written to convey information, or to please its recipient: it may achieve both those results incidentally; but its fundamental purpose is to express the personality of the writer. This is true of love-letters no less than of others. A desperate egotism burns through the passionate pages of Mademoiselle de Lespinasse; and it is easy to see, in spite of her adoring protestations, that there was *one* person in the world more interesting to Madame de Sévigné than Madame de Grignan. Walpole's letters, with all their variety of appeal, are certainly a case in point. They may be read for many reasons; but the final, the attaching reason is the revelation which they contain of a human being. It is, indeed, a revelation of a curious kind— an uncertain, ambiguous revelation, shifty, deceptive, for ever

197

incomplete. And there the fascination lies. As one reads, the queer man gets hold of one; one reads on—one cannot help it; the long, alembicated sentences, the jauntiness, the elegance, the faint disdain—one grows familiar with it all—and the glitter of the eyes through the mask. But it is impossible to stop: perhaps, just once—who knows?—when no one else is looking, the mask may be lifted; or there may be another, a subtler, change in the turn of the speech. Until at last one comes to feel that one knows that long-vanished vision as well as a living friend—one of those enigmatical friends about whom one is perpetually in doubt as to whether, in spite of everything, one *does* know them at all.

1919.

THE EIGHTEENTH CENTURY

DR. PAGET TOYNBEE[1] is to be congratulated on bringing to a close the monumental edition of Horace Walpole's Letters, the first volume of which appeared, under the editorship of Mrs. Toynbee, in 1903. The enormous and exquisite structure stands before us in all its Palladian beauty, and we can wander through it at our ease, conducted, as we go, by the most patient and accurate of scholars. This final volume is the third of the supplement and the nineteenth of the whole collection. Its contents are miscellaneous—the gleanings of the great correspondence: more than a hundred new letters by Walpole, together with a most interesting selection of those addressed *to* him by every variety of person, from the elder Pitt, at the height of his glory, to James Maclean, the highwayman. Walpole's own letters come from every period of his life. A delightful series to Sir Charles Hanbury Williams shows us the first sprightly runnings of that inimitable manner: one dip, and we are in the very middle of the eighteenth century. 'My Lady Townshend,' we learn, 'has taken a room at Brompton to sleep in the air. After having had it eight days without having been there within six hours of the evening, she set out t'other night with Dorcas, and moveables and household stuff, and unnecessaries enough to have staid there a fortnight. Night-shifts, and drops, and her supper in a silver saucepan, and a large piece of work to do, four books, paper, and two hundred crow quills. When she came there it was quite dark: she felt her way up to her bedchamber, felt she did not like it, and felt her way down again. All this before the woman of

---

[1] *Supplement to the Letters of Horace Walpole.* Edited, with notes and indices, by Paget Toynbee, M.A., D.Litt. Vol. III: 1744-1797. Oxford: Clarendon Press.

the house could get candles. When she came down her coach was gone. . . .'

Then there are some excellent examples of the brilliant middle period: 'The spring desires I would tell your Ladyship that it is waiting for you on this side of Chantilly': no one could mistake the author of that phrase. Finally, the mature virtuosity of Walpole's long old age is admirably represented. His last letter turns out not to be the famous one addressed on January 9, 1797, to Lady Ossory. Three days later the old connoisseur was able to dictate some lines to the Rev. Mark Noble. 'Mr. Roscoe,' he characteristically declared, 'is, I think, by far the best of our historians, both for beauty of style and for deep reflections.' So much for Mr. Gibbon! 'I was sorry, sir, I missed the pleasure of seeing you when you called. . . . I should have been glad to see that coin or medal you mention of Lord Arundel. . . .' And so, as is fitting, with no particular flourish—with the ordinary amenity of a gentleman, the fascinating creature passes from our sight.

Amid so much that is perfect it may seem a little ungracious to make, or rather to repeat, a complaint. But it is the very perfection that raises one's standard and sharpens one's disappointment, when expectations, satisfied so long and so continuously, are suddenly dashed. The editor is still unable to resist meddling with his text. The complete edition is incomplete, after all. Apparently, we should blush too much were we to read the whole of Walpole's letters; those privileges have been reserved to Dr. Toynbee alone. It was impossible not to hope that, after so prolonged a *tête-à-tête* with his author, he would relent at last; perhaps, in this latest volume at any rate—but no! the powers of editorship must be asserted to the bitter end; and the fatal row of asterisks and the fatal note, 'passage omitted' occur, more than once, to exacerbate the reader. Surely it would have been kinder not to reveal the fact that any deletion had been made. Then one could have read on, innocent and undisturbed. As it is, when one's irritation has subsided, one's imagination, one's shocking imagination, begins to work. The question must be asked: do these explicit suppressions really serve the interests of the highest morality? Dr. Toynbee reminds one of the man who . . .[1] But enough; for, after all, it is not the fly but the ointment that claims our attention.

And, indeed, the ointment is rare and rich, of a subtle and delicious perfume. The aroma of a wonderful age comes wafting out from these few hundred pages, and enchants our senses. Why is it that the eighteenth century so particularly delights us? Are we perhaps simply reacting against a reaction? Is the twentieth century so fond of the eighteenth because the nineteenth disliked it so intensely? No doubt that is partly the reason; but the whole truth lies deeper. Every age has a grudge against its predecessor, and generally the grudge is well founded. The Romantics and the Victorians were probably right: thay had good reason to dislike the eighteenth century, which they found to be intolerably rigid, formal, and self-satisfied, devoid, to an extraordinary degree, of sympathy, adventure, and imagination. All this was perfectly true. A world, for instance, in which Voltaire's criticism of Hamlet, or Walpole's of Dante—'a methodist parson in Bedlam'—could be meant seriously and taken seriously would certainly have been a most depressing world to live in. The nineteenth century, very properly, revolted, broke those chains, and then —proceeded to forge others of its own invention. It is these later chains that *we* find distressing. Those of the eighteenth century we cannot consider realistically at all; we were born —owing to the efforts of our grandfathers—free of them; we can afford to look at them romantically; we can even ima-gine ourselves dancing in them—stately minuets. And for the purposes of historical vision, the eighteenth century is exactly what is wanted. What would have been, in fact, its most infuriating quality—its amazing self-sufficiency—is precisely what makes it, in retrospect, so satisfying; there hangs the picture before us, framed and glazed, distinct, simple, complete. We are bewitched by it, just as, about the

[1] Passage omitted.

year 2000, our descendants, no doubt, will cast longing eyes towards the baroque enchantments of the age of Victoria.

But, just now, to consider thus is to consider too curiously. With this book in one's hand, it is impossible to be anything but romantic: facts vanish; the hardest heart collapses before this triumph of superficial charm. There is a divine elegance everywhere, giving a grace to pomposity, a significance to frivolity, and a shape to emptiness. The English language takes on new shifts and guises. One discovers a subtle employment of *shall* and *should* as the future indicative in the formal third person singular—a truly beautiful usage, which must send a delicious shiver down the backbone of every grammarian. Nor is it only in the letters of the grand master, of Walpole himself, that these graces are evident; they are scattered everywhere over the pages of his correspondents. This is how, in those days of leisure and urbanity, a Prime Minister said, 'Thank you for your kind letter':—

The impressions I am under from the honour of your letter are too sensible not to call for expression. As often as I have read it, for ('tis best to confess) I do indulge myself in the frequent repetition, I am at some loss to decide.which sort of pleasure such a letter is made to excite most; that delight which springs from wit, agrément and beauty of style, or the serious and deep-felt satisfaction which the possession of so kind and honourable a Testimony must convey.

It was annoying, doubtless, to be held up by highwaymen in the Park; but there were compensating advantages; one might receive, a few days later, a letter beginning as follows:

Sir, seeing an advertisement in the papers of to Day giveing an account of your being Rob'd by two Highway men on wednesday night last in Hyde Parke and during the time a Pistol being fired whether Intended or Accidentally was Doubtfull Oblidges us to take this Method of assureing you that it was the latter and by no means Design'd Either to hurt or frighten you.

These are unusual occasions; it is in the everyday word, the casual gesture, that one perceives, still more plainly, the form and pressure of the time. The Duchess of Bedford asks Mr. Walpole to buy a bust of Faustina for her at a sale. 'If it is tolerable,' she adds; and nobly makes no mention of a price. And then—'Lord Huntingdon with his Compliments sends Mr. Walpole, according to promise, a little Spanish snuff. Having left off taking any, from finding that it disagreed with him, he hopes Mr. Walpole will be so much his friend as to keep possession of his box.' Could delicate suavity go further? Sometimes the ladies' pens frisk and pirouette in irresponsible fantasy. Lady Lyttelton, in a mad letter, all dashes and exclamations, seems to forestall the style of Tristram Shandy; and Miss Mary Carter—unknown to fame—winds up an epistle full of vague and farcical melancholy, with—'I will not take up more of that precious stuff of which Life is composed but to assure You that I am with great Esteem and Respect yr most Obedt Moll Volatile Evaporated.'

The precious stuff of which Life is composed flowed away gaily, softly, without any fuss whatever. The old letter writer and letter receiver, in his fortunate island, with his pens and paper, his Berrys, his gout and his memories, continued, as the century drew to its end, to survey the world with a dispassionate civility. There were changes, certainly; the French had become 'a worse race than Chictaws and Cherokees'; but it hardly mattered. The young men stopped powdering their hair; even that could be met with a lifted eyebrow. Were there other, even more terrible revolutions brewing? Perhaps; but the Earl of Orford would not heed them. Machinery? Yes, he had indeed noticed it, and observed one day to Hannah More, in his clever fashion, that it might be used for making sugar, so that by its intervention 'the poor negroes' could be saved from working. He passed on to more interesting subjects, his tranquillity unshaken; it remained unshaken to the end. He departed, happily unconscious that the whole system of his existence was doomed to annihilation—elegantly unaware of the implications of the spinning-jenny.

1926.

MARY BERRY

'Amor, che a nullo amato amar perdona': there could be no
better summary of the tragic romance of Madame du Deffand,
Horace Walpole, and Mary Berry. For Love moves in a
mysterious way, and the Paolos and Francescas of this world,
though they may be the most attractive of his victims, are not
the most remarkable. Madame du Deffand was blind and
nearly seventy when, after a long career of brilliant dissipation
and icy cynicism, she was suddenly overwhelmed by a passion
which completely dominated her existence, until she died,
fifteen years later, at the age of eighty-three. Horace Walpole, the object of this extraordinary adoration, was a middle-
aged man of fashion, a dilettante, whose heart, like hers, had
never felt a violent emotion, and, naturally enough, was not
induced to do so by this strange catastrophe. He was flattered,
he was charmed; but he was obsessed by a terror of ridicule;
his enemies—worse still, his friends—would laugh if they
ever got wind of this romantic aberration; and so he mixed
kindness and severity, ruthlessness and attentions, in so fatally
medicinal a potion that the unhappy creature in Paris died at
last less of old age than a broken heart. But 'the whirligig of
Time brings in his revenges.' Walpole himself, when he was
over seventy, suffered the same fate as Madame du Deffand.
The egotism of a lifetime suddenly collapsed before the
fascinations of Mary Berry. It was in vain that the old wit
sought to conceal from himself and the world the nature of
the feelings which had seized upon him. He made game of his
vicissitude; he was in love—ah, yes!—but with both the
charming sisters—with Agnes as well as Mary; they were his
'twin wives,' and might share his coronet between them if
they liked. For a short space, indeed, he was almost entirely

happy. Mary was gentle, intelligent, and appreciative; Agnes, gay and sprightly, made a perfect chaperon. They were his near neighbours at Twickenham, and night after night they would sit with him in his Strawberry Hill drawing-room, while, from his sofa, with an occasional pinch of snuff, he discoursed to them for endless magical hours, pouring out before them his whole treasury of anecdotes and reflections and quips and fancies and memories—old scandals, old frolics, old absurdities, old characters—the darling sixty years' accumulation of the most rapacious gossip who ever lived.

It was during these happy days—the spring-time of his passion—that he wrote down for the sisters his *Reminiscences,* which have now been republished, from the original manuscripts, by the Clarendon Press.[1] The volume, elegantly printed, with elucidations by Mr. Paget Toynbee, two portraits, and some interesting 'Notes of conversations with Lady Suffolk,' now produced for the first time, is as delightful in its form as in its matter—delightful to handle, to look at, to browse over for an evening by the fire. In its polished, delicate pages the English eighteenth century is reflected for us, as in a diminishing mirror—St. James's, Sir Robert, a King or two, Mrs. Howard, old Sarah, Queen Caroline—miraculously small and neat; while Dance's admirable drawing shows us the author, almost, one might imagine, in the act of composition, with his face so full of subtlety, experience, reticence, and sly urbanity.

But the happy days were not to last. Love grows cruel as he grows old; the arrow festers in the flesh; and a pleasant pang becomes a torture. Walpole could not be blinded for ever to the essential impossibility of his situation, and at last he was obliged to plumb his feelings to their depths. A dreadful blow fell when the sisters, accompanied by their father, left England on the grand tour. Their decision to do so had stunned him; their departure plunged him in grief; he was

[1] *Reminiscences, written by Mr. Horace Walpole in 1788, for the amusement of Miss Mary and Miss Agnes Berry.* With Notes and Index by Paget Toynbee. Oxford: Clarendon Press.

very old, and they were to be away for more than a year; would he ever see Mary again? Yet he bore up bravely, and his inimitable letters flowed over Europe in an unceasing stream. The crisis came when, on their return journey, the Berrys arranged to go back through France. It was in 1791, and the country was seething with the ferment of the Revolution. Walpole was terrified, and implored Mary to return by Germany; in vain. Then the old man's self-control utterly gave way. Fear, mortification, anger, and solicitude mastered him by turns; his agitation was boundless; he could talk of nothing but the Berrys, rushing from person to person, pouring out, everywhere, to anybody, the palpitating tale of his terrors and his griefs. London shrugged its shoulders: Lord Orford was ridiculous. The grim ghost of Madame du Deffand must have smiled sardonically at the sight.

It was not merely the incompatibility of age that made his case desperate; there was another more fatal circumstance. Mary Berry herself was passionately in love—with General O'Hara. He was a middle-aged soldier of an old-fashioned type, abounding in Irish energy, with a red and black face and shining teeth; and when, in 1795, he was made Governor of Gibraltar, she became engaged to marry him. The marriage itself was postponed, at her wish. She might have left Walpole in his misery; and even her father, who was helpless without her; but she could not leave her sister, who was in the middle of a difficult love-affair, and was every moment in need of her advice. 'I *think* I am doing right,' she told O'Hara. 'I am *sure* I am consulting the peace and happiness of those about me, and not my own.' The General sailed, and she never saw him again. At first their correspondence was all that was most fitting. The General poured out his gallantries, and Mary indulged in delightful visions of domesticity. She sketched in detail the balance-sheet of their future 'establishment.' Reducing their expenditure to a minimum, she came to the conclusion that £2,263 a year would be enough for them both. Of this sum, £58 would cover 'the wages of four women servants—a housekeeper, a cook under her, a housemaid, and lady's maid'; while 'liveries for the three men servants and the coachman' would cost £80 a year, and wine £100. But Mary's castle was all too truly in Spain. Before the year was out, it had vanished into thin air. She discovered that the 'Old Cock of the Rock,' as his military comrades called him, was keeping a couple of mistresses; expostulations followed, mutual anger, and finally a complete severance. She believed to the end of her life that if they could have met for twenty-four hours every difficulty would have disappeared; but it was not to be. The French War prevented O'Hara from returning to England, and in 1802 he died at his post.

Mary Berry was to live for half a century more, but she never recovered from this disaster. There, for the rest of her life, at the very basis of her existence, lay the iron fact of an irremediable disappointment. Thus her fate was the very reverse of Madame du Deffand's; the emotional tragedy, coming at the beginning of a long life instead of at the end, gave a sombre colour to the whole; and yet, in the structure of their minds, the two were curiously similar. Both were remarkable for reason and good sense, for a certain intellectual probity, for a disillusioned view of things, and for great strength of will. Between these two stern women, the figure of Horace Walpole makes a strange appearance—a creature all vanity, elegance, insinuation, and finesse—by far the most feminine of the three.

He died, leaving the sisters a house at Little Strawberry Hill and the interest on £4,000 for each of them for their lives. By a cruel irony of circumstance, her sister's love-affair, which had led Mary, so fatally, to postpone her marriage, turned out no less unfortunately than her own. Agnes had become engaged to a wealthy young cousin; but, at the last moment, the match had been broken off. The sisters never separated for the whole of their long lives. Agnes was cheerful, but a little vague in the head; she painted. Old Mr. Berry was cheerful, but quite incompetent; he did nothing at all. Mary was intelligent, with enough character for three at the very least; and she did everything that had to be done, with consummate ease. Friends surrounded her. Walpole had launched the family into the highest society, where they had at once become very popular. His cousin, Mrs. Damer, was Mary's intimate and confidante. The Berry sisters—Blackberry and Gooseberry they were nicknamed by the malicious—were seen at every social function, and gradually became a social centre themselves. Among her other gifts Mary possessed a marvellous capacity for the part of hostess. Wherever she went—and she was constantly on the move—in North Audley Street, in Bath, in Paris, in Italy—it always happened that the most fashionable and the cleverest people grouped themselves about her. One winter, in Genoa, she seemed to create a civilisation out of nothing; the little community gave a gasp of horror when she went away. Apparently there was nothing that she could not bring about in her drawing-room: she could even make Frenchmen hold their tongues; she could even make Englishmen talk.

But these were not her only accomplishments. Her masculine mind exercised itself over higher things. She read eagerly and long; she edited Walpole's papers; she studied political economy, appreciating Malthus and Free Trade. In Madame de Staël's opinion she was '*by far* the cleverest woman in England.' She had literary ambitions, and brought out a book on 'Social Life in England and France'; but her style failed to express the force of her mentality, so that her careful sentences are to-day unreadable. Had she been a man, she would not have shone as a writer, but as a political thinker or an administrator; and a man she should have been; with her massive, practical intelligence, she was born too early to be a successful woman. She felt this bitterly. Conscious of high powers, she declaimed against the miserable estate of women, which prevented her from using them. She might have been a towering leader, in thought or action; as it was, she was insignificant. So she said—'insignificant!'—repeating the word over and over again. 'And nobody,' she added, 'ever suffered insignificance more unwillingly than myself,'

Yet it was a mitigated insignificance, after all. In 1817

old Mr. Berry died, and for another thirty years all that was distinguished in England and in France passed through the sisters' room in Curzon Street. As time went on, Mary grew ever grander and more vigorous. With old age, something like happiness seemed to come to her—though it was a happiness without serenity. Agnes chirped blithely by her side. Mrs. Damer had vanished, but her place was taken by Lady Charlotte Lindsay, who remained a faithful follower till her death. We catch a glimpse of the three ladies in Paris in 1834, when they were all in the neighbourhood of seventy. 'The Berrys,' Lady Granville tells us, 'run up and down.' Mary was the leader, prepotent, scolding, loud-voiced, and dressed in a pink sash. Agnes and Lady Charlotte fluttered along behind her. There was some laughter, but there was more admiration: Miss Berry was impossible to resist. Everyone flocked to her evenings, as usual, and even critical Lady Granville was at her feet. She was friendly and true, said the Ambassadress, in spite of her frowns and hootings, and her departure would be regretted very much.

The *salon* in Curzon Street lasted on into the Victorian age, and Thackeray would talk for hours with the friend of Horace Walpole. The lady was indeed a fascinating relic of an abolished world, as she sat, large and formidable, bolt upright, in her black wig, with her rouged cheeks, her commanding features, and her loud conversation, garnished with vigorous oaths. When, in 1852, both sisters died, aged eighty-nine and eighty-eight, the eighteenth century finally vanished from the earth. So much was plain to the *habitués* of Curzon Street; but they had failed to realise the inner nature, the tragic under-tones, of that spirit which had delighted them so wonderfully with its energy and power. It was only when Mary Berry's papers came to be examined that the traces of her secret history appeared. Among them was a description of a dream, dreamt when she was nearly eighty, in which she had found herself walking with Mrs. Damer by a Southern shore, young again, and married to General O'Hara. She was perfectly happy—so happy that she prayed to die 'before this

beautiful vision of life fades, as fade it must from my senses.'
Yet no!—she was about to have a child; she must live to give
him a child, she told Mrs. Damer, and then she might die,
'convinced that I have exhausted everything that can make
life desirable. . . . Here I awoke with my eyes suffused with
tears, to find myself a poor, feeble old soul, never having
possessed either husband or child, and having long survived
that friend whom my waking as well as my sleeping thoughts
always recall to me, as the comfort and support of nearly
thirty years of my sadly insignificant existence.'

1925.

LADY HESTER STANHOPE

THE Pitt nose has a curious history. One can watch its transmigrations through three lives. The tremendous hook of old Lord Chatham, under whose curve Empires came to birth, was succeeded by the bleak upward-pointing nose of William Pitt the younger—the rigid symbol of an indomitable *hauteur*. With Lady Hester Stanhope came the final stage. The nose, still with an upward tilt in it, had lost its masculinity; the hard bones of the uncle and the grandfather had disappeared. Lady Hester's was a nose of wild ambitions, of pride grown fantastical, a nose that scorned the earth, shooting off, one fancies, towards some eternally eccentric heaven. It was a nose, in fact, altogether in the air.

Noses, of course, are aristocratic things; and Lady Hester was the child of a great aristocracy. But, in her case, the aristocratic impulse, which had carried her predecessors to glory, had less fortunate results. There has always been a strong strain of extravagance in the governing families of England; from time to time they throw off some peculiarly ill-balanced member, who performs a strange meteoric course. A century earlier, Lady Mary Wortley Montagu was an illustrious example of this tendency: that splendid comet, after filling half the heavens, vanished suddenly into desolation and darkness. Lady Hester Stanhope's spirit was still more uncommon; and she met with a most uncommon fate.

She was born in 1776, the eldest daughter of that extraordinary Earl Stanhope, Jacobin and inventor, who made the first steamboat and the first calculating machine, who defended the French Revolution in the House of Lords and erased the armorial bearings—'damned aristocratical nonsense'—from his carriages and his plate. Her mother, Chatham's daughter and the favourite sister of Pitt, died when she was four years old. The second Lady Stanhope, a frigid woman of fashion, left her stepdaughters to the care of futile governesses, while 'Citizen Stanhope' ruled the household from his laboratory with the violence of a tyrant. It was not until Lady Hester was twenty-four that she escaped from the slavery of her father's house, by going to live with her grandmother, Lady Chatham. On Lady Chatham's death, three years later, Pitt offered her his protection, and she remained with him until his death in 1806.

Her three years with Pitt, passed in the very centre of splendid power, were brilliant and exciting. She flung herself impetuously into the movement and the passion of that vigorous society; she ruled her uncle's household with high vivacity; she was liked and courted; if not beautiful, she was fascinating—very tall, with a very fair and clear complexion, and dark-blue eyes, and a countenance of wonderful expressiveness. Her talk, full of the trenchant nonchalance of those days, was both amusing and alarming: 'My dear Hester, what are you saying?' Pitt would call out to her from across the room. She was devoted to her uncle, who warmly returned her affection. She was devoted, too—but in a more dangerous fashion—to the intoxicating Antinous, Lord Granville Leveson Gower. The reckless manner in which she carried on this love-affair was the first indication of something overstrained, something wild and unaccountable, in her temperament. Lord Granville, after flirting with her outrageously, declared that he could never marry her, and went off on an embassy to St. Petersburg. Her distraction was extreme: she hinted that she would follow him to Russia; she threatened, and perhaps attempted, suicide; she went about telling everybody that he had jilted her. She was taken ill, and then there were rumours of an accouchement, which, it was said, she took care to *afficher*, by appearing without rouge and fainting on the slightest provocation. In the midst of these excursions and alarums there was a terrible and unexpected catastrophe. Pitt died. And Lady Hester suddenly found herself a dethroned princess, living in a small house in Montague Square on a pension of £1200 a year.

She did not abandon society, however, and the tongue of gossip continued to wag. Her immediate marriage with a former lover, Mr. Hill, was announced: 'il est bien bon,' said Lady Bessborough. Then it was whispered that Canning was 'le régnant'—that he was with her 'not only all day, but almost all night.' She quarrelled with Canning and became attached to Sir John Moore. Whether she was actually engaged to marry him—as she seems to have asserted many years later—is doubtful; his letters to her, full as they are of respectful tenderness, hardly warrant the conclusion; but it is certain that he died with her name on his lips. Her favourite brother, Charles, was killed beside him; and it was natural that under this double blow she should have retired from London. She buried herself in Wales; but not for long. In 1810 she set sail for Gibraltar with her brother James, who was rejoining his regiment in the Peninsula. She never returned to England.

There can be no doubt that at the time of her departure the thought of a lifelong exile was far from her mind. It was only gradually, as she moved further and further eastward, that the prospect of life in England—at last even in Europe—grew distasteful to her; as late as 1816 she was talking of a visit to Provence. Accompanied by two or three English fellow travellers, her English maid, Mrs. Fry, her private physician, Dr. Meryon, and a host of servants, she progressed, slowly and in great state, through Malta and Athens, to Constantinople. She was conveyed in battleships, and lodged with governors and ambassadors. After spending many months in Constantinople, Lady Hester discovered that she was 'dying to see Napoleon with her own eyes,' and attempted accordingly to obtain passports to France. The project was stopped by Stratford Canning, the English Minister, upon which she decided to visit Egypt, and, chartering a Greek vessel, sailed for Alexandria in the winter of 1811. Off the island of Rhodes a violent storm sprang up; the whole party were forced to abandon the ship, and to take refuge upon a bare rock, where they remained without food or shelter for thirty hours. Eventually, after many severe privations, Alexandria was reached in safety; but this disastrous voyage was a turning-point in Lady Hester's career. At Rhodes she was forced to exchange her torn and dripping raiment for the attire of a Turkish gentleman—a dress which she never afterwards abandoned. It was the first step in her orientalisation.

She passed the next two years in a triumphal progress. Her appearance in Cairo caused the greatest sensation, and she was received in state by the Pasha, Mehemet Ali. Her costume on this occasion was gorgeous: she wore a turban of cashmere, a brocaded waistcoat, a priceless pelisse, and a vast pair of purple velvet pantaloons embroidered all over in gold. She was ushered by chamberlains with silver wands through the inner courts of the palace to a pavilion in the harem, where the Pasha, rising to receive her, conversed with her for an hour. From Cairo she turned northwards, visiting Jaffa, Jerusalem, Acre, and Damascus. Her travelling dress was of scarlet cloth trimmed with gold, and, when on horseback, she wore over the whole a white-hooded and tasselled burnous. Her maid, too, was forced, protesting, into trousers, though she absolutely refused to ride astride. Poor Mrs. Fry had gone through various and dreadful sufferings—shipwreck and starvation, rats and black-beetles unspeakable—but she retained her equanimity. Whatever her Ladyship might think fit to be, *she* was an Englishwoman to the last, and Philippaki was Philip Parker and Mustapha Mr. Farr.

Outside Damascus, Lady Hester was warned that the town was the most fanatical in Turkey, and that the scandal of a woman entering it in man's clothes, unveiled, would be so great as to be dangerous. She was begged to veil herself, and to make her entry under cover of darkness. 'I must take the bull by the horns,' she replied, and rode into the city unveiled at midday. The population were thunder-struck; but at last their amazement gave way to enthusiasm, and the incredible lady was hailed everywhere as Queen, crowds followed her, coffee was poured out before her, and the whole bazaar rose as she passed. Yet she was not satisfied with her triumphs; she would do something still more glorious and astonishing; she would plunge into the desert and visit the ruins of Palmyra, which only half-a-dozen of the boldest travellers had ever seen. The Pasha of Damascus offered her military escort, but she preferred to throw herself upon the hospitality of the Bedouin Arabs, who, overcome by her horsemanship, her powers of sight, and her courage, enrolled her a member of their tribe. After a week's journey in their company, she reached Palmyra, where the inhabitants met her with wild enthusiasm, and under the Corinthian columns of Zenobia's temple crowned her head with flowers. This happened in March 1813; it was the apogee of Lady Hester's life. Henceforward her fortunes gradually but steadily declined.

The rumour of her exploits had spread through Syria, and from the year 1813 onwards, her reputation was enormous. She was received everywhere as a royal, almost as a supernatural, personage: she progressed from town to town amid official prostrations and popular rejoicings. But she herself was in a state of hesitation and discontent. Her future was uncertain; she had grown scornful of the West—must she return to it? The East alone was sympathetic, the East alone was tolerable—but could she cut herself off for ever from the past? At Laodicea she was suddenly struck down by the plague, and, after months of illness, it was borne in upon her that all was vanity. She rented an empty monastery on the slopes of Mount Lebanon, not far from Sayda (the ancient Sidon), and took up her abode there. Then her mind took a new surprising turn; she dashed to Ascalon, and, with the permission of the Sultan, began excavations in a ruined temple with the object of discovering a hidden treasure of three million pieces of gold. Having unearthed nothing but an antique statue, which, in order to prove her disinterestedness, she ordered her appalled doctor to break into little bits, she returned to her monastery. Finally, in 1816, she moved to another house, further up Mount Lebanon, and near the village of Djoun; and at Djoun she remained until her death, more than twenty years later.

Thus, almost accidentally as it seems, she came to the end of her wanderings, and the last, long, strange, mythical period of her existence began. Certainly the situation that she had chosen was sublime. Her house, on the top of a high bare hill among great mountains, was a one-storeyed group of buildings, with many ramifying courts and outhouses, and a garden of several acres surrounded by a rampart wall. The garden, which she herself had planted and tended with the utmost care, commanded a glorious prospect. On every side but one the vast mountains towered, but to the west there was an opening, through which, in the far distance, the deep blue Mediterranean was revealed. From this romantic hermitage, her singular renown spread over the world. European travellers who had been admitted to her presence brought back stories full of Eastern mystery; they told of a peculiar grandeur, a marvellous prestige, an imperial power. The precise nature of Lady Hester's empire was, indeed, dubious; she was in fact merely the tenant of her Djoun establishment, for which she paid a rent of £20 a year. But her dominion was not subject to such limitations. She ruled imaginatively, transcendentally; the solid glory of Chatham had been transmuted into the fantasy of an Arabian Night. No doubt she herself believed that she was something more than a chimerical Empress. When a French traveller was murdered in the desert, she issued orders for the punishment of the offenders; punished they were, and Lady Hester actually received the solemn thanks of the French Chamber. It seems probable, however, that it was the Sultan's orders rather than Lady Hester's which produced the desired effect. In her feud with her terrible neighbour, the Emir Beshyr, she maintained an undaunted front. She kept the tyrant at bay; but perhaps the Emir, who, so far as physical force was concerned, held her in the hollow of his hand, might have proceeded to extremities if he had not received a severe admonishment from Stratford Canning at Constantinople. What is certain is that the ignorant and superstitious populations around her feared and loved her, and that she, reacting to her own mysterious prestige, became at last even as they. She plunged into astrology and divination; she awaited the moment when, in accordance with prophecy, she should enter Jerusalem side by side with the Mahdi, the Messiah; she kept two sacred horses, destined, by sure signs, to carry her and him to their last triumph. The Orient had mastered her utterly. She was no longer an Englishwoman, she declared; she loathed England; she would never go there again; and if she went anywhere, it would be to Arabia, to 'her own people.'

Her expenses were immense—not only for herself but for others, for she poured out her hospitality with a noble hand. She ran into debt, and was swindled by the moneylenders; her steward cheated her, her servants pilfered her; her distress was at last acute. She fell into fits of terrible depression, bursting into dreadful tears and savage cries. Her habits grew more and more eccentric. She lay in bed all day, and sat up all night, talking unceasingly for hour upon hour to Dr. Meryon, who alone of her English attendants remained with her, Mrs. Fry having withdrawn to more congenial scenes long since. The doctor was a poor-spirited and muddle-headed man, but he was a good listener; and there he sat while that extraordinary talk flowed on—talk that scaled the heavens and ransacked the earth, talk in which memories of an abolished past—stories of Mr. Pitt and of George III, vituperations against Mr. Canning, mimicries of the Duchess of Devonshire—mingled phantasmagorically with doctrines of Fate and planetary influence, and speculations on the Arabian origin of the Scottish clans, and lamentations over the wickedness of servants; till the unaccountable figure, with its robes and its long pipe, loomed through the tobacco-smoke like some vision of a Sibyl in a dream. She might be robbed and ruined, her house might crumble over her head; but she talked on. She grew ill and desperate; yet still she talked. Did she feel that the time was coming when she should talk no more?

Her melancholy deepened into a settled gloom when the news came of her brother James's death. She had quarrelled with all her English friends, except Lord Hardwicke—with her eldest brother, with her sister, whose kind letters she left unanswered; she was at daggers drawn with the English consul at Alexandria, who worried her about her debts. Ill and harassed, she hardly moved from her bedroom, while her servants rifled her belongings and reduced the house to a condition of indescribable disorder and filth. Three dozen hungry cats ranged through the rooms, filling the courts with frightful noises. Dr. Meryon, in the midst of it all, knew not whether to cry or laugh. At moments the great lady regained her ancient fire; her bells pealed tumultuously for hours together; or she leapt up, and arraigned the whole trembling household before her, with her Arab war-mace in her hand. Her finances grew more and more involved—grew at length irremediable. It was in vain that the faithful Lord Hardwicke pressed her to return to England to settle her affairs. Return to England, indeed! To England, that ungrateful, miserable country, where, so far as she could see, they had forgotten the very name of Mr. Pitt! The final blow fell when a letter came from the English authorities threatening to cut off her pension for the payment of her debts. Upon that, after despatching a series of furious missives to Lord Palmerston, to Queen Victoria, to the Duke of Wellington, she renounced the world. She commanded Dr. Meryon to return to Europe, and he—how could he have done it?—obeyed her. Her health was broken, she was over sixty, and, save for her vile servants, absolutely alone. She lived for nearly a year after he left her—we know no more. She had vowed never again to pass through the gate of her house; but did she sometimes totter to her garden—that beautiful garden which she had created, with its roses and its fountains, its alleys and its bowers—and look westward at the sea? The end came in June 1839. Her servants immediately possessed themselves of every movable object in the house. But Lady Hester cared no longer: she was lying back in her bed—inexplicable, grand, preposterous, with her nose in the air.

1919.

MADAME DE LIEVEN

ARISTOCRATS (no doubt) still exist; but they are shorn beings, for whom the wind is not tempered—powerless, out of place, and slightly ridiculous. For about a hundred years it has been so. The stages in the history of nobility may be reckoned by the different barricades it has put up to keep off the common multitude. The feudal lord used armour to separate him from the rest of the world; then, as civilisation grew, it was found that a wig did almost as well; and there was a curious transition period (*temp*. Marlborough) when armour and wigs were worn at the same time. After that, armour vanished, and wigs were left, to rule splendidly through the eighteenth century, until the French Revolution. A fearful moment! Wigs went. Nevertheless the citadel still held out, for another barrier remained—the barrier of manners; and for a generation it was just possible to be an aristocrat on manners alone. Then, at last, about 1830, manners themselves crumbled, undermined by the insidious permeation of a new—a middle-class—behaviour; and all was over. Madame de Lieven was one of the supreme examples of the final period. Her manners were of the genuinely terrific kind. Surrounded by them, isolated as with an antiseptic spray, she swept on triumphantly, to survive untouched—so it seemed—amid an atmosphere alive with the microbes of bourgeois disintegration. So it seemed—for in fact something strange eventually happened. In her case, aristocracy, like some viscous fluid flowing along, when it came to the precipice did not plunge over the edge, but—such was its strength, its inherent force of concentration —moved, as it had always moved, straight onward, until it stuck out, an amazing semi-solid projection, over the abyss. Only at long last was there a melting; the laws of nature asserted themselves; and the inevitable, the deplorable, collapse ensued.

Born in 1785, a Russian and a Benckendorf, Madame de Lieven was by blood more than half German, for her mother had come from Würtemberg and her father's family was of Prussian origin. From the first moment of her existence she was in the highest sphere. Her mother had been the favourite companion of the Empress Marie, wife of Paul I, and on her death the Empress had adopted the young Benckendorfs and brought them up under her own care. At the age of fifteen, Dorothea was taken from a convent and married to the young Count de Lieven (or, more correctly, Count Lieven without the 'particule'; but it would be pedantry to insist upon an accuracy unknown to contemporaries) whose family was no less closely connected with the Imperial house. His mother had been the governess of the Emperor Paul's children; when her task was over, she had retained the highest favour; and her son, at the age of twenty-eight, was aide-de-camp to the Emperor and Secretary for War. Paul I was murdered; but under the new Czar the family fortunes continued to prosper —the only change being the transference of the Count de Lieven from the army to the diplomatic service. In 1809 he was appointed Russian ambassador at Berlin; and in 1812 he was moved to London, where he and his wife were to remain for the next twenty-two years.

The great world in those days was small—particularly the English one, which had been kept in a vacuum for years by the Napoleonic War. In 1812 a foreign embassy was a surprising novelty in London, and the arrival of the Lievens produced an excitement which turned to rapture when it was discovered that the ambassadress was endowed with social talents of the highest order. She immediately became the fashion—and remained so for the rest of her life. That she possessed neither beauty nor intellect was probably a positive advantage; she was attractive and clever—that was enough. Her long gawky figure and her too pronounced features were somehow fascinating, and her accomplishments were exactly suited to her *milieu*; while she hated reading, never opening a book except Madame de Sévigné's letters, she could be very entertaining in four languages, and, if asked, could play on the pianoforte extremely well. Whenever she appeared, life was enhanced and intensified. She became the intimate friend of several great hostesses—Lady Holland, Lady Cowper, Lady Granville; she was successfully adored by several men of fashion—Lord Willoughby, Lord Gower, and (for a short time—so it was whispered) the Prince Regent himself. She was made a patroness of Almack's—the only foreign lady to receive the distinction. Exclusive, vigorous, tart, she went on her way rejoicing—and then there was a fresh development. The war over, the era of conferences opened. In 1818, at Aix-la-Chapelle, where all the ministers and diplomats of Europe were gathered together, she met Metternich, then at the beginning of his long career as the virtual ruler of Austria, and a new and serious love-affair immediately began. It lasted during the four years that elapsed between the Congress of Aix-la-Chapelle and that of Verona; and in Metternich's love-letters—extremely long and extremely metaphysical— the earlier stages of it may still be traced. The affair ended as suddenly as it had started. But this close relationship with the dominating figure in European politics had a profound effect on Madame de Lieven's life.

Henceforward, high diplomacy was to be her passion. She was nearly forty; it was time to be ambitious, to live by the head rather than the heart, to explore the mysteries of chanceries, to pull the strings of cabinets, to determine the fate of nations; she set to work with a will. Besides her native wits, she had two great assets—her position in English society, and the fact that her husband was a nonentity—she found that she could simply step into his place. Her first triumph came when the Czar Alexander entrusted her personally with an overture to Canning on the thorny question of Greece. Alexander's death and the accession of Nicholas was all to the good: her husband's mother received a princedom, and she herself in consequence became a Princess. At the same time Russia,

abandoning the traditions of the Holy Alliance, drew nearer
to England and the liberal policy of Canning. Madame de
Lieven became the presiding genius of the new orientation;
it was possibly owing to her influence with George IV that
Canning obtained the Premiership; and it was certainly owing
to her efforts that the Treaty of London was signed in 1827,
by which the independence of Greece became an accomplished fact. After Canning's death, she formed a new connection—with Lord Grey. The great Whig Earl became one
of the most ardent of her admirers. Sitting up in bed every
morning, he made it his first task to compose an elaborate
epistle to his Egeria, which, when it was completed, he carefully perfumed with musk. The precise nature of their relationship has never transpired. The tone of their correspondence seems to indicate a purely platonic attachment; but
tones are deceitful, and Lord Grey was a man of many gallantries; however, he was sixty-eight. It is also doubtful who
benefited most by the connection: possibly the lady's influence
was less than she supposed. At any rate it is certain that when,
on one occasion, she threatened a withdrawal of her favours
unless the Prime Minister adopted a particular course, she
was met with a regretful, an infinitely regretful, refusal; upon
which she tactfully collapsed. But, on another occasion, it
seems possible that her advice produced an important consequence. When Lord Grey took office, who was to be Foreign
Minister? Lady Cowper was Madame de Lieven's great friend,
and Palmerston was Lady Cowper's lover. At their request,
Madame de Lieven pressed the claims of Palmerston upon the
Premier, and Palmerston was appointed. If this was indeed the
result of her solicitations, the triumphant Princess was to find
before long that she had got more than she had bargained for.

In the meantime, all went swimmingly. There was always
some intriguing concoction on the European table—a revolution in Portugal—the affairs of Belgium to be settled—a
sovereign to be found for Greece—and Madame de Lieven's
finger was invariably in the pie. So we see her, in the Memoirs
and Letters of the time, gliding along in brilliant activity,

a radiating focus of enjoyment, except—ah! it was her one
horror!—when she found herself with a bore. If it was her
highest felicity to extract, in an excited *tête-à-tête*, the latest
piece of diplomatic gossip from a Cabinet Minister, her deepest
agony was to be forced to mark time with undistinguished
underlings, or—worst of all!—some literary person. On
such occasions she could not conceal her despair—indeed she
hardly wished to—even from the most eminent—even from
the great Chateaubriand himself. 'Quand elle se trouve avec
des gens de mérite,' he acidly noted, 'sa stérilité se tait; elle
revêt sa nullité d'un air supérieur d'ennui, comme si elle avait
le droit d'être ennuyée.' She only admitted one exception: for
royal personages very great allowances might be made. A
royal bore, indeed, was almost a contradiction in terms; such
a flavour of mysterious suavity hovered for ever round those
enchanted beings. She was always at her best with them, and
for her own particular royalties—for the Czar and the whole
imperial family—no considerations, no exertions, no adula-
tions could be too great. She corresponded personally with her
imperial master upon every twist and turn of the international
situation, and yet there were tedious wretches . . . she would
not bear it, she would be ruthless, they should be *écrasés*—
and she lifted her black eyebrows till they almost vanished and
drew herself up to her thinnest height. She looked like some
strange animal—what was it? Somebody said that Madame
Appony, another slender, tall ambassadress, was like a giraffe,
and that she and Madame de Lieven were of the same species.
'Mais non!' said Madame Alfred de Noailles, 'ce n'est pas la
même classe: l'une mangera l'autre et n'aura qu'un mauvais
repas'—'One sees Lieven,' was Lady Granville's comment,
'crunching the meek Appony's bones.' Everyone was a little
afraid of her—everyone, that is to say, except Lady Holland;
for 'Old Madagascar' knew no fear. One day, at a party,
having upset her work-basket, she calmly turned to the ambassadress with, 'Pick it up, my dear, pick it up!' And Madame
de Lieven went down on her knees and obeyed. 'Such a sight
was never seen before,' said Lady Granville.

Lady Holland—yes; but there was also somebody else; there was Palmerston. Madame de Lieven, having (so she was convinced) got him his appointment as Foreign Secretary, believed that she could manage him; he was, she declared, 'un très-petit esprit'; the mistake was gross, and it was fatal. In 1834, Palmerston appointed Stratford Canning ambassador to Russia; but the Emperor disliked him, and let it be known, through Madame de Lieven, that he was unwilling to receive him. Palmerston, however, persisted in his choice, in spite of all the arguments of the ambassadress, who lost her temper, appealed to Lord Grey—in vain, and then—also in vain—tried to get up an agitation in the Cabinet. Finally, she advised the Czar to stand firm, for Palmerston, she said, would give way when it came to the point. Accordingly, it was officially stated that Stratford Canning would not be received in Russia. The result, however, was far from Madame de Lieven's expectations. Palmerston had had enough of female interferences, and he decided to take this opportunity of putting an end to them altogether. He appointed no ambassador, and for months the English business in St. Petersburg was transacted by a *chargé d'affaires*. Then there happened precisely what the wily minister had foreseen. The Emperor could support the indignity no longer; he determined to retort in kind; and he recalled the Lievens.

So ended the official life of the Princess. The blow was severe—the pain of parting was terrible—but, as it turned out, this was only the beginning of misfortune. In the following year, her two youngest sons died of scarlet fever; her own health was broken; stricken down by grief and illness, she gave up the Court appointment with which her services had been rewarded, and went to live in Paris. Suddenly she received a peremptory order of recall. Nicholas, with autocratic caprice, had flown into a fury; the Princess must return! Her husband, seeing that a chance of self-assertion had at last come to him, fell in with the Emperor's wishes. A third son died; and the Prince was forbidden to communicate the fact to his wife; she only learnt it, months later, when one of her letters to her son was returned to her, with the word 'mort' on the envelope. After that, there was a hectic correspondence, the Prince at one moment actually threatening to cut off his wife's supplies if she remained in Paris. She would not budge, however, and eventually the storm blew over; but the whole system of Madame de Lieven's existence had received a terrible shock. 'Quel pays!' she exclaimed in her anguish. 'Quel maître! Quel père!'

The instinct which had kept her in Paris was a sound one; for there, in that friendly soil, she was able to strike fresh roots and to create for herself an establishment that was almost a home. Her irrepressible social activities once more triumphed. Installed in Talleyrand's old house at the corner of the Rue de Rivoli and the Rue St. Florentin, with an outlook over the Place de la Concorde, she held her nightly *salon*, and, for another twenty years, revived the glories of her London reign. Though no longer in any official situation, she was still perpetually occupied with the highest politics, was still the terror of embassies, still the delight of the worldly and the great. Still, in her pitiless exclusiveness, she would *écraser* from time to time some wretched creature from another sphere. 'Monsieur, je ne vous connais pas,' she said in icy tones to a gentleman who presented himself one evening in her *salon*. He reminded her of how often they had met at Ems, in the summer—had taken the waters together—surely she must remember him. 'Non, Monsieur,' was the adamantine reply, and the poor man slunk away, having learnt the lesson that friendship at Ems and friendship in Paris are two very different things.

Such was the appearance; but in fact something strange had happened: Madame de Lieven's aristocracy was trembling over the abyss. The crash came on June 24, 1837—the date is significant: it was four days after the accession of Queen Victoria—when, worn out by domestic grief, disillusioned, embittered, unable to resist any longer the permeations of the Time Spirit, the Princess fell into the arms of Monsieur Guizot. Fate had achieved an almost exaggerated irony. For

Guizot was the living epitome of all that was most middle-class. Infinitely respectable, a Protestant, the father of a family, having buried two wives, a learned historian, he had just given up the portfolio of public instruction, and was clearly destined to be the leading spirit of the bourgeois monarchy of Louis-Philippe. He was fifty years old. His first wife had been a child of the *ancien régime*, but he had tamed her, turned her thoughts towards duty and domesticity, induced her to write improving stories for the young, until at last, suddenly feeling that she could bear it no longer, she had taken refuge in death while he was reading aloud to her a sermon by Bossuet on the immortality of the soul. His second wife—the niece of the first—had needed no such pressure; naturally all that could be wished, she wrote several volumes of improving stories for the young quite of her own accord, while reflections upon the beneficence of the Creator flowed from her at the slightest provocation; but she too had died; his eldest son had died; and the bereaved Guizot was left alone with his high-mindedness. Madame de Lieven was fifty-two. It seemed an incredible love-affair—so much so that Charles Greville, who had known her intimately all his life, refused to believe that it was anything but a 'social and political' *liaison*. But the wits of Paris thought otherwise. It was noticed that Guizot was always to be found in the house in the Rue St. Florentin. The malicious Mérimée told the story of how, after a party at the Princess's, he had been the last to leave—except Guizot; how, having forgotten something, he had returned to the drawing-room, and found that the Minister had already taken off the ribbon (the 'grand cordon') of the Legion of Honour. A chuckle—a chuckle from beyond the tomb—reached the world from Chateaubriand. 'Le ridicule attendait à Paris Madame de Lieven. Un doctrinaire grave est tombé aux pieds d'Omphale: "Amour, tu perdis Troie." ' And the wits of Paris were right. The *liaison*, certainly, was strengthened by political and social interests, but its basis was sentimental passion. The testimony of a long series of letters puts that beyond a doubt. In this peculiar correspondence, pedantry, adoration, platitudes, and suburban *minauderies* form a compound for which one hardly knows whether smiles or tears are the appropriate reaction. When Guizot begins a love-letter with—'Le Cardinal de Retz dit quelque part,' one can only be delighted, but when Madame de Lieven exclaims, 'Ah! que j'aurais besoin d'être gouvernée! Pourquoi ne me gouvernez-vous pas?' one is positively embarrassed. One feels that one is committing an unpardonable—a deliciously unpardonable—indiscretion, as one overhears the cooings of these antiquated doves. 'Si vous pouviez voir,' he says, with exquisite originality, 'tout ce qu'il y a dans mon cœur, si profond, si fort, si éternel, si tendre, si triste.' And she answers, 'Maintenant, je voudrais la tranquillité, la paix du cottage, votre amour, le mien, rien que cela. Ah! mon ami, c'est là le vrai bonheur,' La paix du cottage! Can this be really and truly Madame de Lieven?

Yet there was a point at which she did draw the line. After the death of the Prince in 1839, it was inevitable that there should be a suggestion of marriage. But it faded away. They were never united by any other vows than those which they had sworn to each other in the sight of heaven. It was rumoured that the difficulty was simply one of nomenclature. Guizot (one would expect it) judged that he would be humiliated if his wife's name were not his own; and the Princess, though wishing to be governed, recoiled at that. 'Ma chère, on dit que vous allez épouser Guizot,' said a friend. 'Est-ce vrai?' 'Oh! ma chère,' was the reply, 'me voyez-vous annoncée Madame Guizot!' Was this the last resistance of the aristocrat? Or was it perhaps, in reality, the final proof that Madame de Lieven was an aristocrat no longer?

The idyll only ended with death—though there were a few interruptions. In 1848, revolution forced the lovers to fly to England; it also precipitated the aged Metternich, with a new young wife, upon these hospitable shores. The quartet spent a fortnight together at Brighton; until their discreet conversations were ended for ever by the restoration of order; and the *salon* in the Rue St. Florentin was opened again. But a new dispensation was beginning, in which there was no place for the old minister of Louis-Philippe. Guizot stood aside; and, though Madame de Lieven continued to wield an influence under the Second Empire, it was a gradually declining one. The Crimean War came as a shattering blow. She had made it up with the Czar; their correspondence was once more in full swing; this was known, and, when war came, she was forced to leave Paris for Brussels. Her misery was complete, but it only lasted for eighteen months. She crept back on the plea of health, and Napoleon, leniently winking at her presence, allowed her to remain—allowed her at last to re-open, very gingerly, her *salon*. But everything now was disappearing, disintegrating, shimmering away. She was in her seventy-second year; she was ill and utterly exhausted; she was dying. Guizot, a veteran too, was perpetually at her bedside; she begged him at last to leave her—to go into the next room for a little. He obeyed, and she was dead when he returned to her. She had left a note for him, scribbled in pencil—'Je vous remercie des vingt années d'affection et de bonheur. Ne m'oubliez pas. Adieu, Adieu.' At the last moment, with those simple and touching words, the old grandeur—the original essence that was Dorothea Benckendorf—had come into its own again.

1931.

AN ADOLESCENT

THERE is a story in Hogg's *Life of Shelley* of how the poet went on one occasion to a large dinner-party at Norfolk House. He sat near the bottom of the table, and after a time his neighbour said to him: 'Pray, who is that very strange old man at the top of the table, sitting next to His Grace, who talks so much, so loudly, and in so extraordinary a manner, and all about himself?' 'He is my father,' Shelley replied; 'and he is a very strange old man indeed!' Our knowledge of Timothy Shelley has been hitherto mainly based upon Hogg's portrait of him—the portrait certainly of a 'very strange old man'—eccentric, capricious, puzzled, blustering, 'scolding, crying, swearing, and then weeping again,' then bringing out the old port, and assuring everybody at great length that he was highly respected in the House of Commons—'and by the Speaker in particular, who told him they could not get on without him'—and then turning in a breath from some rambling anecdote of poachers in Sussex to a proof of the existence of the Deity, extracted from 'Palley's Evidences,' ('My father always will call him Palley,' the poet complained; 'why does he call him so?' 'I do not know, unless it be to rhyme to Sally,' was Hogg's only suggestion.) And Hogg produces specimens of 'the epistles of the beloved Timothy,' which, as he says, are 'very peculiar letters'—'exactly like letters that had been cut in two, and the pieces afterwards joined at hazard; cross readings, as it were, cross questions and crooked answers.' Such is Hogg's portrait. But Hogg was not always accurate; he was capable of rearranging facts for his own purposes; he was even capable of rewriting letters which he alleged he was quoting from the originals. It seemed, therefore, difficult to accept his presentment of 'the poor old governor' as literally true; the letters especially looked as if they had been delicately manipulated—even an irate and port-bibbing country gentleman of the time of the Regency could hardly be supposed in sober earnest to have been the author of quite so much incoherence and of quite so little grammar. One guessed that Hogg, with his unscrupulous pen, had been touching things up. But now Mr. Ingpen has discovered and published [1] a collection of documents which gives us a great deal of firsthand information upon Sir Timothy and his relations with his son. These documents, drawn principally from the correspondence of the Shelleys' family lawyer, William Whitton, are full of interest; they are concerned with many important incidents in Shelley's career, and they substantiate—in a remarkable way—Hogg's account of Sir Timothy. It becomes clear, in the light of these new and unimpeachable manuscripts, that Hogg's portrait was by no means a fancy one, that 'the epistles of the beloved Timothy' were in truth 'very peculiar'—illiterate, confused, and hysterical to an extraordinary degree, and that his conduct was of a piece with his correspondence—a singular mixture of futility and queerness. Indeed, if in all the other elements of his character Shelley was the very antithesis of his father, there can be no doubt at all where his eccentricity came from.

Of course, Sir Timothy is only interesting from the accident of his fatherhood. It is one of Fate's little ironies that the poor old governor, who in the natural course of things would have dropped long since into a deserved and decent oblivion, should still be read about and thought about—that even his notes to his lawyer should be carefully unearthed, elaborately annotated, and published in a large book—for the sake of a boy whom he disliked and disapproved of, whom he did his best to injure while living, and whose very memory he tried hard to suppress. He is immortal, as the French say, *malgré lui*—an unwilling ghost caught up into an everlasting glory. And as to Shelley himself, it may be hoped that Mr.

[1] *Shelley in England.* New Facts and Letters from the Shelley-Whitton Papers. By Roger Ingpen. Kegan Paul.

Ingpen's book will lead the way to a clearer vision of a creature who, for all his fame, still stands in need of a little understanding. It is a misfortune that the critics and biographers of poets should be for the most part highly respectable old gentlemen; for poets themselves are apt to be young, and are not apt to be highly respectable. Sometimes the respectable old gentlemen are frankly put out; but sometimes they try to be sympathetic—with results at least equally unfortunate. In Shelley's case it is difficult to decide whether the distressed self-righteousness of Matthew Arnold's famous essay or the solemn adoration of Professor Dowden's standard biography gives the falser impression. Certainly the sympathetic treatment is the more insidious. The bias of Matthew Arnold's attack is obvious; but the process by which, through two fat volumes, Shelley's fire and air have been transmuted into Professor Dowden's cotton-wool and rose-water is a subtler revenge of the world's upon the most radiant of its enemies.

Mr. Ingpen's book deals chiefly with that part of Shelley's life which elapsed between his expulsion from Oxford and his separation from his first wife. It is the most controversial period of Shelley's career—the period particularly selected by Matthew Arnold for his high-toned fleerings and by Professor Dowden for his most ponderous palliations. It is the period of the elopement with Harriet Westbrook, of the sudden flittings and ceaseless wanderings to and fro between Edinburgh, York, Keswick, Wales, Ireland, Devonshire, and London, of the wild Dublin escapade, of the passionate correspondence and furious quarrel with Miss Hitchener, of the composition of *Queen Mab*, and of the elopement with Mary Godwin. The great merit of Mr. Ingpen's new letters is that they show us the Shelley of these three years, neither as the Divine Poet nor as the Outcast from Society, but in the painful and prosaic posture of a son who is on bad terms with his father and wants to get money out of him. Now there is one fact which must immediately strike every reader of this correspondence, and which really affords the clue to the whole queer history: Shelley's extraordinary youthfulness. And it is just this fact which writers on Shelley seem persistently to ignore. It is almost impossible to remember, as one watches their long faces, that the object of all their concern was a youth scarcely out of his teens; that Shelley was eighteen when he was expelled from Oxford, that he was just nineteen when he eloped with Harriet, who was herself sixteen, that he was under twenty-two when he eloped with Mary, while Mary was not seventeen. In reality, Shelley during these years was an adolescent, and an adolescent in whom the ordinary symptoms of that time of life were present in a peculiarly intense form. His restlessness, his crudity of thought and feeling, his violent fluctuations of sentiment, his enthusiasms and exaggerations, his inability to judge correctly either the mental processes of other people or the causal laws which govern the actual world —all these are the familiar phenomena of adolescence; in Shelley's case they happened to be combined with a high intelligence, a determined will, and a wonderful unworldliness; but, none the less, the adolescence was there.

That was the fundamental fact which his father, like his commentators, failed to realise. He persisted in treating Shelley's behaviour seriously. The leaflet for which Shelley was sent down from Oxford, *The Necessity of Atheism*, signed 'Jeremiah Stukeley,' and circulated to all the Bishops and Heads of Houses, was obviously little more than a schoolboy's prank; but Atheism happened at that moment to be the bugbear of the governing classes, and Sir Timothy lost his head. Instead of attempting to win over the youth by kindness, instead of sending his mother to him to bring him home, the old man adopted the almost incredible course of refusing to have any communication with his son, save through the family lawyer. And the lawyer, Whitton, was the last man who should have been entrusted with such a task. His letters show him to have been a formal and testy personage, with the disposition, and sometimes the expressions, of a butler. 'You care not, you say,' he wrote to Shelley, 'for Family Pride. Allow me to tell you that the first part of the Family Pride of a Gent is to preserve a propriety of manners and a decency of expression in communication, and your forgetfulness of those qualifications towards me in the letter I have just received induces me to say,' etc. 'The Gent,' Whitton told Sir Timothy, 'is very angry, and has thought proper to lecture me on the occasion.' 'The occasion' was Shelley's innocent suggestion that he should be allowed to resign his inheritance to the family property (worth over £200,000) in return for a settled income of £100 a year. The lawyer was appalled, and easily whipped up Sir Timothy into a hectic fury. 'The insulting, ungentlemanly letter to you,' wrote the indignant, incoherent parent, 'appears the high-toned, self-will'd dictate of the Diabolical Publications which have unluckily fallen in his way, and given this Bias to his mind, that is most singular. To cast off all thoughts of his Maker, to abandon his Parents, to wish to relinquish his Fortune and to court Persecution all seems to arise from the same source. The most mild mode of giving his conduct a thought, it must occur that these sallies of Folly and Madness ought to be restrain'd and kept within bounds. Nothing provokes him so much as civility, he wishes to become what he would term a martyr to his sentiments—nor do I believe he would feel the Horrors of being drawn upon a Hurdle, or the shame of being whirl'd in the Pillory.' If with these views Sir Timothy had decided to cut off his son altogether and let him shift for himself, there might have been something to be said for him. But he could not bring himself to do that. Instead, while refusing to allow Shelley to return home, he doled out to him an allowance of £200 a year; and then, when the inevitable happened, and the inflammable youth, lonely in London, fell into the arms of the beautiful Harriet, imagined he was rescuing her from a persecuting family, and married her, the foolish old man cut off the allowance without a word. Shelley's letters to his father at this juncture reveal completely the absurd ingenuousness of his mind. Penniless, married, in a strange town—he had eloped with Harriet to Edinburgh—and altogether dependent upon his father's good will, Shelley brought himself to beg for money, and yet, in the very same breath, could not resist the opportunity of lecturing Sir Timothy upon his duties as a Christian. 'Father, are you a Christian? . . . I appeal to your duty to the God whose worship you profess, I appeal to the terrors of that day which you believe to seal the doom of mortals, then clothed with immortality. Father, are you a Christian? Judge not, then, lest you be judged . . . . What! Will you not forgive? How, then, can your boasted professions of Christianity appear to the world,' and so on, and so on, through page after page and letter after letter. As Mr. Ingpen says, it is indeed strange that no inkling of the mingled pathos and comedy of those appeals should have touched Sir Timothy. And then when the poor boy was met by nothing but silence, we see him breaking out into ridiculous invective. 'You have treated me *ill, vilely*. When I was expelled for Atheism, you wished I had been killed in Spain. . . . If *you* will not hear my name, *I* will pronounce it. Think not I am an insect whom injuries destroy . . . had I money enough I would meet you in London and hollow in your ears Bysshe, Bysshe, Bysshe . . . aye, Bysshe till you're deaf.' Had I money enough! Truly, in the circumstances, an exquisite proviso!

These are the central incidents with which Mr. Ingpen's book is concerned; but it is difficult to indicate in a short space the wealth of human interest and curious detail contained in these important letters. They may be recommended alike to the psychologist and the historian, to the reader of Professor Dowden and the admirer of Matthew Arnold. Mr. Ingpen is also able to throw fresh light on some other circumstances of interest: he shows for the first time that Shelley was actually arrested for debt; he gives new documents bearing upon Harriet's suicide; and he reproduces in facsimile extracts from the poet's manuscript note-book, found among the *débris* of the *Ariel*. Not the least amusing part of his book is that in which he traces the relations between Sir Timothy and Mary Shelley, after the tragedy in the Gulf of Spezzia. The epistles of the beloved Timothy retain their character to the end. 'To lose an eldest son in his lifetime,' he writes to Whitton, 'and

the unfortunate manner of his losing that life, is truely melancholy to think of, but as it has pleas'd the Great Author of
our Being so to dispose of him I must make up my mind with
resignation.' And Whitton's own style loses nothing of its
charm. After Shelley's death, one of his Oxford creditors—
a plumber—applied to the lawyer for the payment of a bill.
Whitton not only refused to pay, but took the opportunity of
pointing the appropriate moral. 'The officious interference
of you and others,' he informed the unfortunate plumber, 'did
a most serious injury to the Gent that is now no more.'

1917.

MR. CREEVEY

CLIO is one of the most glorious of the Muses; but, as everyone knows, she (like her sister Melpomene) suffers from a sad defect: she is apt to be pompous. With her buskins, her robes, and her airs of importance she is at times, indeed, almost intolerable. But fortunately the Fates have provided a corrective. They have decreed that in her stately advances she should be accompanied by certain apish, impish creatures, who run round her tittering, pulling long noses, threatening to trip the good lady up, and even sometimes whisking to one side the corner of her drapery, and revealing her undergarments in a most indecorous manner. They are the diarists and letter-writers, the gossips and journalists of the past, the Pepyses and Horace Walpoles and Saint-Simons, whose function it is to reveal to us the littleness underlying great events and to remind us that history itself was once real life. Among them is Mr. Creevey. The Fates decided that Mr. Creevey should accompany Clio, with appropriate gestures, during that part of her progress which is measured by the thirty years preceding the accession of Victoria; and the little wretch did his job very well.

It might almost be said that Thomas Creevey was 'born about three of the clock in the afternoon, with a white head and something a round belly.' At any rate, we know nothing of his youth, save that he was educated at Cambridge, and he presents himself to us in the early years of the nineteenth century as a middle-aged man, with a character and a habit of mind already fixed and an established position in the world. In 1803 we find him what he was to be for the rest of his life—a member of Parliament, a familiar figure in high society, an insatiable gossip with a rattling tongue. That he

should have reached and held the place he did is a proof of
his talents, for he was a very poor man; for the greater part
of his life his income was less than £200 a year. But those
were the days of patrons and jobs, pocket-boroughs and
sinecures; they were the days, too, of vigorous, bold living,
torrential talk, and splendid hospitality; and it was only natural
that Mr. Creevey, penniless and immensely entertaining,
should have been put into Parliament by a Duke, and welcomed in every great Whig House in the country with open
arms. It was only natural that, spending his whole political
life as an advanced Whig, bent upon the destruction of abuses,
he should have begun that life as a member for a pocket-
borough and ended it as the holder of a sinecure. For a time
his poverty was relieved by his marriage with a widow who
had means of her own; but Mrs. Creevey died, her money
went to her daughters by her previous husband, and Mr.
Creevey reverted to a possessionless existence—without a
house, without servants, without property of any sort—
wandering from country mansion to country mansion, from
dinner-party to dinner-party, until at last in his old age, on the
triumph of the Whigs, he was rewarded with a pleasant little
post which brought him in about £600 a year. Apart from
these small ups and downs of fortune, Mr. Creevey's life was
static—static spiritually, that is to say; for physically he was
always on the move. His adventures were those of an observer, not of an actor; but he was an observer so very near the
centre of things that he was by no means dispassionate; the
rush of great events would whirl him round into the vortex,
like a leaf in an eddy of wind; he would rave, he would gesti-
culate, with the fury of a complete partisan; and then, when
the wind dropped, he would be found, like the leaf, very much
where he was before. Luckily, too, he was not merely an
agitated observer, but an observer who delighted in passing
on his agitations, first with his tongue, and then—for so the
Fates had decided—with his pen. He wrote easily, spicily,
and persistently; he had a favourite stepdaughter, with whom
he corresponded for years; and so it happens that we have

preserved to us, side by side with the majestic march of Clio (who, of course, paid not the slightest attention to him), Mr. Creevey's exhilarating *pas de chat*.

Certainly he was not over-given to the praise of famous men. There are no great names in his vocabulary—only nicknames: George III is 'Old Nobs,' the Regent 'Prinney,' Wellington 'the Beau,' Lord John Russell 'Pie and Thimble,' Brougham, with whom he was on friendly terms, is sometimes 'Bruffam,' sometimes 'Beelzebub,' and sometimes 'Old Wickedshifts'; and Lord Durham, who once remarked that one could 'jog along on £40,000 a year,' is 'King Jog.' The latter was one of the great Whig potentates, and it was characteristic of Creevey that his scurrility should have been poured out with a special gusto over his own leaders. The Tories were villains, of course—Canning was all perfidy and 'infinite meanness,' Huskisson a mass of 'intellectual confusion and mental dirt,' Castlereagh . . . But all that was obvious and hardly worth mentioning; what was really too exacerbating to be borne was the folly and vileness of the Whigs. 'King Jog,' the 'Bogey,' 'Mother Cole,' and the rest of them—they were either knaves or imbeciles. Lord Grey was an exception; but then Lord Grey, besides passing the Reform Bill, presented Mr. Creevey with the Treasurership of the Ordnance, and in fact was altogether a most worthy man.

Another exception was the Duke of Wellington, whom, somehow or other, it was impossible not to admire. Creevey, throughout his life, had a trick of being 'in at the death' on every important occasion; in the House, at Brooks's, at the Pavilion, he invariably popped up at the critical moment; and so one is not surprised to find him at Brussels during Waterloo. More than that, he was the first English civilian to see the Duke after the battle, and his report of the conversation is admirable; one can almost hear the 'It has been a damned serious business. Blücher and I have lost 30,000 men. It has been a damned nice thing—the nearest run thing you ever saw in your life,' and the 'By God! I don't think it would have done if I had not been there.' On this occasion the Beau spoke, as was fitting, 'with the greatest gravity all the time, and without the least approach to anything like triumph or joy.' But at other times he was jocular, especially when 'Prinney' was the subject. 'By God! you never saw such a figure in your life as he is. Then he speaks and swears so like old Falstaff, that damn me if I was not ashamed to walk into the room with him.'

When, a few years later, the trial of Queen Caroline came on, it was inevitable that Creevey should be there. He had an excellent seat in the front row, and his descriptions of 'Mrs. P.,' as he preferred to call her Majesty, are characteristic:

Two folding doors within a few feet of me were suddenly thrown open, and in entered her Majesty. To describe to you her appearance and manner is far beyond my powers. I had been taught to believe she was as much improved in looks as in dignity of manners; it is therefore with much pain I am obliged to observe that the nearest resemblance I can recollect to this much injured Princess is a toy which you used to call Fanny Royds (a Dutch doll). There is another toy of a rabbit or a cat, whose tail you squeeze under its body, and then out it jumps in half a minute off the ground into the air. The first of these toys you must suppose to represent the person of the Queen; the latter the manner by which she popped all at once into the House, made a *duck* at the throne, another to the Peers, and a concluding jump into the chair which was placed for her. Her dress was black figured gauze, with a good deal of trimming, lace, &c., her sleeves white, and perfectly episcopal; a handsome white veil, so thick as to make it very difficult to me, who was as near to her as anyone, to see her face; such a back for variety and inequality of ground as you never beheld; with a few straggling ringlets on her neck, which I flatter myself from their appearance were not her Majesty's own property.

Mr. Creevey, it is obvious, was not the man to be abashed by the presence of Royalty.

But such public episodes were necessarily rare, and the main stream of his life flowed rapidly, gaily, and unobtrusively through the fat pastures of high society. Everywhere and always he enjoyed himself extremely, but his spirits and his happiness were at their highest during his long summer sojourns at those splendid country houses whose hospitality he chronicles with indefatigable *verve*. 'This house,' he says at Raby, 'is itself *by far* the most magnificent and unique in several ways that I have ever seen. . . . As long as I have heard of anything, I have heard of being driven into the hall of this house in one's carriage, and being set down by the fire. You can have no idea of the magnificent perfection with which this is accomplished.' At Knowsley 'the new dining-room is opened; it is 53 feet by 37, and such a height that it destroys the effect of all the other apartments. . . . There are two fireplaces; and the day we dined there, there were 36 wax candles over the table, 14 on it, and ten great lamps on tall pedestals about the room.' At Thorp Perrow 'all the living rooms are on the ground floor, one a very handsome one about 50 feet long, with a great bow furnished with rose-coloured satin, and the whole furniture of which cost £4000.' At Goodwood the rooms were done up in 'brightest yellow satin,' and at Holkham the walls were covered with Genoa velvet, and there was gilding worth a fortune on 'the roofs of all the rooms and the doors.' The fare was as sumptuous as the furniture. Life passed amid a succession of juicy chops, gigantic sirloins, plump fowls, pheasants stuffed with pâté de foie gras, gorgeous Madeiras, ancient Ports. Wine had a double advantage: it made you drunk; it also made you sober: it was its own cure. On one occasion, when Sheridan, after days of riotous living, showed signs of exhaustion, Mr. and Mrs. Creevey pressed upon him 'five or six glasses of light French wine' with excellent effect. Then, at midnight, when the talk began to flag and the spirits grew a little weary, what could be more rejuvenating than to ring the bell for a broiled bone? And one never rang in vain—except, to be sure, at King Jog's. There, while the host was guzzling, the guests starved. This was too much for Mr. Creevey, who, finding he could get nothing for breakfast, while King Jog was 'eating his own fish as comfortably as could be,' fairly lost his temper.

My blood beginning to boil, I said: 'Lambton, I wish you could tell me what quarter I am to apply to for some fish.' To which he

replied in the most impertinent manner: 'The servant, I suppose.'
I turned to Mills and said pretty loud: 'Now, if it was not for the
fuss and jaw of the thing, I would leave the room and the house this
instant'; and dwelt on the damned outrage. Mills said: 'He hears
every word you say': to which I said: 'I hope he does.' It was a
regular scene.

A few days later, however, Mr. Creevey was consoled by
finding himself in a very different establishment, where 'everything is of a piece—excellent and plentiful dinners, a fat
service of plate, a fat butler, a table with a barrel of oysters and
a hot pheasant, &c., wheeled into the drawing-room every
night at half-past ten.'

It is difficult to remember that this was the England of the
Six Acts, of Peterloo, and of the Industrial Revolution. Mr.
Creevey, indeed, could hardly be expected to remember it, for
he was utterly unconscious of the existence—of the possibility
—of any mode of living other than his own. For him, dining-
rooms 50 feet long, bottles of Madeira, broiled bones, and the
brightest yellow satin were as necessary and obvious a part of
the constitution of the universe as the light of the sun and the
law of gravity. Only once in his life was he seriously ruffled;
only once did a public question present itself to him as something alarming, something portentous, something more than
a personal affair. The occasion is significant. On March 16,
1825, he writes:

I have come to the conclusion that our Ferguson is *insane*. He
quite foamed at the mouth with rage in our Railway Committee in
support of this infernal nuisance—the loco-motive Monster, carrying
eighty tons of goods, and navigated by a tail of smoke and sulphur,
coming thro' every man's grounds between Manchester and Liver-
pool.

His perturbation grew. He attended the committee assiduously, but in spite of his efforts it seemed that the railway Bill
would pass. The loco-motive was more than a joke. He sat
every day from 12 to 4; he led the opposition with long
speeches. 'This railway,' he exclaims on May 31, 'is the

devil's own.' Next day, he is in triumph: he had killed the Monster.

Well—this devil of a railway is strangled at last. . . .To-day we had a clear majority in committee in our favour, and the promoters of the Bill withdrew it, and took their leave of us.

With a sigh of relief he whisked off to Ascot, for the festivities of which he was delighted to note that 'Prinney' had prepared 'by having 12 oz. of blood taken from him by cupping.'

Old age hardly troubled Mr. Creevey. He grew a trifle deaf, and he discovered that it was possible to wear woollen stockings under his silk ones; but his activity, his high spirits, his popularity, only seemed to increase. At the end of a party ladies would crowd round him. 'Oh, Mr. Creevey, how agreeable you have been!' 'Oh thank you, Mr. Creevey! how useful you have been!' 'Dear Mr. Creevey, I laughed out loud last night in bed at one of your stories.' One would like to add (rather late in the day, perhaps) one's own praises. One feels almost affectionate; a certain sincerity, a certain immediacy in his response to stimuli, are endearing qualities; one quite understands that it was natural, on the pretext of changing house, to send him a dozen of wine. Above all, one wants him to go on. Why should he stop? Why should he not continue indefinitely telling us about 'Old Salisbury' and 'Old Madagascar'? But it could not be.

> Le temps s'en va, le temps s'en va, Madame;
> Las! Le temps non, mais nous, nous en allons.

It was fitting that, after fulfilling his seventy years, he should catch a glimpse of 'little Vic' as Queen of England, laughing, eating, and showing her gums too much at the Pavilion. But that was enough: the piece was over; the curtain had gone down; and on the new stage that was preparing for very different characters, and with a very different style of decoration, there would be no place for Mr. Creevey.

1919.

CHARLES GREVILLE

THE fortunate generations are the homogeneous ones—
those which begin and end, comfortably, within the bounda-
ries of a single Age. It is the straddlers who are unlucky.
Charles Greville was a straddler. His life lasted from 1794 to
1865, so that the active part of it was almost equally divided
between two periods of extraordinary discordance—the
period of George the Fourth and that of Queen Victoria.
The discordance was fatal to him. His character had no
strongly marked individuality. He was neither a rebel nor a
prophet. He did not, like Lord Melbourne, live to be an
anachronism—a homesick voyager from a world that had
disappeared. He was amenable to the Time-Spirit; and the
fashionable young man who betted at White's and flirted at
Almack's, and who felt that his wildest dreams had come true
when he was given the management of the Duke of York's
racing stables, became at last a grave, respectable personage,
in black, with a conscience, a follower of Sir Robert Peel, and
an admirer of the Prince Consort. The transition was complete; but it was ruinous. There were the two stools; where
was the man? He himself was aware of a profound discom-
fort. He thought he was a failure, he complained of his circumstances, his temper grew worse and worse. In his youth
he had been 'Punch'; he was 'the Gruncher' in his old age.
On the whole, perhaps his crossness was excusable; perhaps
things had been against him; perhaps he was, indeed, a failure
—it certainly looked like it : with all his great abilities, what
had he done? What indeed?—was all that he and his friends
could echo to that unpleasant question. And yet, by a whim
of destiny, the true answer has turned out to be different.
Posterity discovered that the disappointed, disagreeable,

unsatisfactory man had in reality done a great deal—much more than most of his contemporaries—enough to make him certainly famous and possibly immortal. He had kept a diary.

The diary, which filled ninety-one small quarto volumes (now preserved at the British Museum), was published in three instalments, in 1874, 1885, and 1887, by Henry Reeve, Greville's friend and colleague. Reeve, with great courage and good sense, printed very nearly the whole of the manuscript. His omissions were of three kinds—scandalous stories, which might have given pain to persons then living; observations upon the writer's private affairs; and reflections upon the character and conduct of Queen Victoria. Perhaps the time has now come when a really complete edition of the whole work might be produced with advantage; for the years have smoothed down what was agitating and personal half a century ago into harmless history. When the book first appeared, it seemed—even with Reeve's tactful excisions—outrageous. The later Victorians were shocked. Their sharp noses detected at once, under the odour of Greville's high-mindedness, the pungent whiffs of original sin. He was not as they were; he had been born and bred beneath alien stars; he had come from a strange, undesirable country, ruled by a Regent; he was cynical, malicious, and without a heart. To turn from their horrified comments to the Greville Memoirs themselves is almost disappointing. In those essentially sober pages the envenomed wretch of the Victorian imagination is nowhere to be found. To our more impartial vision, the book seems, if anything, too serious, too measured—a trifle formal, and flat. On reflection, one can understand the cause of this. It is not so much that the subject-matter—the inner workings of the political machine—seems to demand a certain colourlessness in the treatment; it is rather that this colourlessness inevitably followed from the divided nature of Greville himself. Saint-Simon's subject-matter was the same; yet he has managed to illuminate it with all the colours of the rainbow; but then Saint-Simon was the fortunate child of a homogeneous generation, who could express himself with a tremendous whole-heartedness and without a single *arrière-pensée*. With Greville it was otherwise. If, as the Victorians supposed, he had been simply heartless, his case would have been less parlous; but he was, in fact, half-hearted, which was a much more serious matter. His fundamental ambiguity obliged him to wince and relent and refrain. And so his book, in spite of its high intelligence, its easy, vigorous writing, and its immense historical and social interest, remains merely a good book; it is not a great one.

The major part of it is concerned with the mature Greville—the indefatigable newsmonger and sedate politician; and our vision of the earlier incarnation is therefore less distinct. We have a glimpse of him in Oxford, letting himself out of a Christ Church window, to get into a chaise and four and dash to London to see an execution. We catch sight of him a little later at clubs and country-houses—fashionable and extravagant, in an exclusive Tory set. The Duke of Portland was his uncle, and he was properly looked after. He was given a sinecure office, the Secretaryship of Jamaica, and in 1821 he was made Clerk to the Privy Council, in which position he remained for the next forty years. His income was at least £4,000 a year, but he ran into debt. He was fascinated by racing, and owned a number of racehorses himself. On one occasion, he was obliged to borrow £3,000 from his uncle the Duke, and, when he was at last able to repay the money, he provided himself with three Bank of England notes of a thousand pounds each, and went off to discharge the debt. 'Oh, no, Charles,' said the Duke, 'keep the money by all means. It will bring you luck.' Charles made some show of reluctance, and laid the money on the table. Alas! the sight of the bright, clean notes was too much for his Grace, who placed them, neatly folded, in his pocket-book, saying: 'Well, Charles, since you insist upon it——' And poor Charles perceived, too late, that a large, untidy bundle of dirty notes would have been more appropriate to the situation. Another misadventure befell him, of a still more unpleasant nature. Some letters, disclosing an intrigue between him and a lady, were discovered by another lady in a bag which had been left in a shop in Bond Street. The letters flew round everywhere, and Greville was covered with ridicule. The high society of 1824 was delighted by the incident; Punch, they said, was well punished; the whole affair was charmingly absurd; one of the intercepted letters, reported an ambassadress, was 'filled with bitter reproaches at his not seeming pleased to hear that the dear little babe had got a tooth.' Either for this reason, or for some other, Greville never married.

The transition from fashion to politics was accomplished during the agitations of the Reform Bill. Greville was drawn into the vortex; and, having once tasted the delicious fruit of the tree of political knowledge, he found he could eat nothing else for the rest of his life. His intellectual bent asserted itself; he changed his friends, drifting away from his old associates, and becoming intimate with the group of men—Tories who were almost Whigs, and Whigs who were almost Tories: Lord Palmerston, Lord John, Lord Clarendon, Sir James Graham —who ruled England during the first twenty-five years of Victoria. It is in its picture of those years—the later thirties, the forties, and the fifties—that the great value of Greville's journal resides. The details might not be always accurate— for he was sometimes taken in by great ladies, or used by Cabinet Ministers to disseminate convenient falsities—but the mass of his information was enormous, and it was first-hand. He was not exactly a gossip, nor a busybody; he was an extremely inquisitive person, in whom, somehow or other, it it seemed natural for everybody to confide. Thus the broad current of London life flows through his ample pages, and, as one turns them over, one glides swiftly into the curiously distant world of eighty years ago. A large leisureliness des-cends upon one, and a sense that there is plenty of room, and an atmosphere of extraordinary moderation. Reason and in-stinct, fixity and change, aristocracy and democracy—all these are there, but unaccountably interwoven into a circumambient compromise—a wonderful arrangement of half-lights. One's days pass in endless consultations over the intricate eddies of almost imperceptible crises, and, in the intervals, one drives in a brougham to Lady Palmerston's party, or listens for five or six hours, entranced, to a speech in the House of Commons, or walks across St. James's Park and takes off one's hat to the Duke. So Greville unrolls his long panorama; then pauses for a little, to expatiate in detail on some particular figure in it. His portraits, with their sobriety of tone and precision of outline, resemble very fine engravings, and will prove, perhaps, the most enduring portions of his book.

The Gruncher himself could hardly imagine that any of it would endure. He constantly wondered why he continued to keep up the futile diary. His life was a failure; why record it? And the worst of it was, he had only himself to blame. He sat next Sir Edward Alderson at dinner, and 'found him a very agreeable man, Senior Wrangler, Senior Medallist, a judge, a wit; a life all of law and letters, such as I might have led if I had chosen the good path.' But perhaps, after all, the good path was still not inaccessible. He might sell his racehorses, for instance; and, at last, after many hesitations, in 1857, sell them he did. Yet he hardly felt himself the easier. The last relics of youth had gone, and old age brought few compensations. His friends, he complained, deserted him; such, indeed, was his snappishness that one could scarcely be much surprised if they did. 'Ah, M. Greville, est-ce que par hasard vous seriez de mauvaise humeur ce soir?' a French lady of his acquaintance was in the habit of asking him. A very old lady told the story of how she had found him, as a child, in floods of tears after dinner, because he had not been given the 'liver-wing' of the chicken. Mr. Greville had not changed; he was too old to cry now when he did not get the liver-wing; but he grunched. In January, 1865, when he was in his seventy-first year, he paid a visit at Taplow Court, where a lady happened to be ill with scarlatina. From Taplow he went to Savernake; but Lady Ailesbury was so much afraid of infection that she would not allow him into the house. Very angry, he drove on to an inn at Marlborough, where he slept in a damp bed. Next day he returned with a bad cold to Taplow, shaking with fury, and exclaiming: 'I come back here because no one will receive me!' The chill and the vexation together were too much for him, so that by the time he reached London again he was very ill. Henry Reeve went to see him in the house he shared with Lord Granville in Bruton Street, and found the old man propped up in a chair, his large face sunk forward, and his small, sharp eyes, with that peculiar expression in them which only comes from a life-long observation of horses as well as men, fixed on a small quarto book, which he held in his hand. It was one of the volumes of his diary. When he died, he muttered, Reeve was to have the thing, and do what he liked with it. Soon afterwards Reeve left him; he ate a woodcock for his dinner, and then went to bed, and fell into a sleep, from which he never woke.

1923.

CARLYLE

My grandfather, Edward Strachey, an Anglo-Indian of cultivation and intelligence, once accompanied Carlyle on an excursion to Paris in pre-railroad days. At their destination the postilion asked my grandfather for a tip; but the reply—it is Carlyle who tells the story—was a curt refusal, followed by the words—'Vous avez drivé devilish slow.' The reckless insularity of this remark illustrates well enough the extraordinary change which had come over the English governing classes since the eighteenth century. Fifty years earlier a cultivated Englishman would have piqued himself upon answering the postilion in the idiom and the accent of Paris. But the Napoleonic wars, the industrial revolution, the romantic revival, the Victorian spirit, had brought about a relapse from the cosmopolitan suavity of eighteenth-century culture; the centrifugal forces, always latent in English life, had triumphed, and men's minds had shot off into the grooves of eccentricity and provincialism. It is curious to notice the flux and reflux of these tendencies in the history of our literature: the divine amenity of Chaucer followed by the no less divine idiosyncrasy of the Elizabethans; the exquisite vigour of the eighteenth century followed by the rampant vigour of the nineteenth; and to-day the return once more towards the Latin elements in our culture, the revulsion from the Germanic influences which obsessed our grandfathers, the preference for what is swift, what is well arranged, and what is not too good.

Carlyle was not an English gentleman, he was a Scotch peasant; and his insularity may be measured accordingly—by a simple sum in proportion. In his youth, no doubt, he had German preoccupations; but on the whole he is, with Dickens, probably the most complete example of a home growth which the British Islands have to offer to the world. The result is certainly remarkable. There is much to be said for the isolated productions of special soils; they are full of strength and character; their freedom from outside forces releases in them a spring of energy which leads, often enough, to astonishing consequences. In Carlyle's case the release was terrific. His vitality burst out into an enormous exuberance, filling volume after volume with essays, histories, memoirs and philosophisings, pouring itself abroad through an immense correspondence, and erupting for eighty years in a perpetual flood of red-hot conversation. The achievements of such a spirit take one's breath away; one gazes in awe at the serried row of heavy books on the shelf; one reads on and on until one's eyes are blinded by the endless glare of that aurora borealis, and one's ears deafened by the roar and rattle of that inexhaustible artillery. Then one recovers—very quickly. That is the drawback. The northern lights, after all, seem to give out no heat, and the great guns were only loaded with powder. So, at any rate, it appears to a perverse generation. It was all very well in the days when English gentlemen could say with perfect sang-froid 'Vous avez drivé devilish slow' to French postilions. Then the hurricane that was Carlyle came into contact with what was exactly appropriate to it—gnarled oaks—solitary conifers; and the effect was sublime; leaves whirled, branches crashed, and fathers of the forest were up-rooted. But nowadays it hurls itself upon a congregation of tremulous reeds; they bend down low, to the very earth, as the gale passes; and then immediately they spring up again, and are seen to be precisely as they were before.

The truth is that it is almost as fatal to have too much genius as too little. What was really valuable in Carlyle was ruined by his colossal powers and his unending energy. It is easy to perceive that, amid all the rest of his qualities, he was an artist. He had a profound relish for words; he had a sense of style which developed, gradually and consistently, into interesting and original manifestations; he had an imaginative eye; he had a grim satiric humour. This was an admirable

outfit for a historian and a memoir writer, and it is safe to pro-
phesy that whatever is permanent in Carlyle's work will be
found in that section of his writings. But, unfortunately,
the excellence, though it is undoubtedly there, is a fitful and
fragmentary one. There are vivid flashes and phrases—visions
thrown up out of the darkness of the past by the bull's-eye
lantern of a stylistic imagination—Coleridge at Highgate,
Maupertuis in Berlin, the grotesque image of the 'sea-green
Incorruptible'; there are passages of accomplished caricature,
and climaxes of elaborately characteristic writing; and then
the artist's hand falters, his eye wanders, his mind is distracted
and led away. One has only to compare Carlyle with Tacitus
to realise what a disadvantage it is to possess unlimited powers.
The Roman master, undisturbed by other considerations, was
able to devote himself entirely to the creation of a work of art.
He triumphed: supremely conscious both of his capacities and
his intentions, he built up a great design, which in all its
parts was intense and beautiful. The Carlylean qualities—the
satiric vision, the individual style—were his; but how differ-
ently he used them! He composed a tragedy, while Carlyle
spent himself in melodrama; he made his strange sentences the
expression of a profound personality, while Carlyle's were the
vehicle of violence and eccentricity.

The stern child of Ecclefechan held artists in low repute,
and no doubt would have been disgusted to learn that it was in
that guise that he would win the esteem of posterity. He had
higher views : surely he would be remembered as a prophet.
And no doubt he had many of the qualifications for that profession—a loud voice, a bold face, and a bad temper. But unfortunately there was one essential characteristic that he
lacked—he was not dishonoured in his own country. Instead
of being put into a pit and covered with opprobrium, he made a
comfortable income, was supplied by Mrs. Carlyle with everything that he wanted, and was the favourite guest at Lady
Ashburton's fashionable parties. Prophecies, in such circumstances, however voluminous and disagreeable they may be,
are apt to have something wrong with them. And, in any case,

who remembers prophets? Isaiah and Jeremiah, no doubt, have gained a certain reputation; but then Isaiah and Jeremiah have had the extraordinary good fortune to be translated into English by a committee of Elizabethan bishops.

To be a prophet is to be a moralist, and it was the moral pre-occupation in Carlyle's mind that was particularly injurious to his artistic instincts. In Latin countries—the fact is significant—morals and manners are expressed by the same word; in England it is not so; to some Britons, indeed, the two notions appear to be positively antithetical. Perhaps this is a mistake. Perhaps if Carlyle's manners had been more polished his morals would have been less distressing. Morality, curiously enough, seems to belong to that class of things which are of the highest value, which perform a necessary function, which are, in fact, an essential part of the human mechanism, but which should only be referred to with the greatest circumspection. Carlyle had no notion that this was the case, and the result was disastrous. In his history, especially, it is impossible to escape from the devastating effects of his reckless moral sense.

Perhaps it is the platitude of such a state of mind that is its most exasperating quality. Surely, one thinks, poor Louis XV might be allowed to die without a sermon from Chelsea. But no! The opportunity must not be missed; the preacher draws a long breath, and expatiates with elaborate emphasis upon all that is most obvious about mortality, crowns, and the futility of self-indulgence. But an occasional platitude can be put up with; what is really intolerable is the all-pervadingness of the obsession. There are some German cooks who have a passion for caraway seeds: whatever dish they are preparing, from whipped cream to legs of mutton, they cannot keep them out. Very soon one begins to recognise the fatal flavour; one lies in horrified wait for it; it instantly appears; and at last the faintest suspicion of caraway almost produces nausea. The histories of Carlyle (and no less, it may be observed in passing, the novels of Thackeray) arouse those identical sensations—the immediate recognition of the first approaches of the well-known whiff—the inevitable saturation—the heart that sinks and sinks. And, just as one feels that the cook was a good cook, and that the dish would have been done to a turn if only the caraway canister could have been kept out of reach, so one perceives that Carlyle had a true gift for history which was undone by his moralisations. There is an imaginative greatness in his conception of Cromwell, for instance, a vigour and a passion in the presentment of it; but all is spoilt by an overmastering desire to turn the strange Protector into a moral hero after Carlyle's own heart, so that, after all, the lines are blurred, the composition is confused, and the picture unconvincing.

But the most curious consequence of this predilection is to be seen in his Frederick the Great. In his later days Carlyle evolved a kind of super-morality by which all the most unpleasant qualities of human nature—egotism, insensitiveness, love of power—became the object of his religious adoration— a monstrous and inverted ethic, combining every possible disadvantage of virtue and of vice. He then, for some mysterious reason, pitched upon Frederick of Prussia as the great exemplar of this system, and devoted fourteen years of ceaseless labour to the elucidation of his history. Never was a misconception more complete. Frederick was in reality a knave of genius, a sceptical, eighteenth-century gambler with a strong will and a turn for organisation; and this was the creature whom Carlyle converted into an Ideal Man, a God-like Hero, a chosen instrument of the Eternal Powers. What the Eternal Powers would have done if a stray bullet had gone through Frederick's skull in the battle of Molwitz, Carlyle does not stop to inquire. By an ironical chance there happened to be two attractive elements in Frederick's mental outfit; he had a genuine passion for French literature, and he possessed a certain scurrilous wit, which constantly expressed itself in extremely truculent fashion. Fate could not have selected two more unfortunate qualities with which to grace a hero of Carlyle's. Carlyle considered French literature trash; and the kind of joke that Frederick particularly relished filled him with profound aversion. A copy of Frederick's collected works still exists, with Carlyle's pencilled annotations in the margin. Some of the King's poetical compositions are far from proper; and it is amusing to observe the historian's exclamations of agitated regret whenever the Ideal Man alludes, in some mocking epigram, to his own or his friends' favourite peccadilloes. One can imagine, if Frederick were to return to earth for a moment and look over one's shoulder, his grin of fiendish delight.

The cruel Hohenzollern would certainly have laughed; but to gentler beings the spectacle of so much effort gone so utterly awry seems rather a matter for lamentation. The comedy of Carlyle's case topples over into tragedy—a tragedy of waste and unhappiness. If only he could have enjoyed himself! But he never did. Is it possible, one wonders, to bring forth anything that is worth bringing forth, without some pleasure —whatever pains there may be as well—in the parturition? One remembers Gibbon, cleaving his way, with such a magisterial gaiety, through the Decline and Fall of the Roman Empire. He, too, no doubt, understood very little of his subject; but all was well with him and with his work. Why was it? The answer seems to be—he understood something that, for his purposes, was more important even than the Roman Empire —himself. He knew his own nature, his powers, his limitations, his desires; he was the master of an inward harmony. From Carlyle such knowledge was hidden. Blindness is always tragic; but the blindness that brings mighty strength to baffled violence, towering aspirations to empty visions, and sublime self-confidence to bewilderment, remorse and misery, is terrible and pitiable indeed.

Unfortunately it was not only upon Carlyle himself that the doom descended. A woman of rare charm and brilliant powers was involved in his evil destiny. Regardless both of the demands of her temperament and the qualities of her spirit, he used her without scruple to subserve his own purposes, and made her as wretched as himself. She was his wife, and that was the end of the matter. She might have become a consummate writer or the ruler and inspirer of some fortunate social group; but all that was out of the question; was she not Mrs. Carlyle? It was her business to suppress her own instincts, to devote her whole life to the arrangement of his domestic comforts, to listen for days at a time, as she lay racked with illness on the sofa, to his descriptions of the battles of Frederick the Great. The time came when she felt that she could bear it no longer, and that at all hazards she must free herself from those stifling bonds. It is impossible not to wish that she had indeed fled as she intended with the unknown man of her choice. The blow to Carlyle's egoism would have been so dramatic, and the up-heaval in that well-conducted world so satisfactory to contem-plate! But, at the last moment, she changed her mind. Curi-ously enough, when it came to the point, it turned out that Mrs. Carlyle agreed with her husband. Even that bold spirit succumbed to the influences that surrounded it; she, too, was a mid-Victorian at heart. The woman's tragedy may be traced in those inimitable letters, whose intoxicating merriment flashes like lightning about the central figure, as it moves in sinister desolation against the background of a most peculiar age: an age of barbarism and prudery, of nobility and cheap-ness, of satisfaction and desperation; an age in which every-thing was discovered and nothing known; an age in which all the outlines were tremendous and all the details sordid; when gas-jets struggled feebly through the circumambient fog, when the hour of dinner might be at any moment between two and six, when the doses of rhubarb were periodic and gigantic, when pet dogs threw themselves out of upper storey windows, when cooks reeled drunk in areas, when one sat for hours with one's feet in dirty straw dragged along the streets by horses, when an antimacassar was on every chair, and the baths were minute tin circles, and the beds were full of bugs and disasters.

After it was all over and his wife was dead, Carlyle realised what had happened. But all that he could do was to take refuge from the truth in the vain vehemence of sentimental self-reproaches. He committed his confessions to Froude without sufficient instructions; and when he died he left behind him a legacy of doubt and scandal. But now, at length, some enjoyment appeared upon the scene. No one was happier than Froude, with an agitated conscience and a sense of duty that involved the divulgation of dreadful domesticities; while the Victorian public feasted upon the unexpected banquet to its heart's content.

1928.

FROUDE

JAMES ANTHONY FROUDE was one of the salient figures of
mid-Victorian England. In that society of prepotent personages he more than held his own. He was not merely the author
of the famous *History*; he was a man of letters who was also a
man of the world, an accomplished gentleman, whose rich
nature overflowed with abounding energy, a sportsman, a
yachtsman, a brilliant and magnificent talker—and something
more: one in whose presence it was impossible not to feel a
hint of mystery, of strange melancholy, an uncomfortable
suggestion of enigmatic power. His most impressive appearance completed the effect: the height, the long, pale face, the
massive, vigorous features, the black hair and eyebrows, and
the immense eyes, with their glowing darkness, whose colour
—so a careful observer noted—was neither brown, nor blue,
nor black, but red. What was the explanation of it all? What
was the inner cause of this *brio* and this sadness, this passionate
earnestness and this sardonic wit? One wonders, as his after-
dinner listeners used to wonder, in the 'sixties, with a little
shiver, while the port went round, and the ladies waited in the
drawing-room.

Perhaps it is easier for us than for them to make, at any rate,
a guess; for we know more of the facts, and we have our
modern psychology to give us confidence. Perhaps the real explanation was old Mr. Froude, who was a hunting parson of
a severely conventional type, with a marked talent for water-
colours. Mrs. Froude had died early, leaving the boy to be
brought up by this iron-bound clergyman and some brothers
much older than himself. His childhood was wretched, his
boyhood was frightful. He was sent, ill and overgrown, to
college at Westminster, and there—it was, as the biographers

dutifully point out, in the bad old days before the influence of Dr. Arnold had turned the Public Schools into models of industry and civilised behaviour—he suffered, for two years, indescribable torment. He was removed in disgrace, flogged by his father for imaginary delinquencies, and kept at home for two years more in the condition of an outcast. His eldest brother, Hurrell, who was one of the leaders in the new fashion of taking Christianity seriously, and mortified his own flesh by eating fish on Fridays, egged on the parental discipline with pious glee. At last, grown too old for castigation, the lad was allowed to go to Oxford. There, for the first time in his life, he began to enjoy himself, and became engaged to an attractive young lady. But he had run up bills with the Oxford tradesmen, had told his father they were less than they were, the facts had come out, and old Mr. Froude, declaring that his son was little better than a common swindler, denounced him as such to the young lady's father, who thereupon broke off the engagement. It seems surprising that Anthony resisted the temptation of suicide—that he had the strength and the courage to outface his misfortunes, to make a career for himself and become a highly successful man. What is more surprising is that his attitude towards his father never ceased, from first to last, to be one of intense admiration. He might struggle, he might complain, he might react, but he always, with a strange overpowering instinctiveness, adored. Old Mr. Froude had drawn a magic circle round his son, from which escape was impossible; and the creature whose life had been almost ruined by his father's moral cruelty, who—to all appearances—had thrown off the yoke, and grown into maturity with the powerful, audacious, sceptical spirit of a free man, remained, in fact, in secret servitude—a disciplinarian, a Protestant, even a church-goer, to the very end.

Possibly the charm might have been exorcised by an invocation to science, but Froude remained curiously aloof from the dominating influence of his age; and instead, when his father had vanished, submitted himself to Carlyle. The substitution was symptomatic: the new father expressed in explicit dogma

the unconscious teaching of the old. To the present generation
Carlyle presents a curious problem—it is so very difficult to
believe that real red-hot lava ever flowed from that dry,
neglected crater; but the present generation never heard
Carlyle talk. For many years Froude heard little else: he
became an evangelist; but when he produced his gospel it met,
like some others, with a mixed reception. The Victorian
public, unable to understand a form of hero-worship which
laid bare the faults of the hero, was appalled, and refused to
believe what was the simple fact—that Froude's adoration
was of so complete a kind that it shrank with horror from the
notion of omitting a single wart from the portrait. To us the
warts are obvious: our only difficulty is to account for the
adoration. However, since it led incidentally to the publication
of Mrs. Carlyle's letters as well as her husband's, we can only
be thankful.

The main work of Froude's life, the *History of England
from the Fall of Wolsey to the Defeat of the Spanish Armada*,
began to appear in 1856, and was completed in 1870. It is undoubtedly a deeply interesting book, full of thought, of imagination and of excitement, the product of great industry and
great power of writing: whether it ranks among the small first
class of histories is less certain. Contemporary critics found
much to complain of in it, but their strictures were, on the
whole, beside the mark. Among them the most formidable
was Professor Freeman, who dissected Froude with the utmost savagery month after month and year after year in the
pages of the *Saturday Review*. Freeman was a man of considerable learning, and of an ill temper even more considerable; his minute knowledge of the Early English, his passionate devotion to the Anglo-Saxons, and his intimate conviction
(supported by that of Dr. Stubbs), that he (with the possible
exception of Dr. Stubbs) was the supreme historian, made a
strange mixture in his mind, boiling and simmering together
over the flames of a temperamental vexation. Unfortunately
no particle of this heat ever reached his printed productions,
which were remarkable for their soporific qualities and for

containing no words but those of Anglo-Saxon descent. The spirit, not only of the school but of the Sunday school, was what animated those innumerable pages, adorning with a parochial earnestness the heavy burden of research. Naturally enough Froude's work, so coloured, so personal, so obviously written by somebody who was acquainted with the world as well as Oxford, acted like a red rag on the professor. He stormed, he stamped, his fiery and choleric beard shook with indignation. He declared that the book was a mass of inaccuracies and a dastardly attack upon the Church of England. The former accusation was the more important, and the professor devoted years to the proof of it. Unluckily for him, however, the years only revealed more and more clearly the indisputable value of Froude's work in the domain of pure erudition. He was not a careful transcriber, and he occasionally made a downright blunder; but such blemishes are of small moment compared with the immense addition he made to historical knowledge by his exploration and revelation of the manuscripts at Simancas. Froude was dignified; he kept silence for twenty years, and then replied to his tormentor in an article so crushing as to elicit something almost like an apology.

But he was more completely avenged in a very different and quite unexpected manner. Mr. Horace Round, a 'burrower into wormholes' living in Brighton, suddenly emerged from the parchments among which he spent his life deliciously gnawing at the pedigrees of the proudest families of England, and in a series of articles fell upon Freeman with astonishing force. The attack was particularly serious because it was delivered at the strongest point in the professor's armour—his exactitude, his knowledge of his authorities, his undeviating attention to fact, and it was particularly galling because it was directed against the very crown and culmination of the professor's history—his account of the Battle of Hastings. With masterly skill Mr. Round showed that, through a variety of errors, the whole nature of the battle had been misunderstood and misrepresented; more than that, he proved that the name of 'Senlac' with which Freeman had christened it, and which he had imposed upon the learned world, was utterly without foundation, and had been arrived at by a foolish mistake. Mr. Round was an obscure technician, but he deserves the gratitude of Englishmen for having extirpated that odious word from their vocabulary. The effect of these articles on Freeman was alarming; his blood boiled, but he positively made no reply. For years the attacks continued, and for years the professor was dumb. Fulminating rejoinders rushed into his brain, only to be whisked away again—they were not quite fulminating enough. The most devastating article of all was written, was set up in proof, but was not yet published; it contained the *exposé* of 'Senlac,' and rumours of its purport and approaching appearance were already flying about in museums and common-rooms. Freeman was aghast at this last impertinence; but still he nursed his wrath. Like King Lear, he would do such things—what they were yet he knew not— but they should be the terrors of the earth. At last, silent and purple, he gathered his female attendants about him, and left England for an infuriated holiday. There was an ominous pause; and then the fell news reached Brighton. The professor had gone pop in Spain. Mr. Round, however, was remorseless, and published. It was left for his adversary's pupils and admirers to struggle with him as best they could, but they did so ineffectively; and he remained, like the Normans, in possession of the field.

A true criticism of Froude's *History* implies a wider view than Freeman's. The theme of the book was the triumph of the Reformation in England—a theme not only intensely dramatic in itself, but one which raised a multitude of problems of profound and perennial interest. Froude could manage the drama (though in his hands it sometimes degenerated into melodrama) well enough: it was his treatment of the philosophical issues that was defective. Carlyle—it seems hardly credible—actually believed that the Revolution was to be explained as a punishment meted out to France for her loose living in the eighteenth century; and Froude's ethical conceptions, though they were not quite so crude, belonged to the same infantile species as his master's. The Protestants were right and the Catholics were wrong. Henry VIII enabled the Protestants to win, therefore Henry VIII was an admirable person: such was the kind of proposition by which Froude's attitude towards that period of vast and complicated import was determined. His Carlylean theories demanded a hero, and Henry VIII came pat to hand; he refused to see—what is plain to any impartial observer—that the Defender of the Faith combined in a peculiar manner the unpleasant vices of meanness and brutality; no! he made the Reformation—he saved England—he was a demi-god. How the execution of Catherine Howard—a young girl who amused herself— helped forward Protestant England, we are not told. Froude's insensitiveness to cruelty becomes, indeed, at times, almost pathological. When King and Parliament between them have a man boiled alive in Smithfield Market, he is favourably impressed; it is only when Protestants are tortured that there is talk of martyrdom. The bias, no doubt, gives a spice to the work, but it is cheap spice—bought, one feels, at the Co-operative Stores. The Whiggery of Macaulay may be tiresome, but it has the flavour of an aristocracy about it, of a high intellectual tradition; while Froude's Protestantism is—there is really only one word for it—provincial.

A certain narrowness of thought and feeling: that may be forgiven, if it is expressed in a style of sufficient mastery. Froude was an able, a brilliant writer, copious and vivid, with a picturesque imagination and a fine command of narrative. His grand set-pieces—the execution of Somerset and Mary Queen of Scots, the end of Cranmer, the ruin of the Armada —go off magnificently, and cannot be forgotten; and, apart from these, the extraordinary succession of events assumes, as it flows through his pages, the thrilling lineaments of a great story, upon whose issue the most *blasé* reader is forced to hang entranced. Yet the supreme quality of style seems to be lacking. One is uneasily aware of a looseness in the texture, an absence of concentration in the presentment, a failure to fuse the *whole* material into organic life. Perhaps, after all, it is the intellect and the emotion that are at fault here too; perhaps when one is hoping for genius, it is only talent—only immense talent—that one finds. One thinks of the mysterious wisdom of Thucydides, of the terrific force of Tacitus, of the Gibbonian balance and lucidity and co-ordination—ah! to few, to very few, among historians is it granted to bring the κτῆμα ἐς ἀεί into the world. And yet . . . if only, one feels, this gifted, splendid man could have stepped back a little, could have withdrawn from the provinciality of Protestantism and the crudity of the Carlylean dogma, could have allowed himself, untrammelled, to play upon his subject with his native art and his native wit! Then, surely, he would have celebrated other virtues besides the unpleasant ones; he would have seen some drawbacks to power and patriotism, he would have preferred civilisation to fanaticism, and Queen Elizabeth to John Knox. He might even have written immortal English. But alas! these are vain speculations; old Mr. Froude would never have permitted anything of the sort.

1930.

DIZZY

THE absurd Jew-boy, who set out to conquer the world, reached his destination. It is true that he had gone through a great deal, a very great deal, to get there—four volumes by Mr. Buckle and Mr. Monypenny. But there he was. After a lifetime of relentless determination, infinite perseverance and superhuman egotism, he found himself at last old, hideous, battered, widowed, solitary, diseased, but Prime Minister of England. Mr. Buckle's last two volumes [1] show him to us in this final stage—the stage of attainment. The efflorescent Dizzy, Earl of Beaconsfield and Knight of the Garter, stands before us. It is a full-length portrait: twelve hundred pages tell the story of twelve years. Much is revealed to us—much of the highest interest, both personal and public—the curious details of political complexities, a royal correspondence, the internecine quarrels of cabinets, a strange love affair, the thrilling *peripeteia* of world-shaking negotiations, the outside and the inside of high affairs, and yet—why is it?—the revelation seems to be incomplete. Is this really everything, one wonders, or was there something else? *Can* this be everything? Is this, in truth, greatness? Can this, and nothing more, have been the end of all those palpitating struggles, the reward of energies so extraordinary, and capacities so amazing? The sinister, mysterious features return one's stare with their mummy-like inscrutability. 'What more do you want to know?' they seem to whisper. 'I have conquered the world.' 'Yes, you have conquered the world—granted,' we answer. 'But *then*——?' Silence.

[1] *The Life of Benjamin Disraeli, Earl of Beaconsfield.* By George Earle Buckle, in succession to W. F. Monypenny. Vols. V and VI. John Murray.

A moralist, with the pen of a Thackeray, might, indeed, make great play with these twelve hundred pages. He could compile a very pretty sermon out of them, on the text of the vanity of human ambition. He could draw a striking picture of the aged vain-glorious creature, racked by gout and asthma, dyed and corseted, with the curl on his miserable old forehead kept in its place all night by a bandana handkerchief, clutching at power, prostrating himself before royalty, tottering to congresses, wheezing out his last gasps, with indefatigable snobbery, at fashionable dinner-tables; and then, with all his shrewdness and his worldly wisdom, so easily taken in!—a dupe of the glittering outsides of things; a silly, septuagenarian child, keeping itself quiet with a rattle of unrealities, unreal patriotism, and unreal loyalty, and unreal literature, and unreal love. Only, unfortunately, the picture would be a little crude. There would be a considerable degree of truth in it, no doubt, but it would miss the really interesting point. It would be the picture of a remarkable, entertaining, edifying figure, but not an important one—a figure that might, after all, be ignored. And Dizzy could not be ignored. He was formidable—one of the most formidable men who ever lived. His conduct of the European negotiations which reached their climax in the congress of Berlin—laid before us with illuminating detail by Mr. Buckle—reveals a mind in which all the great qualities of action—strength, courage, decision, foresight—were combined to form an engine of tremendous power. It is clear that Bismarck was right in treating him almost, if not quite, as an equal; and to have been almost the equal of Bismarck is to have been something very considerable indeed. Nor, of course, was he merely a man of action. He had the nervous sensibility of an artist, living every moment of his life with acute self-consciousness, and observing the world around him with the quick discrimination of an artist's eye. His letters, like his novels, are full of curious brilliance—an irony more latent than expressed, an artificiality which, somehow or other, is always to the point; and some of his phrases have probably achieved immortality. The puzzle is that so many varied and splendid qualities should, in the aggregate, leave such an unsatisfying impression upon the mind. The gorgeous sphinx seems to ring hollow after all. Never, one guesses, was so much power combined with so little profundity. The intrepid statesman drifts through politics without a purpose; the veteran man of the world is fascinated, by the paraphernalia of smart parties; the author of *Endymion* is more ridiculously ingenuous than the author of *The Young Visiters*. He could not, he said, at the age of seventy-four, 'at all agree with the great King that all is vanity.' One wonders why. It is certainly very difficult to find anything in these twelve hundred pages which is not vanity —excepting, of course, the approbation of Queen Victoria. The correspondence with Lady Bradford is typical of the whole strange case. To pursue, when one is seventy and Prime Minister, a Countess who is fifty-six and a grandmother, with protestations of eternal passion, appears to have presented itself to Dizzy quite genuinely as the secret culmination of his career. Thus, under the rococo futilities of his adoration, a feeling that is not entirely a simulacrum is perceptible—a feeling, not towards the lady, but towards himself and the romantic, the dazzling, and yet the melancholy circumstances of his life. One perceives that in spite of his years and his experience and his cynicism, he never grew old; under all his trappings the absurd Jew-boy is visible till the very end.

But perhaps, in reality, it is a mistake to look at the matter from the moralist's point of view. Perhaps it is as a history, not of values, but of forces, that this long ambiguous, agitated existence should be considered. One would see it then as a mighty demonstration of energies—energies pitted against enormous obstacles, desperately struggling, miracluously triumphant, and attaining at last the apogee of self-expression, perfect and, from the very beginning, pre-ordained. Perhaps it is useless to enquire the object of it all. 'Joy's life lies in the doing.' Perhaps! Only, if that is so, joy's life is a singularly insubstantial thing. 'Condition de l'homme—inconstance, ennui, inquiétude!' Let us moralise with Pascal, if we must moralise at all. And, in Dızzy's case, those three grim spectres seem always to be crouching behind the painted pasteboard scene. Probably, indeed, he never noticed them; for the old comedian, acting in his own private theatre, with himself for audience, preferred not to question the solidity of the fairy palaces in which he played his marvellous part. But we, who, thanks to Mr. Buckle and Mr. Monypenny, have been provided with seats in the wings, can see only too clearly what lies on the other side of those flimsy erections. Such is the doom of the egotist. While he is alive, he devours all the happiness about him, like a grub on a leaf; but when he goes, the spectacle is not exhilarating. 'Le dernier acte est sanglant, quelque belle que soit la comédie en tout le reste. On jette enfin de la terre sur la tête, et en voilà pour jamais.'

1920.

A DIPLOMATIST:
LI HUNG-CHANG

ONE of the favourite dodges of the satirist is the creation of an imaginary world, superficially different from our own, and yet turning out, on further acquaintance, to contain all the familiar vices and follies of humanity. Swift's Lilliput and Brobdingnag are contrived on this principle. The vanity of courtiers, the mischiefs of politicians, the physical degradations of men and women—these things strike upon our minds with a new intensity when they are shown to us as parts of some queer universe, preposterously minute or enormous. We gain a new vision of war and lust when we see the one waged by statesmen six inches high, and the other agitating young ladies of sixty feet. Mr. Bland's book on Li Hung-Chang,[1] with its account of the society and institutions of China, produces—whether consciously or no it is a little difficult to say—very much the same effect. China is still so distant, its language is so incomprehensible, its customs are so singular, its whole civilisation has such an air of topsy-turvydom about it, that our Western intelligence can survey it with a remote disinterestedness hardly less complete than if it were a part of Laputa or the moon. We do so, with Mr. Bland's guidance; and we very soon perceive that China is, after all, only another Europe, with a touch of caricature and exaggeration here and there to give the satire point. Mr. Bland himself, indeed, seems at times to be almost a second Gulliver, such is the apparent ingenuousness with which he marvels at the strange absurdities of Chinese life. This, however, may be merely a Swiftian subtlety on his part to heighten the effect. For instance, he tells us with great gravity that one of the chief misfortunes

[1] *Li Hung-Chang.* By J. O. P. Bland. Constable.

from which China suffers is that she is ruled by officials; that whatever changes of government, whatever revolutions may take place, the officials remain undisturbed in power; and that these officials form a close bureaucratic caste, cut off from the world at large, puffed up with petty vanity, and singularly ignorant of the actual facts of life. He then goes on to relate, with amazement, that the official caste is recruited by means of competitive examinations of a literary kind, and that it is possible—and indeed frequent—to obtain the highest places in these examinations merely through a knowledge of the classics. The foundation of Li Hung-Chang's administrative career, for example, was based on his having been able, in reply to one of his examiners, to repeat a celebrated classic not only forwards, but backwards as well. Then Mr. Bland expatiates on the surprising and distressing atmosphere of 'make-believe' in China; he points out how it infects and vitiates the whole system of government, how it is even visible in works of history—even in the Press: 'They make their dynastic annals,' he says, 'conform to the official conception of the world-of-things-as-they-should-be, with little or no relation to the world-of-things-as-they-are, and the native Press, served chiefly by writers imbued with the same predilection for solemn make-believe in the discussion of public affairs, affords but little material for checking or amplifying the official annals.' It inevitably follows, as Mr. Bland observes, that (in China) it is exceedingly difficult to discover the truth about any public event. Another singular characteristic of the Chinese is their hatred of foreigners. This passion they carry to extraordinary lengths; they are unwilling to believe that anything good ever came from a foreign country; they put high duties upon foreign importations; at moments of excitement the more violent among them clamour to 'make an end, once and for all, of all the obnoxious foreigners, whose presence creates grave difficulties and dangers for the Empire.' Strange to say, too, it is particularly the caste of officials which is infected by what Mr. Bland calls 'this purblind ignorance and pride of race.'

Li Hung-Chang, however—the hero of Mr. Bland's well-informed and spirited book—was different. Though a knowledge of the classics was the basis of his fortunes, it was not his only knowledge; though an official—and in many ways a typical official—he yet possessed a perspicacity which was never taken in by official 'make-believe'; above all, he understood something of the nature and the powers of foreigners. Mr. Bland calls him a one-eyed man among the blind, and by 'the blind' we are to understand the rest of China. But, in truth, the description applies equally well to every leader in thought or action in every community under the sun. In Europe, no less than in China, the vast majority of men are blind—blind through ignorance and superstition and folly and senseless passions; and the statesmen and the thinkers are one-eyed leaders, who see neither very far nor very many objects, but who see what they do see quite clearly. Li Hung-Chang was a leader because he saw quite clearly the nature of China's position in international affairs. But his one-eyedness is amusingly illustrated by the manner in which this perception was originally forced upon his consciousness. It came through the chance of his being thrown together with General Gordon. It was Gordon who gave him his first vision of Europe. Nothing could be more ironical. The half-inspired, half-crazy Englishman, with his romance and his fatalism, his brandy-bottle and his Bible, the irresponsible knight-errant whom his countrymen first laughed at and neglected, then killed and canonised—a figure straying through the perplexed industrialism of the nineteenth century like some lost 'natural' from an earlier Age—this was the efficient cause of Li Hung-Chang's illumination, of his comprehension of the significance of Europe, of the whole trend of his long, cynical, successful, worldly-wise career.

It was particularly in diplomacy that that career achieved its most characteristic triumphs. Of all public servants, the diplomatist and the general alone must, if they are to succeed, have a grasp of actual facts. Politicians, lawyers, administrators, financiers even, can pass their lives in a mist of fictions and go down to posterity as great men. But the general who fails to perceive the facts that surround him will inevitably pay the penalty in defeat. The facts with which the diplomatist has to deal are less specialised and immediate, more subtle, indeterminate and diverse than those which confront the general; they are facts the perception of which requires an all-round intelligence; and thus, while it is possible for a great soldier to be a stupid man, a diplomatist who is stupid must be a failure. Li Hung-Chang's perspicacity was precisely of the universal kind; his cold gaze went through everything it met with an equal penetration. He could measure to a nicety all the complicated elements in the diplomatic game—the strength of his opponents, their intentions, their desires, their tenacity, their amenability to pressure, their susceptibility to bluff—and then the elaborate interactions of international forces, and the dubious movements of public opinion, and the curious influences of personal factors. More than this, he possessed a capacity, rare indeed save among the greatest masters of his craft—he could recognise the inevitable. And when that came, he understood the difficult art of bowing to it, as Mr. Bland pithily remarks, 'with mental reservations.'

His limitations were no less remarkable than his powers. He was never in the slightest danger of believing in a principle, or of allowing his astuteness to degenerate into profundity. His imagination was purely practical, and his whole conception of life was of a perfectly conventional kind. In this he was only carrying out the high diplomatic tradition; he was following in the footsteps of Queen Elizabeth and Richelieu, Metternich and Bismarck. It seems as if the human mind was incapable of changing its focus: it must either apprehend what is near it or what is far off; it cannot combine the two. Of all the great realists of history, the master spirits in the matter-of-fact business of managing mankind, it is difficult to think of more than one or two at most who, in addition, were moved by philosophical ideals towards noble aims.

Another consideration is suggested by Mr. Bland's book. There is something peculiarly fascinating about the diplomatic art. It is delightful to watch a skilled performer like Li Hung-Chang, baffling and befogging the English into humiliation, bluffing all Europe, by means of an imitation navy, into a genuine fear of a 'Yellow Peril,' and, finally, when all sins seem to have found him out, when Japan has 'seen' him, and his stakes are forfeit, 'tirant son épingle du jeu' with such supreme felicity. Certainly, it is a humane and elegant art, essentially intellectual, concerned, too, with momentous issues, and mingling, in a highly agreeable manner, the satisfactions of self-interest and altruism. Yet one cannot help perceiving indications that its days may be numbered. It belongs to a situation of affairs in the world, which there is no reason to suppose will be permanent, and of which the essential condition is the existence of a few strong States, of approximately equal power, interacting in competitive rivalry. This period began with the Renaissance; and it is at least possible that a time may come when it will have ended, and when the diplomatist will appear as romantic and extinct a creature as the mediæval baron or the Italian *condottiere*. Perhaps—who knows?—the subtle Oriental with the piercing eye may turn out to have been the very last of the charming race.

1918.

CREIGHTON

THE Church of England is one of the most extraordinary of institutions. An incredible concoction of Queen Elizabeth's, it still flourishes, apparently, and for three hundred years has remained true to type. Or perhaps, in reality, Queen Elizabeth had not very much to do with it; perhaps she only gave, with her long, strong fingers, the final twist to a stem that had been growing for ages, deep-rooted in the national life. Certainly our cathedrals—so careful and so unæsthetic, so class-conscious and so competent—suggest that view of the case. English Gothic seems to show that England was Anglican long before the Reformation—as soon as she ceased to be Norman, in fact. Pure piety, it cannot be denied, has never been her Church's strong point. Anglicanism has never produced—never could produce—a St. Teresa. The characteristic great men of the institution—Whitgift, Hooker, Laud, Butler, Jowett—have always been remarkable for virtues of a more secular kind: those of scholarship or of administrative energy. Mandell Creighton was (perhaps) the last of the long line. Perhaps; for who can tell? It is difficult to believe that a man of Creighton's attainments will ever again be Bishop of London. That particular concatenation seems to have required a set of causes to bring it into existence—a state of society, a habit of mind—which have become obsolete. But the whirligigs of time are, indeed, unpredictable; and England, some day or other, may well be blessed with another Victorian Age.

In Creighton *both* the great qualities of Anglican tradition were present to a remarkable degree. It would be hard to say whether he were more distinguished as a scholar or a man of affairs; but—such is the rather unfair persistence of the written word—there can be little doubt that he will be remembered chiefly as the historian of the Papacy. Born when the world was becoming extremely scientific, he belonged to the post-Carlyle-and-Macaulay generation—the school of Oxford and Cambridge inquirers, who sought to reconstruct the past solidly and patiently, with nothing but facts to assist them—pure facts, untwisted by political or metaphysical bias and uncoloured by romance. In this attempt Creighton succeeded admirably. He was industrious, exact, clear-headed, and possessed of a command over words that was quite sufficient for his purposes. He succeeded more completely than Professor Samuel Gardiner, whose history of the Early Stuarts and the Civil Wars was a contemporary work. Gardiner did his best, but he was not an absolute master of the method. Strive as he would, he could not prevent himself, now and then, from being a little sympathetic to one or other of his personages; sometimes he positively alluded to a physical circumstance; in short, humanity would come creeping in. A mistake! For Professor Gardiner's feelings about mankind are not illuminating; and the result is a slight blur. Creighton was made of sterner stuff. In his work a perfectly grey light prevails everywhere; there is not a single lapse into psychological profundity; every trace of local colour, every suggestion of personal passion, has been studiously removed. In many ways all this is a great comfort. One is not worried by moral lectures or purple patches, and the field is kept clear for what Creighton really excelled in—the lucid exposition of complicated political transactions, and the intricate movements of thought with which they were accompanied. The biscuit is certainly exceedingly dry; but at any rate there are no weevils in it. As one reads, one gets to relish, with a sober satisfaction, this plumless fare. It begins to be very nearly a pleasure to follow the intrigues of the great Councils, or to tread the labyrinth of the theological theory of indulgences. It is a curious cross-section of history that Creighton offers to the view. He has cut the great tree so near to the ground that leaf and flower have vanished; but he has worked his saw with such steadiness and precision that every grain in the wood is visible, and one can look *down* at the mighty structure, revealed in all its complex solidity like a map to the mind's eye.

Charming, indeed, are the ironies of history; and not the least charming those that involve the historian. It was very natural that Creighton, a clever and studious clergyman of the Church of England, should choose as the subject of his investigations that group of events which, centring round the Italian popes, produced at last the Reformation. The ironical fact was that those events happened to take place in a world where no clever and studious clergyman of the Church of England had any business to be. 'Sobriety,' as he himself said, was his aim; but what could sobriety do when faced with such figures as Savonarola, Cæsar Borgia, Julius II, and Luther? It could only look somewhere else. It is pleasant to witness the high-minded husband and father, the clever talker at Cambridge dinner tables, the industrious diocesan administrator, picking his way with an air of calm detachment amid the recklessness, the brutality, the fanaticism, the cynicism, the lasciviousness, of those Renaissance spirits. 'In his private life,' Creighton says of Alexander VI, 'it is sufficiently clear that he was at little pains to repress a strongly sensual nature. . . . We may hesitate to believe the worst charges brought against him; but the evidence is too strong to enable us to admit that even after his accession to the papal office he discontinued the irregularities of his previous life.' There is high comedy in such a tone on such a topic. One can imagine the father of the Borgias, if he could have read that sentence, throwing up his hands in delighted amazement, and roaring out the obscene blasphemy of his favourite oath.

The truth was that, in spite of his wits and his Oxford training, the admirable north-country middle-class stock, from which Creighton came, dominated his nature. His paradoxes might astound academical circles, his free speech might agitate the lesser clergy, but at heart he was absolutely sound. Even a friendship with that dæmonic imp, Samuel Butler, left him uncorroded. He believed in the Real Presence. He was opposed to Home Rule. He read with grave attention the novels of Mrs. Humphry Ward. The emancipation of a Victorian bishop could never be as that of other men. The string that tied him to the peg of tradition might be quite a long one; but it was always there. Creighton enjoyed his little runs with the gusto and vitality that were invariably his. The sharp aquiline face, with the grizzled beard, the bald forehead, and the gold spectacles, gleamed and glistened, the long, slim form, so dapper in its episcopal gaiters, preened itself delightedly, as an epigram—a devastating epigram—shot off and exploded, and the Fulham teacups tinkled as they had never tinkled before. Then, a moment later, the guests gone, the firm mouth closed in severe determination; work was resumed. The duties of the day were despatched swiftly; the vast and stormy diocese of London was controlled with extraordinary efficiency; while a punctual calmness reigned, for, however pressed and pestered, the Bishop was never known to fuss. Only once on a railway journey, when he believed that some valuable papers had gone astray, did his equanimity desert him. 'Where's my black bag?' was his repeated inquiry. His mischievous children treasured up this single lapse; and, ever afterwards, 'Where's my black bag?' was thrown across the table at the good-humoured prelate when his family was in a teasing mood.

When the fourth volume of the *History of the Papacy* appeared there was a curious little controversy, which illustrated Creighton's attitude to history and, indeed, to life. 'It seems to me,' he wrote in the preface, 'neither necessary to moralise at every turn in historical writing, nor becoming to adopt an attitude of lofty superiority over any one who ever played a prominent part in European affairs, nor charitable to lavish undiscriminating censure on any man.' The wrath of Lord Acton was roused. He wrote a violent letter of protest. The learning of the eminent Catholic was at least equal to Creighton's, but he made no complaint upon matters of erudition; it was his moral sense that was outraged. Creighton, it seemed to him, had passed over, with inexcusable indifference, the persecution and intolerance of the mediæval Church.

The popes of the thirteenth and fourteenth centuries, he wrote, '. . . instituted a system of persecution. . . . It is the most conspicuous fact in the history of the mediæval Papacy. . . . But what amazes and disables me is that you speak of the Papacy not as exercising a just severity, but as not exercising any severity. You ignore, you even deny, at least implicitly, the existence of the torture chamber and the stake. . . . Now the Liberals think persecution a crime of a worse order than adultery, and the acts done by Ximenes considerably worse than the entertainment of Roman courtesans by Alexander VI. The responsibility exists whether the thing permitted be good or bad. If the thing be criminal, then the authority permitting it bears the guilt. . . . You say that people in authority are not to be snubbed or sneered at from our pinnacle of conscious rectitude. I really don't know whether you exempt them because of their rank, or of their success and power, or of their date. . . . Historic responsibility has to make up for the want of legal responsibility. Power tends to corrupt, and absolute power corrupts absolutely. Great men are almost always bad.' These words, surely, are magnificent. One sees with surprise and exhilaration the rôles reversed—the uncompromising fervour of Catholicism calling down fire from Heaven upon its own abominable popes and the wordly Protestantism that excused them. Creighton's reply was as Anglican as might have been expected. He hedged. One day, he wrote, John Bright had said, 'If the people knew what sort of men statesmen were, they would rise and hang the whole lot of them.' Next day Gladstone had said 'Statesmanship is the noblest way to serve mankind.' 'I am sufficient of a Hegelian to be able to combine both judgments; but the results of my combination cannot be expressed in the terms of the logic of Aristotle. . . . Society is an organism,' etc. It is clear enough that his real difference with Lord Acton was not so much over the place of morals in history as over the nature of the historical acts upon which moral judgments are to be passed. The Bishop's imagination was not deeply stirred by the atrocities of the Inquisition;

what interested him, what appealed to him, what he really
understood, were the difficulties and the expedients of a man
of affairs who found himself at the head of a great administration. He knew too well, with ritualists on one side and
Kensitites on the other, the trials and troubles from which a
clerical ruler had to extricate himself as best he could, not to
sympathise (in his heart of hearts) with the clerical rulers of
another age who had been clever enough to devise regulations
for the elimination of heresy and schism, and strong enough
to put those regulations into force.

He himself, however, was never a persecutor; his great
practical intelligence prevented that. Firmly fixed in the
English tradition of common sense, compromise and comprehension, he held on his way amid the shrieking of extremists
with imperturbable moderation. One of his very last acts was
to refuse to prosecute two recalcitrant clergymen who had
persisted in burning incense in a forbidden manner. He knew
that, in England at any rate, persecution did not work. Elsewhere, perhaps, it might be different; in Russia, for instance.
. . . There was an exciting moment in Creighton's life
when he was sent to Moscow to represent the Church of
England at the Coronation of the Emperor Nicholas; and his
comments on that occasion were significant. Clad in a gorgeous cope of red and gold, with mitre and crozier, the English
prelate attracted every eye. He thoroughly relished the fact;
he tasted, too, to the full, the splendour of the great ceremonies
and the extraordinary display of autocratic power. That there
might have been some degree of spiritual squalor mixed with
those magnificent appearances never seemed to occur to him.
He was fascinated by the apparatus of a mighty organisation,
and, with unerring instinct, made straight for the prime
mover of it, the Chief Procurator of the Holy Synod, the
sinister Pobiedonostzeff, with whom he struck up a warm
friendship. He was presented to the Emperor and Empress,
and found them charming. 'I was treated with great distinction, as I was called in first. The Empress looked very nice,
dressed in white silk.' The aristocratic Acton would, no doubt,

have viewed things in a different light. 'Absolute power corrupts absolutely'—so he had said; but Creighton had forgotten the remark. He was no Daniel. He saw no Writing on the Wall.

The Bishop died in his prime, at the height of his success and energy, and was buried in St. Paul's Cathedral. Not far from his tomb, which a Victorian sculptor did his best to beautify, stands the strange effigy of John Donne, preaching, in his shroud, an incredible sermon upon mortality. Lingering in that corner, one's mind flashes oddly to other scenes and other persons. One passes down the mouldering street of Ferrara, and reaches an obscure church. In the half-light, from an inner door, an elderly humble nun approaches, indicating with her patois a marble slab in the pavement—a Latin inscription—the grave of Lucrezia Borgia. Mystery and oblivion were never united more pathetically. But there is another flash, and one is on a railway platform under the grey sky of England. A tall figure hurries by, spectacled and bearded, with swift clerical legs, and a voice—a competent, commanding, yet slightly agitated voice—says sharply: 'Where's my black bag?'

1929.

A STATESMAN: LORD MORLEY

It is obvious that this is an interesting book[1]; it is less obvious in what the precise nature of its interest consists. Like most modern biographies, but in a more marked degree, it appeals to two totally distinct kinds of curiosity: on the one hand, it provides the reader with hitherto unpublished documents of first-rate importance; and on the other, it presents a picture of a man and an age. These two threads of discourse have by no means been woven together into a unity. After more than a volume of general reflections and personal reminiscences, Lord Morley suddenly lifts the curtain upon a high political scene, and reveals, through two hundred pages of private correspondence with Lord Minto, the detailed inner workings of a series of transactions which have made an epoch in the history of the English administration of India. Probably it is this portion of the book which will turn out to be of the more enduring value. The letters of a Secretary of State to a Viceroy are bound to contain material which no future student of Imperial politics can afford to neglect. They are bound to contain authentic information upon important facts, and that is a kind of information very much rarer than is generally supposed—so rare, indeed, that whenever it appears, the world will always treasure it. To take a small example, pp. 331 and 333 of Vol. II give us authentic information as to Lord Kitchener and the Governor-Generalship of India. We there learn that Lord Kitchener stated to Lord Haldane that he expected the appointment, that Mr. Asquith personally favoured it, that King Edward vehemently supported it, and that Lord Morley was so strongly opposed to it that he was prepared to resign if it should take place. Apart from incidental revelations

[1] *Recollections*. By John Viscount Morley, O.M. Macmillan.

of this sort, the whole purport of the letters is of singular interest, owing both to the time of peculiar difficulty at which they were written and to the fact that they give expression to a policy—a policy laid down, elaborated, and at last put into execution with consistency and success. It is possible, no doubt, that the changes in our government of India, which were carried out during Lord Morley's tenure of office, were of somewhat less positive consequence than he himself would seem to suggest; that the 'historic plunge,' of which he speaks with evident complacency, was more of a *beau geste* than one of those great acts of profound reform which affect the fundamentals of national polity; that, in fact, it will be for its *negative* qualities—its allaying of hatreds, its avoidance of extreme measures, its skill in eluding not merely a host of difficulties, but some appalling dangers—that Lord Morley's work will be esteemed by the historian of the future. This may be so; yet it is difficult to read this record without a feeling of pleasure akin to that produced by some admirable example of dramatic art— the situation is so interesting, the developments are so well managed, and the *dénouement* is so satisfactory. The hand of the master is plainly visible throughout. For, though Lord Minto might perhaps be well described as an average Viceroy, Lord Morley was certainly not at all an average Secretary of State.

Indeed, what the reader finally carries away from this part of the book is the impression of a rare political capacity. That Lord Morley possessed the qualities of a strong and skilful ruler was already vaguely realised; it is now made manifest in explicit detail. His attitude towards Lord Minto, for instance, is highly characteristic. Lord Minto had been appointed by a Tory Government, and his opinions were clearly at variance with those of the Secretary of State, upon many vital questions. It is delightful to observe Lord Morley's virtuosity in the treatment of this thorny situation—his gentle persuasions, his tactful acquiescences, the subtle suggestions of his compliments. 'You will not suspect me,' he remarks on one occasion, 'of vulgar flattery.' No, certainly not; who would? But the discerning reader (and of course it is of the essence of the situation that Lord Minto himself could hardly be called one) may be pardoned if he puts a delicate emphasis upon the 'vulgar.' And then, occasionally, amid all the velvet of the correspondence, one catches a glimpse of underlying steel. On one of his visits to Ireland, Lord Morley made the acquaintance of Lord Waterford, who, he was told, was 'of a dictatorial turn.' 'Perhaps,' was Lord Morley's comment in his diary, 'I don't mind that.' One understands very well, after reading the correspondence with Lord Minto, that he would not mind it; he was of a dictatorial turn himself. But with him the determination to have his own way was both veiled and strengthened by an acute perception of the facts with which he had to deal. Thus it is true to say that his policy was that of an opportunist—but an opportunist, not of the school of Walpole, but of the school of Burke. Perhaps the most remarkable feature of these letters is their constant assertion of great principles. They form a running comment, of the highest value, upon the current platitudes of Imperialist doctrine; and will live, if for no other reason, as the exposition of a statesman's handling of the Liberal creed.

The rest of the book is, from some points of view, decidedly disappointing. The recollections of a life passed in familiar intercourse both with the leading men of letters and the leading politicians of the age, a life intimately connected with some of the most agitated events of English history, a life of high achievement in literature as well as in action, could hardly fail, one might have thought, to be exciting. But 'exciting' is really the last word that anyone would dream of applying in these pages. 'And is this all?' is the question which rises to one's lips at the end of them. To have been the friend of John Stuart Mill and Gladstone, to have negotiated with Parnell, to have fought in the forefront of the Home Rule battle, to have worked for ten years in the inner circle of a Cabinet—when all this, and the rest, is added up, what a curiously tame, what an almost obvious affair it seems to come to! If one might hazard the paradox, it is their very lack of interest that makes these reminiscences so interesting. Once or twice, Lord Morley seems to hint that he holds a brief for the Victorian Age; and there can be no doubt that his book is impregnated with the Victorian spirit. An air of singular solemnity hovers over it, and its moral tone is of the highest. Only a Victorian, one feels, would have, on the one hand, allowed Mr. Gladstone to flit like a shadow through his pages, while, on the other, devoting a whole long chapter to a series of extracts from the most esteemed authors on the subject of Death. Only a Victorian, having made his reputation by writing the lives of Diderot, Rousseau and Voltaire, would, on his return from visits to Paris, have thrown, in horror, two French novels out of the railway-carriage window. Such details, slight as they are, depict a period. The Victorian Age, great in so many directions, was not great in criticism, in humour, in the realistic apprehension of life. It was an age of self-complacency and self-contradiction. Even its atheists (Lord Morley was one of them) were religious. The religious atmosphere fills his book, and blurs every outline. We are shown Mr. Gladstone through a haze of reverence, and Emerson, and Marcus Aurelius. We begin to long for a little of the cynicism and scepticism of, precisely, the Age of Diderot, Rousseau and Voltaire. Perhaps—who knows?—if Lord Morley and his contemporaries had been less completely devoid of those unamiable and unedifying qualities, the history of the world would have been more fortunate. The heartless, irreverent, indecent eighteenth century produced the French Revolution. The Age of Victoria produced—what?

1918.

SARAH BERNHARDT

THERE are many paradoxes in the art of acting. One of them —the discrepancy between the real feelings of the actor and those which he represents—was discussed by Diderot in a famous dialogue. Another—the singular divergence between the art of the stage and the art of the drama—was illustrated very completely by the career of Sarah Bernhardt.

It is clear that the primary business of the actor is to interpret the conception of the dramatist; but it is none the less true that, after a certain degree of excellence has been reached, the merits of an actor have no necessary dependence upon his grasp of the dramatist's meaning. To be a moderately good actor one must understand, more or less, what one's author is up to; but the achievements of Sarah Bernhardt proved conclusively that it was possible to be a very good actor indeed without having the faintest notion, not only of the intentions of particular dramatists, but of the very rudiments of the dramatic art.

No one who saw her in *Hamlet* or in *Lorenzaccio* could doubt that this was so. Her *Hamlet* was a fantastic absurdity which far, far surpassed the permitted limits even of a Gallic miscomprehension of 'le grand Will.' But perhaps even more remarkable was her treatment of *Lorenzaccio. Hamlet*, after all, from every point of view, is an extremely difficult play; but the main drift of Musset's admirable tragedy is as plain as a pikestaff. It is a study in disillusionment—the disillusionment of a tyrannicide, who finds that the assassination, which he has contrived and executed with infinite hazard, skill, and difficulty, has merely resulted in a state of affairs even worse than before. Sarah Bernhardt, incredible as it may seem, brought down the final curtain on the murder of the tyrant, and thus made the play, as a play, absolutely pointless. What remained was a series of exciting scenes, strung together by the vivid and penetrating art of a marvellous actress. For art it was, and not mere posturing. Nothing could be further from the truth than to suppose that the great Frenchwoman belonged to that futile tribe of empty-headed impersonators, who, since Irving, have been the particular affliction of the English stage. Dazzling divinity though she was, she was also a serious, a laborious worker, incessantly occupied—not with expensive stage properties, elaborate make-up, and historically accurate scenery—but simply with acting. Sir Herbert Tree was ineffective because he neither knew nor cared how to act; he was content to be a clever entertainer. But Sarah Bernhardt's weakness, if weakness it can be called, arose from a precisely contrary reason—from the very plenitude of her power over all the resources of her craft—a mastery over her medium of so overwhelming a kind as to become an obsession.

The result was that this extraordinary genius was really to be seen at her most characteristic in plays of inferior quality. They gave her what she wanted. She did not want—she did not understand—great drama; what she did want were opportunities for acting; and this was the combination which the *Toscas*, the *Camélias*, and the rest of them, so happily provided. In them the whole of her enormous virtuosity in the representation of passion had full play; she could contrive thrill after thrill, she could seize and tear the nerves of her audience, she could touch, she could terrify, to the very top of her astonishing bent. In them, above all, she could ply her personality to the utmost. All acting must be, to some extent, an exploitation of the personality; but in the acting of Sarah Bernhardt that was the dominating quality—the fundamental element of her art. It was there that her strength, and her weakness, lay. During her best years, her personality remained an artistic instrument; but eventually it became too much for her. It absorbed both herself and her audience; the artist became submerged in the divinity; and what was genuine, courageous, and original in her character was lost sight of in oceans of highly advertised and quite indiscriminate applause.

This, no doubt, was partly due to the age she lived in. It is odd but certainly true that the eighteenth century would have been profoundly shocked by the actress who reigned supreme over the nineteenth. The gay and cynical creatures of the *ancien régime*, who tittered over *La Pucelle*, and whose adventures were reflected without exaggeration in the pages of *Les Liaisons Dangereuses*, would have recoiled in horror before what they would have called the '*indécence*' of one of Sarah Bernhardt's ordinary scenes. Every age has its own way of dealing with these matters; and the nineteenth century made up for the high tone of its literature and the decorum of its behaviour by the luscious intensity of its theatrical displays. Strict husbands in icy shirt-fronts and lovely epitomes of all the domestic virtues in bustles would sit for hours thrilling with frenzied raptures over intimate and elaborate present-ments of passion in its most feverish forms. The supply and the demand, interacting upon one another, grew together. But by the end of the century the fashion had begun to change. The star of Eleonora Duse rose upon the horizon; Ibsen became almost popular; the Théâtre Antoine, the Moscow Art Theatre, introduced a new style of tragic acting—a prose style—surprisingly effective and surprisingly quiet, and subtle with the sinuosities of actual life. Already by the beginning of the twentieth century the bravura of Sarah Bernhardt seemed a magnificent relic of the past. And the generation which was to plunge with reckless fanaticism into the gigantic delirium of the war found its pleasures at the theatre in a meticulous imitation of the significant trivialities of middle-class interiors.

Fortunately, however, Sarah Bernhardt's genius did not spend itself entirely in amazing personal triumphs and the satisfaction of the emotional needs of a particular age. Fortu-nately the mightier genius of Jean Racine was of such a nature that it was able to lift hers on to its own level of the immortal and the universal. In this case there was no need on her part for an intellectual realisation of the dramatist's purpose;

Racine had enough intellect for both; all that she had to do was to play the parts he had provided for her to the height of her ability; his supreme art did the rest. Her Hermione was a masterpiece; but certainly the greatest of all her achievements was in *Phèdre*. Tragedy possesses an extraordinary quality, which, perhaps, has given it its traditional place of primacy among all the forms of literature. It is not only immortal; it is also for ever new. There are infinite implications in it which reveal themselves by a mysterious law to each succeeding generation. The *Œdipus* acted yesterday at Cambridge was the identical play that won the prize two thousand years ago; and yet it was a different *Œdipus*, with meanings for the modern audience which were unperceived by the Athenians. The records show conclusively that the Phèdre of Bernhardt differed as much from that of Rachel as Rachel's differed from Clairon's, and as Clairon's differed from that of the great actress who created the part under the eyes of Racine. But each was Phèdre. Probably the latest of these interpretations was less perfect in all its parts than some of its predecessors; but the great moments, when they came, could never have been surpassed. All through there were details of such wonderful beauty that they return again and again upon the memory —unforgettable delights. The hurried horror of

Mes yeux le retrouvaient dans les traits de son père;

the slow, expanding, mysterious grandeur of

Le ciel, tout l'univers, est plein de mes aïeux;

the marvellous gesture with which the words of Œnone, announcing the approach of Thésée, seemed to be pressed back into silence down her 'ill-uttering throat'—such things, and a hundred others, could only have been conceived and executed by a consummate artist in her happiest vein. But undoubtedly the topmost reach came in the fourth act, when the Queen, her reason tottering with passion and jealousy, suddenly turns upon herself in an agony of self-reproach. Sarah Bernhardt's treatment of this passage was extremely original, and it is difficult to believe that it was altogether justified by the text. Racine's words seem to import a violent directness of statement:

Chaque mot sur mon front fait dresser mes cheveux;

but it was with hysteric irony, with dreadful, mocking laughter, that the actress delivered them. The effect was absolutely overwhelming, and Racine himself could only have bowed to the ground before such a triumphant audacity. Then there followed the invocation to Minos, culminating in the stupendous

Je crois voir de ta main tomber l'urne terrible.

The secret of that astounding utterance baffles the imagination. The words boomed and crashed with a superhuman resonance which shook the spirit of the hearer like a leaf in the wind. The *voix d'or* has often been raved over; but in Sarah Bernhardt's voice there was more than gold: there was thunder and lightning; there was Heaven and Hell. But the pitcher is broken at the fountain; that voice is silent now for ever, and the Terror and the Pity that lived in it and purged the souls of mortals have faded into incommunicable dreams.

1923.

INDEX

[Figures in italics indicate the more important references]

Acton, Lord, 276–279
Addison, 49
Aiguillon, Duchesse d', 182
Ailesbury, Lady, 247
Albert, Prince, 243
Albon, Comtesse d', 154, 155
Alderson, Sir Edward, 247
Alembert, Jean d', 105, 120, 123, 126, 135, 138, 154, 156, 157, 163, 164, 168, 172
Alexander I, Emperor, 220, 221
Alexander VI, Pope, 275, 277
Algarotti, 87, 94, 95
Alleurs, Chevalier des, 60
Amelia, Princess, 193
Anne, Queen, 68
Apponyi, Madame, 223
Argens, Marquis d', 95
Argental, d', 84, 170
Ariosto, 1, 2
Arnold, Dr., 258
Arnold, Matthew, 231, 234
Arundel, Lord, 200
Ashburton, Lady, 251
Ashford, Daisy, 266
Asquith, H. H., 280
Aubrey, John, *11–16*

Bacon, Francis, 35, 46
Baudy, Charles, 116, 117, 119, 120
Bayle, Pierre, 74
Beccaria, 134
Becket, Thomas à, 47
Bedford, Duchess of, 202
Bentley, Richard, 28–33

Berkeley, Bishop, 69
Bernhardt, Sarah, *284–288*
Bernières, Madame de, 59, 60, 70
Berry, Agnes, 203–209
Berry, Mary, 165, 166, 167, 193, 196, 203, *204–210*
Beshyr, Emir, 216
Bessborough, Lady, 213
Bismarck, 265, 271
Bland, J. O. P., *268–271*
Blücher, 238
Boileau, 88
Boleyn, Anne, 50
Bolingbroke, 62, 64, 67, 74
Borgia, Cæsar, 275
Borgia, Lucrezia, 279
Bossuet, 24, 46, 226
Boswell, 16, 107, 141, *147–152*
Boufflers, Comtesse de, 49, 157, 173
Boufflers, Marquise de, 173
Bouillon, Cardinal de, 26, 27
Bourbon, Duc de, 169
Bradford, Lady, 266
Brancas, Comte de, 24
Bright, John, 277
Broome, Major, 64, 65
Brosses, Président de, *112–121*
Brougham, Lord, 238
Buckle, G. E., 264, 265, 267
Buffon, 96, 178
Burke, 174, 196, 282
Bute, Lady, 42
Butler, Bishop, 69, 273
Butler, Samuel (Erewhon), 275
Butler, Samuel (Hudibras), 6
Byron, 188

CABANIS, 136, 137
Canning, George, 213, 217, 221, 222, 238
Canning, Stratford, 213, 216, 224
Caraccioli, 157, 174
Carlyle, 47, 56, 80, 87, 103, 197, *249–256*, 258, 259, 261, 263, 274
Carlyle, Mrs., 251, 254–255, 259
Caroline, Queen (wife of George II), 67, 205
Caroline, Queen (wife of George IV), 239
Carter, Mary, 203
Carteret, Lord, 30, 31, 33, 69
Castlereagh, Lord, 238
Catherine, Empress, 130
Catt, Henri de, *106–111*
Cellini, Benvenuto, 166
Charles I, 50
Charles II, 9, 14, 18
Charlotte, Queen, 191
Chasot, 95
Chastellux, Marquis de, 157
Chateaubriand, 137, 223, 226
Châtelet, Madame du, 52, 53, 76, 84–86
Châtillon, Duchesse de, 157
Chatterton, 196
Chaucer, 249
Chaulieu, 88
Chesterfield, Lord, 52
Choiseul, Duc de, 135, 177
Choiseul, Madame de, 178, 183
Cicero, 166, 197
Clairon, Mademoiselle, 287
Clairvaux, Bernard of, 50
Clarendon, Edward, Lord, 46
Clarendon, George William Frederick, Lord, 246
Clark, Andrew, 16
Colbatch, Dr., *28–33*
Coleridge, 144, 251
Collins, Anthony, 29, 73, 74
Collins, Churton, *56*, 51, 66
Commines, 46

Condé, Prince de, 169
Condorcet, 157, 164
Congreve, 63
Conti, Prince de, 59
Conway, Henry Seymour, 192
Corneille, 59, 116, 177
Coulanges, Emmanuel de, *23–27*
Coulanges, Madame de, 24–27
Cowper, Lady, 221, 222
Cowper, William, 197
Cranmer, Archbishop, 262
Creevey, Thomas, *236–242*
Creighton, Mandell, *273–279*
Cromwell, Oliver, 8, 47, 106, 253
Cunningham, Peter, 187

DALRYMPLE, Sir David, 148
Damer, Mrs., 208–210
Dance, George, 205
Dancourt, 58
Dante, 201
Darget, 95, 97, 102
Dee, Dr. John, 15
Deffand, Madame du, 60, 154–157, *165–186*, 187, 193, 194, 204, 206, 207
Denis, Madame, 91, 93, 98, 99, 119
Descartes, 44, 76
Desnoiresterres, 56
Devonshire, Duchess of, 217
Dickens, 249
Diderot, 113, 123–133, 138, 157, 168, 283, 284
Disraeli, *264–267*
Dodington, Bubb, 64, 67
Domenichino, 190
Donne, John, 279
Dowden, Edward, 231, 234
Durham, Lord, 238, 240, 241
Duse, Eleonora, 286

EDWARD VII, 280
Egmont, Madame d', 170
Einstein, 17

Elizabeth, Queen, 1–4, 15, 46, 263, 271, 273
Emerson, 283
Epinay, Madame d', 122, 124–131
Erasmus, 50
Essex, Earl of, 3
Euler, 97, 98

FALKENER, Everard, 61, 62
Fénelon, 143
Fielding, 177, 189
Fleury, Cardinal, 75
Fontenelle, 74, 167, 170, 171
Forcalquier, Madame de, 182
Foulet, Lucien, 56, 57, 59, 61, 66, 68
Fox, Charles James, 174, 175
Fox, George, 6, 8
Fox, Henry, 194
Franklin, Benjamin, 136
Frederick the Great, 53, 56, 80–111, 114, 253–255
Freeman, E. A., 259–261
Fréron, Elie, 115
Froude, Hurrell, 258
Froude, J. A., 257–263
Fry, Mrs., 213, 214, 217

GALIANI, 158
Gardiner, Samuel, 274
Garrick, 136
Gay, 65
Geoffrin, Madame, 135, 157
George II, 189
George III, 189, 217, 238
George IV, 221, 222, 238, 239, 242, 243
Gibbon, 139–146, 174, 178, 193, 196, 197, 200, 254, 263
Gladstone, 277, 282, 283
Gluck, 162
Godwin, Mary, 231, 232
Goldsmith, 136

Gordon, General, 270
Gower, Lord, 221
Grafton, Duchess of, 190
Graham, Sir James, 246
Gramont, Madame de, 177
Granville, Lady, 209, 221, 223
Granville, Lord, 212
Gray, 192, 193, 197
Greville, Charles, 226, 243–248
Grey, Lord, 222, 224, 238
Grignan, Madame de, 23, 26, 197
Grimm, Baron de, 123–130
Guibert, Comte de, 154, 159–164
Guizot, 225–228

HALDANE, Lord, 280
Hamilton, Duchess of, 193
Hardwicke, Lord, 218
Harington, Sir John, 1–5
Helvétius, Madame, 135–138
Hénault, Président, 120, 170, 173, 175
Henry II, 47
Henry VII, 71
Henry VIII, 262
Henry, Prince, 4
Hervey, Lady, 190
Higginson, Edward, 62, 63
Hitchener, Miss, 231
Hobbes, 11, 19
Hogarth, 189
Hogg, Thomas, 229, 230
Holbach, Baron d', 135
Holland, Lady, 221, 223, 224, 242
Homer, 89, 99
Hooke, Robert, 14
Hooker, Richard, 273
Horace, 29, 31
Houdetot, Madame d', 128
Howard, Catherine, 262
Hume, David, 43–49, 74, 76, 123, 126, 158, 189
Huntingdon, Lord, 203
Huskisson, William, 238

INGPEN, Roger, 230, 231, 234
Irving, Sir Henry, 285

JAMES I, 3, 4
Johnson, Dr., 16, 66, 148, 152, 196
Jourdain, Philip, 97
Jowett, 273
Julius II, Pope, 275

KEATS, 188, 196
Kitchener, Lord, 280
Knox, John, 263
Koenig, Samuel, 97–99

LA BEAUMELLE, 97
La Bruyère, 24, 36
La Fare, Marquis de, 89
La Fontaine, 26
La Mettrie, Julien de, 95, 96, 97
Lanson, 56, 62
La Rochefoucauld, 42
La Trousse, Marquis de, 24
Laud, Archbishop, 273
Lauderdale, Duke of, 18
La Vallière, Madame de, 182
Lecouvreur, Adrienne, 58
Leibnitz, 84, 97, 98
Leicester, Earl of, 2
Lely, Sir Peter, 19
Le Sage, 177
Lespinasse, Mademoiselle de, 135, 138, *153–164*, 168, 169, 172, 183, 197
Lieven, Madame de, *219–228*
Lieven, Prince de, 220, 221, 224, 225, 227
Li Hung-Chang, *268–272*
Lindsay, Lady Charlotte, 209
Locke, 44, 73, 75, 77–79
Long, Colonel, 12, 14
Long, Lady, 12, 15

Lonsdale, Lord, 151, 152
Louis XIV, 25, 50, 88, 169, 170
Louis XV, 109, 252
Louis-Philippe, 226, 228
Louvois, Marquis de, 24, 27
Lower, Dr. Richard, 20
Lucian, 49
Lully, 167
Luther, 6, 275,
Luxembourg, Maréchale de, 156, 173, 180, 183
Lyttelton, Charles, 187
Lyttelton, Lady, 203

MACAULAY, 188, 191–193, 196, 262, 274
Macdonald, Frederika, 123–130
Maclean, James, 199, 202
Maine, Duchesse du, 169, 172
Maintenon, Madame de, 24, 25
Malesherbes, 157
Malthus, 208
Mann, Sir Horace, 188, 194
Marie, Empress, 220
Marlborough, Duchess of, 64, 193, 205
Marlborough, Duke of, 62, 68, 219
Marmontel, 157
Mary, Queen of Scots, 262
Mason, William, 192
Massillon, 172
Matignon, Marquis de, 182
Maupertuis, 96–104, 251
Mehemet Ali, 214
Melbourne, 243
Mérimée, 226
Meryon, Dr., 213, 217, 218
Metternich, 221, 227, 271
Middleton, Conyers, 74
Mill, John Stuart, 282
Milton, 32, 64
Minto, Lord, 280–282
Mirepoix, Maréchale de, 173, 183

Molière, 20, 103
Moncrif, 170
Montagu, George, 189
Montagu, Lady Mary Wortley, 34–42, 211
Montespan, Madame de, 24, 172
Montesquieu, 46, 70, 74, 113, 170
Monypenny, W. F., 264, 267
Moore, Sir John, 213
Mora, Marquis de, 158–161, 164
More, Hannah, 203
Morellet, André, 133–138
Morley, Lord, 73, 124, 280–283
Muggleton, Lodowick, 6–10
Musset, 284

NAPOLEON I, 137, 165
Napoleon III, 228
Necker, 182
Necker, Madame, 139
Newcastle, Duke of, 67
Newton, Sir Isaac, 11, 13, 14, 17, 19, 63, 68, 69, 74–76, 84
Nicholas I, 221, 223, 224, 228
Nicholas II, 278
Noailles, Madame Alfred de, 223
Noble, Mark, 200
North, Dr. John, 17–22
North, Lady, 21
North, Roger, 17, 22

O'HARA, General, 206, 207, 209, 210
Orléans, Duc d', 167, 169, 172, 182
Ossory, Lady, 189, 193, 200
Oughtred, William, 14, 15

PALEY, William, 229
Palissot, 134, 135
Palmerston, 218, 222, 224, 246, 247
Paoli, General, 148, 150
Parnell, 282

Pascal, 75, 145, 266, 267
Paston, George, 35, 36, 40
Paul I, 220
Peel, Sir Robert, 196, 243
Pelham, Miss, 190
Pell, John, 14
Pepys, 147, 236
Peterborough, Lord, 65, 66
Petty, Sir William, 12
Pitt, Anne, 190
Pitt, William, Lord Chatham, 148, 149, 189, 199, 202, 211
Pitt, William, 211, 212, 217, 218
Plato, 18
Pobiedonostzeff, 278
Pöllnitz, Baron, 95
Pompadour, Madame de, 86, 109, 135
Pompignan, Marquis de, 115
Pont-de-Veyle, 170, 173
Pope, 35, 63–66, 69
Portland, Duke of, 245
Potter, Francis, 14
Prévost, 155
Prie, Madame de, 57, 59, 169

QUEENSBERRY, Duchess of, 193
Quinault, 167

RABELAIS, 2, 22
Rachel, Mademoiselle, 287
Racine, 59, 88, 89, 108, 109, 177, 286–288
Raleigh, Professor Sir Walter, 38
Randolph, Dr., 145
Ray, John, 13
Reeve, Henry, 244, 248
Reeve, John, 7, 8, 10
Rémusat, Madame de, 137
Retz, Cardinal de, 227
Reynolds, Sir Joshua, 34, 189
Richardson, 155, 177
Richelieu, Cardinal, 271

Richelieu, Maréchal de, 120, 170
Richmond, Duke of, 190
Rimbaud, 147
Robecq, Princesse de, 134, 135
Robespierre, 251
Robins, John, 7, 8
Rochester, Lord, 70
Rogers, Lady, 3
Rohan, Chevalier de, 52, 57–59, 61
Roscoe, William, 200
Rosebery, Lord, 110
Round, Horace, 260, 261
Rousseau, Jean-Jacques, 115, *122–
132*, 140, 141, 148, 167, 182, 283
Ruffey, Président de, 117, 119
Ruffhead, Owen, 66
Russell, Lord John, 238, 246

Sainte-Beuve, 124, 160
Saint-Lambert, 128
Saint-Simon, Duc de, 178, 236,
244
Sanadon, Mademoiselle, 182
Savonarola, 275
Scott, Sir Walter, 13
Ségur, Marquis de, 153–156
Sévigné, Madame de, 23–27, 189,
197, 221
Shaftesbury, Lord, 73
Shakespeare, 67, 69, 74–76, 178,
201, 284
Sheffield, Lord, 145
Shelburne, Lord, 136, 158
Shelley, *229–235*
Shelley, Sir Timothy, 229–235
Simiane, Madame de, 27
Smith, Adam, 134
Somers, Lord, 78
Somerset, Duke of, 262
Spencer, Lord, 146
Staël, Madame de, 208
Stanhope, Earl, 211, 212
Stanhope, Lady Hester, *211–218*
Sterne, 189, 203

Strachey, Edward, 249
Stubbs, 259
Suard, 157
Suffolk, Lady, 205
Sully, Duc de, 58, 67, 70
Swift, 35, 64, 65, 67, 69, 197, 268
Swinburne, 147

Tacitus, 251, 263
Tallentyre, S. G., 54
Talleyrand, 225
Tawny, John, 7, 8
Temple, Lord, 63
Temple, William, 149, 151
Tencin, Cardinal de, 154
Têtu, l'Abbé, 24, 25
Thackeray, 209, 252, 265
Thanet, Lord, 15
Thévenart, 168
Thieriot, 60, 61, 62
Thucydides, 263
Tindal, Matthew, 74
Tinker, C. B., 147, 148
Toland, John, 73, 74
Tonge, Dr., 14
Townshend, Lady, 199
Townshend, Lord, 31
Toynbee, Mrs. Paget, 165–167,
173, 187, 188, 194, 199
Toynbee, Paget, 194, 199–201, 205
Tree, Sir Herbert, 285
Tronchin, Dr., 180
Turgot, 126, 136, 137, 156, 157,
168

Vichy, Comte de, 154, 155
Victoria, Queen, 202, 209, 218,
225, 236, 242–244, 246, 266, 283
Virgil, 89
Voltaire, 46, *50–105*, 107, 109,
110, *114–121*, 131, 134, 138,
145, 167, 168, 170, 173, 176–
179, 181, 196, 201, 283

WALLER, Sir Wathen, 194
Walpole, Horace, 41, 60, 147, 165–
    168, 172–174, 176–178, 180,
    181, *183–209*, 236
Walpole, Horatio, First Baron, 66
Walpole, Sir Robert, 66, 68, 69,
    189, 205, 282
Warburton, 66, 189
Ward, Mrs. Humphry, 276
Waterford, Lord, 282
Watt, James, 51
Wellington, Duke of, 197, 218,
    238, 239, 247
Westbrook, Harriet, 231–233
Whitehead, Professor A. N., 17, 22
Whitgift, Archbishop, 273
Whitton, William, 230, 232–235
Wilkes, John, 148

Williams, Sir Charles Hanbury,
    199
Willoughby, Lord, 221
Wollaston, William, 74
Wood, Anthony, 12, 15
Woolston, Thomas, 74
Wortley, Edward, *36–42*
Wren, Sir Christopher, 12, 14
Würtemberg, Duke of, 98
Wylde, Edmund, 12

XIMENES, 277

YORK, Duke of, 243
Young, Edward, 64